FORBIDDEN EMBRACE

Emma turned around to face Revelstoke. "Do you make it a practice at every ball you attend, my lord, to single out an unattached female for your particular attention, or have I the honor of being the only one to whom you have made your outrageous proposal?"

"You are the only one, never doubt it."

Without warning, he set his glass aside and, unfolding his long body from the chair, crossed to her with a purposeful stride. Emma fought the impulse to back away from him as his tall form loomed suddenly, large and forbidding, over her. Strong fingers closed about her arms. "But then," he said, drawing her deliberately to him. "You already knew that, or you would not be here."

Emma arched an inquisitive eyebrow. "Here, at Revelstoke?" she queried, a devil in her eye. "Or, here, in your arms, my lord?" Resolutely ignoring the persistent voice in the back of her head that warned against giving rein to irresistible impulse, Emma ran her hands upward over Revelstoke's chest and clasped her arms provocatively about his neck. Her hand at the back of his head, she lifted her face to his and pulled him down to her.

At that moment, she did not care where her actions might lead. Her lips parted to meet his. "Tell me, sir, do you intend to kiss me or not?"

"I intend to do much more than kiss you, Lady Blythe," he whispered, relishing the sudden leap of her pulse at the base of her throat.

—from "Dark Shadows," by Sara Blayne

ROMANCE FROM JANELLE TAYLOR

ANYTHING FOR LOVE   (0-8217-4992-7, $5.99)

DESTINY MINE   (0-8217-5185-9, $5.99)

CHASE THE WIND   (0-8217-4740-1, $5.99)

MIDNIGHT SECRETS   (0-8217-5280-4, $5.99)

MOONBEAMS AND MAGIC   (0-8217-0184-4, $5.99)

SWEET SAVAGE HEART   (0-8217-5276-6, $5.99)

Available wherever paperbacks are sold, or order direct from the Publisher. Send cover price plus 50¢ per copy for mailing and handling to Penguin USA, P.O. Box 999, c/o Dept. 17109, Bergenfield, NJ 07621. Residents of New York and Tennessee must include sales tax. DO NOT SEND CASH.

LORDS OF THE NIGHT

Monique Ellis
Sara Blayne
Janice Bennett

Zebra Books
Kensington Publishing Corp.
http://www.zebrabooks.com

ZEBRA BOOKS are published by

Kensington Publishing Corp.
850 Third Avenue
New York, NY 10022

Copyright © 1997 by Kensington Publishing Corp.

"The DeVille Inheritance" copyright 1997 by Monique Ellis
"Dark Shadows" copyright 1997 by Sara Blayne
"The Full of the Moon" copyright 1997 by Janice Bennett

All rights reserved. No part of this book may be reproduced in any form or by any means without the prior written consent of the Publisher, excepting brief quotes used in reviews.

If you purchased this book without a cover you should be aware that this book is stolen property. It was reported as "unsold and destroyed" to the Publisher and neither the Author nor the Publisher has received any payment for this "stripped book."

Zebra and the Z logo Reg. U.S. Pat. & TM Off.

First Printing: March, 1997
10 9 8 7 6 5 4 3 2 1

Printed in the United States of America

CONTENTS

THE DEVILLE INHERITANCE
by Monique Ellis — 7

DARK SHADOWS
by Sara Blayne — 143

THE FULL OF THE MOON
by Janice Bennett — 237

The DeVille Inheritance

Monique Ellis

Seven Dials

He lurked in the shadows of one of London's vilest stews, watching and waiting, his patience born of necessity.

One would have believed him a libertine seeking the usual entertainments, given the polish of his dress, and the area and hour—Seven Dials, long past midnight—but that his face was unmarked by dissipation, his silvery eyes unclouded. His hair, too, was silver. Dark winged brows slashed across an alabaster forehead. Long-fingered hands, elegant and powerful, caressed the slender swordstick he carried as he observed the girl he'd been following.

She was pausing, staring about her as if perplexed, shoulders hunched against the cold. The raw March night was moonless, parish lights nonexistent. Most would have been unable to read the consternation on those gentle features, but both his night vision and hearing were preternaturally keen.

And his need? That, too, was preternaturally keen. The time of feeding was on him.

The girl's breath came in shallow gasps. Moments before she'd been running over the filth-slickened cobbles, her horror at the sodden derelicts snoring in doorways speaking of a kinder life *than this place offered. Not an habitué of Seven Dials then, nor anywhere even remotely resembling it.*

At last, after nights of searching, and with his strength showing the first signs of ebbing, one who might serve.

He'd bleed her into the chalice, choke down the revolting contents, find her a husband and set them up in some business far from London. It was, he insisted for the twelfth time in three centuries, a better fate than one such as she had a right to expect did he not enter her life. In time her memories would fade to little more than a garbled family legend. That had been the pattern until now. No reason for it to change.

With a sigh of regret, Henry Frye stepped from the shadows.

It was cold—so cold!

Ann Leighton shivered in her abigail's there-is-work-to-be-done dress and Ann's own third-best cloak, peeping over her shoulder from the deep hood.

Tendrils of fog snaked through the coarse brown wool, raising the hair on her arms and pinching her fingers, but it wasn't the cold that made her shiver. Footsteps had dogged her since the hackney abandoned her on the fringes of this awful place. They might be muffled, but the steps were clear, stopping when she stopped, continuing when she continued. She was being followed.

Dear heaven, what had possessed her? Surely some crony of Tom's would've served equally well, and not minded the place half so much, being more or less acquainted with it. And yet her brother's words had been despairing, as if she were his last hope. Not surprising. They were everything to each other, left as they always had been to each other and the ministrations of servants.

"I will not be lily-livered," she muttered, glancing up and down the crooked way and squaring her shoulders.

His note had said Mother Hinchey's in Catspaw Alley behind a place called Old Sedgewick House. Typically, he'd neglected to say whether there were a New Sedgewick

House, what either might resemble, or what purpose they served. Tom's instructions were vague to the point of uselessness at the best of times. Pressured as he'd been, and probably foxed into the bargain? Her only hope lay in desperation having lent a touch of accuracy to his hasty scrawl.

She slipped her hand back through the cloak's deep slit, fingers seeking the crisp bank notes in the dress pocket that were all of her quarterly pin money.

She believed she'd followed the jarvey's directions precisely, if precision were possible in this warren of twisting streets that seemed to lead nowhere, doubling back on themselves until they put the most devilishly conceived maze to shame. Behind her buildings leaned over the narrow passageway, cutting off the night sky. The air hung still and dank, fetid with the refuse of human squalor.

"Are yer lost, dearie?"

Ann spun, nose wrinkling at the odors of stale sweat, cheap spirits, and cheaper perfume assailing her. The crone had appeared from nowhere, barely visible in the penumbra, bent and crabbed, her voice slyly insinuating. Behind her stood three bully-boys muffled to their ears against the cold, greatcoats dragging on the filthy cobbles, arms dangling at their sides.

"Well, watcher looking fer, dearie?" the old woman repeated, seizing Ann's forearm through her cloak with a wizened claw. "I knows these parts like the back o'me hand, as the saying goes. Be it a man er be it a place? Glad ter help."

"Please release me."

"My, but yer unfriendly!" the woman cackled, fingers digging more sharply. "Be yer looking fer yer sweetheart? Er might it be yer looking fer young Master Tom Leighton, what's got hisself in bad odor with certain folks as it ain't wise ter cross?"

Ann stilled, heart pounding. "What do you know of

Tom?" she demanded with a combination of disbelief and disgust. "Are you Mother Hinchey?"

"Could be I am. Could be I'm not. Could be I know precise who y'are, pretty lass, arriving just when yer supposed to. Accommodating of yer. Here we goes, me boyo's! Sharp, now." With a force belied by her apparent decrepitude, the hag spun Ann toward the men, simultaneously catching her across the shins and tumbling her to the gutter. "And get them yeller boys in her pocket. No sense turning 'em over ter his nibs along with her sweet self. He's got pounds enough a'ready."

Breath driven from her lungs, Ann lay gasping in the muck as a sack redolent of drains and rotten cabbages engulfed her, cutting off what little air there was. Rude hands lifted her into the air. She kicked feebly, then writhed in desperation. Suddenly she was in the gutter once more, feet stumbling over her as the air resounded with thuds and muttered curses. Frantically she attempted to roll out of the way, ribs aching, head pounding, trapped by her cloak and the sacking.

Dear heaven, what a fool she'd been to venture here at any time, let alone in the dead of night! What could Tom've been thinking? Unless he hadn't been thinking at all, which would be nothing unusual these days. Where Ambrose DeVille led, Tom followed. There was no doubt in her mind she had her unappealing suitor's influence to thank for Tom's current predicament as well as his perpetually emptied pockets. If there was trouble these days, the earl always seemed at the back of it.

Ann fetched up against a hard barrier, her stomach churning vilely. And still the invisible battle raged just beyond her. Never, *never* had she felt so helpless—not even when the great Brummell looked her up and down, raised his brows, lowered his quizzing glass, and turned his back.

What a paltry comparison!

She broke into a hysterical giggle at the notion of likening the fastidious Beau to her brutish assailants. Yet his power to destroy utterly was equally great—witness the slights to which she'd been treated since that humiliating night, and the arrogance with which DeVille had three times made his offer, unable to fathom why, like Brummell, she turned her back on what she considered unappetizing.

"You're able to laugh in the midst of all this? Stap me, but you're a plucky one!"

Ann froze at the sound of the pleasantly husky tenor voice, its tone at once amused and dubious, its accent educated. Strong hands seized the fabric that held her bound as securely as the sturdiest ropes, pulled.

"That," the voice grunted, "or you've lost your wits."

The sensation as she was lifted to a sitting position without her own muscles having anything to do with the matter, then set on her unsteady feet, was akin to what a netted fish whisked from its watery home must experience: total disorientation, her head swimming, her breath coming in unpleasant gulps that did her not the least good.

An arm was around her shoulders, holding her erect as a hand tugged at the noisome canvas sack. Then it was gone. She blinked, glancing about her. There was a heap of refuse where there'd been none before.

She turned to her rescuer, trembling uncontrollably.

"I haven't lost my wits," she managed with a touch of humor, pushing away the hood of her cloak. She'd had enough of fabric about her face to last her a lifetime. "At least I don't believe I have. Not yet, at any rate."

He stiffened at her words. There wasn't much she could see of the man—merely indistinct features that appeared pale in the darkness, dark clothes that might or might not fit, and a silvery glint to his hair. A long-fingered hand seized her chin, gently turned her head first this way, then that.

"Blast!" the stranger muttered as he bent to retrieve what appeared to be a slender walking stick from the uneven cobbles.

"I disappoint you, sir?" she said, taking refuge in bravado and pertness, both of which would've earned her a severe scold from her governess only months before.

"Disappointed? Not in the least. Rather a comely wench I've managed to rescue." White teeth flashed in a broad grin. "I've always had a predilection for golden curls and hazel eyes with a touch of golden green to them."

"You can see so much in this darkness?"

"Always had exceptional night vision. Come—we'd best get you where you can regularize your appearance. Your cloak appears sodden."

"I dread to think with what. That heap over there, is it—"

"It'll never trouble anyone again, 'an end tenaciously to be sought after', as my friend Will said before I suggested a trace of consonance and a few less words might serve his purpose better."

Ann found herself being propelled up the twisting lane, her upper arm gripped firmly.

"Such inaccurate citing of Shakespeare in pretense the saying's one's own is a bit presumptuous, don't you think?" she protested, grateful for the inconsequence of the conversation. "You speak like an educated man. I'm surprised you didn't correct your friend."

"Oh, I did," he chuckled as he hurried her over the rough cobbles. "Constantly. He took most of my suggestions in good part, being not unintelligent himself. Charming fellow, and an excellent drinking companion. Always with a tale or two to regale the company."

"Has he, indeed?"

"Had, not has, though he's achieved immortality of a sort, I suppose—a much more comfortable one than the usual," he said with genuine amusement. "No demands on him, you see, after a lifetime of importunings at every turn. This way, if you please."

"Indeed? Fascinating," she snapped at his mocking flourish. "This isn't how I came. Are you certain you know where you're going? And do we have to go so fast? My boots have thin soles, and—"

"You wish to encounter more of the louts who accosted you moments ago? Your abbess is sure to return with reinforcements."

"My—? Oh, dear heaven! Is that what she was?"

"Unless the world's changed more than anyone has a right to expect. I just managed to dispatch those three, one permanently, which example caused the others to take to their heels temporarily. Such ruffians don't fight like gentlemen, and I definitely do not have the strength of ten. More to the point, I've only two arms, two legs and two eyes, like any ordinary mortal. A superabundance of attackers, and I might have a problem. You wouldn't care for that."

"No, I wouldn't."

"Neither would I," he agreed dryly. "It doesn't suit me to slough off this 'too, too solid flesh' just yet, though when cessation leads to sleep eternal rather than eternal wandering, I'll be glad enough to make my farewells.

"Through here," he instructed, pulling her into an alley that appeared as blind-ended as the others she'd tried. "Watch your step. Crossing sweeps don't frequent this part of London, and there's a mews of sorts down the way. My carriage is just beyond."

"Thank heavens for small mercies," she murmured, tripping over what felt like a pile of rags but was certain not to be, lurching into the stranger as she shuddered at scrabbling sounds that, if she was lucky, were only cats foraging for a midnight snack. "Is it everywhere like this? You know the area well, I gather."

"This isn't my first foray, if that's what you mean. Now, hush. We don't want to call attention to ourselves. I've had enough exercise for one evening."

He pulled her on, a solid shadow comfortably close to her own modest height, yet enough taller and with shoulders sufficiently broad to give at least the illusion of security. They reached a jog in the alley, great wooden doors in a dilapidated building directly before them catching the feeble light of a lantern on an iron stanchion. The alley angled to the right, carriage lamps glowing on the pavement at its mouth.

Her rescuer hesitated, then gathered her roughly against his side and covered her mouth with a surprisingly cool ungloved palm as he glanced first at the alley's end, then back the way they'd come.

"That's not my carriage," he murmured. "It's at the next corner unless my coachman's ignored my instructions—a most unlikely occurrence—and I do believe we're being followed. Not your abbess, and not her minions. Someone else. A gentleman, or one who purports to be a gentleman, from the sound of his boots. At a guess, he's somewhat disgruntled."

"But how—"

"Hush!"

With what to Ann appeared a magician's quickness, he opened a small door camouflaged within the larger, pulled her through, eased the smaller door closed on well-oiled hinges, then slid a trap aside to reveal a minuscule window. Behind them came a soft whicker, and the homely sound of horses shifting in their stalls.

"A convenient bolt-hole," he murmured as he peered through the slit. "The only problem would've been if it no longer existed. D'you have enemies in high places, my dear young lady?"

"I? Don't be foolish!" she stammered. "How could you tell—"

"Superior boot-making always has a certain ring to it when heel strikes pavement or cobbles. Someone dear to you who is possessed of enemies, then?" he interrupted without regard to social niceties. "I believe I heard a certain Tom mentioned."

"My brother."

"Truthfully?"

She nodded, incensed. "I don't know the conventions where you customarily reside, but in London it's not considered the thing for a young unmarried woman to indulge in assignations."

"But it is for older, married ones? No, don't bother to answer. You may not be aware of the less publicized activities of the *ton,* but I am. *Le plus ça change, le plus c'est la même chose.*"

"I beg your pardon?"

"Crudely, the more things change, the more they remain the same—according to the French, at least. We British, on the other hand, tend to act with either consistent inconsistency, or else in a mad lockstep chained to outworn traditions—which I suppose goes to prove the French adage."

"What infinite cleverness," she snapped, irritated by his almost schoolmasterish air and tone of boredom. "I'm overawed. Shouldn't we attempt to leave?"

"I'd like nothing better, but here comes our friend now," he murmured. "Best we permit him the illusion that we've vanished if it's indeed you he's searching for, and you truly don't know who he is."

"Let me see," she whispered, tugging on his sleeve and standing on tiptoe. "Perhaps I'll recognize him."

"I rather doubt it. He's muffled like a mendicant leper. All he lacks is the traditional bell to warn of his approach. One would almost suspect his lordship didn't want his presence noted."

"His lordship?"

"A figure of speech."

As she peeped over his shoulder the tattoo of rapid footsteps came closer, but she could see nothing. The stranger was right: the tap of heel against cobbles did sound angry. "D'you know who it is?" she whispered.

"I was about to make the same inquiry of you."

"How can I tell? I can't see him."

"There's that, of course."

"You don't believe me?"

"Experience has taught me when a young lady's not where she's supposed to be at this hour, it's rarely her brother who's the reason," he retorted wryly. "And in a place such as this? My dear child, I cut my wisdoms years before you were born."

"I'm not a child! I'm eighteen, and've made my come-out."

"You're in your infancy," he chuckled, clearly diverted despite the location and their predicament, "for all I realize girls your age are not infrequently many years wed, and mothers several times over. Heavens—my own mother was barely fourteen when I entered this vale of sin and tears."

"Surely not!"

"That, too, was many years ago."

She snorted inelegantly.

"Customs have changed," he insisted. "It was nothing out of the way where we lived back then."

The footsteps passed, receded. From the street beyond the alley came the indistinct echo of voices. The man's arm stiffened, his muscles bunching with sudden power beneath her hand. Then, as if with a tremendous effort of will, they relaxed.

"One thing I can tell you," he said. "That one's definitely not best pleased, and is exceeding unpleasant when roused. Annoyed him by missing your rendezvous, did you?"

"I wouldn't know," she snapped, "for those definitely weren't Tom's steps, and he's the only one I hoped to see here."

"So you say."

The clatter of carriage wheels jolting over rough cobbles cut off Ann's sharp retort. "I'd hate to spend life being such a cynic," she said more mildly than she'd intended as the sounds faded.

"Guilty as charged, my dear," he returned, a smile in his voice. "I've seen a bit more of the world than you, and've learned to beware of apparent innocence. It usually masks the most devious of souls."

He shut the peephole, eased the door open, glanced up and down the alley. Satisfied, he pulled her into the open and shut the door behind them.

"Whoever and whatever you are or are not," he said dryly, glancing at her begrimed cloak, "there's one thing I can tell you without fear of contradiction: You return home in this condition and there'll be explanations demanded you'll find it devilishly difficult to come up with. No matter what the truth is, I suspect it's something you'd rather hide. My man's a marvel at salvaging garments one would've thought past praying for, so with your permission I'll be taking you to my home."

"The cloak and dress don't matter," she sighed, stumbling toward the mouth of the alley at his side with the sense of being trapped in a fantastical dream world bearing no resemblance to reality. "They're merely my abigail's. I'll replace them with something better. She'll be delighted. My real concern is Tom. I dread to think what he'll imagine when I don't appear."

"Bother Tom—if he exists. I doubt you'd get within leagues of your home perfumed as you are. The Watch doesn't encourage derelicts in the environs frequented by *tout Londres,* anymore than the *gendarmerie* do in Paris."

"Probably not." She wavered, all of it crashing down on her at once. "I—thank you, sir," she managed in a disgustingly small voice. "I'd've been in dire straits had you not intervened."

"You'd most likely be lying drugged in a magdalen, about to be auctioned off to the highest bidder," he specified brutally. "I want your word you'll not be coming here again, no matter who Tom is or what problems he faces."

"But I can't abandon him!"

"Leave rescue missions to those who're equipped to handle them. That, or I'll catch up the carriage that just departed and turn you over to whoever's inside. Perhaps he'll be able to teach you sense!"

The trip to his bachelor establishment was swift and silent once Henry Frye had overridden the girl's half-hearted protests regarding the impropriety of a young lady visiting a gentleman's home unchaperoned.

He wasn't particularly proud of the way he'd snapped at the child, but he found her lack of common sense wearying, especially as he'd had to give up his own highly essential plans for the evening in favor of coming to her assistance. That he'd at first thought she offered the answer to his recurring predicament was immaterial.

Frye leaned against the squabs, observing the intriguing play of emotions on the piquant face across from him as parish lamps cast uneven bands of light through the lowered windows. This one apparently didn't follow her vapid sisters' pattern. The determinedly erect figure screamed exhaustion and despair. Yet, beyond the one protest, she'd complained neither of her own situation nor his high-handed insistence that she regularize her appearance before attempting a return to her home.

What, beyond thwarted young love *à la* Romeo and Juliet—a pair of idiots if ever there were one—could've brought the child to such a pass? The tale of a brother in dire straits didn't wash, not if his experience of the animosities more often to be found among siblings was a measure.

"Sir?"

Frye's head snapped up.

Had he been dozing? Impossible. He almost never wasted the night sleeping. This era, with the *beau monde* snoring the mornings away recovering from its evening dissipations, had proved more accommodating than most.

"Yes, my dear?" he said with a forced smile as he stifled

a yawn. He was, dammit, not accustomed to playing the soothing *pater familias*.

"I believe I owe you a full explanation as well as my thanks."

"Plenty of time for that. We've arrived."

He leaned forward, gratefully inhaling the slightly cleaner winter air beyond the carriage's window. Those same senses that made him a superb hunter when the need was on him had rendered this journey across the city acutely unpleasant. He could have told the girl, had she any desire for the information, the exact origin of each damp stain on her cloak. As for the clay-like clumps encrusting her boots, even she could have no doubt as to their nature.

With a sigh of relief he opened the carriage door and leapt to the pavement as John Coachman pulled up in front of the area. Frye turned, lowered the steps and offered his hand with an abbreviated bow.

Behind him he knew Springer, his infinitely punctilious man, would be opening the sea green front door with its gargoyle's head brass knocker. He also knew the likely reaction of that very proper gentleman's gentleman when he realized Frye had arrived with a highborn girl in tow. A doxy Springer would've accepted as being consistent with how bachelors conducted themselves on occasion, albeit not customarily in their own homes. But arriving with a girl of quality, and an innocent into the bargain? For what his valet would assume was dalliance of the more energetic sort?

Springer wouldn't approve.

"Come now," Frye said, attempting to insert a reassuring note in his voice. "There truly are no evil demons waiting you within, nor any of the sort who had designs on you earlier. When all's said and done, I'm the most ordinary of fellows, and not in the least given to, ah—"

"To lecherous improprieties at the expense of others?"

"What a charming way of stating the not-so-obvious. I

could be every bit as heinous as those delights who accosted you earlier, you know."

At least the girl wasn't hanging back as he'd first feared she would. She merely gave him a trusting, slightly shy glance from those remarkable eyes traced with green and gold, placed her hand in his and gracefully stepped to the pavement.

"I don't believe so," she said, a pair of dimples twinkling on either side of her prettily-shaped mouth.

Definitely the chit wasn't going to be a bore, which was a blessing.

"Scrape your boots on the curb," he cautioned. "You don't want to bring in any more of what you've partially deposited on the carriage floor than you can help."

She complied, clinging tightly to his hand and treating him to what could only be termed a minxish, amused peep from beneath partially lowered lids whose lashes were so luxuriant he wondered she could open them at all. The child might not know it, but with a little tutelage she could become a devastating flirt.

"That's all of it, I believe," she murmured. "I'm quite good at curbs."

A glance at her boots proved her right. He gave a nod, turned her toward the entry steps and the front door.

"John, stable 'em," he tossed over his shoulder, "but I'll be wanting the carriage again in an hour or so. Have it swept out and fresh straw laid."

The irony of their mounting those steps hand in hand like a pair of schoolchildren wasn't lost on Frye. Neither, apparently, was it lost on Springer, waiting just beyond the open door with a lamp held high, his features a mask of correctness more chilling than the loudest reproof.

"Good evening, sir," he said, quite as if Frye returning at such an hour with a young lady were a common occurrence.

"Came upon a bit of a to-do," Frye explained, divesting the girl of her cloak and dumping it on a chair as Springer closed the door. He removed his greatcoat, tossed it at another chair along with his hat, gloves, and swordstick. "That'll require cleaning," he said, pointing to the weapon. "See to it, would you? I've been a little busy this evening."

"Have you indeed, sir."

"We'll be needing Mrs. Finch, and please see what you can do about salvaging this young lady's cloak. Both she and it've been through something of an ordeal."

"Indeed, sir." Springer held the lamp up, nostrils pinching as he examined the offending garment without touching it. "Sponging won't set this to rights, nor yet an iron. Might be best," he frowned, turning to his master, "if we arrange for the young person to be given one of the housemaid's cloaks, sir. This is ready for the dustbin."

"Whatever you think best, Springer," Frye shrugged, already bored with the topic. He wanted nothing so much as his bed, but suspected he wouldn't be seeing it soon. "Bring me brandy after you've seen to the young lady. She'll want to regularize her appearance. At bit blowzy at the moment, which I suspect is grossly out of character."

"I believe you're correct, sir. If you'll be so good as to follow me, miss, I'll show you below stairs and fetch the housekeeper."

Springer held his lamp high as he indicated the back of the house and the stairs leading to the servants' rooms. Then he stiffened with as close to a look of surprise as ever graced his features and turned back to Frye.

"Sir, are you aware this lady is the honorable Ann Leighton, youngest daughter of Viscount and Viscountess Leighton? The family is rather well-known."

"Is she? Interesting. We hadn't time for introductions. You are indeed Miss Leighton?" At the girl's distressed nod he gave a slight, ironic bow, murmuring, "Your servant," as he straightened.

So this was one of the famous Leighton Hodge-Podge: two much older girls long wed, then the son and heir, then this Ann. He eyed the furiously flushing child dispassionately. Swinard Leighton was a gamester of the more devoted and less successful sort. And his rib? It was barely possible the viscount's blood flowed in his heir's veins—and the Leighton sprig, a young idiot who bid fair to become his father's equal, did indeed go by the name of Tom. A double cuckold was the viscount, one horn the gift of his lady wife, Carlotta, as the club wags put it, the other of Lady Luck.

This youngest of the brood? Most anyone could be her father. One *on dit* hinted Sally Jersey had called the woman Harlotta to her face. Poor girl, indeed. Given she appeared to have a character entirely different from her mother's, she had a great deal to live down.

Springer was drawing himself up, turning to Frye.

"I will return immediately, sir," he said, a touch of threat in his voice.

Frye almost laughed. Every proper and improper gentleman's gentleman since the days of Hadrian stood at Springer's back in that moment, supporting the man's the unspoken reproof.

"I'll be waiting for you, but there's no rush," Frye returned with a weary grin he could no more suppress than he could banish the appreciative glint from his eyes. "If you were to ask Miss Leighton, you'd find she's more grateful than not for my intervention. As for coercing her to join us for a bit, she couldn't return home in that condition."

Springer's bland expression proved nothing had changed as far as that worthy was concerned. Miss Ann Leighton, daughter of a viscount, had no business in his master's residence, no matter what the circumstances. Head high, the valet indicated the elliptical marble staircase at the front of the house.

Frye watched Springer, wispy-haired and spindle-shanked, lead Miss Leighton away with a deference as unaccustomed in that household as it was genuine, murmuring smooth civilities all the while. Then, with a wry twist to his lips, Frye strode down the short corridor leading to his bookroom at the back of the house. The fire was not only laid, but glowing gently on the grate. He need not have asked for brandy. A full Waterford decanter and half a dozen goblets waited on the hunt table between the velvet-draped windows.

But the draperies were drawn.

Frye looped them back with a resigned sigh. Neither Mrs. Finch nor her efficient staff accepted that, unlike most employers, he wanted the draperies open at night, closed during the day.

He poured himself a generous portion of brandy, then glanced at the ceiling, hope lighting his eyes. With an air of determination, he crossed to the nearer of the massive cabinets flanking the fireplace, set his glass on the mantel, pulled a key from his waistcoat, unlocked the doors and eased them open. The shelves were crammed with moldering folios and manuscripts. The drawer under the middle shelf opened at the turn of another key. Frye slid it out and dropped the facing. Within were three ranks of compartmentalized, velvet-lined trays. He pulled the bottom tray forward, eyes narrowing. Only the rear compartments still held sparkling silver cubes, each a quarter inch on a side. Soon he'd have to replenish his supply.

Jaws clenched, he took a pair of wooden tongs from the shelf above the drawer, retrieved a single cube and set it on the mantel. Then he replaced the tongs, shut and locked the cabinet, and took a gulp of the brandy. Finally, eyes closed, he groped along the mantel, feeling for the cube. Something clattered to the floor. He knelt, opened his eyes, and cursed. The cube, lying on the hearth, was now black as ebony. With a muttered curse he hurled the thing across the room. Then, shoulders sagging, he retreated to one of the deep chairs flanking the fireplace. The entire situation reeked of irony.

Cocking his head, he studied the portrait of himself as

Martin Frye, Cavalier. The blue velvet costume with its froth of gold lace and gold buttons had favored him, as had the style for long curling wigs. His gaze shifted to Ben Cellini's gold chalice set with rubies the size of pigeon eggs where stem met bowl. Ben'd had a wonderful sense of the tricks life played, and hadn't been the least dismayed when Frye—another Henry, or Enrico, as Ben'd called him—had explained his predicament and made his request.

"I will create for you the most exquisite chalice the world has ever seen," the goldsmith said. "Even the Holy Father won't have its equal, for if you must exist without a soul and be invisible to God, you must have a recompense. Only one request I make of you, *amico mio*: Should you one day acquire a soul, give my cup to a church, that it may be used for the purpose for which such vessels are customarily intended."

Not much chance of that as things stood, and he was so tired, so blasted sick of this life that dragged on from day to day without so much as the slightest indisposition to relieve the monotony.

What, he wondered for the millionth time, did a nose that ran feel like? Was a cough a truly unpleasant thing?

Ann gazed about her in curiosity as Springer—a wiry little man with the face of a well-bred hake and the protruding eyes of a carp—placed the lamp on the mantel, then softly closed the plain door and vanished on velvet feet.

The bedchamber was small, its scant furnishings—a narrow bed with mended hangings, a dressing table in one corner, a wash stand with Staffordshire basin and ewer in the other—ordinary to the point of vapidity. The painting over the mantel followed the tone set by the rest of the spotless room: a lackluster "portrait of a lady" that paid more attention to fabric and jewels than to features and expression. She'd expected something more worthy of notice in the home of the gentleman with the sweeping black brows, silvery gray eyes and prematurely silver hair. Why? She couldn't've said, but the mundane room, its furnishings crying out "for hire," seemed incongruous even if he employed it only for the accommodation of the occasional visiting friend. And the occasional waif rescued from the stews, she added with a wry grin.

She wandered to the window and parted the faded rose damask curtains. Behind her coals glowed on the grate, reflecting orange and red in the night-darkened panes, her face a pale smudge haloed by their warmth. The fog pressed like cotton wadding against the moist surface, cutting off the world. Anything could lie beyond—lands of horror or delight, or only the most everyday sort of world, one that resembled hers in all its depressing details of isolation, loneliness, and futility.

With a rueful smile she let the curtains drop.

Eulalia Bowditch, who had been until last summer Ann's governess, would've claimed she was again indulging in fantasies out of keeping with her position. They'd never admitted openly such dreams were the only pleasant ones Ann was likely to have, but her last letter to Eulie, telling of Ambrose DeVille's suit, had received an immediate response containing an invitation to spend the spring months in Yorkshire. If only she could! But, all else aside, her mother would never grant permission.

Behind her the door opened hard on a firm knock. Ann turned to find Springer carrying a steaming copper can. He was followed by a plump, gray-haired woman in a gown of black bombazine whose outmoded full skirts swept the gleaming, uncarpeted floor with a soft hush.

"This is Mrs. Finch," Springer said, striding across the room to pour the can's contents in the pottery basin, "the housekeeper. She'll be fetching you anything else you need."

"Miss Leighton."

The woman's features might be a mask of correctness

as she set a stack of towels and a bar of soap on the bed, but her black eyes snapped with fury. If Springer was a hake, she was a grouper—albeit a fierce, somewhat elderly and fast-moving grouper—Ann decided with no little amusement. Apparently Mrs. Finch had no liking for being summoned from her bed to attend a stranger. Well, and who would?

"You'll want comb and brush, and pins," Mrs. Finch continued, managing to inject a world of accusation in her tone. "You'll find them in the top drawer of the dressing table. Can you arrange your hair, or do you require assistance?"

"I can manage for myself. Thank you for asking."

"Because if you require assistance, I don't know what we'll do," the woman scolded as if Ann hadn't spoken. "Not accustomed to females needing the services of an abigail here. Of course, maybe you're expecting the master to see to you. Wouldn't be the first to try it. Will you be wanting this bed made up, or will you be—"

"I'll be returning to my parents' home as soon as I've put myself to rights," Ann interrupted, blushing furiously.

"Y'won't be spending the night?"

"Hardly!"

"Then what's she doing here?" the housekeeper bristled to Springer in a clearly audible aside, arms folded under her generous bosom. "D'you think she intends to follow in her mother's footsteps? Certain, she has the look of her. She's famous, that one is. And a quick worker, from all reports."

"Now, Mrs. Finch—no call for such assumptions," Springer reproved softly, poking the fire and adding some coal from the scuttle. "Miss Leighton has the air of a true lady. That the master—"

"What's she trying to do, compromise the poor lad?" the housekeeper hissed. "Force him into marriage? Has someone primed to break in at the right moment, like as not, skulking about the garden and listening at keyholes.

She wouldn't be the first t'try it. Right wealthy, the master is, and with no more sense than a babe. Have to watch over him every minute of the day."

"Master's well able to see to himself," Springer broke in with an apologetic glance at Ann. "You shouldn't be talking this way, Mrs. Finch, for all your loyalty's admirable. Master wouldn't be in the least pleased. Young lady's more'n what you think. Come to that, I imagine she's more'n what he thinks."

"I'll warrant she is! That don't mean she's honest, or the *more* she is is fit for him to consort with."

"I don't so much as know the gentleman's name," Ann insisted, entering the unseemly fray, "nor have I ever seen him before tonight."

"And I'll be taking dinner at Carlton House tomorrow with Prinny," Mrs. Finch scoffed, eyes narrowed. "No better than she should be," the woman muttered, turning back to Springer, "that much I can tell you without fear of contradiction. Those pasty-faced, butter-wouldn't-melt-in-their-mouths sorts are the worst. Trap a man with their innocent looks, and before he knows what's happened to him he's paying deep. Well, the master has troubles enough without that, wasting away before our eyes as he is."

"He's not your son, that you can regulate his activities," Springer protested mildly.

"If he was, I'd see to him better than whatever woman gave him birth. Needs a keeper, and that's the truth of it."

"Mrs. Finch," Ann said, straightening her shoulders and stepping forward, tired of the woman's accusations and innuendoes, and realizing only she could put an end to them, "I'm not my mother, any more than you are yours."

"What's that supposed to mean?"

"It's a simple statement of fact. Each person is an individual, and should be judged on the basis of his or her actions, not those of others."

"And she's prosy into the bargain!" Mrs. Finch said with a sniff. "Well, she won't last long. Master can't abide prosiness, for all he indulges himself on occasion."

"I'm merely quoting my governess," Ann returned amiably, if with a touch of aloofness of which she would never've believed herself capable moments earlier. "Miss Bowditch was all that was kind and everything that wasn't prosy."

"Gave a fair imitation of it, then."

"My only business here is to put myself to rights following an extremely unpleasant experience," Ann continued, ignoring the woman's effrontery. "It was my good fortune your employer happened upon me as I was being accosted in the stews. Had he permitted it, I would've returned directly home.

"Now, if you'd be so kind, Mrs. Finch, I'd appreciate a little privacy in which to put that water to use before it must be reheated."

"I'll see you don't succeed, missy, no matter what you think," the housekeeper snapped. "The master's the greatest gentleman I've known in all my years, even if he hasn't a handle to his name nor yet a fancy country seat. Not one hair on your head will he harm, for all his odd looks and odder habits. Be sure you don't harm a hair on his."

On those words the housekeeper stalked from the room, back rigid, gray curls bobbing with indignation.

"My apologies, miss," Springer said, expression long-suffering. "Mrs. Finch has a habit of speaking her mind that keeps her from being employed in the very best establishments. As for the master, she's beyond reason. Reminds her of someone she knew when she was a girl, she says, for all she won't say who."

Ann sighed, exhaustion claiming her now the unpleasant little scene had played itself out. "Her partiality's obvious, and I suppose her loyalty's to be commended," she responded with a familiarity that was as unaccustomed when dealing with one of the servant class as it was honest. "Certainly were I one of the sort Mrs. Finch believes me to be, I'd hope someone would see to your master's protection. I owe him my safety, very possibly my life. That's an enormous debt, one I'll never be able to repay."

"He's a good man," Springer agreed, easing toward the door. "Mrs. Finch has that right, for all he hasn't the slightest sense of style, nor yet does he entertain sufficient to enhance his position or ours, which is something of a disappointment. His man of business and solicitor, who're one and the same, no one else. As for the invitations he receives, the ladies might as well not waste the ink.

"Well, miss, I'll leave you to it, with your permission. If you need anything, just give that rope by the bed a tug and I'll be back on the instant. And if you'll summon me when you're done I'll show you to the master's bookroom."

"I can find my own way," she said with a gentle smile. "I'm sure you're wanting to seek your bed now your master's home."

"And leave him to fend for himself?" Springer was through the door, closing it firmly on the single incensed word, "Never!"

"What an odd household," Ann murmured, staring at the door, "but then I suppose allowances must be made for an unmarried gentleman of reclusive habits."

Strangely, not once had either valet or housekeeper mentioned her host's name. Neither, come to that, had he made any attempt to introduce himself. Odd? Incredibly bizarre. Once more she had the sensation of having slipped through reality's cracks to find herself in a place where neither custom nor reason prevailed.

Frye rolled his head against the chair back at the gentle tap on the bookroom door.

"That you, Springer?" he called, knowing full well it wasn't. Springer, old-fashioned to a fault, scratched rather than knocked. "Find out anything more about why that girl was traipsing about Seven Dials as if she were taking an afternoon stroll?"

He watched from beneath lazily lowered lids as the door opened, revealing Miss Leighton more or less set to rights. Certainly her hair no longer straggled about her face in witch's wisps, and her gown had been given a thorough brushing. He'd been right: the little creature was uncommonly pretty once a touch of color was restored to her cheeks and a bit of precision to her person.

"Well, don't just stand there," he said with calculated irritability. He was damned if he'd permit himself to be cast in the role of hero, fawned over and expected to rescue the girl from more than stews toughs. It'd happened before. Surliness depressed such expectations more effectively than any other method he'd been able to devise. "Come in and shut the door behind you. I don't make it a practice to heat the halls and stairs, and I don't care for drafts."

Her incoherent apologies were all he could've desired. The confusion clouding her eyes at his incivility was even better.

"Been poking about where you've no business?" he continued the attack. "Took you long enough to see to yourself. What are you—a vain little thing who spends half the day in front of her mirror tarting herself up, and the rest admiring the results?"

"I don't believe so," she murmured politely, "but perhaps you would be the best judge."

"A primper!" he crowed, for all he could tell it wasn't true. "And a snoop into the bargain, I'll warrant. Been grubbing about in the hall cabinets? And examining the contents of every room into the bargain. Well? Have you?"

"I did look at a chest that appears Egyptian in origin. It has whippets carved on it, and gilt ladies in their nightgowns at the corners."

"Ha! What else did you notice in your spying?"

"It wasn't spying," she protested mildly.

"It wasn't? Strange, how the meanings of words change without one's being in the least aware of it," he returned unpleasantly.

"I touched nothing."

"And that makes all right? My dear girl, you've an odd notion of what constitutes proper behavior in a stranger's home."

"And you have odd notions regarding courteous discourse."

"My-my, the little butterfly has a sting. What else did you paw?"

"I touched nothing! I merely looked, and only in the hall on the way to the stairs. The paintings of your ancestors are wonderful. One had the air of a Gainsborough and another of a Michelangelo, for all I'm not certain he did portraits as a general thing."

"Fine artists, both. My, ah, ancestors had excellent taste and deep pockets."

"Are they like? Certainly you have the look of them."

"I do?" he asked, diverted. "And what of this one over the mantel? It's a Rembrandt, by the bye."

"He appears to have the same long-fingered hands, and the same sweeping brows."

"Family traits," he murmured. "Nothing unusual in that."

"Nothing in the least. The Hapsburg lip is famous, and runs true."

"And is excessively unattractive, especially on a woman."

"The cup beneath is exquisite," she breathed, apparently noting it for the first time. "Is it medieval? It has a barbaric look to it, for all its delicacy."

"Sixteenth century, actually. It's the heaviness of the gold that lends it a slightly crude look. I drink from it on occasion."

"The garnets are huge."

"They're rubies," he said, then chuckled at her gasp.

"Well, stop hovering by the door. I don't bite, you know. Come into the light where I can see you."

Her steps were hesitant, her blush deep. Her eyes betrayed her, flashing a green fire reminiscent of lightning over a stormy sea. Interesting. This was no spineless miss—but then he'd already determined that, hadn't he? No girl would've survived the experience in the stews without hysterics unless she were most unusual, and possessed a more highly developed vertebral column than was common in an era when vapidity in females was the preference. For her kind of bottom one had to look to the Elizabethans, starting with Gloriana herself.

"You're not entirely unprepossessing, you know," he continued with every intention of unnerving her as much as possible as he gestured at the chair across the hearth from him. "Well, sit down. We'll be here a bit. Would you care for a sip of brandy to warm you?"

"I think not."

He came close to laughter at the sight of her delicate little nose wrinkling at the idea, but she took the chair as instructed, automatically arranging her skirts as if she were in a ballroom rather than a bookroom, and her gown of finest silk rather than cheap wool.

"Well, let's have it now you're a bit more yourself," he barked, studying her with every appearance of coldness. "What were you doing in Seven Dials?"

She pulled a crumpled piece of paper from her pocket, handed it to him. Frye's brows rose, but she met his eyes with apparent candor, hands now calmly folded in her lap. Meticulous training showed. She must've had a superior governess at one time, however little attention her progenitors paid her otherwise.

"I know you didn't believe me earlier," she said. "This may convince you. It's a good thing I have it with me, though what business any of this is of yours I can't fathom. You did rescue me from the results of my own folly, but that doesn't give you the right to hold me against my will."

"Excellent point," he said on a yawn, not bothering to open what was apparently a note, and gesturing at the door. "You may go. No one's holding you here. Inform your parents of your—brother, isn't it?—your *brother's* predicament. I'm certain your father will know what to do."

"He might were he at home and cared to bestir himself. Then again, he might merely curse and throw things."

"Or you can depend on one who's already proved his abilities in the rescuing department," Frye continued dryly, "but I insist on honesty."

"Read the note."

Frye cocked his head, narrowed his eyes. Lud, but she had the air of his mother when she'd caught him in some *bêtise*. Was that long-suffering expression infused with the slightest touch of amusement a female characteristic? Heaven knew he'd seen it in other female eyes besides his mother's, ignored it as beneath notice. With this one, however, it was particularly effective. She must've learned the gambit from one who used it to perfection.

With a long-suffering sigh of repressed irritation to match her long-suffering look of determined patience, he unfolded the crumpled paper. It wasn't much, just a few words in an unsteady, but definitely masculine scrawl. With misspellings corrected and illegible words guessed from context, it read:

Nanette—

Went out with his lordship as planned, and stumbled on a new hell. D refused to stay—said he didn't like the look of the place—but I wanted to try my luck. Now my pockets're to let and they won't accept my vowels, so I need you to ransom me. I'm at Mother Hinchey's in Catspaw Alley behind Old Sedgewick House. Any jarvey'll know the way.

Don't fail me, Nan. They've been talking of press gangs and that's the least of it. Don't alert Father.

He'd come after me with a whip or leave me to rot. I don't know which'd be worse at this point.

                                                    Tom

"Irresponsible whelp," Frye muttered.

"I beg your pardon?"

"Nanette?"

"A pet name from our childhood. No one else calls me that."

He glanced at the golden-haired girl, his eyes narrowing. "This is your brother's hand?"

She nodded.

"And his mode of expression?"

"More or less, especially when in his cups."

"Which you suspect he was when he penned it?"

"There's no question. Tom's generally most sensible about not outrunning the constable, but I've found that in him, at least, sense takes a holiday when his faculties are impaired by a touch too much wine. Unfortunately, that's been happening rather often of late given the company he keeps."

"What a delicate way of saying he's an idiot when foxed and selects his friends with the usual lack of wisdom to be found in the infantry." Frye scanned the note again, frowning. "How did you come by this?"

"It was left at the stables. The messenger disappeared without even waiting for a coin or two. 'Took ter 'is 'eels like the devil war arter 'im,' was how my groom put it."

Frye's brows rose. The impish copying of a servant's diction was unexpected. Indeed, the girl was proving in every way unexpected—witness her refusal to be put out of countenance by his incivilities. That might be due to lack of perception, but he rather doubted it. A trace too much perception was the more likely answer.

"And your groom gave it to your abigail, with whom he's on excellent terms," he said, lolling comfortably—and rudely—in his chair. She appeared unimpressed. He sat up. He'd never found lolling as comfortable as people claimed. "That's usually the case. She brought it to you. You convinced her of your brother's peril, contrived your 'disguise,' and ransacked your horde of shillings and pence. Once the house was asleep she fetched you a hackney. Now she awaits you and your cup-shot brother at a side door, probably with a tankard of some repulsive remedy for those who overindulge."

"It was the front door, almost twenty pounds, and I found the hackney, not Meg. Beyond that, yes. I don't know about the tankard."

"It never occurred to you to request assistance of your brother's friends?"

"Their pockets're generally to let as well," she sighed, "so they wouldn't've been much use. Besides, who would've known where to find them at this hour, or if they're even in Town? There's to be a mill somewhere between Little Stoking and Crivenden tomorrow. Tom doesn't care for such things, but most of his friends do. And before you ask, our father is from home. He's visiting his, ah, *friend* tonight."

"The term's *chère amie*, if you must insist on being unmissishly accurate about these things. Milicent Sinclair," Frye murmured absently. "Quite a fetching little thing in her youth. Dimples on her—ah—"

His gaze flew to little Miss Leighton. Aha! That'd discomposed her, for a miracle. He'd begun to fear nothing would shake that imperturbable calm.

He shook his head, grinning ruefully. Dealing with females, except on a strictly professional basis and with the parameters clearly set, was exhausting work. Dealing with such a young one? Debilitating in the extreme. They never reacted as one had every right to expect. At least this one wasn't.

"Who's this lord to whom your brother refers? D-something," he said, convinced of the answer. "And yes, I've come to accept your motive for being in the stews was indeed your brother, however unlikely that explanation is."

"Thank you."

"You're welcome. The lord with whom he was disporting himself this evening—who is he?"

"Ambrose DeVille, the Earl of Denbigh."

"That dissipated lecher?"

"You don't like him either?"

"No, I don't like him. How the devil did a young cub like your brother come to be acquainted with a rotter like DeVille?" Frye exploded, unable to help himself. "The man isn't known for bear-leading striplings."

"You'd be surprised. Lord Denbigh seems to enjoy the company of anyone who'll pay him proper deference. He's introduced Tom to all sorts of dreadful people and amusements. Tom pays him extremely proper deference, you see."

"Has your father taken leave of his senses to permit such a connection?" Frye spluttered. Then he in turn flushed. "Forgive me," he said. "I have no right to ask you such a question, nor to cast aspersions on your father's probity."

"You have every right, none better. Were Papa more of a father, Tom could've turned to him and you'd've not become involved. Actually, Papa encourages the connection and hopes for a closer one."

"You can't possibly mean—"

"The earl has three times honored me with an offer of marriage," she said primly.

"And?" he thundered, surprised by his own vehemence.

"I have three times refused him."

"If you're wise, you'll keep on refusing," Frye snapped. "For the rest of your life, if necessary."

"I will as long as I'm able, but Papa doesn't mislike the idea, and with Tom's debts mounting at every turn I may have little choice. Lord Denbigh is excessively wealthy, and his offer includes a generous wedding settlement that would pay off Tom's debts, and most of Papa's as well.

Besides, with no other suitors in the offing, I may not have much choice."

"And they claim slavery no longer exists in England," Frye muttered.

"I've considered joining my former governess," she continued as if he hadn't spoken, "but that's the first place they'd look for me, and positions are hard to find. The one advertisement I answered? Well," she said with a shudder, "I'd rather die!"

"Oh? And with whom were you seeking a post?"

"A Mrs. Carson Doncastle, as her companion."

"Good Lord!"

"You're acquainted with her?"

"I was, once," he chuckled. "What's Gertie like now?"

"Odorous. No—I mean it. She reeks, as if she were so impregnated with perfumes and dirt that, well, it's not pleasant being in the same room with her. And raddled, and crippled with rheumatism, and so unpleasant one would rather die than spend more than five minutes in her presence."

"Poor old Gert! A strapping fine female when I knew her."

"And then there's her husband. Mr. Doncastle is, was, well—"

"Still peeping down ladies' corsages and up their skirts, is he?" Frye chuckled. "He'll never change. You were wise to avoid employment there."

"At least they don't move in the same circles as my parents and the earl. I should've been safe."

"The same circles? My dear child, Gertie Doncastle was nothing but an expensive lightskirt in her best days. Donny Doncastle was her procurer, pure and simple. Rather good at it, too. Always got her top wages. The Doncastles, move among the *ton*? Hardly! At least not in the way you mean. Gertie moved under its male members vigorously enough.

"But you as Gertie's companion? Either Donny'd've had you in his bed the first night, or else he'd've sold you to the highest bidder. Virgins fetch a pretty penny, and I assume you're untouched. Certainly you have that air."

"And you're certainly blunt," she snapped. "I've never heard such words spoken except in whispers, and then never by a gentleman."

"What's the good of pretending reality is other than it is? Men will always be men, and women will always be either virtuous and boring, or else everything that's the opposite. Besides," he added at her look of disbelief, "I've spent most of my life traveling, and am more used to Continental manners than British."

"I suppose you've never heard one should do as the Romans do when in Rome?"

"London isn't Rome, not by a long shot. You'd like Rome," he said with a wicked grin. "Lively and uninhibited despite the Holy Father's omnipresence. The Via Appia by moonlight, now—that's where you should be tutored in the arts of love, driving slowly under the pines as the wind that caressed Caesar's cheek sighs against your own. Wonderful sense of treading where others have already trod that makes the adventure all the more delightful."

"Shocking!" she murmured, for all her eyes were sparkling. "I do believe you're flirting with me in a highly improper fashion, Mr.—dear me, what is your name? You've never mentioned it, and neither did Springer or Mrs. Finch."

"Frye," he said. "Henry Frye, at your service."

Trimble House

Frye stared at the blackened silver cube lying in his palm as the rumble of his town carriage's wheels faded. Within that carriage? One Ann Leighton, more familiarly known to her brother as Nanette. And Mrs. Finch, to play propriety. And Springer, because he'd demanded it and Frye had seen no reason to say him nay.

What the devil had come over him during this odd night?

Yes, it infuriated him that his many-generations-removed half-nephew was apparently behind the girl's attempted abduction. Nothing new in that. The DeVilles were famous for their dedication to the art of seduction—witness his own presence in this vale of tears. When seduction didn't work they resorted to cruder methods, none with more determination than Ambrose, whose vile career he'd been following since his return to London in an attempt to undo some of the man's worst crimes.

Just how greatly the DeVilles, man and woman, excelled in the sport accounted for Frye's unusual nature: the seventh son of a seventh son, not all of them legitimate by any means, and the bastard son of bastard parents. The latter had come as a surprise, fitting the final piece into the puzzle he'd been so long assembling: not that his mother sprang from the wrong side of the blanket, but randy Reginald DeVille, every inch the *grand seigneur*?

Frye had come across that tidbit a century ago in the tattered diary of a gossip-loving priest who'd recorded every blanket secret whispered in the confessional. According to Father Timothy, his grandmother's manner of seeking consolation with a willing neighbor following her lord's death had been a trifle direct. Reginald was her bonus. The usual would have been for mother and ten-month babe to be smothered by some hanger-on anxious to keep the DeVille strain pure, but Frye's grandmother's family was powerful. They had ensured Reginald's accession to his "father's" honors by marrying their widowed daughter to a loutish baron with an arm strong enough to defend Reginald's rights, keeping infant far from stepfather so that defending sword wouldn't slip at an inopportune moment. It was a common enough tale in those days, if not the sort generally bandied about.

No, he'd come by his problems naturally, if such an unnatural condition could be termed "natural." That had taken more than a trace of bad luck. The odds? Heaven alone knew—and must—but the chances of a creature such as himself existing had to be so slim as to be close to nonexistent.

Born to this state, dammit, with not even the opportunity to make a bad decision and so have no one to blame but himself. No soul, though the traditional banes of church and cross, of rose thorn and garlic affected him not at all. Forced to ingest blood—the perfect food, some wag'd claimed in his early days—or crumble to dust. He'd learned that much from all his reading.

No, other than willful self-destruction he was immortal, or so close to it as made no difference. He'd aged precisely ten years since he discovered his nature at the age of nineteen. Ten years apparently, three hundred in point of fact. If he were fortunate, he'd reach his allotted span of three score and ten in another eighteen hundred, and be permitted to stop. To cease to exist. To fade into blessed nothingness. Perhaps, but only perhaps. In the Year of Our Lord 3611. If he didn't go mad first.

He was as tired of people and their eternal sameness, of his solitary and peripatetic existence, as it was possible to become. Was that why he'd played the fool tonight, breaking every rule he'd set down over two hundred and seventy years ago when the less obvious but more annoying aspects of his problem became evident? Because he had broken them, every one. He'd spoken with little Miss Leighton as if she were one of his sort, more than hinting at friendships with those too aged for him to have known at the times he'd indicated. He'd more than hinted at friendships even more impossible with those already gone to their eternal rest.

And why?

Because eyes touched with green and gold had gazed trustingly into his. Because hair the color of sunlight striking through broken clouds had tumbled about a face as pretty and pert as any he'd ever seen, and he'd seen a lot of pretty faces over the years. Because a voice as light as a spring zephyr, and as seductive, had laughed with him.

He was a fool. A certifiable fool. Fit for Bedlam. As callow as any mooncalf.

Apparently even a man with three hundred years and more in his basket could fall prey to female charms if they were fresh enough.

Of course there was some excuse. What man wouldn't find excuses where he could? The feeding frenzy was on him again, not crucial yet, but naggingly insistent nevertheless, and he was never quite rational when it struck. Cow's blood and raw beefsteak wouldn't hold him much longer. Then it would be a case of feed or go mad and perform acts that, when he recovered, would drive him into another form of madness.

With an angry shrug he headed for the bookroom and the comfort of brandy while he waited for his carriage to return, cramming the silver cube in his waistcoat pocket. The cube that had bruised Ann Leighton's foot through her boot, and that she'd handed him asking him what it could be. An unusual die, he'd told her, for an esoteric game of chance.

Well, that hadn't been so far off the mark. It and its brethren were his touchstone of normality. Of a soul, a normal life span, perhaps even a wife and children and the joys available to every other man with a soul had the fools the wit to realize how infinitely precious they were, how meaningless the wealth and power most sought as the greatest rewards of life. To a time when the mere touch of his hand wouldn't turn such bright silver cubes a lusterless, impenetrable black.

A disgusted growl at the back of his throat, Frye splashed a liberal portion of brandy in his glass and turned to study the portrait over the mantel. Martin, he'd called himself then. And he'd believed then he'd uncovered the secret that would make him as weak and mortal as any other man, and far more content: To drink his own blood spilled in a noble cause. That hope had proved as false as all the others. So had choking down water strained through gobbets of earth soaked with a king's blood. Desperation led to mad actions that made his gorge rise each time he thought of them.

Martin Frye had obtained quite a reputation for valor in support of King Charles. His "son" had served poor beheaded Charles's son well during the Restoration until he found it wise to go voyaging abroad again, eventually reporting his "marriage," the birth of his "son" Lemuel, and his own death to the MacDougal firm. Lemuel had received an invitation to Court on his arrival in England, but had refused it, claiming unworthiness.

More accurately, Lemuel had been determined nothing would distract him from poring over tomes obtained in the

Carpathians. Such dedication had perhaps been rewarded, for Lemuel believed he'd discovered the only way to gain a soul. Henry suspected he was right.

Should one born to the condition, accursed through no fault of his own, perform a genuinely selfless act, God would see both the act and the man who performed it, and grant that man a soul. There was only one problem. If one knew one must perform a selfless act to gain a soul, and one desired a soul above all else, how could any act be truly selfless? The very impossibility had to make this solution the true one.

But he was trying, always trying. He'd thought he might've unwittingly managed it that night, rescuing the girl from old Mother Hinchey with the intention of bleeding her only to discover she was an innocent, and so of no use to him. Only after the silver cube turned black had he realized his motives had been self-serving all along.

And if he died soulless at the end of his unnatural span? Or of debility caused by lack of ingestion of human blood? Or from injury sustained from a silver weapon? Then he'd wander the earth until the stars grew cold, and God Himself either died of boredom or indulged in a new fit of creation.

And what would happen to him then? No way to know.

Jaws clenched, eyes haunted by the futility of his situation and its unachievable remedy, he gazed with loathing at the single most beautiful and valuable object he owned: Benvenuto Cellini's chalice, into which he'd so far bled eleven girls only too glad to exchange a pint of blood for a life of comparative ease, and so extended his pathetic existence to this grand and glorious year of 1811 which found England embroiled with Napoleon on the Continent and his minions in the Peninsula, and stumbling toward another war with her former American colonies.

Little Ann Leighton had only minutes earlier offered to be the twelfth, had she but known it.

"You'll truly go back there and rescue Tom?" she'd

said, then attempted to force her twenty pounds on him. "You're the bravest man I know, and the kindest"

When he'd refused her largesse, she'd offered him anything he wished in recompense. His bemused chuckle at her innocent offer, his response that there was nothing she could grant him he could as an honorable man accept, had taken her aback. Moments later, tears of gratitude tangled in her dark lashes like dew in France's poplars at dawn, she'd placed a hand on his shoulder, stood on tiptoe and kissed his cheek, the two of them reflected in the mirror by the entry door. It'd been clear she saw him in it as she saw him in person: a vigorous man of twenty-nine, silver-haired perhaps, but youthful for all of that. Her sweet smile had made him want to cry out in horror

For he? He'd seen the reality none saw but himself: a corpse-like thing so wizened it was scarcely recognizable as human. His shudder at the hideous reflection of those rosy lips pressed to his mummy-like sunken cheek, the contrast between firm young flesh and aged decrepitude, had brought the slightest of frowns to her brow. He'd shrugged off her puzzlement, claiming a sudden draft, and she'd been gracious enough to at least pretend to accept his shallow explanation.

Springer and Mrs. Finch'd bustled into the entry. The carriage arrived, the door opened, and closed. That quickly Ann Leighton was gone from his life.

With a snarl of fury, Frye drew his arm back to hurl the goblet into the fire, thought better of it. Lord knows he'd indulged in enough fits of wanton destruction in the past to last any man a lifetime, even him. They accomplished nothing—except creating a mess for one of his ever changing stable of servants to clean up. There was even a small dent in the lip of Ben's chalice bearing witness to one of those blind rages.

Frye set the goblet down with a resigned sigh as a scratch sounded on the door.

"I'm coming, Springer," he called.

In the event, wresting young Tom Leighton from his jailers proved more annoyance than effort unless one counted carrying the unconscious boy up a set of rickety stairs and then to his carriage—not that the lad was particularly heavy, being little more than half-formed and lacking a man's solid bulk, but a nerveless collection of muscle and bone made for an awkward parcel.

The would-be Thuggees, six of them this time, proved gratifyingly amenable to persuasion in the form of cudgel blows and shillings distributed with equal liberality and impartiality. DeVille hadn't been generous, a common error among those of high social standing when rewarding the services of those they considered beneath notice.

Mother Hinchey protested more vehemently at Frye's absconding with her charge, but only slightly and only for form's sake. Young Leighton had merely been bait. With his sister flown the coop, his sole value lay in the extra crown she could cadge for specifying his precise whereabouts given Frye's disinterest in searching the place. That those whereabouts proved to be a heap of refuse in a cellar where the lad'd been dumped was no surprise to Frye. That Tom wasn't merely cup-shot, but drugged into the bargain, was even less of a surprise.

Frye strode back through a warren of evil-smelling passages and into what Hinchey called her parlor, where he set the boy on the floor. Then he turned to her, Springer at his back, his two burly grooms, Jem and Phinny, hovering in the doorway.

"What did Ambrose DeVille want with Miss Leighton?" he asked. "Don't bother to protest his innocence. I happen to know he was at the back of it. He was here earlier, and I recognized him."

"Why, bless yer, dearie," the crone cackled, "course he were here. Going ter tup her all the night, he was. Refused him twice, and he wanted ter leave his mark on her. Said he'd let m'boys have a turn once he was done, and watch 'em at it."

"Three times," Frye muttered, fists clenched, jaw rigid. "She refused his offer three times."

"That so? Two er three, it don't matter—'cept to you and him. Ain't wise ter refuse a nob like him, and he wanted her ter know it. All she'd've been good fer after's a coop. Said he was going ter claim he saw as how she looked like a Miss Leighton what he were acquainted with, but couldn't believe she'd be in such a place."

"You don't say."

"Oh, I do indeed, dearie. Didn't manage it, but there's always the next time."

It was all Frye could do to keep from throttling the hag. That Tom lay in a jumbled heap at his feet, giggling and warbling snatches of song between snores, made not the slightest difference.

"Have an interest there yerself?" Mother Hinchey leered with a gap-toothed grin. "Nice armful. Keep a feller amused of a cold night."

Frye gave a noncommittal shrug and slung Tom over his shoulder. If he disposed of the witch, there'd be a dozen waiting to take her place.

"If you're wise," he said, "you'll avoid dealings with DeVille in the future. You attempt something of this sort again, and I won't bother to alert the authorities. I'll take care of the matter myself, and I won't do it slowly, if you catch my drift. Word of warning: I have a way of learning about things that interest me."

He spun on his heel, ignoring her babbled protests, and signaled for Springer and the two scrappy grooms to precede him.

"Here now, what about me money," she shouted after them. "I was ter get the young toff's togs and whatever the girl brought with her, and double the usual fer me trouble as well."

"Present your bill to Lord Denbigh if you dare," he shot over his shoulder. "You'll not be seeing another farthing from me."

"He won't pay me neither. Pullet got away," she grumbled.

"It's a chancy world, and one must take one's chances in it," he said, forcing a laugh, and then he was in Catspaw Alley, Old Sedgewick House behind him, the lane where he'd found Ann Leighton ahead.

The trip to his home was swift, dawn streaking the sky with garish fingers of red and gold, peddlers already out hawking their wares. There followed hours of forcing coffee and emetics on Tom Leighton, of holding his head over a basin and then walking him up and down the hall, of pacing the downstairs rooms with him and then repeating the process while the worst of the drugs and alcohol worked themselves out of his system. By the time Frye had Ann's fool of a brother settled in the same featureless bedchamber where she'd earlier set herself to rights the sun was well up in the sky and Frye was feeling the effects of a long day and longer night.

He gave Springer instructions not to let the young man depart before he had a chance to confer with him, then sought his own bed after penning a note to Ann informing her Tom was safe, if a bit the worse for wear. She was not to worry. He'd see to everything. But—and he was adamant on the point—she was not to leave her parents' home until he'd spoken with her. He'd call later in the day.

Ann Leighton glanced up, her fingers stilling on the yellowed keys of the old pianoforte at the flirtatious feminine laughter beyond the back parlor door. The responding masculine drawl set her shuddering.

And then came her mother's voice, the words as damningly clear as their intent.

"Why, naturally Ann is receiving callers this afternoon, Brosie. And one so distinguished as yourself? She'll be positively thrilled."

Again came the condescending, deep drawl, the words

incomprehensible, the tone insufferably arrogant. Ann's hands twisted at her mother's next words.

"A drive in the park? How thoughtful. The silly child quite misses the country, which bodes well for when she's a mother for all it's a dreadful inconvenience just now. Country's much healthier for children—and far more convenient for a husband who has, shall we say, *business* that keeps him in Town. Beaton, show his lordship to the drawing room. Do make yourself comfortable, Brosie, while I fetch Ann."

Ann cast a longing glance at the garden, but the parlor door was already opening. She slumped against the piano, doing her best to appear vaguely ill as Carlotta Leighton glided into the room, the hem of her fuchsia afternoon costume slightly higher than customary to reveal trim ankles, its tight bodice and plunging décolletage more in keeping with boudoir assignations than receiving morning callers.

"Such a delightful treat's in store for you," she gushed, clearly intending for their caller to hear her.

As soon as the door was closed she descended on Ann, pulling her from the piano with far more force than was required. Ann stumbled, catching herself against one of the worn chairs that formed part of her favorite retreat.

"What a clumsy mouse you are," Carlotta Leighton snapped. "I'm amazed a gentleman as exacting as Brosie would cast a glance at you. Certainly in my day that wouldn't've been the case, and his latest unofficial interest is all that's most graceful."

"I'm certain she is."

"And you in that dowdy wool from before your comeout. It positively hangs on you, and the neck's so high one would think you were a nun! I don't know what your abigail is about to let you appear in public so."

"I'm hardly in public here."

Ann glanced guiltily at her reflection in the tarnished mantel mirror. No, the jonquil merino wasn't suitable to

London, but it was warm and bright. When she'd finally risen after fretting over Tom for what seemed a lifetime, she'd felt a need of something cheerful. Even Mr. Frye's note hadn't totally reassured her, hinting as it did of severe indisposition.

"Besides, Mama," she added, "I'm not feeling well."

"Not feeling well? On such a fine day? Don't be silly!"

Lady Leighton treated her daughter to her famous trill of laughter as she strolled to the fireplace and toyed with a chipped china bulldog, the slightest of frowns puckering her brow.

"It slipped my mind until just now, but Cecily Trimble was kind enough to include you in my invitation to her rout this evening," she said as if the matter hadn't any consequence. "What shall you wear? I suppose I'll have to play duenna, worse luck. I do wish you'd accept Ambrose and have done with it."

Ann retreated to the paired window seats overlooking the garden, a mulish set to her firm little chin.

"Cecily always has dancing, you know," her mother rambled on, "and calls her balls routs so she can skimp on decorations and refreshments. Quite the skint, Cecily, for all she's one of my dearest friends, but her eccentricities have made her all the rage so one must adapt or be out of the running. Imagine me, sitting on the sidelines unable to dance or have the least fun. How ridiculous! Why, I'm barely past my own girlhood."

" 'Barely' thirty years past it," Ann muttered.

"I suppose we'll have to resurrect your governess—what was her name? something impossible, I do remember that—should your spinsterhood last much longer. When I think you could already be wed, and most advantageously, I could scream!"

"Well, I'm not wed yet, and I'm not likely to be wed anytime soon."

"We'll see." Carlotta Leighton joined her daughter at the windows, and twitched the draperies. "Firing off a daughter's the most dreadful bore. Reminds everyone precisely how old one must be. Once you're gone, I believe I'll turn this into a music room. Musicales're all the rage. It'll want redecorating, of course, and we'll have to purchase a decent instrument. This old thing never has held its pitch. Well, which gown will you wear, the ice blue sarcenet or the blush rose?"

"I shan't be wearing either, Mama."

"Oh? You purchased something new? High time you took an interest in your wardrobe! Perhaps there's hope for you yet."

"No, Mama—I've purchased nothing. I have far too many gowns as it is."

"Then what will you wear? For I'll tell you this: Not a gown of mine may you borrow. They're none of them suitable to a chit in her first year."

"I shan't be wearing any of them," Ann sighed, "yours or mine."

"Now, that'll be novel! And sure to create a stir, though I'm not certain it's the best way to acquire serious suitors. Appearing at a rout in one's chemise and petticoats hasn't quite become the style as yet."

"I shan't be attending, Mama. I wasn't able to sleep last night." Ann made her eyes huge, doing her best to appear both ill and innocent. "I'm truly most unwell."

"Well, you can forget that now." Her ladyship's laughter was brittle. "Quickest thing to put roses in a girl's cheeks and a spring in her step is a gentleman's attentions. Brosie DeVille has called to take you for a drive."

"I know. I overheard you in the hall. I won't go, Mama," she said, crossing her fingers under her skirts. "Papa's agreed I needn't receive his lordship anymore."

"You're impossible! And your devil of a father runs you a close second, let me tell you. Well, I shan't be put to the rout by those muddy eyes of yours. You'll receive him, and you'll drive out with him. Brosie is handsome, and rich as he can stare, and adds to your consequence. Indeed, he gives you the only consequence you have! What more could a girl ask in a suitor?"

"Kind eyes. A gentle voice. A warm heart. A sense of the ridiculous. Above all, a respectful and courteous manner, and a modicum of affection."

"*Affection?* Don't be more foolish than you can help!"

"Lord Denbigh's been unpleasantly forward when we've been alone—which you've engineered at every turn."

"D'you mean he tried to steal a kiss? Let him! You might find you enjoy it, and he has every right to make sure it won't disgust him to bed you once you're wed. There's a deal of pleasure to be found between the sheets if one's partner is vigorous enough."

"He disgusts me, Mama," Ann pleaded in a small voice. "His hands are damp, and his eyes slide over one like slugs, and he moves his tongue like a worm, and he's infinitely cold and arrogant, and he never hears a word one says."

"You think your father's any better? Most men disgust their wives. The thing is to endure with a smile, and amuse oneself elsewhere whenever possible. That's what the gentlemen do. Why shouldn't the ladies have the same right, so long as we're circumspect about it?"

"I wouldn't care to live like that, Mama."

"It's the only life there is for a woman who desires to cut a dash. That requires considerable funds, and considerable funds and those qualities you demand rarely march together." Carlotta Leighton spun on her heel, heading for the door. "There'll be no more of this foolishness. Having to see to you rendered the Little Season a total bore. Motherhood doesn't mean one hasn't a right to one's own pleasures, or that life should come to a halt merely because one's cursed with a daughter who's missish beyond all that's reasonable."

She paused at the door, fingers gripping the handle, and glanced at her daughter over her shoulder.

"Go change your gown," she snapped. "I expect you

in the drawing room in half an hour. Fifteen minutes would be better. Put on a carriage dress. You *will* go for that drive, and you *will* attend Cecily Trimble's rout, and you'll be married by April or you'll be gone from this house in some other manner. Resign yourself and do your duty."

"I'm suffering from my monthly courses," Ann pleaded desperately as her mother turned her back.

"And you think no other woman has ever suffered the same? Wear the cherry poplin. If you have an accident, no one will notice."

One couldn't say her mother had slammed the door, Ann decided as she glanced about her helplessly, but it certainly hadn't been a whisper-soft closing. As always, the room seemed to have lost much of its vitality upon her mother's exit, but it'd gained a peace that never existed in that lady's vicinity.

Ann leaned against the window embrasure, eyes seeking the sere garden with its puddled paths and empty flower beds, pondering how best she might avoid his lordship and the drive in Hyde Park. If only Mr. Frye would bestir himself and pay his calls at the accepted hour! That, however, would make her life too simple. Gentlemen, no matter how much they prattled about deferring to the ladies, nevertheless marched to their own drummers. She'd have to manage to send DeVille packing without assistance from anyone. The penalty for success, once he departed, could be most anything her mother chose to invent, and Carlotta Leighton was extremely inventive these days.

No, her mother hadn't been funning when she said she favored Lord Denbigh's suit, and what she favored had a habit of becoming reality. Much easier all around. Besides, her father hadn't said she needn't receive DeVille. He'd merely said he'd consider the matter, which meant precisely nothing.

* * *

"You said to waken you as soon as the lad stirred," Springer enunciated clearly, tugging on the tangled bottom sheet of Henry Frye's bed. "He's stirring, sir."

Frye rolled over with the sensation of floundering in a sea of fog so thick it possessed substance, staring around his bedchamber with bleared eyes. The blasted place wasn't foggy at all. Instead it was preternaturally sharp-edged and harsh.

"What the devil've you opened the draperies for?" he grumbled.

"Merely an attempt to assist you in waking, sir. I find such encouragement generally routs a gentleman from his bed when there's a need."

"You should've learned by now it won't rout this one. Close 'em," Frye groaned. "Young Leighton really awake, or is he merely—"

"He's ordered a bath, and a breakfast the Regent himself would be hard pressed to consume."

"Blast! But that's ever the way with young cubs. They make you think they're dying one moment, and the death of you the next. Remind me not to involve myself with such should I prove unforgivably foolish in the future. How much sleep've I had?"

"Almost four hours, sir. It's going on two in the afternoon."

"I shan't be able to keep this pace much longer, not as things stand." Frye reluctantly pushed the covers aside, squinting at the sunlight reflected by every polished surface in the bedchamber, doubling and tripling the glare until he was near blinded. "Close those draperies, blast it, Springer! I shouldn't have to repeat myself."

"Perhaps not, sir, but you'll notice you've been effectively routed."

"I have at that." Then somehow he was shuffling to the

windows, feet arched against floorboards so slick and cold they might've been ice rather than wood. "You could've at least lit the fire," he grumbled.

"Cozy doesn't make for fast waking."

"There's that. I wish you'd break this habit of being right more often than not."

As usual, nothing had changed during the night. He'd often wondered if acquiring a soul were an instantaneous thing or if, like physical birth, it involved considerable time and effort on at least one person's part, and was possibly painful into the bargain. He had yet to learn the answers to those questions. As things stood, he wasn't likely to ever learn them.

Frye pulled the draperies closed, eyes slitted against the impossibly bright afternoon sun. Unfortunately, rescuing young Leighton hadn't been a selfless act, any more than rescuing the lad's sister had. A favor to foolhardy little Ann was a favor to himself, ludicrous as that would've sounded to the few who'd known him well over the years: Will, Ben Cellini, Leo DaVinci, a handful of others.

He'd stopped indulging in close friendships by the mid-sixteen hundreds. It was too painful to watch the treasured few wither while his vigor only increased, almost as if he sucked the vitality from them in some incomprehensible manner. Each had promised to put in a good word for him with the One who counted. Apparently none had. Probably forgot him the moment they acquired haloes and harps.

One could, he insisted, stumbling to the wash stand behind its sheltering screen as Springer lit a branch of candles, survive a friendless existence. He was living proof of that truism, wasn't he? He, and every monarch who'd ever lived, every man of extraordinary intellect or ability or wealth. It'd been among such he'd found a bitter sort of companionship before he'd decided to forgo the dubious luxury of watching those for whom he cared pass eternally beyond his reach. Others might bid farewell to those they loved with the hope of eventual reunion, at least if they believed their priests and vicars. For him, unless everything changed, no reunions. Not ever. Not with anyone.

Of course he could've found social intercourse of a sort among those supposedly of his own kind if he'd truly desired it, but seek the companionship of those who were what they were by choice rather than chance? One encounter had been a thousand times too many.

"'Ill met by moonlight,' indeed," he muttered, pouring the icy water Springer had provided in the basin and thrusting his head beneath the surface, holding his breath and waiting for the cobwebs to be swept from his mind. "Will," he spluttered, emerging more awake than he had any right to be at that hour, "had that one right, at the least, even if he gave it an entire new meaning. Ill met, indeed!"

"Sir?"

"Nothing, Springer. Merely talking to myself—a very bad habit, but one I find it impossible to break. Bear with me."

No, beyond that one highly unpleasant encounter—having a woman snarl he was a fool as she bared genuine fangs dripping with the blood of her latest victim wasn't precisely to his taste—he'd avoided those whom mortals would consider his equals and brethren because they were neither.

Frye seized the towel Springer was holding and buried his face in it with the usual sensation of being suffocated in a sack he'd never escape. The girl had had all his sympathy the night before.

"Order a beefsteak galloped past the grill for me, and have both meals served in my bookroom," he said, tossing the sodden towel aside and pulling his nightshirt over his head. "And coffee. The lad may not need it, but I do. Dress me for paying a morning call—though why the devil they're called 'morning calls' when they're paid in the afternoon I'll never understand. You managed to restore Leighton's clothing?"

"Wasn't set upon the way the young lady was. Nothing to it, sir—just a bit of brushing and sponging, and a good press."

Within half an hour Frye was seated before the glowing fire in his bookroom. On the table between the windows a repast of incredible proportions awaited Tom Leighton. He glanced at the clock in the bookcase, then consulted his watch. The sprig was taking his own sweet time.

Frye lifted the domed cover from his own plate, sighed. The beefsteak was so rare the grill marks barely showed. Good. It might keep him going for the requisite few hours, boring though it was as a steady diet.

He managed to consume the quivering purple slab before Ann's brother made his appearance, golden curls prettily arranged, a restrained buttonhole of pinks gracing his lapel. Springer had been right. Given the lad had been dressed informally the night before, he might've just risen from his own bed after an evening spent reading to an aged aunt.

"How're you feeling, Leighton?" Frye asked, covering his plate with a napkin after sopping up the last of the meat juices with a corner of bread.

"More or less restored." The boy was peering about him as if perplexed. "Oh, there you are. Seem to remember you from last night. Was you, wasn't it?"

"It was. The name's Henry Frye, in case you've forgotten. Got yourself in something of a mess, didn't you."

"Oh, I say—don't natter like m'father or I'll be taking my leave," Leighton protested. "Why hasn't someone opened the curtains? Dark as midnight in here."

"Leave 'em be," Frye barked. "I said leave 'em be, you graceless whelp! I have weak eyes, and can't tolerate the midday sun. Where'd you start out yesterday evening, and with whom?" Not that he needed to ask, but he wanted confirmation. "You were drugged, you know. Rather efficiently."

"I was? Y'don't say!"

"I do indeed say. Who was your companion in crime?"

"A friend. A good one. Couldn't be responsible. Besides, we parted company early on. Is that my breakfast over there? Can't hardly see in this dark."

"Yes, that's your breakfast."

"Then I'll be helping myself, if you don't mind. Gut-foundered, and that's the truth of it. Never did have dinner last night, and I seem to remember pu—"

"If you're suffering from a cavernous sensation," Frye cut him off, "there's a good reason for it. You were rather unwell, shall we say."

"Hope I wasn't too much of a bother."

The boy was striding over to the hunt table, lifting the covers and sniffing appreciatively. He picked up a plate, began loading it with everything in sight: bacon, gammon, mushroom fritters, eggs, grilled kidneys, sirloin, muffins, stewed fruit, cold pork pie, the whole mingling until one item was indistinguishable from the next.

"When did you write that note to your sister? And what in blazes gave you the idea she'd be safe in Seven Dials?"

"Note?" Tom Leighton turned, brows puckered. "I never wrote Nan. Never write anybody if I can help it. Bit of a bore, trying to remember how to spell things."

"Well, you wrote her last night."

"Not I," the boy said sunnily, turning back to the dishes set over warmers. "Fluff in your cockloft, that's what you've got. Planned on White's for dinner after a bit. Never got there. Went to this hell Brosie'd heard tell of and never left, for all he did his best to get me to quit the place. Claimed it wasn't honest."

"Brosie?"

"Wouldn't call him that to his face, of course," the boy shrugged, reddening a bit as he took his place across from Frye. "Ambrose DeVille—Earl of Denbigh, don't you know. Particular acquaintance of mine."

"He is, is he? Take a look at this." Frye pulled the note

that'd sent Ann flying to her brother's rescue from his pocket, shoved it across the table. "Ever seen it before?"

Tom shoveled a massive forkful of eggs into his mouth, then picked up the note and held it close to the single candle burning on the table.

"That's my hand, by Jove!" he mumbled through the eggs.

"Is it? Look carefully."

"Well, I generally make m'T's a bit differently," he admitted after a gargantuan swallow that set his Adam's apple to bobbing like a nubbin of pumice caught in the Gulf of Naples's sharp chop. "All the big ones, in fact. Bit more of a flair, don't you know? These're plain as churchmice."

"So this isn't your hand?"

"Oh, it could be," Tom shrugged, returning the note to Frye and attacking the pork pie. "Could've been foxed when I wrote it. Probably was, given what it says. Not such a noddy I'd ask Nan to come to such a place—not that she wouldn't if I asked her. Most accommodating girl, Nan. Do just about anything for me."

"Including risking her own safety, as it happens. Whose idea was it to go to this hell of which you speak? And which one was it?"

"Brosie DeVille—already told you that. The Tinker's Bum."

"Good God! Have you no sense whatsoever?"

"I say, if you're going to play Grand Inquisitor, I'll be taking my leave."

"Not very grateful for being retrieved from Mother Hinchey's cellars, are you."

"That where you found me?"

"That's where."

"Old besom," Tom muttered. "Never did care for her above half. Smells of mold, and the fellows say her girls and her cards're marked. How'd I end up there?"

"You were apparently escorted in some manner."

"Sod it! Wonder who had it in for me? Still, all's well that end's well, I suppose."

Frye leaned back, watching as Leighton shoveled his breakfast down his gullet. Trying to bring the young fool to a sense of his culpability would be impossible until that cavernous maw was filled. The fellow must be three quarters stomach, with storage extending into all four limbs. Even then, given his apparent lack of concern for anyone but himself, the task would be gargantuan. Hedonism might be the order of the day—a custom in which the Regent led the way—but Tom Leighton carried the taste to extremes.

Leighton kept casting Frye uneasy glances as he attacked first one jumbled mess and then another, clearly convinced Frye wasn't done with him yet. Frye let the boy stew—and boy he was, for all he'd supposedly reached the age of manhood. How a girl, a young woman really, as clear-minded as Ann Leighton could be related to this cub was a matter for the angels to ponder.

"Done?" Frye asked when the last scrap was gone from the lad's plate.

"Not really. There's more."

"There's always more in any well-regulated household. Doesn't mean you must consume it all to survive."

"But it'll go to waste if I don't eat it up," Tom protested, casting a longing glance at the hunt table.

"No, it won't. All leavings are taken to an institution in the stews that sees to those deserving assistance. Starving children, for instance, who find themselves parentless and homeless through no fault of their own and must steal to eat, risking transportation and worse, or die."

"Oh, I say, claiming I'm taking food from the mouths of babes is a bit much, don't you think?"

Frye smiled enigmatically as he shrugged at Leighton's colorful flush. There was the possibility of compunction there. He hadn't counted on even that much.

"Why not give your stomach a chance to catch up with

your eyes," he suggested. "Otherwise you'll end up resembling poor Prinny before you're much older. Bit of puffiness to your face already."

"Isn't the thing—to indulge in personalities."

"Maybe not, but someone had better or your youth will be over before it's fairly begun. Wouldn't want that, would you?"

"I suppose not," Tom admitted grudgingly.

"I thought not, so let's return to yesterday evening's adventures, and your part in them."

"I'd really rather not, you know," Tom said, pushing away from the table as if to distance himself from his host. "Don't remember much of anything. Won't do the least good to ask me about it."

"Ever study geometry?"

"Theorems and such? For my sins. Dreadfully dull stuff."

"Then you understand the principles behind geometric proofs?"

Tom shrugged. "I suppose so, for all the good they'll ever do a fellow."

"Try this. You didn't write that note to your sister. Who did, then? She was at great risk down there. About to be abducted, in fact, for what purpose you can imagine without my belaboring the point."

"No one'd dare! Why, m'father's a—"

"Given his reputation, your father is as uncaring a parent as I've encountered, and I've encountered a few in my time—witness your current career, and the company in which you elect to pursue it."

"If you're going to lecture," Tom said airily, this time pushing his chair from the table and rising, "I'm scarce as saints in hell."

The speed with which Frye moved was astonishing, even to himself. In a flash a highly cowed Tom Leighton was back in his chair, what he grumbled would be bruises that would disable him for months already forming on his shoulders.

"Do I tie you there," Frye demanded, "or will you behave yourself?"

The sullen eyes, the forward-thrusting jaw, the pouting lower lip almost had Frye laughing. Had he ever been this young? He didn't think so, for by Leighton's age he'd been contending with his unusual nature while desperately trying to hide its oddities from others. That hadn't left much time for childish arrogance or fits of the sulks. Genuine adversity had a way of leaching away the less endearing qualities of youth.

"Well, what's it to be?" he snapped.

"Y'can't hold a fellow against his will," Leighton protested. "Just isn't done."

"I can't? What leads you to this fascinating opinion? I believe you were most efficiently held only a few hours ago. At least you'll find no rats here."

The silky smile, the cold silver eyes, the fingers of steel would've silenced a hardened warrior. As it was, Leighton subsided, the slightest of shrugs indicating his acquiescence as his eyes dropped guiltily.

"Good—I'm glad to see you're reasonable. Now, let's return to the point at hand, shall we? I'm not your enemy, no matter what you may think."

"If you're not, y'have an odd way of proving it."

Frye gave Leighton's shoulder a reassuring slap, carefully tempering it to the lad's bone structure, and returned to his seat across the table. He had, he knew, been a trace more forceful than'd been strictly necessary moments before. It was difficult to remember others had neither his strength nor his immunity to such frailties as bruised flesh and shattered bones.

He shuddered at the memory of almost crushing Ben's hands during a rare and joyful reunion. The poor fellow hadn't been able to work for weeks, excusing his incapacity to his apprentices as rheumatism. A commission for the fifth Pius had been late and almost refused, along with payment. Popes had a habit that way, believing everything they ordered to be done for God and so not requiring greater recompense than the honor of creating the work itself. The Medicis had been almost as bad, considering themselves temporal gods.

"Now," Frye said, "let's examine this situation like rational men, if you please. You are a man, I presume, and not still in leading strings?"

The glare from beneath beetling brows would've been his undoing had Frye's knowledge of Ambrose DeVille not been so deep. As things stood, he was terrified for both the lad and his sister.

It had been years since Frye had attempted the role of tutor. The last time it had been with a willing pupil, a lad who'd gone on to make a name for himself in mathematics before descending into the ephemera of alchemy.

Isaac never had an apple fall on his head. It had been bird droppings. They'd made a proper mess, but along with the feathers fluttering from the tree following a cat's successful attack on a dove, they had suggested the notion objects might be attracted to the earth—after considerable encouragement. At first the boy had insisted, child-like, that it was only his head to which they were attracted. Fact, unfortunately, had a tendency to be discarded when the honor of a revered graybeard was at stake. That had most definitely been the case when a revisionist Cambridge don cleaned up the tale in more ways than one, however much posterity might've preferred the truth about a slender lad and bird's droppings to a portly man and an apple.

This latest pupil was anything but willing, besides not possessing Isaac's acumen and penchant for logic. Still, the job had to be attempted.

"Who's in Town among your cronies?" Frye asked patiently. "Your sister mentioned a mill near Crivenden."

"They've all gone, every last one."

"And you didn't accompany them?"

Tom Leighton shrugged. "Don't care much for such things," he mumbled, shamefaced. "Know I'm supposed to, but I never have. Sickening, watching men pummel each other for sport. End up with less than half the sense they were born with if they go at it long enough. Tom Cribb stopped in time. So did The Gentleman. Most don't because they can't afford to."

Frye's brows rose. Not so callow after all. "What about cockfights? Bear baiting? Hunting?"

Leighton shuddered.

"Let's leave that issue aside for the moment," Frye said dismissively, understanding the boy's unease. Blood sports were *de rigueur* among the aristocracy, for all their insistence on rituals for everything from compounding boot blacking to the correct way to blend and take snuff. Well, the blood sports had their own rules as well, he supposed. "The issue is, none of your usual companions are in Town. Your drugging and abduction wasn't a lark gone sour then, correct?"

"I suppose."

"Then what was it? Were you truly the target?"

"Must've been. Was me they took, wasn't it?"

"Why? You were never truly at risk, for all you were in sad case when I found you, and if we hadn't seen to ridding you of most of what you'd ingested I suspect you'd be in even sadder case this morning."

"Had to've been me," Leighton protested. "Who else could it've been?"

"Then why the note to your sister?" Frye pressed.

"I've no idea. Fellows wouldn't pull such a prank, that I can tell you."

Frye's brows rose encouragingly. Tom frowned, clearly deep in thought.

"They like Nan, for all she's naught but a mouse," he said finally. "No harm to her, y'see, and not the least threat to 'em. Not ready to get leg-shackled, any of us. Besides, m'mother's holding out for deep pockets. M'father's expensive, and so's she. I'm not precisely cheap goods, come to that. Most of m'friends are forever skirting dun territory when they're not plunging deep. Not a one of 'em'd be suitable."

It tallied, though heaven knows he hadn't expected the sprig to be quite so honest about it. Ann Leighton was on the auction block. So far there'd been only one bidder.

"Who's in the running?" Frye asked for form's sake.

"Brosie's m'mother's favorite. Only candidate there is, come to that. Nan didn't make much of a splash at her come-out. Bloomed on the walls, and there wasn't much competition—Little Season, y'understand. She hasn't the foggiest how t'flirt with a fellow or make him feel more important than he is, and nothing m'mother or I say makes the least difference. She'll end up on the shelf or worse, she doesn't watch her step."

"They're betrothed, then?"

"Brosie and Nan? No, the more fool she! Turned him down cold. Three times."

"Has she, now. Why?"

"Doesn't care for the cut of his coats, I expect, or some such nonsense. Sterling fellow, Brosie DeVille," Tom insisted. "A knowing 'un. That grateful he ain't given me the cut direct, for he'd every right to the way Nan's been acting. Men've been cut for less, and it'd've been the end of me in Town for years."

"Surely you exaggerate."

"Not a bit of it. First time there was maybe an excuse—shyness, or something of the sort—but y'don't turn a fellow down *three* times, don't y'see? Then there's no question but it's *him* you're turning down. Brosie's been far more patient than he'd any need to be. Can't understand what he sees in her, anyway. Sweet little thing, of course, Nan—devoted to her—but she ain't the sort to set a fellow's blood running hot. Brosie's opera dancer, now, she's something like!"

"Has it occurred to you that your sister might've been last night's target?"

"Nan?" Leighton guffawed. "Who'd want Nan? And for what?"

"Revenge," Frye said succinctly, then let the word hang in the air.

It took Tom Leighton a bit, but he got there. When he did, his complexion turned ashen.

"Impossible," he said on a pleading note. "It is, ain't it?"

"I'm afraid not. According to Mother Hinchey, your friend and mentor intended deflowering your sister, then claiming he hadn't believed it could be she in such a place—and that's if she was ever returned to her family. She might've spent the rest of her life down there, had I not happened along."

"I don't believe it."

Frye shoved the note across to Tom. "That's not your hand. You've admitted as much. Whose is it, then? And who would've known your sister would come running to your rescue at the first sign of trouble, did you but request her assistance?"

"Dammit, no!" Tom roared, leaping to his feet. "I refuse to believe it! In fact," he snarled, "I'm calling you out. Name your seconds!"

"It's not your sister's honor I'm impugning. The man you're so anxious to defend is known as a loose fish all over Town," Frye countered mildly. "Fuzzes the cards, among other things. A disreputable scion of a not always reputable family."

"But—"

"Sit down, cawker. I'm not meeting you at dawn, or anyone else."

Ann Leighton was delighted with both the effect she'd achieved and the amount of time she'd expended in the effort. The juice of an onion delicately applied to the lids could render eyes most unattractively red. And, to the nose? Again red, and both watering copiously. As for Lord Denbigh, he'd been cooling his heels in the drawing room for close to an hour. With any luck, his sense of insult had burgeoned to the point where he'd already rescinded his invitation.

She paused to inspect herself in one of the mirror-paneled niches lining the entry rotunda. The shawls were the perfect touch, all four of them, and her nose and eyes clashed wonderfully with the cherry poplin her mother had ordered her to don. With a minxish grin she pulled a handkerchief from her reticule and inhaled deeply. Pepper was a preservative? Then let it preserve her from Ambrose DeVille! She gave Beaton, the butler at Leighton House since before time began, a watery smile and a nod.

"I'm ready," she choked between sneezes.

The antiquated Beaton's eyes signaled empathy as he gave his young mistress the slightest of minatory frowns. Her responding wink was for him alone, her back to both doors and flanking footmen.

"Not to worry," she mouthed. "I know what I'm about."

Beaton emitted a stentorian cough, paused magnificently to permit the echoes to cease circling the reception area's domed ceiling, then nodded. As if to the blare of invisible trumpets and the roll of phantom drums, the footmen swept the doors open. A languid Lady Leighton lingered by the marble fireplace absently adjusting her corsage, her eyes vacant. On the table at her side reposed an enormous silver tray, its burden of tea and cakes untouched. Lord Denbigh was by the windows, his back to the room, fumbling hurriedly with something at his waist. It was all Ann could do to keep from giggling.

Instead, expression listless, she dragged herself across the sill as the doors whispered shut behind her.

"Good afternoon, Mama, Lord Denbigh," she sniffled. Then, as DeVille turned, she managed another horrendous sneeze as she bobbed a serving maid's curtsy and took the chair nearest the fire, shivering as if she'd contracted an ague. "Do keep your distance, Lord Denbigh. I'm most dreadfully unwell, but Mama insisted I come down to greet you at the least."

"Rose fever," Lady Leighton declared, throwing her daughter a furious glance. "Naught but rose fever, Brosie. Ann's suffered from it since infancy according to Nurse. Regrettable, but not in the least contagious."

"At this season? When there isn't a rose anywhere? Are you certain the chit hasn't taken a chill? Weather's been inclement of late, particularly in the small hours."

The shrewd glance he threw Ann, the sardonically lifted single brow had her trembling. How could Ambrose DeVille know she'd been out last night? Was her abigail in his pay? It wouldn't surprise her, for the servants' wages were constantly in arrears, and they had to live somehow.

She brought her handkerchief and its hidden burden of pepper to her nose with excellent results. Then, fearful her mother would spot the source of her indisposition, she crammed the handkerchief in her reticule, cast DeVille a pathetic glance through streaming eyes, and huddled among her shawls.

"Where's young Tom?" DeVille drawled in the silence following her awesome sneeze, negligently swinging his quizzing glass from long, elegantly-tapered fingers. "I'd hoped to find him at home."

"Thomas?" Carlotta Leighton shrugged, gesturing DeVille to the seat beside her. "Goodness, Brosie, you expect a son to keep his mother abreast of his activities? Thomas is his own master, and could be most anywhere."

"But surely *you* know his whereabouts, Miss Leighton," DeVille probed as he glided across the drawing room, pausing on his way to retrieve a glass of Madeira from the mantel, then carefully separating his coattails before taking his place beside her mother. "I have it on the best authority you're unusually devoted to one another—Tom's own, in point of fact."

"Tom is with friends," Ann wheezed.

"Amazing! And here I thought all his cronies had abandoned him for Crivenden and a bit of sport that held no appeal for him. Certainly that's what he told me yesterday. We spent the earlier part of the evening in each other's company, you understand."

"I wouldn't know, my lord," Ann insisted, coughing and wishing she could bolt and knowing she couldn't. Pepper might be efficacious. It was also most wonderfully unpleasant.

"Pity. How did you come to contract such a shocking cold, Miss Leighton? And so quickly?" DeVille studied her above the rim of his glass, eyes hooded, expression enigmatic, as he took a sip of wine. "You have all my sympathy, for moments ago your lovely mother insisted you were blooming rather than dropping petals all over the place."

"I hardly know, my lord. These things are in the air."

"I'd planned to take you for a drive in the park, but that appears quite impossible now," he drawled offensively, setting his glass on the table and reaching for the snuff box in his waistcoat pocket. "Pity, for we have much to discuss."

"Perhaps Mama might drive out with you in my stead? Certainly you appear to've been finding each other's company all that is pleasant while awaiting my arrival."

Stony silence on her mother's part and a loftily irritated glare on his lordship's met Ann's improper sally. Indeed, the expression in his ice-blue eyes would have been enough to send her pelting from the room had she the courage. As it was, she shrank in her seat, wishing she'd learn to govern her often unruly tongue. Far from giving him a disgust of her, she was somehow increasing DeVille's incomprehensible interest.

"Would it be permissible for me to ring for fresh tea, Mama?" she asked. "What's here appears to've been sitting forever."

"Will you be attending Cecily Trimble's rout this evening?" Carlotta Leighton inquired, ignoring her daughter as she turned to DeVille with fluttering lashes.

"I doubt it," he drawled. "Such gatherings are infinitely tedious, don't you agree? *Tout Londres* in attendance, and *tout Londres* has a pernicious habit of having not an idea in its collective brainbox beyond the latest *on dits* and crim. cons."

"What a shame, because I'll be in attendance. Ann, too," she pouted. "Your company'll be greatly missed, Brosie."

DeVille's eyes sought Ann's. She shuddered, then forced herself to sit rigidly erect rather than cowering in her chair.

"You'll be there, Miss Leighton?" he said with a belittling parody of surprise and respect, dark brows raised in arch exaggeration. "Despite your current indisposition? Now that shows true evidence of a lady's commitment to social duty. Is this admirable trait one of your more persistent characteristics, Miss Leighton?"

"I hardly know," Ann murmured, blanching.

"For if you have the courage to attend, perhaps I should reconsider my own plans, boredom being a far less serious indisposition than an inflammation of the lungs."

"It's merely rose fever, I tell you," Carlotta Leighton insisted. "Ann will be totally recovered by evening. She always is—the effect of the setting of the sun, you understand. It's positively miraculous! We can depend on your escort, Brosie?"

"I think not, but I'll look for you there if the idea of lending Cecily Trimble the consequence of my presence doesn't overly disgust me when the time comes."

Behind them the drawing room doors whispered open.

"Hallo, all," Tom's voice caroled. "Lord Denbigh! Well met. Should've listened to you last night. Tinker's Bum's no place for an honest gamester."

Ann froze, then turned her head. It was Tom all right, looking as if he'd just quitted his club rather than having spent half the night in the stews and the rest in Henry Frye's spare bedchamber. Behind him stood Frye, and behind them both Beaton, a most peculiar expression on his customarily impassive face.

"No, it's not," DeVille agreed affably, "but show me a youth who'll believe his elders in such matters, and I'll show you a molly-coddled fribble of no use to anyone."

"Couldn't agree more."

Ann's gaze flew from her despised suitor to her brother. That DeVille's eyes should be coldly calculating was no surprise. The unaccustomed fury in Tom's brown ones, so greatly at variance with the good-humored grin with which he was favoring DeVille, was terrifying. Behind them, Beaton announced, "Mr. Henry Frye," in a hollow voice that bore no relation to his usual mellifluous tones, then stood in the open doorway as if turned to a pillar of salt. As Ann watched, Frye somehow got the poor dear to fade into the rotunda. The doors closed. Her eyes sought Frye, not precisely lurking behind her brother, but not putting himself forward, either. By contrast with Tom's, his silvery eyes were expressionless, almost as if he were absorbing the tensions in the room while wasting no energy on unproductive emotions himself.

She shivered at the odd notion, gaze mutely pleading for reassurance. Frye offered none, his eyes passing over her as if she didn't exist. While she realized that was only proper, it hurt unbearably. However well she felt she knew him, and after yesterday evening she felt she knew him very well indeed, for him to show recognition would put her mother on the alert. That might not be so serious, but the possibility such recognition might alert Ambrose DeVille to something, never mind what, terrified her.

"Brought a friend with me," Tom babbled, quite as if he hadn't changed beyond recognition and were still the carefree rattle who'd left the house the previous afternoon intent on discovering new methods of dissipation. "Sterling fellow. Met him at Tatt's couple days ago.

"Don't know how to go about it properly—all nonsense anyhow, precedence is—but this is Henry Frye, everybody.

Member of Brooks's, which establishes his *bona fides*. Frye, that's Ambrose DeVille, the Earl of Denbigh, and that's m'mother sitting beside him. She's Lady Leighton, if y'want to be formal about it. And," he said, pointing as if he were at a racecourse, "that one over there's m'younger sister, Nan. Miss Leighton, I guess that'd be. Made her come-out last fall for all she looks like a schoolroom chit, so you're permitted to admit she exists."

"Thomas! You weren't raised among savages, you know," Carlotta Leighton reproved with a laugh that was as gay as it was false. "Dear heaven, Mr. Frye, what must you think of us? Believe me, we're not customarily so ramshackle."

Frye was bowing, then striding across the room, his trim, athletic figure and youthful features in strong contrast to his silver hair, his manner, his dress everything that was elegant. Ann watched as he bent over her mother's hand murmuring pleasantries, then nodded to DeVille. The air bristled with unvoiced accusations. And then he was turning to her. She barely remembered to extend her hand.

It was seized in one that was cool and dry, unlike DeVille's perpetually sweaty palms. Why hadn't she remembered Mr. Frye's hands were so pleasant to touch?

"An honor, Miss Leighton," he was saying. "I hope I find you well?"

Her answer was a traitorous and explosive sneeze.

"I say, Nan, y'look like death," Tom said. "Must be sickening for something."

"Merely rose fever," Carlotta Leighton insisted.

"Nonsense! Y'belong in bed, Nan. Never had rose fever in her life," Tom informed the company at large.

"Thank you, Tom," Ann murmured, blushing furiously. "That's what a lady always likes to hear."

"I'm not certain which of your brother's comments that's in response to," Frye murmured too low for any but Ann to hear, especially as Tom and her mother were now engaged in an acerbic discussion of Ann's susceptibility—

or lack thereof—to rose fever, "but I'd watch myself if I were you. There could be a rather naughty implication at the back some of your words."

Dear heaven—he was right. She gazed into his eyes, found there the same warmth that'd enchanted her the night before. The slightest of smiles quirked her lips. "I'm not ill, you know," she whispered. "It's merely the lingering effects of inhaling too much pepper. You did say not to leave the house until you'd spoken with me, and I couldn't think how else to manage it as Lord Denbigh had come to take me driving and Mama wouldn't hear of a refusal."

"Clever girl," he approved. "Tom'll explain later, as it's quite obvious we won't have a chance to be private."

"But he's all right?"

"Fully restored to his own inimitable self, as you can see, with no aftereffects other than a salutary dose of instant maturity. Your brother's no fool, for all he gives every appearance of it."

"You understand why, ah, last night—"

"I understand perfectly, and commend your loyalty. Not your fault things weren't as they seemed."

"Mr. Frye!"

"Oh, dear," he murmured. "Now I'm for it, I fear. Your brother did caution me."

He gave her an intent, bracing glance, turned to her mother.

"My apologies for not better attending, your ladyship," Frye said smoothly, "but I was commiserating with your daughter regarding her current indisposition. Most unfair she should be felled by the inclement weather we've had of late."

"Do have a seat, Mr. Frye. There's no need for you to concern yourself with Ann, none in the least. Here, beside me," Carlotta Leighton simpered, kohled lashes quivering like hummingbird wings. "You'll have to cede your place, Ambrose. I was merely wondering," she continued once the company was rearranged, DeVille lounging against the fireplace and scowling, Tom making depredations among the tea things, "from what part of England your family springs, Mr. Frye? I don't recognize that family name as figuring among my acquaintance."

"A minor branch of a minor family, actually, and I its last representative. Not unusual that you don't know of us. I've lived much of my life abroad for reasons of health, as did my father, and his before him."

"But you are fixed permanently in Town?"

"For the nonce."

"How positively delightful," she cooed. "A handsome gentleman is always a welcome addition to any gathering. May we expect to see you during our social rounds?"

"If you mean am I received, I believe I am. Certainly my desk is littered with invitations, though I rarely enjoy the society of ladies. More likely to make the rounds of my clubs, quite frankly."

"Now, *that* will have to change! It simply won't do, a gallant gentleman such as yourself playing the misogynist. Not at all in your nature, I'm certain. Merely modesty, which does become a man, I must say."

"He's modest? That what you call it?" DeVille drawled. "Then the encroaching bumpkin probably has something to be modest about."

"Oh, la—we all have things about which we should be modest." Carlotta Leighton gazed pointedly at the spot on DeVille's anatomy where, in former times, padded codpieces supplemented Nature's lack of generosity. DeVille's jaws clenched, his fingers tightening on the stem of his glass until Ann thought it would snap. "Come, Brosie," she insisted, "you must encourage Mr. Frye to take advantage of London's more civilized pleasures or I'll think you're jealous."

"Frye can see to himself," DeVille snapped, eyes narrowed. "No need for you to encourage mushrooms, Carlotta—not that this one requires much encouragement."

"Why, I don't believe he's a mushroom at all. He has

such an air! Are you a mushroom, Mr. Frye?" Lady Leighton asked, turning the full force of her eyes and splendid décolletage on her new acquaintance.

"I don't believe so," Frye returned with a smile. "Certainly that's one failing of which none of my acquaintance have ever accused me."

"Meaningless." DeVille's hard blue eyes narrowed as he looked Frye up and down as if he were a piece of spoiled fish. "Pounds to pence he's a basket-scrambler out to feather his nest."

"Then he's come t'the wrong house," Tom guffawed. "Not looking for us to frank you, are you, Frye?"

"Not in the least."

"Didn't think y'were. I say, Mama, this swill's colder than a—well, it's cold. Tea's not my tipple best of times, but this's undrinkable. Couldn't you ring for fresh?"

"See to it yourself," Lady Leighton snapped, then turned back to Frye, suggestive languor in every gesture. "I'm attending Lady Trimble's rout this evening," she simpered. "As Lord Denbigh finds himself unable to escort me, might you lend me your protection? And the chit, of course. I'm taking her with me. I'd be eternally grateful, as Tom's never available for such duties."

"Going to foist this Cit on Cecily?" DeVille laughed nastily. "She won't thank you, being rather particular about whom she acknowledges and whom she doesn't."

"Cecily Trimble? I already have an invitation," Frye interrupted before DeVille could say more. "No need to offer me yours, Lord Denbigh."

"I certainly won't abandon you ladies to this parvenu's mercies," DeVille snarled, all pretense at civility flown. "If I must endure an evening of crushing boredom, so be it, but I do intend demanding recompense for my tolerance, Carlotta."

"Think I'll go, too," Tom threw in.

"You?" His mother whirled on him, eyes widening. "I

can't believe it! Thomas, there may be hope for you yet. Have you proper evening wear?"

"Course I do! Very latest stare, as it happens."

"Not from Nugee, I hope," Carlotta Leighton dithered, naming the premier tailor to the fops and pinks. "His creations are so *farouche.*"

"Good Lord, Mother, what d'you take me for, a flat?"

"So long as you present a suitable appearance. Isn't this delightful?" she gushed. "I'll have not one, but *three* handsome escorts!"

In the end Ann selected the ice blue sarcenet with spider gauze overlay, crystal flowers flowing gracefully to the hem in rivers of light. The neckline was marginally higher than the blush rose and the trim, while intricate, wasn't as garish as the blond lace embroidered with purple pansies—her mother's favorite, and a gown Ann detested.

Her abigail eased white kid gloves up her arms, fastened a demure crystal collar at her neck, then draped a white shawl over Ann's elbows.

"You do look a treat in that one, miss," Meg breathed. "Like a snowflake kissed by the moon, maybe."

"More like a cheap goblet lying shattered at the bottom of a well," Ann chuckled, "but it doesn't matter. I'm not hoping to cut a dash, merely be overlooked. My reticule, Meg, and my fan, and I'll be on my way. Don't wait up for me. We're likely to be very late, and after last night's excitements you need your rest."

She was out her bedchamber door and down the stairs before she permitted herself to think about the coming evening. With Tom and Mr. Frye present—so long as Tom eventually put in an appearance and then didn't vanish into the card rooms or become foxed the moment he did, and Mr. Frye, who'd seemed at the end of his strength when he left that afternoon, didn't snore the evening away in some palm-sheltered corner—she should be safe enough.

And if they failed her? She shuddered at the thought.

As luck would have it, she arrived in the rotunda at the very moment Beaton was admitting Henry Frye. Her rescuer appeared only slightly more rested: eyes sunken and lacking the sparkle that graced them as recently as that afternoon, complexion far paler than was usual even in a society that valued pallor as proof of elevated rank, and there was a weariness to his steps that appeared bone-deep.

She waited for him at the bottom of the stairs as a footman took his hat, gloves and walking stick, then removed the black evening cloak that swirled around him like raven's wings. It was almost, she decided, as if mist had filled the space between them, rendering his figure wraithlike. A trick of the light, no doubt, and her own depleted condition.

She smiled, holding her hand out in welcome as Frye turned to her.

"Well met, Mr. Frye," she said. "I see our concepts of punctuality are similar."

"You look charmingly, Miss Leighton," he returned with a wan smile as he bowed over her hand. "Dew on a spider web at dawn, I think, or moonlight striking a delicate moth's wing."

"How lovely, and how original! They shimmer so. Thank you."

"Only the truth, and not particularly original, unfortunately. You deserve better." He extended his arm as Beaton signaled the footmen to open the drawing room doors. "You're quite recovered from this afternoon's debility?"

"Totally, as its cause is no longer about. You appear even more exhausted than I," she murmured, careful to let her words blend with Beaton's susurrus of instructions as she gazed into Frye's face with concern and accepted his proffered arm. "Are you certain you should be attempting an evening party?"

"I'll do," Frye responded, the slightest of rueful glints at the back of his silvery eyes. "Just a bit off my feed, is all."

And then they were crossing the polished marble floor.

"You should be able to remedy that at Lady Trimble's, no matter what my mother claims about her ladyship's cheese-paring ways," Ann said with a giggle. "Lady Trimble's chef is far superior to ours, and Mama hasn't been able to lure him away or steal his recipes, for all she bribed one of Lady Trimble's scullery maids who's since been dismissed. Lady Trimble's table offers every delicacy conceivable."

"Does it, indeed? Perhaps I'll play the green 'un when we arrive, and raid her offerings rather than doing the pretty by the ladies."

"Why not do both? Certainly I'd be glad of a lobster patty and some white soup. There's nothing served here when our mother's going out, especially if Papa's from home—which he most generally is—and I'm famished. It's so much more comfortable approaching a refreshment table with a companion. One's depredations are then viewed as social, rather than stemming from acute starvation."

Frye chuckled, his hand tightening over hers where it rested lightly on his arm.

"You haven't seen your father, then?" he asked more seriously.

"It's my understanding Papa has journeyed to the country with a companion," she said primly, "and will be absent from Town for some time."

As they moved toward the drawing room doors, Ann caught a hint of movement in one of the niches. She glanced over her shoulder. The mirrored backing seemed to swirl with the same fog that blanketed London only hours before. Frye's figure was totally hidden, hers partially. She shivered, and the illusion vanished.

"Are you cold?" Frye asked, pausing in the doorway. "I keep forgetting ladies aren't permitted to dress for the weather at these do's, given display's the goal."

"No, not at all," she said, smiling perhaps a trifle too brightly. "It's anticipation, I think, or else dread. I do so wish Mama hadn't insisted on going tonight."

"Tom cautioned you regarding DeVille?"

She nodded. "I'm to avoid him, though Tom claims there isn't any need for him to do so, that there're those a gentleman may acknowledge whom a lady must cut."

"Ensuring others are about when DeVille importunes you may be all that's possible given his friendship with your mother. Certainly you've the right to refuse him dances and such. Better to face a problem forthrightly, I've learned over the years."

"You're correct, of course. It's just—"

"Stop fretting," Frye insisted. "Tom will be there, and so will I. Once DeVille accepts you're not unprotected there'll be no more trouble. The man isn't entirely unintelligent, merely gripped by an *idée fixe* he must be persuaded to discard as impractical. Quite a lovely little *idée fixe*, in point of fact, all starlight and moonbeams flowing together. His problem's entirely understandable."

Ann blushed furiously. How could it be one man's compliments caused her heart to race so delightfully while equivalent phrases spoken by another would've rendered her rigid with indignation?

They entered the drawing room together, he in corbeau evening clothes, his neckcloth tied to perfection, his embroidered gold waistcoat mirroring her golden hair just as her shimmering gown echoed his silver locks.

"Where's Tom?" Frye asked, dropping her hand and glancing about him in surprise as the doors whispered shut.

"I did mention there's no dinner served on the nights

our mother gallivants. Both Tom and Lord Denbigh are aware of the fact. Being gentlemen, they fancied a substantial repast and intend to join us later. I do hope you've eaten, for you'll get nothing here."

"Tom's with DeVille?" Frye scowled.

"You don't approve?"

"I'm not certain. It depends."

"On what?"

"On your brother's purpose in going about with the blackguard. DeVille isn't the thing, all else aside. A notorious rakehell with more by-blows than the sea has sand and abandons 'em all, not to mince words—a new twist to the time-honored Denbigh pastime, for customarily that tribe sees liberally to their chance-gotten offspring. And that's only the beginning. He was—" Frye paused, surveying the room. "Your mother's not here, either?"

"Naturally not. Mama delights in making an entrance. How could she do that lacking an audience?" Ann explained with a soft gurgle of laughter. "Don't worry—this is how things customarily go. I've entertained her cicibeos for hours while waiting for her to judge the moment propitious. Once she appears, I fade into the woodwork. Mama does *not* like competition."

"I draw the line at being classed with those fools," he said with a smile that managed to lessen the insult of his words. "Lady Leighton may delay as long as she wishes, for her arrival will detract rather than add."

Ann glanced about her, not quite certain what to say or do. This wasn't the same as last night, or even that afternoon. Her mother's customary escorts treated the place as if they owned it, even on those rare occasions when her father was present. As for the attentions they paid her, the pats on the head and the "jollying" accorded misses not yet out of the schoolroom were her usual fare—when they noticed her at all. Claiming she was accustomed to entertaining her mother's friends was a gross exaggeration at best.

"Do have a seat by the fire," she said with a touch of nervousness. "May I offer you a glass of claret, or some brandy perhaps, while we await her pleasure? You do appear fearfully fagged."

"When I'm this tired, alcohol'd merely lay me flat," Frye said, striding to the fireplace and gripping the mantel as he stared into the glowing coals.

"Oh, dear! And here I've always heard gentlemen mention it as a restorative. Ladies, too. Even my governess, if one beats an egg in it."

"Depends on what you're trying to restore," Frye grinned.

The doors were flung open with the usual silent flourish. Frye and Ann turned.

Carlotta Leighton posed between bewigged footmen, head high, color higher, scarlet silk gown lasciviously caressing every curve, décolletage leaving little to the imagination. Spangled scarlet and gold plumes soared from a bandeau of brilliants and fire opals circling her brassy curls. Fire opals plunged between breasts whose improbable elevation had nothing to do with Nature and everything with Art. More opals and brilliants trickled from lobes, circled fingers and wrists.

"Good God!" Frye murmured. "No wonder she favors DeVille. They're a matched pair."

Apparently satisfied she had Frye's full attention, Carlotta Leighton swept into the room, hips undulating, fan fluttering, hand regally extended.

"Mr. Frye," she cooed. "How delightful to see you again! May I be permitted to say you are all one could desire in an escort? So elegant, especially with your youthful features and wonderfully unusual silver hair."

"And you, my lady, are a veritable Gloriana of the sunrise." Frye strode forward and bowed over her hand, leaving Ann beached before the fire. "Or, should I say the goddess of that perfect sunset which so enchants sailors, carrying with it the promise of a perfect dawn and delightful sport upon energetically billowing waves? What wonders, what intimations of heavenly bliss you offer we poor mortals!"

"Very prettily done," Carlotta Leighton simpered, tapping his pale cheek with her fan. "I do believe you're rapidly becoming one of my favorites, you naughty man!"

Ann gripped the back of the *tête-à-tête* where earlier her mother had entertained first DeVille and then Frye, embarrassingly aware of the meaning lurking in Frye's fulsome compliment. Comprehension had apparently escaped her mother, however, who had a tendency to take everything as it appeared on the surface. Then Ann's eyes widened as she grasped the implication of her mother's sultrily beckoning expression.

Frye was offering her mother his arm, escorting her toward the fire just as he'd escorted Ann barely minutes before. And yet his manner was totally different. With her Frye had been all open ease, permitting his exhaustion to show, as with one with whom one had shared adversity and survived, and so is on the easiest of intimate terms. With her mother something quite other hung in the air making it almost impossible to breathe, and his expression was guarded for all his feverishly glittering eyes seemed to drink the woman in as if she were his life's blood. No exhaustion about him now.

And it was her mother who'd caused this amazing metamorphosis. Her mother! And she might as well not even be present, given the attention either was paying her. A cold, hard knot formed in the vicinity of Ann's heart and traveled outward, chaining her in place, drained of all energy and spirit.

She dropped her eyes in confusion, unwilling to watch any longer, as her mother's silvery laughter filled the air, Frye's melodious tenor offering her accompaniment. Dear heaven, what'd happened to change everything so?

"What're you doing here, Ann, lurking about like an awkward gawk?"

Ann lifted her eyes, gaze traveling to her mother, then in despair to Frye. He was ignoring her, attention focused on the woman clinging to his arm, a hectic flush on his high cheekbones.

"Your daughter is accompanying us to Lady Trimble's," he shrugged. "Don't you remember, my lady?"

Frye's words didn't appear to soothe her mother. Well, that wasn't surprising. They didn't soothe her, either—not when he employed the same tone Eulie had when offering her an undeserved treat.

"I suddenly find myself unwell," Ann quavered in a voice that sounded close to tears even to her as she eased toward the doors. "I believe I'll excuse myself if you don't mind, Mama, and return to my bedchamber."

"Don't be such a tiresome chit, Ann," her mother snapped. "As you're here and dressed for an outing, an outing you'll have. The project merely slipped my mind. You're rather easy to forget, you know. Take a seat and content yourself with being in the presence of superior company.

"Now," she said, voice softening as she turned back to Frye, eyes traveling his length in unabashed assessment as her hand traveled his arm and shoulder in more practical exploration, "shall we share a glass of wine, Mr. Frye? There's nothing more delightful to my mind than sharing a single glass of wine with a gentleman."

The next minutes were agony for Ann, for when her mother'd said "share a single glass," she'd meant precisely that. The young woman retreated to the farthest corner of the room as instructed, and from there became an unwilling witness to that shared glass as lips replaced lips on the rim. It was a humiliating experience. It was demeaning. It was depressing. It was infinitely painful—to discover one suddenly didn't exist in a gentleman's eyes.

At last her mother tired of the game. Carriages were summoned, wraps donned.

"What an exquisite conveyance," Carlotta Leighton

trilled as she descended the steps on Frye's arm, pausing to examine his town carriage in the uncertain light of the parish lamps.

"Rather cramped and ill-sprung, actually," Frye caviled.

"Too modest by half! Why, it's the very latest stare. Entirely superior to our decrepit barouche, but Lord Leighton won't hear of replacing it until the blasted thing falls apart. Why, the stuffing's literally spewing from the squabs. I'd give most anything to arrive at Cecily's in such an elegant equipage," she hinted, batting her lashes and stroking Frye's arm.

Ann turned away, feeling his eyes on her at last, sensing his amusement at her mortification.

"Unfortunately, your gown would be crushed beyond remedy, my lady," he said, "and those plumes would be snapped off on the instant."

"Bother my feathers! Do grant me the treat? Ann will do very well by herself in the barouche."

"I'm afraid that will be impos—"

"You there, groom, lower the steps, if you would. I'm coming with you, Frye," her ladyship laughed, "and there's not a thing you can do to stop me! Not and still pretend to be a gentleman, there isn't. Ann, get yourself into our carriage. Be sure you don't gawk at the sights as you go along. It isn't the thing to peer from the windows like a common trollop inviting custom."

Just how he managed it Ann wasn't certain, but in the end it was she and her mother in the barouche, and Mr. Frye who traveled solo. It was also she whom Henry Frye handed into the Leighton carriage, her mother who had to make do with the assistance of a groom—small recompense for agonies endured.

The trip to Lady Trimble's home was unpleasant in the extreme, Carlotta Leighton nattering and complaining when she wasn't sulking, and sulking when she wasn't nattering and complaining. On and on it went.

Ann leaned against the squabs and, not in the best of

humors herself, permitting her mother to scold as she wished. Not the best of humors? What idiotic prevarication. She'd counted on Tom, and now Tom was off carousing with Lord Denbigh—whom he'd more than hinted had been responsible for last night's alarms and terrors. She'd counted on Henry Frye, even after less than a day's acquaintance, but from the moment her mother undulated into the drawing room he'd been a willing trout, not even attempting to free himself of the hook. Much good either "gentleman" would do her! As for their reassurances, their promises of protection?

Ann gave an unladylike-like snort.

Tom's defection didn't matter. He was generally more hindrance than help in any case—witness last night's misadventures. As for the cynical, soft-spoken Mr. Frye with his practiced compliments and his lying eyes, he could throw himself in the Serpentine, or fall into a man-trap, or dispose of himself in any other manner he wished, including hanging on her mother's every word like the besotted moon-calf he'd become, and later disport himself in her mother's bed. It might be a bit crowded, but the gentlemen never seemed to mind.

The carriage lurched to a halt, cutting Carlotta Leighton off in mid-diatribe.

"Sit up," she snapped, eyeing Ann in the flickering lights as they joined the line of conveyances inching toward the Trimble House gates. "Straighten your shoulders and remove that sulky look from your face. You're about as appetizing as a witch."

Ann did as instructed, but the rebellious set of her shoulders, the defiant tilt of her chin were apparently not quite what Carlotta Leighton was seeking. The silence in the carriage grew, punctuated by the calls of linkboys and the shouts of coachmen. Ann sat determinedly rigid, eyes on the chaos just beyond the coach widows.

"I hope you aren't under the misapprehension Mr. Frye has the least interest in you merely because he handed you into the carriage," her mother said, breaking a silence she clearly found either unnatural or uncomfortable, or both. "Is that the cause of your sullens, you silly child? That he showed you a moment or two of courtesy, and has moved on to more intriguing fare?"

Ann continued to stare at the scene before her as her mind wandered among inconsequential matters, almost as if she were avoiding an issue she didn't want to consider right then.

"Don't be more foolish than you can help," Carlotta Leighton snapped at Ann's continued silence. "A sophisticated man of the world, interested in a schoolroom chit? His only reason for seeking Tom's acquaintance was to gain an introduction to me," she preened. "I do hope you'll behave yourself with seemly modesty this evening, and be a credit to me rather than proving yet again what an awkward ninny you are. At the very least, please refrain from yawning in the gentlemen's faces, no matter how flat you find their conversation."

Ann persisted in her silence. She had never once—not once—yawned in a gentleman's face, no matter how great the provocation. Neither had she committed any of the other solecisms of which her mother regularly accused her, and which supposedly doomed a young miss to spinsterhood.

"As for Mr. Frye, I positively forbid you to seek his company, or to accept so much as a single cup of punch from him. He intrigues me, and I won't have you muddying the waters."

"I wouldn't presume to swim in your stream, Mama. The feeding you offer is incomparably richer than any I could provide," Ann returned with an unaccustomed edge to her voice. "As for Mr. Frye, I'm amazed you find him of such interest. An untitled nobody of uncertain fortune? Your friends will say you're losing your touch."

"The kitten has claws," Carlotta Leighton murmured, apparently not in the least put out. "You shouldn't speak to me as an equal. Not in the least *comme il faut.* As for Mr. Frye's attractions, if you can't see them for yourself you're even more cloth-headed than I believed."

"But then neither your behavior nor your words are precisely those one would expect from a mother to her daughter, are they, Mama."

"At least you're slightly less boring in this guise," her ladyship said with a brittle laugh as they turned in at the gates and drew up before the imposing facade of Trimble House. "I despise mealy-mouthed chits. Just see you don't go beyond bounds even I would consider inappropriate."

"Not to worry, Mama," Ann bit out. "Unlike some, I have a sense of what is owed the conventions, and an even clearer sense of what is due my hostess. You may be certain I have no desire to give the *ton* a greater disgust of me than circumstances beyond my control have already fostered."

And there was Henry Frye unlatching the carriage door and lowering the steps, for all the world as if he were a well-trained footman or a befuddled beau. Amazing he wasn't laying his cape on the cobbles to protect her mother's dainty sandals and sculptured hem from the inevitable equine deposits, or offering to carry her to the door.

Ann's lip curled with contempt as she watched him bow deeply and extend his arm to her mother. Gushing and twittering, movements as practiced as those of a professional dancer, Carlotta Leighton quitted the carriage. With a speed that surprised even herself and clearly startled Frye, Ann was on the courtyard cobbles before he could turn to assist her, settling her skirts and adjusting her wrap.

"Are you both quite done?" she snapped with the air of an irritated governess. "We're blocking the way, and unconscionably inconveniencing those behind us. You can exchange compliments while we wait to greet our hostess."

She spun on her heel and headed for the steps sweeping up to the overblown marble portico, her head high, her stride more suited to a country lane than Mayfair. Behind her, her mother protested her rudeness in incensed tones, which troubled Ann not in the least. It was Henry Frye's tolerant chuckle that set her teeth grinding and her fists clenching within their casing of soft kid.

Then she was at the soaring front door, only too aware that grand exits following which one is unable to proceed had a tendency to decline into the farcical.

The girl was, Frye realized, jealous. Not just miffed. Not just insulted by his apparent defection. Deeply and painfully jealous.

Flattering, that he could cause such feelings at his age—but then his age wasn't apparent. Would Nan be repulsed were she to see him as he saw himself? Probably, though she'd try to hide it. As for the girl's mother, she'd faint dead away.

And, he thought with a wry twist to his lips as he assisted Carlotta Leighton up the steps, the girl had no notion what ailed her. The evening might prove interesting. It was also going to prove difficult. He wasn't certain he was up to the exertions required in such situations as Nan was likely to cause in her current mood, especially were DeVille to appear on the scene.

"You see fit to await us after all, Mademoiselle Temper?" Carlotta Leighton trilled from his arm, voice carrying not only to the footmen flanking the doors, but to those following them up the shallow marble steps. "How wise, as I have the card of invitation and you'd've been turned from the door without me."

Nan's dignified silence, her glance of contempt at first her mother and then Frye, spoke volumes.

"Perhaps we should move inside?" Frye murmured, restraining himself with difficulty. Any woman who'd bait her own daughter in front of others deserved dunking in a pond. A pity such punishments were out of style. "My lady?" He gestured at the portals—"doors" was a far too plebeian term for structures that would've done justice to Saint Peter's.

After a hard look at her daughter, Carlotta Leighton swept in on Frye's arm, leaving Nan to follow or not as she wished. Frye glanced over his shoulder, gave a peremptory jerk of his head.

He wasn't about to go chasing the girl all over London. Fortunately other guests crowded close behind her blocking any hope of escape short of an ignominious bolt. Her pride came to his rescue as she condescended to follow him and her mother. Frye gave a relieved sigh. For some unaccountable reason the debilitation lack of feeding caused was progressing more rapidly this time. He'd have to solve the problem soon or fall where he stood.

The very thought made him shudder. To have spent close to three centuries seeking a solution, to have apparently found one only to lose the game at the last minute through lack of time to search the stews for his usual sort of donor, didn't appeal. The easy remedy to his increasing weakness—hinting to Carlotta Leighton his disgusting ritual was a method of enhancing sexual enjoyment—would succeed without question, but the mere thought of ingesting her blood made him gag.

He did the pretty, again playing besotted swain to the woman's bewitching enchantress when his preference would've been to squire the genuinely enchanting daughter rather than the vain and posturing mother. Then, as Carlotta Leighton fawned over the newly-arrived Emily Cowper, Frye turned to Nan with what he hoped was a convincingly apologetic smile.

"One so often has to do things one would rather not," he murmured. "May I help you with your wrap?"

"And do something you'd rather not? I believe I'll depend on a footman."

"You deliberately mistake me," he murmured.

"I do?" Her gaze traveled from him to her mother, then back. "Did you enjoy sharing a glass with the famous

Harlotta?" she snapped, head high, cheeks flaming, eyes slashing him like daggers. "Certainly you gave every appearance of it!"

"You shouldn't call your mother that," he reproved mildly, hoping no one could overhear them in the general brouhaha.

"Why not? Everyone else does, thanks to Lady Jersey. Was the wine particularly delicious?"

"It was rather inferior, actually, the whole thing a repulsive experience," he said with an attempt at a smile.

"Oh, really? And here I was thinking you preferred sunrise to moonlight! And billowing waves, naturally. Bliss, I believe you called them."

"My dear girl—"

"I'm not your dear anything, Mr. Frye. Please remove yourself. I find the air in your vicinity distinctly malodorous."

"Ann, listen to me—"

"I suppose now you're going to inform me tantrums aren't the thing at routs?"

"If the shoe fits," he said irritably, instantly regretting the words.

She turned her back, signaling a hovering footman. Frye sighed. Difficult? The evening was going to prove impossible. The girl was beyond reason, and there'd be no chance to set things right in such a crush. Normally he wouldn't've cared in the least. This time, unaccountably, he did.

"Precisely when did Lord Denbigh and your son say they'd join us?" he asked Carlotta Leighton a few moments later as they inched forward in the press.

"La, how should I know?" she laughed. "They'll arrive when they arrive. Certainly you'll ensure I don't pine for their company?"

Her fluttering lashes and flirtatious glance made his palm itch—not gentlemanly of him, but understandable. Just beyond them Nan watched and waited, eyes blank, nose in the air. Frye gave the slightest of shrugs. She turned her back, gazing up the stairs as if in wonder at being admitted to fairyland.

The place was imposing, he granted it that, if one's taste ran to copies of Greek statuary and ornate carvings, but hardly worthy of Nan's rapt gaze.

He offered Lady Leighton his arm, attempting at the same time to capture Nan on his other. Futile. The girl was truly miffed—that, or disgusted. He couldn't find it in him to blame her, but if he didn't pander to her mother there'd be a scene. He'd be sent packing, and there'd be no way he could lend Nan the protection of his presence.

The first part of the evening passed as all such entertainments did, no matter what the century or venue. Frye found himself being dragged from one clot of bores to the next, the latest trout to be displayed on Carlotta Leighton's arm. Preening like a plump pullet in peacock's feathers, she made her way through the reception rooms, a clever general waging a campaign against superior forces, avoiding those whose notice she would never be granted, toadying the more approachable and relaxing her guard briefly with her set. Keeping an eye on Nan was close to impossible. When she disappeared for the fifth time, Frye turned to the female on his arm, expression carefully schooled.

"Don't you think it might be wise to keep Miss Leighton with us in such a mixed gathering?" he murmured. "There're several here with whom I doubt you'd want her to associate. Albert Scanlon, for one, is termed a gentleman only by virtue of ancestors who marginally deserved the designation."

Carlotta Leighton treated Frye to another example of her silvery laugh and another sharp rap of her fan.

"So touching," she trilled, "this concern for my daughter. A little green for you, though, isn't she? Surely riper charms hold greater appeal for a man of your experience. Besides, I've already informed you Ann's spoken for," she snapped, eyes narrowing to icy needles. "I doubt you can match her suitor's attractions: a title, wealth beyond imagining, and a handsome face and well-formed person into the bargain. You could offer the last two, but the first pair? I doubt it."

"My interest is purely avuncular, I assure you."

There wasn't much else he could say under the circumstances without causing a scandal, unfortunately. And, if truth were told, current circumstances also dictated that what he claimed had, perforce, to be the truth.

"See it remains so," she said, revealing more of her true character than she intended. "I shouldn't care to think you playing fast and loose with my affections merely to gain a few half-fledged feathers to soften your nest. Believe me, Ann's only attractions lie in her own sweet self, and quite soon Ambrose DeVille will ensure those belong to him in fact as well as by law, such as they are."

"Quite a cozy arrangement," he murmured enigmatically, seething with disgust.

It took some doing, but a heavy purse to fritter at loo and a deal of fulsome compliments regarding Lady Luck's preference for females who matched her fatal beauty finally saw Carlotta Leighton installed in one of the chambers devoted to gaming, indulging in her second-favorite pastime. Frye took a quick survey of the rooms where the majority of the company had gathered. Nan was nowhere. Neither were her brother or DeVille. Unfortunately that meant nothing, for all he'd done his best to keep track of new arrivals. If Carlotta Leighton's peripatetic habits, her insistence on lingering in locations from which the stairs couldn't be seen hadn't been planned to make his self-imposed task impossible, they might as well have been.

Carefully skirting the benches and chairs where dowagers who might remember his "father" had gathered to trade insults and gossip, Frye made another rapid circuit of the overcrowded rooms. Nothing. It was too opportune, this disappearance of Nan's, this absence of Thomas's. He didn't like it any more than he enjoyed the shrill cacophony of voices doing battle with a lackluster performance of *Eine kleine Nachtmusik* in the state drawing room. Worse yet, Carlotta Leighton had disappeared from the gaming table, replaced by a septuagenarian nabob with a florid complexion, a booming voice, and a bottomless purse.

Persistent inquiries and considerable pocket generosity to a lackey toting a tray of champagne elicited the information that certain rooms on the floor above had been set aside for private revelries. Further generosity to one of the footmen flanking the entry confirmed Lady Leighton had departed on a gentleman's arm. Her daughter? No one knew who the miss might be, but the Leightons' carriage hadn't been requested, and no young lady of the description Frye gave had departed with Lady Leighton—or anyone else, for that matter. Whatever DeVille had planned, the harpy was leaving him a clear field.

Frye checked the ballroom a last time, the stench of cavorting bodies and heavy perfume almost overcoming him, then made his way to the great open space where Lady Trimble was still greeting her late-arriving guests, hair a trifle less *soigné*, a considerable rent in her gown. He sagged against the newel post as he studied the marble stairs sweeping to the next floor. The ceilings of Trimble House were excessively high in this central block, and while the steps were both broad and shallow there was a superabundance of them. The strain of entertaining Carlotta while masking his real anxiety combined with all the rest was once more telling on him. Scaling the blasted things seemed a task fit for Hercules rather than a gentleman of the nineteenth century. Of course the problem lay in his also being a gentleman of the eighteenth, seventeenth, and late sixteenth centuries as well.

Frye attacked the stairs with a resigned sigh, placing one foot in front of the other and using the balustrade to pull himself up. Saving someone's life made one responsible for it, Eastern legends claimed, and technically he'd done that and more for little Ann. He was still on duty, as it were. Certainly no one else appeared either competent to see to her, or interested in assuming the responsibility. Tom Leighton, his one hope for an ally, was proving as feckless as any other youth when his sister's well-being conflicted with his amusements.

The stairs might as well have been the Alps, the Urals, even the Himalayas—all of which Frye had traversed at earlier stages in his long career. He struggled onward, knowing all too well the sort of "private entertainments" in which gentlemen indulged in such secluded venues, an unaccustomed anger rather than his usual wry amusement at the repetitiveness of human folly lending urgency to his halting steps and labored breath. Young Thomas's dressing down, when it occurred, would be a paradigm of the art.

A knot of giddy debutantes passed him, giggling behind their fans and casting assessing glances over his person and attire. Then, on the landing where an oversized footman lurked—presumably to render assistance to the infirm and the cup-shot—it was a gaggle of fops who inspected him disdainfully through ornate quizzing glasses. He paused, staring them down as he caught his breath and gave the footman a quick shake of his head. He was damned if he was going to accept assistance, not yet at any rate.

Then it was on to the next level. With a sense of unreality, he passed niched busts and fulsome portraits of Trimble ancestors, realizing with a start he'd been in this house before, at least part of it, long ago when it had been well out in the country. A portrait of bulbous-nosed General Sir Anthony Thwaite, a Trimble cousin, sitting a prancing war horse of improbable musculature just prior to leaving for France with the Duke of Marlborough provided the clue. In truth, the old sot had been drinking himself silly in a waterfront tavern, terrified at the thought of facing cannon fire. In the end, both Thwaite and his balky horse had been embarked by means of a rope sling—undignified, but efficacious. Poor old Thwaite. Still sodden, he'd tumbled over the ship's rail in mid-Channel, never reaching the Continent.

Paired corridors extended from the staircase's central trunk. Frye paused at its head, trying to remember how the pile had been laid out when newly built. It seemed to him the family bedchambers had been at the far end of the west wing, with nearer rooms devoted to guests and family living quarters. The east wing had held offices, sitting rooms, a library, a gun room, and a slew of other miscellaneous chambers. Nurseries and servants' quarters were still another floor above, sharing space with attics that were infernos in summer and rivaled Alpine peaks in winter.

The lackey had specified the nearer rooms of the west wing as those set aside for debauches. DeVille, if he'd managed to arrive unobserved, would try for something still less public. It had to be the east wing, which had apparently been redone since his last visit. Marble there had been in the old days, quarries of it, but not this excess of coy gilded *putti* toting garish plaster garlands, and not these everlasting mirrors, each of which reflected his true age with unforgiving accuracy.

The stairs had just about done for him. Battling as if against a surging earth such as he'd experienced in the Levant, knees protesting, heart thudding painfully against his ribs, knowing only too well what ailed him and refusing to succumb to weakness, Frye staggered down the broad, well lit corridor. If this was what old age brought with it, heaven preserve him from being forced to endure the experience—which it probably would by the simple expedient of ignoring his existence.

The first two doors opened easily enough despite his palsied grip. Within lingered none who mattered. The next three chambers, two on one side of the corridor, one much larger on the other which, if he remembered correctly, had once been a music room, were empty.

He stumbled on, doing his best to ignore infirmities

he'd never before suffered. The foolishness had to end. As soon as Nan Leighton was safely returned to her parents' home he'd hire the first woman he encountered, no matter how repugnant the process, no matter how deeply he despised it. The syrupy, metallic tang of blood still warm from the vein was a taste he couldn't seem to acquire. A creature of the night who despised the flavor of blood? Unheard of, and beautifully ironic.

An unfamiliar secondary corridor met the first at right angles, this one unlit. Another new addition to the monstrous sprawl? Probably.

He peered down first one passage and then the other, vision clouding as his condition deteriorated, trying to understand how DeVille might've planned. A muffled cry from far along the branch corridor gave him his answer. Frye took off at an awkward lope, joints complaining, heart now beating irregularly. His hearing might be less acute than customary, but the roar of fury from behind a door at the end of the dim passage gave him all the answer he needed. That was young Leighton. Not so feckless after all? A heartening possibility.

Frye lurched to a halt, seized the door handle with both hands and twisted. The damned thing was locked, but he could smell fresh-spilled blood through the cracks. He lunged against the inset decorative panels, desperation lending him a trace of his customary strength. The upper panel splintered with the crack of dry wood. Reaching inside, he turned the key, thrust the door open and stumbled into the room. A single branch of candles burned on the mantel of what appeared to be the secluded bedchamber of an indigent relative, the tarnished mirror above doubling the scene.

It was DeVille, all right, *sans* coat and dancing pumps, neckcloth discarded. And young Leighton, panting even harder than Frye, a crimson patch growing on his sleeve. The hot scent seared Frye's nostrils. The two men had squared off before the fire, furniture knocked aside, De-

Ville armed with an elegant swordstick, Tom brandishing a poker. Nan hovered just beyond them, clutching a heavy ewer with which she'd clearly been attempting to bash DeVille. Her bodice might be torn, her hair tumbling down, her cheeks tear-stained and ugly bruises darkening her slender neck, but she was as uncowed, as indomitable as ever, whirling at the sound of the door crashing open.

"Oh, thank heaven," she gasped. "Do something, Mr. Frye. Please! He'll kill Tom, and it's all my fault."

Frye gave Nan a nod and waved his hand for her to step back from the combatants.

"Not very sporting, DeVille," he managed, amazed at the strength of his voice when the floor was lurching beneath him like the deck of a ship trapped in a North Sea storm, "an armed man in his prime taking on a cub with no training and nothing but a piece of household equipment to defend himself."

"You, again, Mr. Impertinence? What a thick-skulled marplot! I thought you understood your lack of welcome this afternoon." The point of DeVille's swordstick wove an intricate pattern clearly intended to confuse Tom. "And you last night as well, I suppose. Why don't you keep to the stews from which you doubtless sprang?"

"Oh, my ancestry's a bit better than that."

DeVille's sardonic laugh was accompanied by a lightning lunge. A rent appeared from neck to waist in Tom's shirt, followed by a thin trickle of blood. Tom stared at his chest in amazement as the next three slashes drew no blood, but left his shirt hanging in ribbons. Another flick of the blade, and his watch fobs went flying.

"Raise your head, gape-seed!" the earl drawled. "It's not your nose I'm after."

He stepped back, the point of his swordstick resting on the floor, its blade slightly bowed, as he cocked a single brow.

"I keep trying to do this properly," Tom grunted, swinging hard with the poker, and missing DeVille by a mile, "but the blackguard's refused my challenge."

"No, instead he intends to murder you where you stand if he doesn't geld you first." Frye closed what remained of the door and crossed the room. "It won't wash, DeVille. You continue in this manner, and I'll see the tale's in every club in Town before dawn. You can't kill us all. Ann, go stand behind your brother. DeVille, I'm stepping behind you. On the count of three, you'll hand me your swordstick and Tom will give his sister the poker."

"I think not. This uncouth puppy needs to be taught a gentleman doesn't brook interruption when amusing himself."

DeVille accompanied his taunting words with another swift flash of his swordstick Tom was helpless to parry. The reddening crease on the boy's face extended from brow to chin, spider web thin, so delicate had been the rotter's touch.

"And now," DeVille gloated, "for a matching mark so you'll remember to stay out of the affairs of your betters."

"I think not," Frye mocked.

He whirled on the ball of one foot, stiff arm striking first high and then low as he wrenched the swordstick from DeVille's light grip. DeVille fetched up against the chimney breast, shaking his head to clear it and snarling with rage. Frye snapped the slender blade in two and tossed it contemptuously on the grate.

"Little trick I learned in my travels," he explained at the stunned look on Tom's face. "Give your sister that poker, if you please, and then take off your shirt and sit on the bed. Ann, if you'll fetch a basin of water and a rag? And Lord DeVille's neckcloth. It's on that chair behind you, and will make an excellent bandage."

DeVille launched himself at Frye's back with a wordless roar. Frye sidestepped neatly, leg lashing out. Ann stared in horror from the mirror to Frye as DeVille flipped top over tail, crashed into the wall and slid to the floor.

"What's that called? I've never seen anything like it," Tom gasped.

"It's unpronounceable, but highly efficacious."

"I'll say! Would you teach me how?"

"Perhaps," Frye grinned weakly. "Are you all right, Miss Leighton? No damage beyond what one can see?"

"None, but—" Her gaze flew once more from Frye, slightly disheveled but otherwise very much himself for the moment, to the mirror. "I don't understand," she said haltingly, eyes wide with a terror that had nothing to do with her brother or the earl. "Am I losing my mind? Is it a dream, all of it?"

"A nightmare, which you'll forget as soon as it's over. I'll explain later if it proves necessary—which I doubt it will."

There was no mistaking the look in Nan's eyes. She'd seen him in the mirror as he saw himself whenever he passed one of the pernicious things—a mummified travesty of a man about to dissolve into his parent dust. No one else had ever seen him so, not even his mother. What it meant Frye wasn't certain, but he'd've wagered his last chance of acquiring a soul that her ability boded ill for that project. Perhaps the illusion existed only when he was at full strength? He'd never experienced such debilitating weakness in his life. But no, Tom clearly had no idea what terrified his sister, nor did he see anything out of the ordinary for all his gaze had followed Nan's to the mirror.

Frye turned to watch as DeVille laboriously pulled himself to his knees, head hanging low. "Had enough?" Frye said.

"I'll tend to you both later," DeVille growled, pushing his pale gold locks from his eyes and standing effortlessly.

"Just so long as you see to us yourself, rather than hiring others to do your dirty work for you."

"I'd call you out for that were you a gentleman. As for you?" DeVille turned to Tom, ice-blue eyes hardening. "I do believe I'll accept your previous invitation. Do you intend to remain here, or do you plan to return home?"

"When and where?" Tom snapped, drawing himself up.

DeVille bared his teeth. "I'll get word to you." He retrieved pumps and coat and limped to the door, then turned back, looking Nan up and down. "You've made a serious error," he snarled, "just how serious you'll eventually come to appreciate. For the moment I bid you adieu, but you and I shall also have a reckoning. I anticipate the experience with considerable pleasure. You should not."

Then he was gone.

"A basin of water, Ann," Frye repeated, exhaustion gripping him now the crisis was past.

"Mr. Frye, are you quite all right?" she said, gaze once more flying in confusion from him to the mirror.

"I'll do."

"But why—"

"I don't know. A basin of water, Ann. Your brother's hurts must be seen to, and you must both be gotten home. The rest we'll sort out later."

"I'm coming with you, sir," Tom insisted from the bed. "If you don't mind, I'd be a deal more comfortable if Nan came, too. There's something deucedly havey-cavey about this whole business, for Nan swears our mother told her to stop being a silly nodcock and go see what I needed when DeVille sent word I required assistance. It wasn't me at all, you understand, any more than it was before."

"I've already told you Tom," Nan sighed from the wash stand. "Mama's determined to see me wed, she cares not how so long as it's to Lord Denbigh. I interfere with her amusements. She made that very clear this morning."

As Frye watched, the young woman fussed with a flask set on a shelf over the wash stand. Then she was at his side, proffering a chipped goblet.

"You appear far more done in than my brother," she murmured, eyes shadowed with concern. "This has all been my fault. Was there ever such a goose? I'm so sorry for everything I said earlier. I didn't mean a word of it, you know."

"I'll let you off lightly this time, as the fault is at least partly mine. I had no idea I was such an excellent actor. It was a game, the business with your mother," he said gently as he accepted the goblet, losing himself in the depths of her eyes. "You told me yourself she wouldn't accept competition. Had I not played it, she would've had me chased from the place and DeVille would've succeeded tonight. I couldn't permit that."

"I understand that now," Nan whispered haltingly. "Can you ever forgive me?"

"You're forgiven," he said, setting the goblet aside, capturing her hands and bringing them to his lips. "Just be sure you don't leap so quickly to unwarranted conclusions in the future, dear one. Examine all the evidence at your disposal, including the past actions and characters of those involved."

"You may be certain of that, at least," she said with a tremulous smile. "Are you quite sure you're recovered?"

"There never was anything wrong with me other than the usual infirmities one might expect in one of my advanced years," he said with a bitter chuckle. "Now that you're satisfied I shan't turn into a cloud of vapor before your eyes, let's see to your brother, shall we?"

Green Park

"Damn and blast," Tom Leighton grumbled as Frye sponged the cut on his face with a soap-laden cloth. "That stings! Can't you be more careful?"

"Fortunes of war. So do salt and vinegar. Sting, that is. So will this."

As Nan emptied the basin in the slops jar under the wash stand, Frye soaked a fresh cloth in the red-tinted cordial and dabbed it on.

"What the deuce?" Tom yelped, jerking away. "Is that really necessary?"

"D'you know where DeVille's swordstick has been? Neither do I, and the problems caused by uncleansed wounds include infection, gangrene, and death. There're two standard battlefield remedies: half a bottle of brandy outside and half inside, or piss on it. I presume you'd prefer brandy, but as there's none in this lady's bedchamber we'll make do with the cordial in deference to your sister."

"You've been in the Peninsula?"

"Among other places."

"What glorious luck! Want to go m'self, but m'father won't hear of it."

"First evidence of sense in Swinard Leighton I've ever heard of. Believe me, there's nothing glorious about a battlefield. There, that should do it." Frye leaned against the bedside table as he examined his handiwork. Only determination was holding him erect, a fact of which Nan seemed fully aware. "Now for the bandages."

"But these're nothing but scratches! I'm not willing to parade through that crush looking like a guy. Wouldn't be able to show my face for a month of Sundays!"

"Tom, you'll do as Mr. Frye says," Nan snapped, tugging her gown over her shoulders and pinning it together at the front. "If you'd think about someone besides yourself for a moment, you'd know we can't go down the main stairs. It's not only you whose appearance isn't quite the thing. There's certain to be a back way."

"And what then? Walk home? These pumps're pinching like the very devil. M'feet must've grown again. Besides, I'm feeling more than a trifle above par, for all I had barely a drop at dinner."

"Servants' stairs and back passages." Frye collapsed beside Tom and downed what was left of the cordial in two gulps. "I'll bring my carriage to the side gate and come back for you since I'm the only one able to show himself in public."

"How d'you know there's a side gate?"

"I've been here before, as it happens. Put on the remains of your shirt and your coat. We don't want unnecessary questions, and servants are gazetted gossips—their revenge for endless boredom, poor pay, and impossible hours. The less said about this night, the better." Frye smiled sadly as he turned to Nan, who'd joined them by the bed. "That gown has passed its prime," he said. "Pity. I liked you garbed in moonbeams."

She blushed, the concern in her eyes so palpable it caused an odd wrenching in his chest.

"I've found an old shawl no one'll miss," she said. "As for the gown, what a silly thing over which to concern yourself. You mustn't worry about me."

"I've done little else since last night—a most unaccustomed experience. I doubt I'll do much else for the rest of my life," he grumbled as he gripped the bedpost and struggled to his feet. "Unusual habit for one of my sort—generally we're quite selfish—but I find I like it. Don't leave this room," he cautioned, scowling at Tom. "DeVille's sure to be lurking about in hopes of catching one of you alone. I sincerely doubt he has much in the way of gentle feelings for either of you at the moment, and he strikes me as the type who'll be even more determined to mete out what he'd term justice in the service of his self-consequence than he was before."

"I'm not a nodcock," Tom bristled.

"No?" Frye went to the door, muttering about the idiocies of social custom, then turned and looked Tom up and down, shaking his head. "And what did you think you were about, taking on one of the premier fencers in England with only a poker?"

"Wasn't much else I could do, blast it! The blackguard was mauling Nan. Would you've preferred I let him continue?"

"I suppose you alerted him to your arrival, and issued the customary gentlemanly challenge. Well, did you?"

Tom nodded, reddening about the ears.

"The goal in such situations is to disable the attacker, rescue the one being attacked, and concern oneself with the niceties of honor at a later time," Frye snapped. "The way you were going about it, you were likely to get yourself killed. What good would that've done your sister?"

"Not much," Tom mumbled.

"None at all, in fact. She holds you in considerable affection. You come to grief, and you'll break her heart. From what I've learned of her in the past day, she has a considerable heart to break. She'd not thank you for leaving her friendless. Neither would I."

"And what of you? Are you so trustworthy?"

"I invariably abandon those about whom I care the most," Frye muttered bitterly. "Indeed, I'm famous for it, and will probably repeat the process shortly."

"What was that? I couldn't quite understand you."

Frye gripped the door handle. "Nothing important," he said. "Just talking to myself—dreadful habit, I know. Please excuse me. Lock the door, Ann, and drape something over the hole. If someone attempts to enter, discourage them with Tom's poker or pretend you're a pair of lovers. That should chase 'em off, *faute de mieux*."

And then he was out of the room, the door with its shattered panel closed on the problems behind him, the challenge of somehow remaining on his feet before him.

He leaned against the wall, eyes glazed with exhaustion, planning his route and the explanations he'd give Jem, Phinny, and John. The truth would probably serve, he realized through the haze clouding his mind. John'd been with him when he rescued Nan, all three there when he went back for Tom. Another rescue of brother and sister wouldn't seem in the least out of the way, for all he was certainly developing what they'd consider a quixotic bent. Fortunately DeVille had a poisonous reputation among the servant class. Far from wishing to avoid aiding any who'd earned the earl's enmity, coachman and grooms would probably be only too glad to lend any assistance necessary to thwart the schemer. If not, he'd offer pocket inducement.

"He'll be back as soon as possible, Tom," Ann snapped. "Don't complain so."

"Overbearing, opinionated, insufferable fellow," Tom grumbled.

"He does have a nasty habit of being right about things more often than not."

"All I can say is y'show Frye more loyalty and consideration than y'do me."

"Yes, I suppose that's true." She fumbled her way to the door, turned the key, then stuffed the shawl she'd found in the hole. "Seven Dials is such an amusing place, and the company so delightful. I can hardly wait for my next excursion."

"Should've known better!"

"As for this evening—"

"T'night don't count," Tom admitted grudgingly from the bed. "Whatever possessed you? Should've known better than to come running at DeVille's beck. I was like to stick my spoon in the wall, indeed! Played the same trick last night, for pity's sake, only it was my pockets were supposedly to let. Why didn't you check with Frye?"

"We'd had the most dreadful row. Well, not precisely a row, but I didn't know where to turn when Mama had me fetched. She said she was having tremendous luck at the tables and to see if you were really ill. He'd sent the note to her, after all, and so I thought it was safe enough. I wasn't thinking clearly, I suppose."

"Why not? Y'normally have more wit than hair—not that your hair's not pretty, even if it is a mess at the moment."

"I, ah, I wasn't quite myself."

"Why not?" he repeated.

"Mama'd been importuning Mr. Frye most dreadfully, if you must know," she said hesitantly, blushing until she thought the room would light up with it.

"And y'didn't like it? Not surprised."

"Well, I was. I was tremendously surprised. I've never cared a whit before when she played her games, and she's played them with every gentleman who's shown the slightest interest in my company."

Ann anchored her hair in a rough knot, then turned in the darkness and groped her way to the bed where her brother waited for their rescuer to return with reinforcements. She'd just extinguished the candles over Tom's vociferous objections. With only the dying embers of a coal fire to give them light, the unprepossessing bedchamber had taken on the atmosphere of a medieval dungeon, reverberations of the revelries echoing ghost-like from below.

"What're you going to do?" Tom asked more calmly. "Mama's determined to see you leg-shackled to DeVille. Thought it was a capital notion m'self until this morning."

"I don't know—except nothing will ever induce me to accept him. I'd die first."

"Fustian!"

"No, Tom, I'm serious." She perched beside him, reaching for his hand. "That's what it would come to in the end, one way or another. Better to avoid the process of getting there, which would be most unpleasant. First I'd try to run away, of course, or marry anyone else who came to hand."

"Such as Frye?" he asked hesitantly. "Y'seem awful fond of him."

"I am," she sighed, grateful for the darkness that hid her blushes and permitted her to be frank even as tears welled in her eyes, "but I'm afraid that'd be impossible. Mr. Frye's seriously ill. I'm most dreadfully concerned about him, for I fear he's done himself a lasting disservice in being of service to us."

"Tumbled top over tail, have you?" Tom's arm was about her shoulders, his voice gruff. "Well, if it's the least comfort, I suspect you've planted him a facer from which he ain't likely to recover. Prime fellow, too. Not the least like Brosie. When Frye says something, y'can trust it's so."

"That only makes it worse," she gulped. "To look at him, one would think he's in the best of health. Yet he's dying—I know it. Nothing's possible under such circumstances."

"Oh yes, it is. Ask him, if he won't ask you," Tom suggested, cramming a square of cambric in her hand. "I know it ain't the thing, but I'd rather see you Frye's widow, no matter who he is or what the state of his health, than wed to Brosie DeVille. Not the man I took him for, and that's the truth. I think he and Mama are, well—"

"I think so, too, and with even better reason than you could have."

"Caught 'em at it?"

"Almost," she sighed, dabbing at her swimming eyes and then blowing her nose. "This afternoon in the drawing room, just before you and Mr. Frye arrived. It was rather amusing, actually—watching them try to pretend nothing untoward had been occurring. You should've seen poor Beaton harrumph and then wait before having the doors opened. I'd always wondered about his harrumphing. Now I know."

"Both of us know a lot of things we didn't until today. It ain't pleasant—this becoming what Frye calls a reasoning adult. Ain't easy, either. Don't worry about DeVille," Tom said abruptly, his arm tightening as her head rested against his chest. "It shan't come to taking your life, that I swear. One way or another, he'll not importune you again."

"Don't do anything foolish, Tom."

"And face one of Frye's tongue-lashings afterwards? Hardly! Enduring his bear-garden jaws ain't my idea of a pleasant time. Y'know how he is."

"Yes, I know."

And then they sat in the dark, abstracted and silent. It seemed to Ann they waited interminably for Frye to return, though she supposed it was only a matter of a few minutes, but at last came the muffled thud of heavy footsteps in the corridor, and the sibilant hiss of whispers. She was at the door on the instant, Tom crowding behind her as she retrieved the shawl and pulled it around her, then turned the cumbersome key.

"Shouldn't've unlocked it until you were positive it was us," Frye scolded, his face gray in the uncertain light.

"Well, out with you both. I, for one, have no desire to be caught by one of Lady Trimble's other guests. The questions would be close to endless and endlessly unanswerable."

They made a strange procession, Frye leaning on Phinny's arm as he led the way, Ann in the middle with Jem, Tom bringing up the rear carrying the poker he'd surreptitiously retrieved from the fireplace. Their path was tortuous and, to Ann's mind, needlessly complicated, further exhausting Frye as they climbed stairs only to descend others and doubled back along parallel passages, pressing against the walls as they came to branches for all the world as if they were housebreakers. Repeatedly she suspected he'd lost his way only to find it again after striking out blindly in first one direction and another. Once she caught a glimpse of a door opening at the end of a dim green corridor that stretched for what seemed like miles. The sudden blast of sound, the brilliant golden light streaming through the distant doorway held an unreality that had her shivering.

They finally arrived at a service door. Frye paused, turned. Ann glanced over her shoulder. Tom had vanished. Then she glimpsed two figures she'd at first thought were one in the penumbra. She wrenched free of the groom's grip and darted back down the corridor, ducking behind a tall storage cabinet as soon as she could hear voices. It was Tom, all right, and a gentleman she'd seen in DeVille's company. Only a few words were distinct, but they were enough: Dawn. Green Park. Rapiers. Heart in mouth, she joined the others, shrugging at Frye's narrowed glance.

"An acquaintance of Tom's," she said dismissively. "I suppose he's curious as to our reasons for skulking about."

Frye doubted that most sincerely, but he was too exhausted to argue. Instead he instructed the door be opened, detailed Jem to wait for Tom and guide him to the carriage. They wouldn't leave without him. With superhuman effort, Frye relinquished Phinny's support and offered Nan his arm.

"I believe we'd best make ourselves scarce," he croaked.

His hand might be trembling, but it was as unmarked by age as ever, smooth and firm-muscled, for all the muscles had less strength than those of a babe. He shuddered at what he knew must be happening. Someone else would have to see to Nan's happiness, another guide Tom until he reached the age when wisdom overrode impulse. He'd played his game. Well, he'd played it with the best, and if this was to be the idiotic end of him, too busy living to ensure his continued existence, so be it.

Nan was gripping his arm without the least attempt at pretending to accept support rather than give it. And she was signaling Phinny to take his other arm again. No, pretenses were over between them. Sad, that. There should always be a touch of mystery between a man and a woman.

"Don't concern yourself about me, my dear," he managed. "I'll do."

"You'll not do in the least," she said with heartbreaking gentleness. "We've got to get you home. If Tom delays, he'll have to join us as best he can."

Damn it, he felt younger, stronger than ever in whatever constituted his mental as opposed to his physical being. Nan had created that miraculous change, for his world-weariness had been incalculable just before he'd encountered her. Now he wanted nothing more than he wanted to live. Unfortunately, wanting wasn't enough.

An unwelcome tear formed in the corner of his eye. He wanted to tell her only she mattered, that somehow he'd guard her. The words wouldn't come, frozen deep within him. Because, no matter what he wanted to believe, he knew he was powerless? And then he realized he wasn't quite as powerless as he seemed. All those houses—Paris, St. Petersburg, Rome, Bombay, Montreal, Shanghai. And the properties, rich ones, scattered here and there across the face of the earth: mines, manufactories, estates, plantations, shipping lines, trading companies. The almost incalculable fortune he'd built over the years thanks to careful husbanding of DeVille's Reginald's initial generosity—there'd be no "son" of his to claim them this time.

"By damn!" he muttered. "By damn, that's the solution!"

A hundred thousand pounds sterling to Swinard Leighton so long as Ann was permitted to wed where she wished, or to remain a spinster all her life. Given the position of women, she might well prefer that sort of independence. Another hundred thousand to Harlotta to fritter so long as she never again importuned her daughter. Two hundred thousand to Tom upon the birth of his first child, and the property in Kent. It was a pleasant place, the land in excellent heart. And the rest? The rest would go to Nan, all of it, with the proviso that should she wed her husband could touch the income, but never the principal. He'd do it, by damn! He was about to cheat fate.

So delighted was he that he barely noticed the insult of Phinny swinging him up in his arms and carrying him through the garden, or Nan opening the gate. He wasn't conscious of Tom joining them, except in a dreamlike manner. The rattle of carriage wheels, the clop of horses' hooves seemed to come from a great distance. As for sights, only one interested him: the beloved face bent over him in concern.

She was murmuring something, what he wasn't quite sure.

"Don't worry, my dear," he croaked, "I've figured it out. You'll want for nothing, and no one will ever be able to coerce you again. Got your future in hand as well," he said, rolling his head against the squabs to stare at Tom. "See to it you justify my trust."

And then they were at his house, Springer opening the door, Mrs. Finch hovering in the entry behind him. Strong arms were lifting him, carrying him up the steps.

"Bookroom," he yelped as Nan instructed that he be taken upstairs to his bed. "My bookroom, dammit! Not ready for a coffin yet. And no blasted physicians. Couldn't do anything for me anyhow."

It was strange to watch the world pass him by from this unaccustomed position. The coffered ceilings were rather pretty, he decided. As for the endless images of himself across the centuries, they amused him. Those, too, would go to Nan.

He smiled bitterly as Phinny deposited him on a divan across the room from his desk. Twenty-four hours before he'd just arrived with Nan, still in command of himself and his world. So few hours for so great a change. And yet? And yet, in a strange way he was still in charge, never more so. Now he knew what he was doing rather than casting about in desperation for the solution to his nature—not that it would do him the least good. As ever, he was acting because it pleased him. No chance of gaining a soul for that. As for his not taking time to see to his needs, and so now being beyond help, that too had been for his own sake rather than for some altruistic motive.

"Paper and a pen," he said irritably, "and prop me up, blast it, Springer. Not about to loll the dregs of my life away."

"But isn't there anything we can do?"

Nan again, not willing to give up. That pleased him, too—her perpetual refusal to accept that which she found unacceptable. Poor way of putting it, but there, his mind wasn't functioning up to par. It was almost as if he were cup-shot, though not quite. He couldn't find an adequate description, gave up the effort. Everything was too much effort at the moment, or almost everything.

"Fraid not," he said with a touch of his former vigor now he didn't have to fritter energy holding himself erect or bend his mind to anything but seeing to her future. "A bit too late, unfortunately, my dear. Should've seen to m'sclf yesterday, or this morning. Knew it could happen. Ignored it. Now it has."

"But what sort of disease can it be that could claim you so rapidly? Yesterday you were—"

"Yesterday was yesterday. Today is today. Most profound statement, don't you agree? Not a disease. Just the way I am. I'll explain if there's time. Told you that. If there isn't? Well, then that's the way it is. No real need for you to understand in any case. But, I'm afraid we shan't be meeting again, not even when time stops."

Springer was placing a portable desk on his lap, complete with paper and a small standish. Frye started to wave away the brandy Mrs. Finch was holding to his lips, thought better of it. He wanted a bit more time than Nature seemed willing to grant him, all the time he could have, in short. The stuff tasted oddly vile, but he could sense a small warmth creeping through his veins.

Simple was best, Niccolo had said, when it came to instructions to be carried out by others, if one wanted them carried out properly and wouldn't be there to oversee the process. Clever fellow, Niccolo Machiavelli. Where was he now, Frye wondered.

"Always thought we were more similar than met the eye," Frye muttered fretfully. "There was that 'nephew' of his, Pietro What's-His-Name, whom he saw to most liberally. Fellow never showed up until after Nicco died, and I don't care what anyone says about a corpse not resembling the living person: Nicco never had a mole the size of a florin on his cheek the way his corpse did, nor a wart on his nose. Neither had Pietro, and his hair was just like Nicco's when I first knew him."

Then, at Nan's puzzled glance, he smiled ruefully. "An old friend. Predeceased me by some years. At least, he's supposed to've. Maybe not, though. Maybe not."

By damn, but this was an odd situation. Here he was, chattering on as if he were going about his customary business, while in reality he was bidding final farewells to people who'd come to mean more to him than he would've dreamed possible only two days before. They must believe him mad, all of them.

"Haven't thought of Nicco in I don't know how long. No one you'd've known. Wrong country, and," he tossed off as if it were meaningless, "wrong century. Now," he said, gaze moving from Nan to Tom, then to Springer and Mrs. Finch, "go sit by my desk. I'll need you and Springer to witness my will, Mrs. Finch, which I'm about to write. Get Jem and Phinny in here as well, and John. The more, the better. Don't worry, there's the wherewithal in the safe behind my desk to see to you all most comfortably."

Apparently coachman and grooms had been hovering in the entry, for Springer had them there almost before the words were out of his mouth.

Writing the thing took no time: The usual claim regarding being of sound mind; instructions to discharge any outstanding debts; three sentences for Leighton *père* and his rib with attendant cautions, and two sentences for Tom. Nan, as the most important, took but a single line, her potential husband another, and it was done. He signed it with a trace of his old flourish, handed the single page to Springer.

"You all know me," he said. "You can see no pressure's been placed on me regarding the terms. Witness it, if you please. There'll be no problems. No heirs of my body, no potential claimants on my consideration. James MacDougal'll see to carrying out the provisions. Clever solicitor, MacDougal. So was his great-grandfather. The others haven't been worth much, but I kept 'em on for the old man's sake."

He watched, eyes narrowed, as first one and then the next affixed mark or signature according to degree of education, overseen by Springer. Then, as the room seemed to swim about him in a misty fog, Nan stumbled to where he lay, tears streaming down her face.

"None of that, Nanette," he murmured as she gripped

his hands, kneeling beside him. He tried to smile at her, found it damnably difficult. "Always did like your brother's pet name for you. How I've thought of you. Always will. The dearest Ann in the world. Nanette. My dearest little Nan."

She was pressing her lips first to his cheek, then branding his with her own as her tears scalded him.

"Here now, you'll never have to worry about DeVille again," he chided tenderly, stroking her hair with a trembling hand. "That's the main thing isn't it, my love?" His gaze shifted slightly. "Tom, see to her. You don't, and I'll haunt you to the end of your days."

The room was cold, so cold, as if heat had never existed anywhere. As if he were in a place before time began, or perhaps after it ended. And dark, as if every light in the universe had been extinguished. He could barely make out her features and, gleaming on the mantel behind her, Ben Cellini's chalice.

"Forgot," he mumbled over her sobs. "Ben's cup—want it given to a church. Where it belongs. See to it, Nanette."

Her hand was slipping away. And the room, and everything in it. And her voice, pleading for him to linger, sobbing out she loved him.

"Must be why y'saw me as I truly am," he mumbled. "Nothing else explains it. Nasty consequence, that."

He gripped her fingers convulsively, and then it was over, whatever "it" was, and he was whirling through a dimensionless darkness so thick, so impenetrable, so silent that at first he thought he'd lost all ability to hear or see. And alone—more alone than he'd ever been.

So he'd played his game to the end, and emerged as he'd begun. Would this pain endure for all eternity, infinitely personal, infinitely futile, containing as it did the vision of all the joys he'd glimpsed only to have them torn from him? He could imagine no truer hell. So must Adam and Eve have felt when chased from the Garden. So must Lucifer have felt, plunging through a different darkness to eternal damnation. Poor Milton, for all his blindness, had had the keenest of visions. Paradise lost, indeed.

A single cry of agony broke from him in the soundless place that held him in its grip, at once pleading with all that existed or didn't exist to grant him forgetfulness while insisting memory of the last day never be taken from him.

Sound reached him: an answering cry of despair so profound it seemed composed of all the torment endured by all the people who'd ever walked the earth, reverberating in the void like the collision of stars.

He centered on that silent, heartrending cry, desperately following it to its source.

And found himself in his bookroom once more, though the perspective confused him, so odd and shifting it was. He reached out, grasped the lip of Ben's golden chalice as it spun by, clung to it without hands, panting without breath. Dear heaven, what was he now? Some whirling, dervish-like thing?

He glanced over his nonexistent shoulder. Nan still knelt by the divan, but she was dry-eyed and silent now. From whence had come that anguished plea, then? Yet he could feel her despair, her longing as clearly as if they were his own, which perhaps they were: the twinned sorrow for what could never be.

And that which had been himself? As he watched, it dissolved into the dust from which it had sprung, the slightest of sighs disturbing the bookroom's air, his true age revealed for all to see now the motive force had fled, features crumbling, that "too, too solid flesh" melting indeed. Was time itself compressed? But no, voices and movements were at the usual human pace. Somehow he knew that, though just how he wasn't certain. Only he was out of step.

He turned with infinite care, still gripping the chalice's lip, so he could watch more comfortably rather than having room and figures spin insanely about him. Given Mrs.

Finch's wails—who'd have thought the old scold had so much emotion in her, and it was genuine, by damn—he could only catch one word in ten, but Tom and Springer were by the windows conferring. He had to hear what they were saying, blast it, though he had a pretty good idea what was to do. He might've been at the end of his strength at Trimble House, but he'd seen Tom clearly enough, toe to toe with Bertie Scanlon, one of DeVille's viler cronies. The young fool'd gotten himself in a position where either he met DeVille or he'd never be able to show his face in London again.

And that meeting? DeVille had already butchered several, getting away with it heaven alone knew how, for dueling had been outlawed at last. Baksheesh, probably—and plenty of it—in the right places. Greasing palms was the time-honored expedient of those with the wherewithal, and DeVille had it in plenty.

Sparing only a glance for Nan—he'd do his best by her later, though what that best might be in his current condition he had no notion—Frye released the cup. The room careened past him. Desperately he reached out, latched onto Tom's collar as he whirled past, gripping desperately. Then, with great care, he settled on the lad's shoulder and bent his attention to the conversation.

"You'll see my sister gets home safely, then," the boy was saying. "And you understand about the other? And will come as soon as you can?"

"I understand, not that I like it," Springer grumbled. "The master'd've called you a fool, and then some. Y'sure you don't want her to wait here?"

"With that lying there?"

Frye followed Tom's gesture of repugnance. The clothes he'd been wearing were crumbling now, following him into whatever place it was he'd landed, and was only escaping for the moment. Dear God, what an ending for a man! Justice didn't exist.

"Can't harm her," Springer said, "and she doesn't seem to mind it."

"Well, I mind it."

"Besides, this isn't the only room. Sure your parents' house is the best place for her? This place is hers now, and most everything else Mr. Frye owned. Took a moment to read what I was signing before I signed it. Short-winded enough when the mood was on him. And clear enough."

"My sister's Frye's heir?"

"What I said, isn't it? I'll vouch for her safety. So will the lads, should worse come to worst, and I'll have Mr. MacDougal fetched soon's I can. Once he's here, I doubt there's any who'd dare try to harm her."

"Do what you think best," Tom sighed, glancing at his sister. "I'm beyond decisions at the moment. Totally confused, if you want to know. What was it just happened here?"

"A man died."

"But—"

"Best leave it at that. Probing too deep isn't wise sometimes. Y'want him to have a decent Christian burial, don't you, friend that he's been to you both?"

"There's that, I suppose. Trifle preoccupied, you understand."

"That I do. Take care of yourself, y'young fool. She has a need of you."

"I know."

Tom crossed to where Nan was kneeling beside—beside what? Frye didn't know quite how to characterize what remained on the divan. Certainly it wasn't himself. Never before had the old saying regarding the body being naught but a meaningless shell providing transportation for the essential self held greater meaning.

Lightning quick he attempted to reach out to her, take her pain into himself, failed.

It'll get better, little Nan, he whispered soundlessly. *Even the deepest wound heals in time.*

"Nan?"

She was gazing up at her brother now, eyes haunted.

"Nan, I've got to take care of some business. Then I'll be back. Springer and Mrs. Finch'll see to you until I return. You're to trust them as if they were myself, or—or Frye."

"I loved him, you know," she said as if it she were announcing the time of day.

"I know. He was quite something, wasn't he? A friend, and more."

"And much, much more."

"You'll not do anything foolish?" the boy asked hesitantly.

"No, I'll not do anything foolish."

She was rising, throwing her arms about Tom, giving him a fierce hug. Frye risked reaching out again, touching her cheek, all of his love in that simple, impossible gesture. A spangle of light lingered there for a moment like the memory of a dying star, and was gone.

"I love you, Nanette." Tom said the words for him, voice harsh with emotion.

And then he was turning, heading for the door.

Don't fear for him, my love, Frye whispered, not daring to look back, whatever constituted his heart aching unbearably. *I'll not fail you.*

The grooms fell in behind young Leighton at Springer's signal. The street door was opening. Frye caught a glimpse of Tom in the entry mirror. There was a golden glow on the boy's shoulder precisely where he clung. Was that what he was now? A mote of light so faint at first even he hadn't noticed it? He tried to inspect himself, but it was hopeless. Whatever his appearance, he hadn't the ability to see it directly. Was that how it had always been—seeing himself reflected in the eyes of others?

Phinny lingered to guard the entrance. Then Tom and Jem were on the pavement, Tom turning toward Green Park as Jem turned in the direction of the City.

Damn the young idiot to everlasting perdition, Frye fumed helplessly, squinting without eyes as glaring fingers of light painted the sky garish rose and gold.

Ann stood beside what was left of Frye as the bookroom door closed. Then, with a sigh, she went to Mrs. Finch and placed a comforting arm around the housekeeper's heaving shoulders.

"He wouldn't want you to cry like this," she said, voice low and gentle. "Excess was anathema to him."

"I knew you'd be the death of him," Mrs. Finch complained bitterly, shrugging the girl's arm off. "You were trouble from the moment you walked through the door. Said so then, and I say so again."

"Don't you think I realize that, and would gladly change the past day if I could?"

"Here now," Springer threw in, "twas young Mr. Leighton caused the problems, Mrs. Finch. You know that, too. And behind all those problems? His fine lordship, Ambrose DeVille. You want someone to blame, look to him and mayhap Lady Leighton. A fine pair, they are."

"They'd've been no problem without these two."

"Master smiled this last day as he'd never smiled before."

"There's that," Mrs. Finch admitted grudgingly. "Here now," she said, giving herself a shake and wiping her eyes on her apron, "look at me, upsetting you when I know you're as distressed as ever I am, Mr. Springer. Pure selfish of me."

"He was the best master I ever had, or any of the rest of us either, and he's seen to our futures as well," Springer insisted as Ann listened impatiently, desperate for them to be done so she could confer with the valet privately. "How many fine gentlemen d'you know who'd do that?"

"Nary a one but him, which is why—"

"A few extra pounds is generally all we see at the end

of a term of service, if that. He'd cautioned us he'd be on his travels again, soon or late. Happen it was sooner than any of us expected is all. Master wouldn't thank you for nattering on at Miss Leighton for what she couldn't help."

"I still say she was the death of him, and should be chased from the place!"

"He had a great fondness for her. This is hers now, and most of the rest."

The peppery housekeeper glanced from Ann to the divan, then back at Springer, her shoulders sagging.

"Call it by its rightful name. It was love, pure and simple. Besotted, he was. Men lose all sense when that happens," she grumbled, "for all it was natural as could be: Pretty, sweet thing like her and a fine, strong gentleman like him. Pity it ended this way. What ailed him do you think?"

"I've no notion," Springer said, not entirely truthfully. "Some condition he picked up in his travels, probably."

"What do we do now? Why, this room's a disgrace!"

As Ann watched with a sense of unreality, Mrs. Finch swiped at Frye's desk with the corner of her apron. Nodding to himself, Springer crossed to the windows, swept the heavy draperies aside. The sun was gilding the topmost branches of the trees in the little garden behind the house, the sky directly above a clear deepening blue, the faintest of gold-touched mists twining through the barren rose bushes. The scene seemed like a stage setting, all contrivances and artifice.

"The master won't be minding if we open these now," Springer said. "Going to be a fine winter's day, for a blessing." He went to the fireplace, glanced at the portrait, then took the chalice down from the mantel and strode to the divan. "If you'll both be absenting yourselves, I'll see to him."

"Whatever are you—"

"He had a special feeling for this cup, Mrs. Finch," Springer explained. "Call me fanciful, but I think he'd've considered it a proper resting place until we find something more usual. Made by a friend of his, he said once, and whatever it was caused the master's death, nothing but dust remains now. That quick Nature reclaimed her own, almost as if he was too good to tarry here in any form."

Ann sighed, her eyes in their turn seeking the portrait over the mantel. It was so lifelike she almost expected Frye's ancestor to leap onto the desk and sweep his plumed hat in a grandiloquent bow.

"I'm not leaving, Springer," she said in a small voice, "so you might as well permit me to assist you. And we need to discuss a minor matter. Papa may be excellent *ton*, but he's rather improvident, feeling providence beneath him." She turned, smiling sadly at Mrs. Finch. Strange, how one could be shriveled inside, without the slightest desire to think or move, and yet the most practical things intruded on sorrow. "I'm hoping you and Springer won't be seeking other positions just yet, if this house is truly mine. I suspect Mr. Frye would've wanted you to remain with me, at least for a bit."

"Here now, don't you go worrying yourself about a thing, miss," Mrs. Finch scolded. "Been a dreadful time for all of us, this last day has. Confusing. We'll sort things out for the best once the dust settles."

The housekeeper's gaze flew guiltily to the divan, and she shuddered.

"Well," she sighed, "those of us as are left behind must see to the usual things, such as feeding ourselves. Way it always is when a death happens, no matter whose: First we wail a bit, and then we blame a bit, and then must needs we start living again. You've told Phinny as how there's none to be admitted?"

Springer nodded. "Especially Lord Denbigh, though what business he'd have here I'm not certain. I doubt his lordship has any notion how deep the master was involved in his business or how close an eye he trained on him, but those were the master's orders and I'm keeping to 'em."

"Oh, Lord Denbigh knows," Ann said. "He knows far too much."

"That the way of it? You're still safe as houses here. We won't have it any other way, given that's what the master wanted." Mrs. Finch gave Ann a motherly smile far warmer than any she'd ever received from Carlotta Leighton, and bustled to the bookroom door, red-eyed and sniffling, but clearly determined life would get back to normal as rapidly as possible. "I'll be bringing you a pot of tea and some muffins," she said. "Something light to see you over the next hours, that's what's needed."

And then she was gone. Ann joined Frye's former valet by the divan.

"There's a problem," she said hesitantly. "My brother—"

"Instructed me you were to stay here," Springer said flatly, "and here you'll stay. How the master would've wanted it, as well."

"Tom's meeting Lord Denbigh in Green Park, and it's all my fault."

"Don't see how, unless you were prepared to be Denbigh's convenient," Springer countered bluntly as he began scooping the dust on the divan into the chalice. "Were you ready for that, and anything else his lordship cared to dish out?"

Ann shook her head, eyes once more swimming with tears. "But if I'd've accepted him as Mama wanted, none of this would've happened, and Mr. Frye would still be alive."

"He might, or he might not. The past day has a feeling of must-be, if you think on it. I've said before you can call me fanciful, but nothing's happened that was ordinary or as it should be, almost as if we capered to a tune we couldn't hear."

The last of what had once been a silver-haired gentleman with twinkling silvery eyes and sweeping dark brows now reposed in the chalice, so little had remained. Springer rose, went to the mantel and placed the chalice directly beneath the portrait.

"I suppose you're wanting to go to Green Park," he sighed.

"I can't bear to wait here. I've just lost one of the two people I care for most in the world, and may be about to lose the other. Not knowing is worse than anything, don't you see?"

"I see quite clearly. Your brother won't like this, you know. There'll be the devil to pay when he realizes I permitted you to come. *He* wouldn't like it a bit more." Springer's gesture encompassed the chalice, and the portrait above it.

"They'll both forgive me," Ann said with more assurance than she felt as she went determinedly to the bookroom door. "They'll forgive you, too. Shall we go?"

Frye sighed with relief.

The world was beginning to steady itself around him, perhaps because it had finally accepted that he refused to be expelled from it, or else it was he who was in some manner making the transition from the placeless "place" where he'd found himself for a few moments to these more accustomed environs. The dizziness that had accompanied the transitions had been annoying in the extreme, the inability to synchronize his actions with the world around him even more so.

He settled himself more securely on Tom's shoulder and glanced about as they entered Green Park. Tom was making for a secluded knoll far from the usual paths, cutting across sere lawns and leaf-strewn walks with the determination and terrible courage of youth. About them bare-branched trees soared in the growing light, and the sky was of a blue so clear and sharp it was almost painful. Tom's breath was clouding before him, painted by the rising sun, and the mists trapped in the hollows and among the trees were like the finest golden tissue. It was going to be what ordinary mortals called an exceptionally fine winter's day.

This place God had given man to live was indeed beautiful—a thing he'd rarely taken the time or trouble to notice before. Familiarity bred contempt, he supposed, and three hundred years and more had led to an excess of familiarity. Only when it had been taken from him had he realized its infinite value, its infinite dearness.

And Nan? "Dearness" didn't even approach that reality. To have come so close! And to have lost everything. All he could do for her now was ensure her fool of a brother survived the next hour. How he'd manage such a thing Frye had no notion. He only knew he must or the sorrows and joys of the last thirty-odd hours would turn to ashes as surely as the shell he'd carted around so long had faded to dust.

With an excess of determination, he essayed a minuscule solo voyage, releasing Tom's collar and snagging a passing twig, then quickly flying back to the security of the lad's shoulder. Not bad. He was apparently capable of independent movement. That could be handy. He tried a longer voyage, this time to a solitary leaf clinging on a branch above Tom's head, and forced himself to wait for a count of three before once more seeking security and safe transport.

So far, so good. Now, could he affect things as well as move between them?

Very carefully, he reached out and grasped a few fine golden hairs on the back of Tom's neck, then gave them a sharp tweak. Tom swore, swatting his neck as Frye went tumbling into a tangle of bushes.

Damn!

But he'd managed to grasp something somehow, though precisely how eluded him, and move it. He could affect the material world. It could also apparently affect him. That wasn't quite as pleasant, but it was a good thing to know. So, he wasn't precisely a spirit or a ghost, or whatever this decorporealized state should be called. As ever, he was "other"—a bitter irony, perhaps, but useful.

Frye dodged through the twigs and dry suckers and rejoined Tom, attempting to fly a parallel course just above his head rather than clinging to him like a limpet. That too worked, even if his progress was somewhat unsteady and a passing starling gave him a bad moment, apparently believing he constituted a delectable morsel. A quick blow to the starling's beak disabused it.

Satisfied, he returned to the boy's shoulder, riding along contentedly. Heaven alone knew how much strength he really had, and he didn't want to squander his resources before they were needed.

They entered a small spinney, the trees and underbrush clustering so thickly London's morning sounds faded to a dream-like murmur. Frye glanced behind them, and spotted two figures hurrying along in the golden dawn light. No need to fly back to determine who they were. He'd already sensed Nan's approach.

Blast and damn! She had no business here. Why couldn't Springer've tied her up, if he'd had to? But of course that would've made things too simple.

The distraction of the girl's presence was something he definitely didn't need given what he and Tom were facing. How the devil did one stop two men from killing each other when each had every intention of putting *finis* to the other's existence, and one was further hampered by the distracting presence of the female one adored, and still further hampered by a state whose limitations were unknown? If Frye failed, Tom, lacking seconds, would be left to rot where he fell, the purported victim of a bloodthirsty stews tough with more than purloining a purse on his mind, for no one would take a servant's word over that of a belted earl, and Nan would be accused of fabricating tales to rid herself of an unwanted suitor.

Tom was entering a clearing through a break in the trees, staring about him. Across the way two gentlemen garbed in black waited: DeVille and Scanlon, the latter cradling a long mahogany case. Just beyond them, back turned, was another figure, a small bag at his feet—doubtless a surgeon. So DeVille was taking precautions, was he? Not quite as cocky as customary? That boded well for Tom, for all Frye didn't like the implications of the horsewhip DeVille was snapping against his boot.

Behind them, Nan and Springer were creeping through the thick undergrowth. Frye shuddered. Tom shook with an answering shudder, then strode manfully across the clearing.

"Morning, my lord," he was saying, voice ringing with youthful bravado. "Glad t'see you didn't fail me."

DeVille looked him up and down, fair hair stirring in the slight breeze that had come up now the sun was risen, as Frye flew to a branch over the earl's head.

"Fail you?" DeVille sneered. "Hardly, whelp. You've a choice: Accept the whipping you deserve for involving yourself in the activities of your betters, and then apologize to me publicly at White's this evening with every welt showing. It's that, or you'll be measuring your length on this little sward within minutes, and you'll not rise from your grassy bed, that I promise you."

"Let's get this over with. A weapon, if you please," Tom said, turning to Scanlon. "I presume that's what you've got there?"

"Anxious to be transformed into a sieve, are you?" Scanlon jeered. "Far be it from me to delay your achieving your doubtless laudable goal. It's considered quite the thing to be perforated by Brosie, y'know. He does it so elegantly—a prick here, a deeper prick there. Leaking one's lifeblood at the dawn of a perfect day's a fine way to finish, I'm told. One sees incredible visions."

"Stubble it, Scanny," DeVille snapped. "I want my breakfast. Let's get this over with, since the boy insists on playing the fool. Then," the earl grinned, "I believe we'll pay a call on his sister. Might even let you have a turn at her."

Tom had found wisdom and dignity somewhere, for he ignored the taunting words as he selected his weapon. It was a beautiful thing: an antique rapier of finest Toledo steel, the grip exquisitely chased, the blade plated with silver—one of Reginald's famous dueling pair, and well-accustomed to drinking blood. So they were still in use, Frye noted with bemusement.

"Aren't you going to remove your coat and boots?" DeVille gibed as he divested himself of his own, handing them to Scanlon. "See these don't get soiled," he cautioned. "I don't want to waste time changing before we breakfast. Always famished after one of these affairs."

Tom, after a narrowed glance at his opponent, was removing his hat, coat, and boots. He set them neatly on a stump, then turned, rapier in hand.

"En garde," DeVille ordered, taking his stance. "I don't want to waste any more time than I must on you, puppy. Give us the signal, Scanny."

And so it began, the two men circling in the pearly dawn light. At first they seemed surprisingly well matched, but Scanlon's chuckles told Frye the earl was merely toying with his prey. Slowly he maneuvered the boy until the sun was in his eyes. Frye saw it coming, that lightning-quick thrust about to end Tom's life. He was on the blade on the instant, merely a glint of the sun, deflecting the tip, the silver gilt turning to gleaming ebony at his touch, traveling the blade's length to the grip.

"What the devil?" DeVille grunted, twisting his weapon the better to examine its strange alteration, for once stunned out of his supercilious hauteur.

In that instant Tom lunged clumsily, and the world seemed to hesitate in its course. Slowly, so slowly, Tom's blade was sinking into DeVille's chest as the earl stared down at the silvery blade in bewilderment, then at his own blackened weapon. Weakened from his first effort, Frye watched helplessly, hanging in the air above the combatants.

"Not wise," DeVille murmured. "Oh, most highly unwise, my young friend. Your mother'll have your liver and lights for this, to say nothing of our revered monarch's customary penalty."

And then he was sinking to his knees, the rapier slipping from his slack hand, his complexion graying.

Frye wasn't conscious of thought, of decision, of action. He only knew if DeVille expired on that honorless field of honor—as he surely would from such a perfectly aimed thrust, however fortuitous the perfection—Tom would either spend the rest of his life on the run or swing at the crossroads. Either way his Nan would be protectorless, bereft, forever mourning the brother she loved almost more than life itself.

With a cry of desperation that was no louder than the whisper of a feather falling to the ground, not caring what price he might be forced to pay to save Nan from such doubled misery, Frye flew along the blackening blade, merely a golden spangle in the misty morning air, following the rapier's gleaming length into a place that was hot and dark as the weapon's tip slipped from the wound. He could sense the neat hole where no hole should be, hear the rushing river of blood as it coursed through the earl's veins, slowing now, and a strange clacking that was becoming ever more hesitant and irregular.

Then came a silent shriek of fury, and a presence he'd sensed trying to expel him was gone. Was that what death was for a common mortal? He didn't have time to consider. The golden shimmer that was Frye twisted and turned, trapped within the stilled heart, grasping, tugging, sealing, not certain what he was doing or how, only knowing he had to do it, bathed in the lifeblood of his many times removed half-nephew.

And then came a furious wrenching, painful beyond the most excruciating torture. He seemed to be everywhere in

DeVille's body at once, the blood absorbing him into itself so that he was torn first this way and that: squeezed through the most minute spaces only to explode into great caverns, scattering bits of himself as he was rushed on. Whimpering at the agony of it, feeling as if he were being burned by all the fires in the universe, he fled the incredible booming that filled every space, no matter how small.

The sudden silence, the accompanying absence of darkness were a greater shock than all the rest of it. He seemed to be lying on ground that was cold and hard, shoving sharp needles through his fine lawn shirt.

Fine lawn shirt? A golden spangle couldn't wear a shirt. It couldn't feel ground, soft and warm or hard and cold. A golden spangle couldn't—

There was light pressing against closed lids, red from the sun, and a finger twisted awkwardly against the ground. It pained him.

Very carefully, not daring to believe, he moved the finger. It wasn't an hallucination. There was one there. Dirt was becoming imbedded beneath its nail—the neatly trimmed and polished nail of an index finger. How the devil could he know that?

He tried a breath. It came, smelling of dried grass leavened by a touch of sandalwood and a whiff of the usual London miasma compounded of horse droppings, bad drains, coal smoke, and the effluvia of the Thames.

He'd never worn scent in his life, dammit, no matter what fashion dictated. Slowly, in total disbelief, he opened the eyes. Above him soared the sky's clear blue hemisphere, decorated at the periphery by the tangled black lace of winter branches. He lay there a moment, glorying in the acute discomfort, the light that didn't pain him, the sounds that were coming to him now: Nanette, pleading with Tom; Springer, arguing with Scanlon and the physician. Dear God, but they were joyous sounds, though what it meant he had no idea.

He sat with immense effort, as if he were clumsily manipulating limbs unfamiliar to him, lifted the hand before the eyes. He recognized the signet ring instantly. His father had worn it centuries ago on a hand equally long-fingered and slender and powerful. As the arguments continued just beyond him, he forced himself to the knees, then to the feet, took first one tentative step, then another, wincing as he stubbed a toe against a small rock.

"Here now, Springer, I'd be grateful for my coat and boots, if you don't mind," he managed, forcing the words out in a voice that was deeper-toned than usual.

A triumphant carillon echoed in his ears, as if all the bells in London had decided to ring at the same moment, all of creation joining in as the earth paused in its course that mountains and seas and deserts, too, might sing, the tune of such incredible sweetness it brought tears to his eyes.

"I say, d'you hear that?" he exclaimed. "I don't remember a church with bells like those near here, nor a ringer so adept."

"Bells? What bells?" Scanlon snapped, whirling to face him, color draining from his features. "What're you doing, standing there? Thought you were dead, Brosie."

"I despise that diminutive, always have," Frye growled as the bells' last peal echoed and faded. "You'll cease to employ it, d'you hear, unless you want a taste of cold steel. Now, get yourself gone, Scanlon. I've no more need of you, as it happens."

"But what about our breakfast? You said as soon as you'd dispatched the lad we'd—"

"Growing deaf, Scanlon? I said make yourself scarce!" Frye barked. "On the instant, if you don't mind. You as well, Mr.—Ah—I don't recall your name, for which I apologize, but as you can tell, your services won't be needed."

"Watrous—Charles Watrous. B-but I examined you not a moment ago," the surgeon stuttered. "That lad pinked you straight through the heart. You were deader than Caesar's ghost when they were done with him."

"Merely a scratch, Mr. Watrous."

Frye smiled as he pulled up the shirt. Just as he claimed, only the slightest of nicks marked the well-muscled chest, a single drop of blood dewing its lower edge. "Hardly a fatal wound, that," he chuckled. "Now, if you don't mind, I'd rather you departed, and took that milk-sop with you. You came in your own carriage, I presume?"

"You know I did," Watrous said with narrowed eyes. "You're talking in a mightily odd fashion. Certain you're not suffering from a brain fever or an excitation of the spleen? Glad to bleed you."

"God, no!" Frye spluttered, repulsed. "No bleeding, not now, not ever. I've seen enough of that pernicious practice to last me several lifetimes."

"See here, Brosie," Scanlon blustered, "I'll not lower myself by riding in a carriage with a menial! Why surgeons're no better'n tradesmen, working with their hands as they do."

"Oh, really?" Frye retrieved Tom's blackened rapier. "Are you certain of that? Because I can think of several methods of encouraging you on your way while teaching you to no longer employ that abominable diminutive."

"Don't sound like yourself, nor yet are you acting like yourself, Brosie. What's come over you?"

"Perhaps I'm not myself, then," Frye grinned. "Interesting possibility, that."

"He's seen God, that's what it is, or thinks he has," Scanlon muttered viciously to the others. "Thought he was a goner, and got religion. Disgusting! Next thing you know, he'll be endowing churches and rescuing sluts from magdalens."

"Think what you wish, Scanlon, so long as you make yourself scarce. Ah, thank you, Springer." Frye extended arms that were obeying him with ever greater precision, his heart singing with the unalloyed joy of it all. "Are those buttons silver? They are? Here—let me."

He stared down at the front of DeVille's coat for what

seemed an eternity. Then, jaws clenched, eyes shut, he grasped the first one gingerly by its edge and attempted to slip it through its matching hole. He fumbled, lost it, sighed. Then, with all the courage and determination at his command, he opened his eyes.

The button was untarnished—a pure, gleaming miniature mirror, reflecting the blue of the sky and the deep gray of the trees. He touched it again. Now it was reflecting the pale flesh of the finger. Nothing more. No black. No tarnish. The sigh that escaped him was like a prayer, so deep it was.

"Thank You," he murmured, then shook himself and turned back to Springer.

"And I'll need help with those boots. Ground's devilish cold. I don't," he chuckled, voice hollow, casting his eyes briefly to the sky, "want to catch my death at this point. Sure to infuriate Someone. That took a deal of effort, I imagine. Besides, there're too many places I want to go on this fine, beautiful morning.

"Ah—they're making their departure. Good," he said, sitting on a small boulder and extending a foot to be shod as he glanced at Tom and Nan, "for there're matters we must discuss, and I'd rather we discussed 'em with only Springer to overhear. He already has a fair notion of what I'll be saying, I believe."

"Could be, sir," Springer said, carefully keeping his eyes on his business. "Then again, mayhap I don't."

"Never one to commit yourself before you're certain which way the wind blows, eh, Springer? Can't say I blame you. Odd situation—distinctly odd. Well, come on over here. I don't want to shout, Tom. And get your coat and boots on. I've no desire to have Nan nursing you through consumption or worse."

"I've nothing to discuss with you, my lord," Tom bristled, "nor has Ann, either. Now, if you don't mind, we'll be making our departures as well."

"To go where?"

"I doubt that's any of your business, my lord."

"Because if you're going to, ah, Mr. Frye's place, I'm coming with you. If you're not, that's still where I'm going. No place else I can go at the moment. Not enough information at my disposal. Being someone else isn't easy." Properly garbed, Frye rose to his feet. "Retrieve the rapiers, will you, Springer? As I'm sure you observed from the bushes, they belong in that mahogany case Scanlon left behind. What a nonentity! Wonder what DeVille saw in him."

"A kindred spirit, possibly. Or a sycophantic one."

"You've that right. What the devil d'you think you were about, permitting Miss Leighton to come here? I told you to keep her at the house."

"She was that determined, sir. Not much I could do," Springer said with a wry smile. "I'm sure you understand how it was."

"No, I suppose there wasn't."

Frye turned, gazing first at Nan, drinking in the sight of her. Then he glanced at her brother. Both were pale beyond the ordinary.

"Confused?" he said with a gentle smile. "So am I, though I thank every power in the universe for what's happened."

Still smiling, gaze as intent as it was both tender and anxious, he strode over to where they stood and knelt before Nan, taking her trembling hands in his own.

"There's no need for you to shrink from me," he said at her involuntary cringing. "I'd never willingly cause you an instant's distress, my dear. Springer'll vouch for that, I believe. Been in my employ for some time, and can attest to my sterling character."

"See here, you rotter, you leave my sister alone!" Tom growled, trying to force himself between them. "Haven't you done enough harm?"

Silently, Frye kissed first the fingers of her right hand, then those of the left, gripping them tightly. "Nanette, my dearest little Nan," he said, voice shaking, "will you grant this poor enfeebled mortal the great honor, the ineffable joy of becoming his wife after all? He loves you above life itself, and has since he first laid eyes on your lovely face. That's a pretty good recommendation, for all it's been barely above a day."

She was gazing into his eyes, the puzzlement in her own clear.

"It's all right, Nanette," Frye said, standing and placing his hands on her shoulders. "It's I, not him. He's gone for good."

"Your eyes are warm gray," she said in wonder. "I'd always thought them the coldest blue in the universe."

"Perhaps I've suffered a sea change."

"And your hands—they're no longer damp."

"Here now, enough of that!" Tom snapped. "I'm taking my sister home, and I'll thank you to stay away from her from now on, DeVille."

"That'll be rather difficult," Frye smiled "as I believe we're to be wed, which will please your mother no end— at least at first. Later I doubt she'll be so pleased."

"Where were you last night?" Nan asked, eyes glued to his.

"Lady Trimble's, just as you were."

"No, the night before."

"The stews, again just as you were. Seven Dials, to be precise."

"Of course he was," Tom roared, dancing about them on his toes, driven beyond endurance. "Frye told us that, Nan. You remember he did!"

"In an ancient stables with a small door hidden within a larger door, Nanette," Frye continued, ignoring Tom, whom Springer was now desperately attempting to restrain. "I slid open a peephole, and you tried to peer through it over my shoulder, and complained because you could see nothing."

"I'm not to ask questions, am I," she said, reaching up

to touch his cheek with a trembling hand. "I'm to accept it, just like that."

"No, I've promised you an explanation, and an explanation you shall have in so far as I can give you one. There's much I don't understand myself, but I do know I've been granted the greatest gift any man has ever received—one most take for granted, not comprehending what the lack means."

"I can't believe this!" Tom spluttered in disgust. "Here I go risking my life so you won't have to marry him, and then I think I've killed him and that I've got to take to my heels and live any way I can, and now you're going to marry the rotter after all since I *didn't* manage to kill him?"

"Yes, Tom," Ann Leighton said, turning to her brother with a blinding smile as she clung to Frye's hands, "I'm going to marry the rotter as soon as ever I can."

In the event, "as soon as ever she could" was a matter of a week as Carlotta Leighton insisted Ann would march to the altar on her father's arm in the most beautiful gown seen in London in that or any year, rather than that very day as both Ann and Frye would've preferred. The gown wasn't the major problem. Any modiste worth her hire was able, given sufficient financial inducement, to produce an exquisite gown in three days' time. Rather Swinard Leighton had to be found and convinced his youngest daughter's nuptials were of sufficient importance to drag him from the arms of his latest *chère amie*.

By the time the festivities took place, Carlotta Leighton had forgotten her interest in Ambrose DeVille, being far more intrigued by the bequests she and Swinard had received from such an unlikely quarter as a bachelor who spent most of his time abroad and rarely went about in society. Ann's sudden accession to immense wealth infuriated her—such charity on Frye's part being, she fumed, inexplicable and even more unnecessary as DeVille was shod and hosed, and then some—but James MacDougal at last convinced her that should she try to appropriate some of that immense wealth to herself, the pittance she was to receive would be forfeit. Not being a total fool, Carlotta Leighton took what she could get immediately and planned to badger her daughter into eventual greater largesse.

Frye's explanation of what had happened? Those who knew him best—Ann, Tom, and Mrs. Finch—recognized him on the instant once the possibility was made clear. Beyond Springer no one else mattered, and Springer had always harbored his own suspicions regarding his master's nature, being rather more well read in esoterica that didn't customarily fall into the hands of valets than even Frye'd suspected. Indeed, it was Springer who opened the bookroom cabinets and retrieved the appropriate references when Tom protested impossibility one too many times.

The day following the ceremony the bride and groom departed on an extended wedding journey, ostensibly so Ambrose DeVille could inspect the far-flung properties bequeathed to Ann by the reclusive Frye. Their companions on that journey? The *beau monde* tittered at the unusual expedient of a newly-wed husband employing his bride's brother as courier, but Frye's breezy explanation that he was a firm believer in the Grand Tour silenced the more importunate. The presences of the earl's new valet (a fellow by the name of Springer), of a housekeeper named Finch to see sheets were aired and accommodations dustless, of Lady Denbigh's abigail, and of the Leightons' former butler, were perhaps more understandable.

Naturally that journey included a leisurely carriage ride along the moonlit Via Appia, just as Frye had described it to Ann on the first night of their acquaintance. She found it every bit as delightful as he'd prophesied.

And so, dead and yet not dead, bodiless and yet able to see and hear and sense, without hope, trapped between heaven and hell with no chance to acquire a soul, believing he had nothing to lose and nothing to gain, Henry Frye at last managed to perform a genuinely selfless act, and was rewarded with a human body possessing only the usual human needs, a soul, and a normal life span. True, his body also possessed an unsavory reputation, but that he eventually managed to live down. He was also at last the possessor of his father's lands, titles and fortune, and it was Frye and Ann's son, born some thirty-six months following their marriage, who would one day gain those honors, their children who would inherit not only from the DeVille line, but from the Frye.

Upon his marriage to Ann Leighton, Frye placed the dust he had been in a tiny golden coffer to one day be buried with him, and presented the emptied Cellini chalice to the church near his father's estates where he was christened nineteen years before his nature manifested itself. And, from memory he transcribed the carillon tune he heard on the morning of his second birth, giving it to the sacristan. It is said no other bells in all of England can play that exquisite carol, not even the great bells of Saint Paul's in London. The DeVille Carol has since then rung out to signal the great events in the lives of Henry and Ann Frye, known incorrectly as Ambrose and Ann DeVille.

Locals claim, should you happen on the village near by the DeVille estates when their carol is being played, you will hear the angels sing and glimpse the gates of heaven through the clouds. They also claim you'll forever long to hear the tune again, never quite able to recapture the elusive melody, its notes ringing forever in your heart, but unreproducible on any instrument.

Author's Note

Monique Ellis lives with her husband, popular watercolorist Jim Ellis, in Tempe, Arizona. She is the author of four Zebra Regency romances: *The Fortescue Diamond, Delacey's Angel, The Lady And The Spy,* and *The Marquess Lends A Hand.* Monique is currently working on her next Zebra Regency romance, *The Colonel's Courtship,* to be published in August 1997. She loves hearing from her readers; you may write her at PO Box 24398, Tempe AZ 85285-4398. Please include a stamped self-addressed envelope if you wish a response.

Dark Shadows

Sara Blayne

Chapter One

The arrival of Emma, Lady Blythe, countess of Wynford at Moorsgate at the edge of Kielder Forest on the Tyne was as unexpected as it was, to most of the inhabitants of the manor at least, unwelcome. Of the Family, only Lady Eleanor Headley, the mistress of the house, and Mrs. Mawbrey, the prodigal daughter's elderly Aunt Amelia, had demonstrated the least pleasure in seeing on their doorstep their long-absent kinswoman; and for Eleanor, it was a mixed blessing at best.

As fond as she was of her husband's cousin, Eleanor could not but think Emma's timing was rather less than fortuitous. Eleanor, after all, was engaged in entertaining an entire houseful of guests, none of whom could possibly be in ignorance of the reputation for daring that had earned her cousin the unhappy epithet of "scandalous."

Neither could Eleanor entertain the faintest hope that the latest tale of ignominy to accrue to that worthy would not have by this time become common knowledge among the families of note in the remote fastness of Northumberland. She, after all, had been made privy to it more than a se'ennight before by no less a personage than Lady Ulverston, who, prey to a chronic inflammation of the joints, was confined to her house!

It was bad enough that Emma's presence promised fair to put a pall on the festivities, reflected Eleanor, observing her husband's ominous change of color, but as mistress of the house, it had fallen to her to give the news to Wilfred, who, out on his morning ride upon the occasion of Emma's unheralded arrival, had been blissfully unaware of events going forth in his absence.

"So," pronounced Mr. Wilfred Headley grimly to his wife. "She has come home to Moorsgate."

Eleanor steeled herself for the storm that was sure to follow. It was not long in coming.

"After all these years. By God," thundered Headley, slamming his riding crop down on the giltwood console table in the Queen's Room with enough force to set the gimcracks rattling, "she is not lacking in nerve."

Eleanor winced at her husband's harshness. "But of course she has come to Moorsgate, Wilfred," she answered, clasping her hands before her. "Where should she go, but here? She lived all her life in this house until her ill-fated marriage. Her roots are here at Moorsgate."

Headley uttered a blistering oath at that gentle observation. "Her roots. Good God, woman. You need not remind me. I suppose she does not dare to show her face again in London. But here. Now? After the scandal with Kittering. She might at least have had the decency to take herself out of the country until the latest talk had the chance to die down. I daresay a decade or two would not have been too soon in light of her latest peccadillo."

"Wilfred, I beg you will not be too harsh in your judgment," interjected Eleanor, stung into a defence of her husband's kinswoman. "It is not as if she has not been more sinned against than sinning. I cannot but think it was wrong of your papa to force her into marriage with a man like Wynford, and her, only just turned eighteen. For a colder, more disagreeable man I should not hope to meet. Nor can you deny that, if not for Emma, we should not now be so comfortable as we are. Indeed, we should be living in quite different circumstances."

Headley, who little liked to be reminded of things that might cause the smallest prick to his normally insensible conscience, reacted to that unsubtle prod with a thunderous expression. "Poppycock," he declared unequivocally. "The days of forced marriages are long since past, Eleanor. Emma consented to marry Wynford, knowing full well what he was. And she has profited from it to the excess of seven thousand a year. Not a paltry income for a widow, you will admit."

"No, we may be grateful that Wynford was too proud to wish it ever to be said he did not provide his wife with a generous marriage settlement. I wonder, however, if Emma sees it as sufficient recompense for the two years she was made to live with him."

If her husband's face had been red before, Eleanor had the dubious satisfaction of seeing it go positively livid at such an absurd suggestion. "If she does not, then she is an ungrateful wretch, and I cannot bring myself to pity her. She did what she did for the good of the Family. That in itself should be recompense enough for a penniless orphan who, owing to my father's generosity, was taken in and provided a home."

It was an old theme, one that Wilfred was used to espousing whenever the disagreeable subject of his cousin was forced to his attention, an event which Eleanor made certain was not often. The very mention of Emma was enough to cause Wilfred to fly immediately into the boughs. In the circumstances, it would hardly have done to add fuel to the fire in a useless attempt to correct any fallacies in his logic, Eleanor wisely decided. She had, perforce, to bite her tongue to keep from pointing out that Moorsgate was Emma's home before ever it was Wilfred's or his father's.

"Yes, well," Eleanor said instead, "you will admit that Emma has never made the least mention of it in all these years. She has never asked anything of us until now. It is only for a week or two. Surely it can do no harm. Unless, of course, you are of the mind that our credit is not great enough to carry us through."

Wilfred, who never forgot that he was seventh in line to inherit the duke's title, a position which, though it made it unlikely that he would ever step into his uncle's shoes, was not so far removed from the realm of possibility as to utterly discourage him of all hope, bridled with indignation at the very suggestion that his standing in the county should be in the least affected by his cousin's ill-timed visit.

"I wish you will not be absurd, Eleanor," he retorted, mounting on his high horse. "We are Headleys. I should hope you are not suggesting that *our* name could be anything less than respected no matter how many black sheep might graze in our paddock. I suppose if Emma agrees to conduct herself with decorum, I can have no objection to allowing her to stay on for a brief visit. However, I shall depend on you to instruct her how to go on while she is at Moorsgate."

The first battle having been won for the moment, Eleanor gave vent to a beam of approval. "I knew that is what you would say," she exclaimed ingenuously. Leaning her palms against her husband's chest and, raising herself on tiptoe, she awarded him a fond buss on the cheek. "You are everything that is generous, Wilfred."

"Yes, and you, my dear, are a complete hand," pronounced that worthy, regarding his lady wife with a sapient eye. Eleanor might pride herself on her subtlety, but he was not such a slow top as not to realize when he had been masterfully outmaneuvered. Still, short of kicking up a dust, he really could not see what else he could have done. Little as he might like it, the Scandalous Lady Blythe was his kinswoman, and he, as head of the family, owed it to her to serve as an example of what it meant to be a Headley.

A pity his cousin had failed to provide Wynford with an heir, thought the proud father of five young hopefuls. Children had a way of proving a stabilizing influence. But then, what would you? No doubt Emma could not be blamed for the stillborn son that had forever dashed all such hopes. From all accounts she had been brought near to death's door herself.

It came to him then that there was little point in postponing the inevitable. "Where is my cousin?" he asked, putting on a hearty front. It was not that he disliked Emma, he told himself, recalling a time when he had been more than fond of a mischievous little sprite who had led him into deep waters with his father more than a few times. It was only that people changed, and he was a man now with a family of his own to consider. "No sense keeping Emma in suspense. Bring her in, Eleanor. I promise I shall give her a proper welcome."

If he had thought by that to elicit a gladsome response in his normally forthright wife, he was to be sadly disappointed.

"Yes, I was sure you would, Wilfred," replied Eleanor, moved, suddenly, to adjust the position of the Staffordshire lion on the mantlepiece, a seemingly innocent action, which served to inspire the beginnings of an ominous pressure in Wilfred's broad chest. "Unfortunately, she has taken it in her head to visit some of the places that she was used to haunt as a child. I'm sure you understand. It has been ten years since last she was at Moorsgate. I daresay you would have smiled to see how eager she was to renew old acquaintances."

Wilfred, however, was not smiling, Eleanor noted. He had, on the contrary, assumed a rigid expression. "She has gone to Dunnecombe, has she not. She has gone to see the cursed grave."

"I shouldn't call it a cursed grave," Eleanor answered, seeing little use in further evasive tactics, since they had proven wholly ineffectual. "Maggie Macpherson was only a poor, grief-stricken woman. The English murdered the man she loved, Wilfred."

"And Maggie Macpherson rode into battle and helped to slay any number of Englishmen before she was mercifully brought down," Headley did not hesitate to point out. "Do you think I don't know the legend? The point is, it happened two-hundred-fifty years ago. It is ancient history, long dead and forgotten by everyone, except Emma. I have never understood her fascination for the place."

"Neither have I, Wilfred, but it is harmless, surely?"

"Harmless? By God, it will have everyone talking again, as if there were not already talk enough. You know what they used to say about Emma. All that nonsense about being touched by the devil. And all because she was of an adventurous nature, slipping out in the middle of the night, the way she did. Making up stories about Maggie Macpherson's bloody grave. Everyone said it was a rare stroke of fortune that Wynford was brought up to scratch, and not a few blamed her for his untimely demise. And now she is at it again. Dash it all, Eleanor. Why in heaven's name did she have to come back again!"

The stone was just as Emma used to think of it, usually at night, when she lay awake with the memories crowding around her in the darkness. It was tall and craggy with lichen and stood alone at the center of the clearing, which, hugged by the encroaching wood, appeared to have grown smaller since last she came to Dunnecombe. The combe was a wonderfully wild and isolated place, and yet the stone seemed neither desolate nor brooding. On the contrary, it appeared strangely at peace in the sylvan glade, as if it had simply sprung up out of the earth itself, like the violets at its base and the tangled vines of ivy that clung to its weathered surface. Unlike Gloaminggate Castle, she thought, which brooded on its weathered hill in the distance, a somber reminder of the battle that had taken place long ago here in this very place.

Slipping from the saddle, Emma dropped the mare's reins and strode with a light step through tall grass rife with yellow celandine and pink and white daisies. Before the stone, she knelt and, parting the ivy, ran her fingertips over the crude lettering cut into the stone's face.

"Maggie Macpherson," she murmured. "I have come back, just as I promised I should. It took me longer than I expected, and a deal has happened since last I was here, but I've never forgotten Dunnecombe or you."

As it came to her that at the very least she would undoubtedly have been thought strange had anyone overheard her talking to a gravestone, a dimple peeped forth at the corner of her mouth, which demonstrated a habitual tendency to curve upwards in humorous appreciation of the world around her. Lady Blythe, as a matter of fact, had been accused more than a few times of displaying a lamentable tendency toward levity, a quality which, while it endeared her to her intimates, was held in the general opinion to be an unfortunate flaw in her character, one of many as it happened. But then, an impish grin would seem peculiarly well-suited to laughing eyes the green of highland moss, a short, dainty nose, slightly retrousse, and hair the color of polished copper.

In the norm, no one who knew her well would have been at all taken aback to see Lady Blythe garbed in a shockingly pink gown that should have been disharmonious, to say the least, with her coppery colored curls, but strangely was not. That on this occasion she wore a riding habit of subdued bottle green would have occasioned more than a few speculative glances from those very same intimates. Indeed, it would have stimulated not a little discussion as to what devilry the Scandalous Lady Blythe was up to this time. As it happened, however, it was not devilry that brought Emma to Dunnecombe, but a promise made long ago to a dead woman from the Scottish highlands.

Emma felt a kinship to Maggie Macpherson. In Emma, on the distaff side of the family, ran the blood of Scottish highlanders.

Her mama's Scottish roots had been greatly deplored by the members of the Family, who had never quite gotten over the border wars in which the Headleys had taken a long and active part, never mind that the lady had brought into the marriage a fortune derived from Scottish textiles, which had served to replenish largely depleted coffers. On the contrary, burdened with an unfortunate bloodline and tainted by trade, she had hardly been the sort of match a Headley would have looked for for a Headley heir.

Emma did not doubt that it was considered of little or no consequence that Albert Headley had been proud to show off his beautiful highlander wife or that, losing her to the fever when Emma was only ten had largely contributed to his own untimely demise little more than six months later. It had mattered to Emma. With the death of her mama and her papa, she had lost everything—even her beloved Moorsgate, which, entailed to the male line of descent, had gone to her uncle. As for her mama's fortune, that had gone long since into the many improvements her papa had put into the land to secure his family's future.

She supposed that, in spite of everything, Moorsgate would always seem like home to her, never mind that she had never been allowed to forget that she owed the roof over her head to her profligate uncle, who in eight years' time had brought them all once more to the brink of ruin. It was certain that rather than see everything her papa had worked to build come to naught, she had agreed to sell her body, if not her soul, to the devil.

All that, however, was water under the bridge, she reminded herself. If nothing else, Wynford had done her the favor of demonstrating how little the proprieties mattered. Life was to be lived to the fullest and the devil with the consequences.

DARK SHADOWS

A wry smile touched her lips at how little her Cousin Wilfred would have agreed with her. But then, Wilfred had had his own way of rebelling against the example set by his papa. Rather than emulate his sire's excesses, he had sunk his roots deep into the soil at Moorsgate, until he was grown to resemble a stout English oak. Indeed, a staider, more unimaginative creature, she could not think to meet. On the other hand, she could not have wished for a better caretaker for Moorsgate, especially as she herself had come to say her final good-byes.

"Farewell, Maggie Macpherson. You are my kin more than any Headley ever was, save for Papa. You must not think that because I shall not come back again that I have forgotten. It is only that my spirit beats at the bars of its cage for something it cannot name. England has grown too small for me. Still, you may be certain that, when I go, I shall leave a part of me here with you in Dunnecombe."

Hardly had the words left her mouth, than Emma felt an odd prickle of cold at the nape of her neck. Carefully, she rose to her feet and studied the woods around her. She saw nothing untoward. Only the breeze sweeping down from the Cheviots and Gloaminggate Castle disturbed the stillness, setting the tree branches into motion. Still, she had the strangest feeling she was not alone, that, indeed, there were eyes on her even then.

Well, if there was someone there, it would seem the mysterious watcher meant to do no more than watch, she decided, shaking off her unease with a wry laugh. Perhaps it was only the spirit of Maggie Macpherson roused from her eternal rest by the voice of a fellow Scot, she told herself. Nevertheless, Emma did not fail to note that the mare, which had been quietly grazing, had suddenly lifted its head to stand with ears pricked forward and nostrils flaring.

"Softly, Molly, my girl," Emma murmured, going quietly to the mare. She gathered up the reins and, running a soothing hand over the animal's neck, glanced over her shoulder in search of what had disturbed the normally placid beast.

Emma's breath caught at sight of the still shape in the half-light of forest and shade. It seemed an insubstantial thing, wrought solely of shadow—save for the eyes. They glowed, yellow-gold and feral, and yet seemingly keen with intelligence. A wolf, she thought, knowing how absurd was such a notion. Wolves no longer roamed the English countryside. No, a dog, then, one that had run from its master and turned to the wild. It was not all that uncommon an occurrence in the forests and moors of Northumberland.

Molly snorted and sidled, pulling at the bridle. Emma tore her eyes away from the watching figure and turned her attention to the mare.

"I see it, Molly," she crooned. "Softly, now. I believe it means us no harm." The mare trembled and grew quiet, the fright leaving its eyes; and, when Emma looked to the forest again, the figure had vanished.

"Well, now," she breathed, absurdly aware of the wild throb of her pulse. "Fanciful or not, it is probably the most stimulating adventure I shall have while I am at Moorsgate. I wonder what Cousin Wilfred would say to such a tale. Poor, dear Wilfred. I daresay he would find little in it to amuse and much to deplore."

Smiling to herself at the thought of her staid cousin's probable reaction to an account of her strange encounter, Emma mounted and turned the mare's head toward Moorsgate, forgetting in her preoccupation with her unlooked for adventure to bid Maggie Macpherson a last farewell.

Chapter Two

It was undoubtedly the desire to see the expression on Wilfred's face when he saw her descend into the ballroom that prompted Emma to don the French tunic gown of feather-light transparent tulle. Of a shade of pink known as "blushing rose," it was cut up the side to reveal Roman sandals with gold cords wound about her shapely ankles and calves. There was a gold ankle bracelet in the Egyptian style of an asp as well, which complemented the gold ring on her little toe. The gown, along with its accoutrements, was, according to *La Belle Assemblee*, of the first stare in French fashion.

It was made immediately clear to Emma, however, that, to the English gentry of Northumberland, her attire was merely shocking.

She was hardly surprised to be met in the wake of a startled high-pitched trill of laughter from a blushing miss just out of the schoolroom by a general, stunned silence. It was, after all, only the sort of thing that Emma had expected. Nor was she in the least amazed to find herself subsequently surrounded by a bevy of eager young bloods ready to prostrate themselves before her in the hopes of earning the boon of a smile or at the very least a glance from their newly enshrined goddess. She knew from experience that untried youths ambitious of establishing themselves as distinct from their forebears tended to be easily dazzled by any striking vision of originality. Their enthusiasm was more than counterbalanced by the disapproval of their elders, who would not have hesitated to give the Scandalous Lady Blythe the snub direct had she allowed them the opportunity. As it was, she sailed blithely past the assembled personages of obvious distinction as if they had been no more than various upthrust boulders strewn along the course she had set for herself.

Emma had, after all, long ceased to look for approval from those who were blinded by the view of their own pedigreed noses. Nor, ever scrupulously honest, would she have denied, had she been asked, that she enjoyed shocking those who preached the gospel of appearance for appearance's sake.

As a child in her uncle's house, she had learned that she was, for all practical purposes, invisible, save in the case of her childish infractions. These, more often than not, had earned her a scrutiny through the magnifying glass of her betters. Nor had her subsequent marriage proven in any way different, except that the Earl of Wynford, who had relished administering punishment, had been ceaseless in his search for wifely transgressions and, upon discovering them, had not hesitated to administer punitive lessons on the subject of disobedience, whether such disobedience was actual or not. That he had been regarded by his peers as a paragon of virtue, based upon such irrefutable evidence as the inestimable fit of his coat and waistcoat cut by Weston, the perfection of his neckcloth tied in the Osbaldeston, the faultlessness of his unmentionables, which hugged undeniably muscular thighs, and the inimitable gloss of his Hessians, achieved by a much sought-after secret formula known only to his valet, had served to convince Emma of what she had long suspected—that virtue, like clothing, was something worn in public and easily shed in private. She had little use for the former and employed the latter solely for her own entertainment.

That was not to say she was without the finer feelings or that she held in contempt those like her Cousin Wilfred who placed great store in the opinions of others. Acutely aware of the short-comings inherent in the human condition, she was not of the self-righteous sort to hold herself above the imperfections of others. Quite the contrary, it was her nature to view the world as a compilation of absurdities at which she would far rather laugh than weep. Tears, after all, would not only have been wasted, but had too much the savor of defeat, and defeat was the one thing to which she had never yet lent herself.

As for Wilfred, Emma had ever a fond place in her heart for her cousin, who, in her orphaned youth, had been the only Headley, other than her dearest Aunt Amelia, who had ever forgiven her her unfortunate Scottish heritage sufficiently to treat her with sympathy, if not always with kindness. Which was why she had made a special effort tonight to make a stunning impression on Wilfred.

Jarring him out of the complacency into which he had settled she viewed as an act of human kindness. She knew from experience that it was when one's settled existence was disturbed that one was made to view the world with new and different eyes, and only in such a way were one's horizons broadened beyond the narrow confines imposed by a life of unruffled contentment. It was then, in the midst of strife, that one came to truly appreciate what one had.

It was readily apparent from the purplish hue of her cousin's face that she could pride herself on *un fait accompli*, Emma noted with no little amusement as she stepped gaily out on to the dance floor in the company of a youthful escort. She was aware, too, of Lady Eleanor's Herculean efforts to calm her agitated spouse.

Poor Eleanor. No doubt she was as close as she had ever come to losing her temper with her troublesome cousin-in-law. Still, Eleanor, one of those rare beings with a truly discerning heart, was perhaps the only one of Emma's acquaintances who actually understood what motivated her to do the things she did. Eleanor would eventually be brought to forgive her this one final jest at Wilfred's expense, thought Emma, unconsciously dazzling her partner with a smile. Then determined to make the most of what was likely to be her one and only fling at Moorsgate, she forgot Eleanor and Wilfred.

As the evening progressed, it appeared the Scandalous Lady Blythe was enjoying herself immensely. It would hardly have occurred to anyone observing her lovely face alight with laughter or her glorious eyes sparkling with gaiety that the evening had begun to pall on Emma. Indeed, only the most insightful of observers or one particularly well acquainted with her proclivity for restlessness would have surmised that the novelty of the situation had long since worn off, leaving her slightly bored with both her youthful admirers and their disapproving elders.

Emma, herself, occupied with making sure none of the young gentlemen who hovered admiringly around her was made to feel one was favored above any of the others, still could not fail to note the late arrival of a newcomer to the ballroom. If anything, his entrance created at least as great a stir as her own had done, but for apparently different reasons.

In no little amusement Emma observed the sudden twitters of excitement from the matrons ensconced on the sidelines, the instantaneous preening of feathers among the single, unattached females who flocked together in groups like gaggles of agitated geese, and the puffing off of consequence among the gentlemen more or less in general. From the manner in which Cousin Wilfred appeared on the verge of bursting his stays, she could not doubt that this was a personage of no little distinction whose appearance at Moorsgate Wilfred counted as a coup of the first water.

His name, one of her young admirers was quick to inform her, was Leopold Smith, Earl of Revelstoke. A strange title, she thought, but hardly so strange as the man himself.

She could not but admit that she had never seen anyone quite like the Earl of Revelstoke, though she could not have explained even to herself what, exactly, it was that made him seem different from any other male of her acquaintance.

Tall and magnificently built, with broad shoulders accentuated by a long torso that tapered to a narrow waist, slim hips, and muscular thighs, he was undeniably striking in elegant, if subdued, black evening dress, but she had known men before who displayed to similar advantage, Wynford among them.

No, it was not his physique that distinguished him in her eyes, she decided, no matter how compelling he was to look upon. Nor was it his remarkably handsome countenance with its arrogant black eyebrows set in a high intelligent forehead, the long straight nose and high, aesthetically cast cheekbones, or the somewhat ruthless slash of the thin-lipped mouth underscored by a lean, masculine jaw. She had known strong, arrogant men before.

What commanded her attention was an aura about him, she realized, aware of a chill that carried with it the savor of excitement and the presentiment of danger.

It was an aura of darkness, a shadow that was not a shadow, not really, since he was just then bathed in the full light of the chandeliers, she reflected humorously. Indeed, their brilliance appeared to strike blue glints from his hair, which, the intriguing color of midnight, was worn unfashionably long and bound in a black riband at the nape of his neck. He was, at least in the matter of fashion, an Original, she thought, which could only make him more interesting in her eyes. As for the shadow that enshrouded him, she mused, her brow puckered in a frown, it came to her inexplicably that it was a darkness of concealment, a pall of secrets that, like knowledge of things beyond the understanding of lesser beings, separated and set him apart from those around him.

"Strange," she commented to Lord Stanworthy, who had proven the most persistent of her would-be suitors. "I do not recall an Earl of Revelstoke in these parts."

"Daresay you wouldn't, Lady Blythe," replied Stanworthy, bridling with pleasure at being thus singled out. "The family holdings are somewhere in the south of England, I hear. Revelstoke's reputed to be rich as Croesus, for all he stays mostly to himself. He only just purchased Gloaminggate Hall, which went under the gavel at old Mr. Derne's demise, though why he should want it, I couldn't say. A wilder, more wretched spot could scarcely be found. Calls the old pile Revelstoke's Gloaminggate."

Emma's glance went thoughtfully to the earl, who was in the act of bowing over Eleanor's hand. "It would seem," she said, gently waving her plumed fan before her face, "his lordship is possessed of a dark humor."

"I shouldn't argue with that, m'lady. As it happens, Revelstoke's a strange, fascinating sort of chap. A pity he isn't one to go out much. I expect he's the most sought after man in the county, for all the good it does anyone. You may be sure his presence here is a feather in Headley's cap."

"Indeed, I am certain of it," Emma agreed, smiling absently in response to Stanworthy's grudging championship of a man he obviously viewed in the light of a rival for whom he entertained a reluctant admiration.

Her smile froze ever so slightly as Revelstoke, straightening, glanced up and with seeming deliberation looked directly into Emma's eyes.

Emma felt, to her consternation, a flush suffuse the entire length of her body. Indeed, she had the most peculiar sensation of having been caught, like a child in the act of plotting to steal a freshly baked pie cooling on a windowsill, a feeling which was not in the least alleviated by observing the slow upward curve of the gentleman's lips. The devil, she thought, swept by a mixture of emotions, chief of which were resentment, confusion, a wholly unexpected quickening of any number of internal organs, and an almost overwhelming urge to laugh at her wholly absurd reaction to a simple meeting of glances.

Calling herself to hand, Emma regally inclined her head in acknowledgment of the earl before coolly returning her attention to her youthful admirers to whom she displayed every evidence of one wholly engrossed in the subject of how Revelstoke managed to achieve the perfection of his neckcloth which, tied in the Waterfall, was just then in discussion.

If she had been expecting the intriguing earl of Revelstoke to approach her and ask for the pleasure of a dance, she was to be sadly mistaken. But then, she noted with wry amusement, she was hardly alone in her disappointment. Revelstoke, far from making himself available to the female contingent, appeared satisfied to view the festivities from the sidelines.

Indeed, while his lordship demonstrated a willingness to exchange pleasantries with anyone who approached him for that purpose, he stood for the most part in compelling solitariness, presumably indifferent to the frequent assessing glances cast his way from beneath luxurious eyelashes or over the tops of provocatively fluttering fans.

Emma, entertained by the sensation the enigmatic nobleman was creating among the numerous guests, told herself she was perfectly content to remain a distant observer. Had she been honest with herself, however, she could not but have admitted that a deal more than her curiosity was piqued by his seeming aloofness.

She was vexed to discover that she could no more ignore Revelstoke's magnetic presence than she could cease to ponder his enormous effect on her consciousness, not to mention on her physical being. She was acutely aware that her pulse rate tended to be ridiculously rapid, that she was experiencing a peculiar queasy sensation in the pit of her stomach, and that she had developed an unaccustomed tendency to succumb to gay trills of laughter. She was, in fact, acutely aware that she was suffering all the symptoms that usually presaged one of her irresistible impulses, and these all too often had the lamentable result of landing her in a bumblebroth of her own making. Worse, however, was her growing certainty that the maddening Earl of Revelstoke was perfectly aware of his odious power to fascinate.

No doubt it was out of a sense of self-preservation that she had come at last, with the approach of midnight, to the decision that she had had enough amusement for one evening.

"You are very kind, *mon ami*," she said, smiling at young Stanworthy, who had eloquently protested that to rob the assembled company of her presence would be equivalent to banishing the stars and moon from the heavens. "However, I believe you will find that I have little influence over the heavenly bodies. You, on the other hand, have it in your power to brighten the evening of a certain young lady who is most certainly wishing me at Jericho just now. Miss Branscomb, I believe, is not so indifferent to you as she might wish you to think she is."

"I fear you are mistaken if you mean Miss Laura Branscomb," returned Stanworthy, casting a doubtful glance in the direction of a young beauty who was studiously ignoring the couple standing before the doors that opened on to the terrace. "Miss Branscomb has made it clear that she can never look upon me in any other light than that of a friend or a brother."

"I see. But then, that was *before* she saw you with me. I believe if you put your fate to the touch, you will discover that Miss Branscomb may have suffered a change of heart."

"But then no less have I, Lady Blythe," asserted the

youth, availing himself of Emma's hand. "Until I saw you, I did not know truly what beauty was. You eclipse every other female I shall ever hope to meet. Knowing that you are far above my touch, I shall teach myself to be content with worshiping you from afar as my ideal of womanly virtue if only you will grant me the favor of one last dance."

Emma, who had not the least desire to be worshiped as an ideal of anything, let alone one of womanly virtue, was forced to conceal a smile behind her fan. Faith, had she ever been so absurdly young? she wondered with a sudden pang that took her quite unexpectedly. Sternly quelling the ridiculous lump that had risen inexplicably to her throat, she drew breath to let her ardent swain down kindly.

She was interrupted by a tall shadow looming over her.

"Ah, Stanworthy," interjected a thrillingly soft masculine voice at Emma's shoulder. "I beg your pardon, but if I'm not mistaken, I believe this dance with the lady is mine."

"I beg your pardon," murmured Emma, glancing up, a pointed retort on her tongue to the effect that the gentleman had taken a great deal upon himself to assume any such thing.

The comment died unspoken the instant she looked into the Earl of Revelstoke's eyes. They were light and piercing and of a peculiar transparency of color, resembling amber or topaz or liquid fire. She stared, then blinked, startled, and looked again, this time into hooded eyes of a compelling, if wholly unexceptional, tawny gold.

Revelstoke arched a single, arrogant eyebrow. "My lady?" he drawled. Insufferably, he waited, a strong, shapely hand extended palm up.

The devil, she thought, shaken in spite of herself. For the briefest instant, she had had the most dreadful sensation of having been pierced through to the dark core of her secretmost self. But how absurd. No doubt her initial impression had been due to a trick of the candlelight, she told herself with a wry twist of the lips at what she conceived as a flight of fancy on her part.

"Damme, Revelstoke," objected Stanworthy in plaintive tones before Emma could voice an answer. "You know perfectly well it is no such thing. It's only a ruse to cut me out with the lady. Blamed if I'll let you get away with it."

"On the contrary, my lord," Emma smoothly interjected, "I did promise the gentleman this dance." She favored Stanworthy with a smile. "I find I am suddenly thirsty. Indeed, I should like nothing better than a glass of punch. If you would be so kind, Stanworthy."

Stanworthy flushed. "Well, naturally, my lady. If you wish it. You know I should gladly do anything you asked of me."

"Then I do ask it." Emma smiled gently. "Never fear, Stanworthy. I daresay I shall be perfectly safe in this gentleman's company until you return."

"Yes, well, I should not be too sure of it," asserted Stanworthy, favoring Revelstoke with a baleful look. "I shall be back directly," he added grudgingly and, bowing, left Emma alone with the earl.

Emma turned a coolly appraising glance on the nobleman. "I believe, sir, that we have not been properly introduced," she observed pointedly. "No doubt it will not surprise you, however, to learn that I already know your name. You are Revelstoke, of course."

A gleam of appreciation shone briefly in the remarkable orbs. "And you are the charming Lady Blythe," he responded, taking her proffered hand in his. "Do you really care to dance?"

"I am not the least in the mood for a country dance, and you, my lord, are too kind," Emma returned, laughing. She, to her confusion, was experiencing an unwitting thrill at the touch of his palm, which was both supple and strong and yet, strangely, soft as a woman's against hers. She had never felt anything quite like it before or like the prickly heat of excitement, for that matter, that was just then coursing along her veins. Hell and the devil confound it.

Revelstoke would seem to exude strength not to mention power of a sort that had a most damned unsettling effect on her, she thought as she added, "*Charming* is hardly the word most people would choose to describe me."

Revelstoke smiled. No, he thought, but then, most people were fools, who could not possibly know or understand who or what she was. "I daresay there are any number of other adjectives that could be ascribed to you," he answered, "none of which would do you justice. You are, if anything, an Original, Lady Wynford."

Emma gave the earl a searching look. "I have the feeling the same might be said of you, my lord. Certainly you are the most intriguing man here. I am afraid you have just caused me to sink most alarmingly in everyone's estimation by singling me out for your attention. You must know there is scarcely a single female here who would not give her quarterly allowance for so much as a word or a glance from the elusive Revelstoke."

The earl lowered his eyes to hide the leap of fire in their depths. There was only one woman here for him—the eternally beautiful Emma, who alone could have drawn him out of his solitude. By the devil, he burned to possess her. "But you are not one of them, I take it, Lady Wynford," he said, drawing her, unprotesting, out on to the terrace where he might have her to himself.

"I, my lord?" Relieved to be free of the lights of the ballroom and the stares of the onlookers, Emma leaned her hands against the terrace wall and inhaled the sweet scents of lilacs and dew-laden grass. Overhead, a full moon shone through a rift in a thickening ceiling of clouds, which promised rain before morning. "Someone told you who I am, my lord, which means you must know perfectly well that I am hardly 'one of them.'" Deliberately she leaned her back against one of the fluted columns and peered through the silvery half-light at Revelstoke. "I am not called the Scandalous Lady Blythe for nothing, my lord. I have been little more than a source of embarrassment to my family, which is no doubt my goal in life. I daresay you should consider what it might do to your reputation to be seen talking to me."

Revelstoke smiled, apparently unmoved at such an eventuality. "You know as well as I what a fruitless exercise that must be. You care as little for my reputation as I do," he observed baldly. "Or for your own, for that matter. If it were otherwise, you may be sure I should not be here with you now. A spotless reputation, after all, is only a page upon which nothing of note has been written. Dull reading, you would agree, and I, I confess, am easily bored."

Emma's eyes widened in astonished disbelief. Indeed, she hardly knew whether to laugh or deliver the earl a scathing rebuke. "I must assume that was meant to be flattering," she retorted, marveling at the effrontery of the man. "No doubt I am pleased that I, it would seem, am in no danger of incurring your ennui."

Had she thought by that to put him in his place, she was soon to learn she was far short of the mark.

"On the contrary," Revelstoke smoothly rejoined, "you are not in the least pleased. Nor do I deal in flattery. I was merely making an honest assessment of your character." His eyes lifted to impale her. "The truth is, Lady Blythe, the moment I saw you, I decided I must have you."

"Have me!" Emma blurted on a gasp of startled laughter. Good God, she thought, wondering if she were in the presence of a Bedlamite. The earl, however, gave every indication of being in perfect control of his faculties. If nothing else, his lordship would seem to have a unique approach with women, she decided, an observation which served perversely only to whet her curiosity. "You, sir, are not lacking in arrogance."

"No doubt," he agreed softly. "On the other hand, I have told you the simple truth. It is the one thing of which you may always be certain. I will never lie to you. Nor do I hesitate to warn you. You have no idea who or what I am. You should run from me, Lady Blythe, as fast and as far away as you can."

The look that accompanied that assertion left her little doubt that he meant what he said. His peculiar eyes gleamed in the moonlight, sinister, somehow, and deadly serious.

"Should I, my lord?" Emma felt a chill explore her back. "Unfortunately, I am not in the custom of running away. But then, I think you know that or you would not have bothered to warn me off. You did say, did you not, that you intended to have me. Tell me, am *I* to have no say in the matter?"

No "say" in the matter? By the devil, she held his life in her hands, if she only knew it, thought Revelstoke grimly, savoring the subtle scent of her, the pulsating warmth of her body, the purely feminine vitality that shone from her with such brilliance that he was amazed the others could not see it for themselves. But then, *they* were not possessed of his sight, he reminded himself cynically, nor were they driven by his singular need.

With an effort he quelled the dark leap of desire that explored his vitals with a cold, searing heat.

"On the contrary, the choice is yours," he said easily. "You may be certain I should never take a woman who did not give herself willingly. I am not in the custom of indulging in rape." He paused and looked at her, his eyes gleaming in the moonlight. "You will come to me. It is hardly in your nature to do otherwise."

Emma stared at Revelstoke in mute fascination. Damn his impudence! she fumed. How dared he presume to anticipate her probable reaction to his outrageous proposal. If only he were not so damnably intriguing, she reflected, she would not have deigned to grant him so much as the time of day. But then, she did not doubt that was the very thing upon which he was counting. The devil! She had never in her life refused a challenge.

"I'm afraid that you are doomed to be disappointed, my

lord," she said, however, when she had got her composure back. "My impulsive nature aside, I cannot think of a single reason why I should do any such thing."

It was, perhaps, the wrong thing to have said, she was to reflect later. Hardly were the words out of her mouth than Revelstoke loomed over her.

"No," he said, and she stood suddenly still, her heart pounding beneath her breast, as he lifted his hands to frame the sides of her face. She was acutely aware of his body, lean and powerful, against hers. And, good God, his eyes, she noted distractedly. They appeared to glow amber in the moonlight as if lit by an eerie fire of their own. "But you will, Lady Blythe," he whispered. Deliberately, he lowered his head to hers. "You will, I promise you."

The next moment his mouth closed over hers, and with a shuddering groan, Emma felt herself melting in his arms.

Chapter Three

Emma stared, unseeing, at the silent march of trees outside the coach window.

She was still more than a trifle shaken after her row with Wilfred. In truth, she had never meant for things to go quite so far, she realized with a hollow pang somewhere in the vicinity of her breastbone. Still, she *had* come home for the sole purpose of taking her final leave of Wilfred and Eleanor and, most particularly, of Moorsgate. They were the ties that bound her to the past, a past that held little in the way of fond memories and much from which she had determined once and for all to free herself.

Well, she had done that with a finality from which there would be no turning back again, she acknowledged with a wry twist of her lips. She was dashed if she would cry over spilt milk.

It was not that she regretted the irreparable parting of ways. She had not since the death of her father been made to feel like a Headley of Moorsgate, and it was a relief to know she need never again feel the least obligation to any of them. She regretted only the bitterness of words that could never be called back again.

Not that she could blame Wilfred for calling her a "doxy with a heart of jade," among other terms of a similar nature, she reflected wryly. She could not deny that she had invited just such an aspersion on her character when she chose to appear at his ball in the French tunic gown of transparent tulle. And *then* to have been discovered by Stanworthy in what could only be construed as compromising circumstances with Revelstoke! Really it was all simply too absurd. Still, she should, perhaps, have made an effort to treat the matter with the seriousness that Wilfred obviously felt it deserved. She had to admit that succumbing to the impulse to laugh in his face might very well have been the feather that tipped the scales against her.

That, however, was neither here nor there, she told herself, her eyes hardening to the color of jade. She could forgive Wilfred's display of temper and the less than flattering names he had called her. What she could neither excuse nor countenance, however, was that, in his heated avowal that no Headley would behave in so reprehensible a manner, he had, in the most unforgivable terms possible, ascribed her profligate nature to her Highlander mama!

It was inevitable, given such provocation, that Emma would strike back in the one way most calculated to add to her already tarnished reputation. She had not hesitated to announce on a gay trill of laughter that Wilfred was undoubtedly in the right of it as regarded both her parentage and her character. Certainly no Headley, other than her dear departed papa, had ever been tempted to go beyond what it meant to be a Headley. Clearly all the evidence pointed to the fact that she was not a Headley at all in any sense of the word, in which case Wilfred need no longer feel the slightest responsibility toward her. Nor need he feel in the least put out that she had decided to forego his hospitality in favor of an invitation to remove herself at once to Revelstoke, she had added lightly before breezing out of the breakfast room to the accompaniment of a stunned silence.

Her exit from Moorsgate had been executed with the pointed absence of her abigail, who, frightened by the tales she had heard about Gloaminggate Castle, had elected to remain behind, or by any guest or member of the family to wish Emma godspeed, save for her Aunt Amelia, who, gesturing to Emma from behind the cover of an hibiscus shrub, had breathlessly assured her that had she been thirty years younger, no doubt she would have been tempted to fling all away for a kiss from one as compellingly handsome as the Earl of Revelstoke.

Emma flushed from the tips of her toes to the top of her head at the memory of that stolen embrace from Revelstoke.

As a widow, she was hardly inexperienced in the physical aspects of love-making, if one could use such a term to describe the nuptial activities in which she had engaged with her late husband. Nor had she forbidden herself an occasional dalliance since fate had intervened to set her free of her wedded state. Though she had yet to take a man to her bed since entering widowhood, she knew what it was to be kissed by one who was not her husband.

Nevertheless, nothing had prepared her for what she had been made to feel in Revelstoke's embrace.

She recalled with a sense of unreality feeling caught in a dream in which, though she was acutely aware of the music from the ballroom, the drift of cloud shadows across the moon, and Revelstoke, her will was peculiarly suspended. It was perfectly absurd, she told herself, but even now, in the cooling light of day, she could not dispel the wholly bizarre notion that had come to her as she lifted her face to his.

She had been waiting an eternity for that moment— waiting for that kiss from Leopold Smith, Earl of Revelstoke. She had realized it at once, somewhere deep in the darkest corner of her being. She simply did not know why or what it had all meant. What she did know was that Revelstoke's kiss had seared her soul with a hunger so intense that even now her blood burned with the memory.

He had been right of course, the devil take him. She could no more stay away from Revelstoke now than she could make things right again with Eleanor and Wilfred.

Poor, dear Eleanor. Emma would have spared her that final dissolution of faith had it been in the least possible.

It had not been an act of defiance, she realized, but one of affirmation, that prompted her to declare to Wilfred in front of his scandalized houseguests that she had accepted the invitation to join the earl at Revelstoke, never mind that she had been left little choice in the matter. She could not but think it was singularly unfortunate that Stanworthy had been so foolish as to precipitate the entire scene. A man with more Town Bronze would have known to quietly withdraw rather than make a cake of himself upon discovering a lady in the arms of a gentleman. Certainly only a callow youth or an idiot would choose to kick up a dust over something that was clearly none of his affair. But then, she supposed it really made little difference in the long run that the young fool had chosen to lay the whole before Wilfred the next day at breakfast. While the storm had raged outside her window in the night, she had lain awake until the wee hours before dawn. Her decision to accept the earl's invitation had already been made when she rose from her bed that morning.

The truth was inescapable. Revelstoke and the thing he had awakened inside her were an irresistible force that drew her irrevocably to Revelstoke's Gloaminggate.

Still, neither green nor a fool, she was perfectly aware that the mysterious earl was not only dangerous, but that he would seem to have an uncanny ability to know precisely how to persuade her to disregard her own better judgment.

Indeed, Emma had the oddest feeling that he was

beyond the touch of mere mortals. But then, when one thought about it, so was she, she reflected with sardonic amusement. She, after all, was the Scandalous Lady Blythe.

Revelstoke's Gloaminggate crouched on the craggy brow of a hill overlooking the North Tyne and bounded by forest. Obviously built during the Border Wars, it had once been heavily fortified to withstand the raids of Scottish chieftains. Now, the great stone fortress appeared besieged by the sheer weight of the centuries through which it had stood guard over the wooded gateway to the Cheviots and Scotland. The outer walls had long since fallen to disrepair, leaving crumbling gaps in their fastness through which the octagonal keep could be glimpsed, stark and brooding, like some grim and ancient warrior stubbornly refusing to concede that time had long since passed it by.

Still, there was a strange beauty about the decaying fortress and the wooded slopes sweeping down from it to the rushing waters of the Tyne, a wildness that appealed to something deep inside Emma—the spirit of adventure, perhaps, that not even Wynford or ten years in London society had been able to eradicate from her. Or something stronger, she thought, more elemental—a hunger or an emptiness, a dissatisfaction with her life that had been growing more noticeable of late.

The truth was that, while she thoroughly enjoyed playing the Scandalous Lady Blythe when it suited her, she had grown more than a little disenchanted with the farce as a whole. She could not help but think that there must be something more to life than the endless round of meaningless games she played to fill her hours.

Instantly she chided herself for such maudlin thoughts. Her life might not be precisely the one she had wanted and dreamed for herself, but it certainly had its bright side. She was, after all, one of those rarities—a woman, both free and financially independent, who need look to no one for guidance. What more could one possibly wish, save, perhaps, to have a wholly intriguing and deliciously sinister stranger crop up out of nowhere with the offer of an irresistible challenge? If nothing else, she told herself, as the coach swept through crumbling gates and came to a halt in the bailey, her stay at Revelstoke promised to be anything but boring.

In spite of the less than prepossessing appearance of the castle's exterior, Revelstoke's staff was more than up to snuff. Emma, helped from the coach by a footman smartly appareled in black livery, was conducted immediately inside. There she was greeted by one whose somber dress and appearance of having been freshly dipped in starch proclaimed him to be one of that most august breeds of superior servants, a butler trained in London. In ponderous tones he introduced himself as Clarence and informed her the earl was out at the moment. Having anticipated her arrival, however, Revelstoke had ordered everything made ready for her. It was his lordship's wish that Lady Wynford treat Revelstoke as her home.

The devil, she thought, torn between a shiver and a quickening of her blood. How dared Revelstoke be so certain of her!

Some fifteen minutes later, Emma found herself instated in rooms, which, if not precisely modern or convenient, were at least sumptuously furnished. No doubt it was some perversity in her character that caused her to find the atmosphere of elegance in the midst of decay strangely appealing, she reflected, ruefully surveying the windows and bed draped in heavy damask, which perfectly complemented the ornately carved wainscoting, woodwork, and fireplace, all of which were done in the grotesque style of gargoyls, lions' heads, shells, and swirled vines laden with fruit. At least it was wholly in keeping with what she had seen thus far of the rest of the castle.

Her initial impression had been one of high-vaulted ceilings painted in murals, legions of armored suits standing guard, chandeliers of brass, tapestry wall-hangings, and massive tables and chairs of a bygone era. It was true the chambers and hallways might have benefited from exposure to sunlight and fresh air if only to dispel the gloom and the musty scent of what must have been years of neglect. Still, she could not deny that she had felt the moment she stepped into the Great Hall an attraction to the castle that was as powerful as it was inexplicable. It was, after all, a cold, dank, dismal place when one went right to the heart of the matter. But then, she could hardly have asked for a more stimulating interlude before she bade farewell to England forever, she reminded herself, as she quickly changed her travel-stained carriage dress for a fresh morning gown of green jaconet. Then, snatching up a wrap against the chill damp that permeated the thick stone walls and a candelabra to light her way through the maze of corridors, she slipped out of her room to satisfy her curiosity about Gloaminggate.

It soon became apparent to Emma that the castle offered little in the way of comfort and a great deal in the way of curiosities. She had never been acquainted with its previous owner, Rupert Derne, a recluse who had had a reputation for eccentricity. By all accounts he had been obsessed with any number of macabre notions, chief of which was his belief that Gloaminggate was haunted by the spirit of an ancient lord of the keep, who, executed for the sin of witchcraft, had had his name struck from any living record.

It was not difficult to imagine why a man of Derne's questionable rationality might have been persuaded to believe the castle was haunted, Emma reflected, as she pulled her wrap close about her against the drafts that breathed through the corridor. With sardonic appreciation, she beheld a tapestry that recorded in vivid detail an account of a mounted knight in mortal combat with a dragon writhe on the wall as though possessed of a life of its own. In addition to the whispers and groans characteristic of large houses of great longevity, there was a distinct scuttering in the dark recesses beyond the candlelight. Rats or mice, speculated Emma with a grimace of distaste. But apart from those undeniably unsettling, if easily explained, disturbances, there was about the castle a sense of something beyond her merely physical apprehension—a sense of brooding, perhaps, or a feeling that the castle itself was aware of her.

As hard as she tried, Emma could not rid herself of the absurd notion that her wanderings were not entirely aimless. Indeed, she could not dispel the feeling that she had been drawn to the very spot on which she stood.

The tapestry rippled and moved to the invisible touch of the prowling drafts, and Emma hesitated, her attention caught by something briefly glimpsed in its writhing shadow. Surely she could not be mistaken, she thought, moved by curiosity to draw the tapestry aside.

The door concealed behind the wall-hanging looked as if it had been sealed for all eternity. What appeared to be the cobwebs of several generations of spiders clung to it, giving mute testimony to the fact that it had not been disturbed for a very long time, as did the carvings on the door panels, nearly obscure in accumulated dust and dirt.

It would seem that the housekeepers employed by Revelstoke, not to mention Derne and very possibly any number of owners of the keep preceding them, had been something less than assiduous in their duties, Emma reflected. Pulling the mass of cobwebs aside, she turned the doorhandle and shoved against the heavy oak barrier.

The door, much to Emma's surprise, opened, but with a protesting shriek of hinges that must surely have alerted Gloammingate's slumbering ghosts, not to mention the servants. Emma slipped hastily through the opening and, pulling the door to behind her, waited for the sound of hurrying footsteps along the corridor.

When several moments had passed without the arrival

of either waking spirits or outraged servants, she breathed a sigh of relief and turned to look around her.

She could not but be a trifle surprised to discover herself in what gave every evidence of being the family picture gallery. Indeed, she could not but think it more than a little odd. After all, most families, rather than hide them behind concealed doors, displayed the likenesses of their ancestors with at least the pretence of pride.

There would seem little to distinguish these from any number of other ancestral portraits she had seen, mused Emma, lifting the candelabra to examine the first in the procession of paintings—that of a female dressed in a red brocade gown over a velvet underskirt and farthingale, which placed their wearer firmly in the Elizabethan era. There were other, even older likenesses from a time preceding that of Good Queen Bess. Derne, it would seem, had been an ancient house. Strange that she had never heard of them, save for the rather undistinguished Rupert Derne, who had been the very last of his line.

She was to discover something even stranger, however, when she came at last to a likeness presumably of one of the lords of the castle. Costumed in a black velvet doublet and robe embroidered in gold in a style reminiscent of the early sixteenth century, a nobleman of singularly striking appearance drew a sharp gasp of surprise from her.

The chiseled countenance was framed in hair the black of ravens' wings, the lean jaw made to appear leaner still by a small pointed beard in the style of a Spanish prince. The eyes, light and piercing, shone with a peculiar amber intensity the likes of which she had seen only once before.

"Good God," she breathed. "Revelstoke!"

"Sir Leopold Smith, actually," corrected a dry masculine voice out of the gloom. "A soldier and an adventurer with a knack for making the most of his opportunities." Emma's breath caught as Revelstoke stepped out of the darkness into the light cast by the candelabra, his tall form seeming to materialize out of the shadows themselves. "The earldom came later—for a particular service to King Henry VIII."

"I see," said Emma, sardonically aware that her pulse rate was considerably elevated. "Is it your usual custom to appear before your guests out of thin air? You never came through that door. I should have heard you. And pray do not say you were waiting for me here, for I shan't believe you."

"No, why should you," Revelstoke answered smoothly. "I had just gone into my study when I heard the gallery door open. Naturally, I was curious. I entered at the other end and saw you, obviously absorbed in the painting of my ancestor. Forgive me if I startled you. That was not my intent."

"No, I did not suppose it was," breathed Emma, annoyed at herself for having let fancy run away with her. Really, the earl, not to mention his castle, would seem to have a most unsettling effect on her. Struck by the absurdity of her suspicions, she lifted rueful eyes to his. "Pray do forgive me. I am not usually such a peagoose. But you did take me by surprise. I fear I was lost in trying to puzzle out what Sir Leopold Smith should be doing hanging in Rupert Derne's picture gallery."

"Gathering dust, I should think," drawled Revelstoke, with what Emma supposed was meant to be a whimsical attempt at humor, but which somehow struck a hollow note. "Like all the others of the long line of Leopold Smiths."

"That much, at least, is obvious," Emma retorted dryly. "You know very well that was not what I wished to know. Why, my lord, are they here?"

Revelstoke smiled faintly to himself. She had arrived at the heart of the mystery, just as he had meant for her to do. The game had begun.

Revelstoke elevated a single arrogant eyebrow. "Where else should they be," he murmured, "but in the castle Sir

Leopold Smith caused to be raised by the command of his king nearly three centuries ago?"

Revelstoke's off-handed declaration seemed to reverberate in the stillness, arousing a multitude of unanswered questions.

"I don't understand." Emma stared at the nobleman's baffling countenance, trying to make sense of what she had just heard. "If this is your ancestral holding, I find it curious that Derne and numerous of his forbears have been in possession of it for as long as anyone can remember. I do not suppose you would care to explain that, would you, my lord?"

Revelstoke's broad shoulder lifted in a shrug. "Why not, Lady Wynford?" The disturbing eyes glinted in the candlelight, amused and yet maddeningly unfathomable. Emma, staring into them, had the curious sensation of being drawn into their depths. Indeed, she could feel her very breath suspended, not to mention her power of mobility. With a sense of dismay at her own lack of feminine discretion, she knew she was on the point of swaying into Revelstoke's arms. Worse, she could see that Revelstoke was perfectly aware of it.

To her surprise, Revelstoke himself broke the spell.

"It is a relatively simple matter, really," he answered, casually turning her away from Sir Leopold's portrait. He placed Emma's hand in the crook of his arm and began to stroll along the gallery. "From the beginning there has always been a Derne in the service of the Lords of Revelstoke. For reasons which shall soon be made clear to you, it became necessary for awhile that the servant appear to be the master. That time is past now. An Earl of Revelstoke is once more rightful lord of the castle."

Abruptly Emma halted, her gaze incredulous on Revelstoke. "Time, my lord?" she queried, wondering if she could possibly have heard him aright. "How much time? I daresay there has not been an Earl of Revelstoke in residence for the past hundred years or more."

"Longer. As a matter of fact, it was in the time of Henry VIII's wooing of a Scottish princess to wed his son Edward. He ordered the border raids that led to the Battle of Ancrum Moor and, finally, to the disastrous Tenth of September."

Emma drew sharply away. "Black Saturday," she said, remembering her history. "The Duke of Somerset, Protector of England, crossed into Lothian and did battle with the Scots in 1547." She turned and walked a pace and then came back again to face the earl. "Ten thousand Scots died that day."

Revelstoke smiled wryly at the accusation in her voice. Over two and a half centuries, he thought, and, still, the feelings were there. But then, he had hardly expected anything less. The blood of the Highlander clans flowed in her veins, and she had little reason to love her English blood-kin. How much less cause would she have to feel in the least generous toward Leopold Smith once she knew all the truth?

"They did so," he answered, shrugging off the somber thought, "without Revelstoke's participation. It was just as well. He was not the sort to tolerate stupidity in battle, and it was the height of folly for the Scots to initiate an attack across the river. With the River Eske before them as an impregnable defense, they might have stood and won the battle. As it was, they stood not a chance on the open plain against the English cavalry and artillery. Revelstoke was better off at home, fighting his own demons than slaughtering Scotsmen like cattle."

Emma lifted her head in surprise. "Are you saying he refused to take up arms against the Scots? An English earl? But why?"

Revelstoke's lips twisted in cynical amusement. "Not for love of the Scots, if that is what you are thinking. As a king's man, he had met them in battle, many times. One might say it was a difference of opinion concerning the king's policy. A soldier, if he is a man, does not butcher women and children. Not even for his king. Leopold Smith was an adventurer and a soldier of fortune, but even he had no stomach for razing whole villages. He could see, if Henry could not, what the king's 'rough wooing' would buy. Instead of a Scottish daughter-in-law, he earned the hatred of Scottish lords who had previously been friends to England. Henry's policy united Scotland against him."

"And what was Revelstoke's reward for his lone stand against King Henry?" Emma persisted, sensing that he was not telling her everything. A professional soldier, after all, did not readily commit an act of what must clearly amount to mutiny against his king. There had to be something more, something that had made the sacrifice of his name and honor worth losing everything. "One does not refuse to obey a king's commands with any hope of impunity."

A flicker of cynical amusement crossed Revelstoke's impassive features. "No, hardly that. On the other hand, it was not so simple a matter as one might have supposed. Revelstoke had made himself useful to Henry on any number of occasions. He was, in fact, in the position to prove something of an embarrassment to the Crown, even with Henry in his coffin. Leopold Smith was pronounced guilty, not of treason to the king, but of being a practitioner of the black arts. He was executed here, at Revelstoke, in 1548."

Revelstoke, watching her, saw the doubt in her eyes vying with the birth of a myriad questions. He wondered if Myrna Headley had glimpsed in the face of her newborn infant something of what lay in store for her daughter. She had named the child Emma Eilidh—the first, a royal name in England, out of a wish, no doubt, to honor her new, English family, and the second, out of a pride in her own Highlander roots. The "healer" and the "light"; together, they made a powerful combination against the dark lord of Revelstoke, but would it be enough?

In sudden impatience with the doubts that crowded him, he brushed such pointless musings aside. In time all would be made clear to her, and then would come the final judgment. In the meantime, he could only wait, as he had already waited, bound in darkness through the slow passage of the centuries, for the one to come who would feed the hunger in him or send him back into his cursed eternity of night.

Still, she was here now, her beauty as potent as wine, her woman's scent a powerful drug to his senses. She fed his desire, like a raging torment, within him. Hastily, he turned away to hide the betraying leap of fire in his eyes.

"You are cold," he said, sensing a shiver course through her slender frame. "I suggest we remove to more congenial surrounds. I have ordered tea laid in the Burgandy Room."

As he spoke, he pressed his palm against a panel in the wall. Emma gave a low gasp of surprise as a large section of paneling slid open giving admittance to the earl's private study.

"No doubt," he added, "you would not be averse to some refreshment after your journey."

Stepping aside, Revelstoke waited for her to go before him.

Chapter Four

Emma gazed wonderingly around her at what appeared to be a veritable treasure trove of old and exceedingly rare books, among other curiosities of antiquity, including maps, swords and various other weapons, an old sextant, a spy glass, and an intriguing host of additional oddities. With a low gasp of delight, she crossed to a small terrestrial globe mounted in an oak stand and ran her fingertips over the engraved copper surface.

"Oh, but this is exquisite," she exclaimed, her face alight with pleasure. "Are you a collector, my lord?" she queried. Then, before he could answer, she went peculiarly still, her eyes fixed in rapt fascination on a portrait that hung over the fireplace at Revelstoke's back.

The likeness of a young woman with flaming red hair stared back at her out of emerald eyes lit with what would seem a sparkling vitality. She was draped in the green and yellow Tartan of a clanswoman, and on her bright curls she wore a Glengarry cap with a short feather.

"I did not see her with the others in the gallery," Emma said softly after a moment. "She is really quite extraordinary." Turning her gaze on Revelstoke, she said simply, "Who is she?"

"A young woman of Badenoch who was promised to a man of Lothian—to join their two clans in prosperity." Revelstoke added cynically, "Their mistake was in failing to take into account the intervention of fate. A common error among mortals."

Emma frowned, puzzled at his seeming harshness. "Fate?" she prodded when it seemed he did not intend to elaborate.

A log fell with a hiss and crackle of sparks on to the hearth. In unwitting fascination, Emma watched as Revelstoke crossed to it and, kneeling, thrust it back on to the fire. Only then did he voice an answer. "Her parents had the misfortune to die," he said, still on one knee before the fireplace. Deliberately, he rose to his feet. "She was sent to England to live with her guardian. The portrait was commissioned shortly after her arrival in London."

"And what happened?" Emma asked, intrigued as much at Revelstoke's seeming reticence as by the story left as yet unfinished. "Did she never go back to Scotland or wed the clansman of Lothian?"

"She went back," Revelstoke said shortly. "But she never married. The young man of Lothian met an untimely demise—before the vows could be exchanged."

Emma stared at the nobleman in no little perplexity. "Oh, come now, Revelstoke," she said, laughing a little. "You cannot mean to leave me dangling. Pray tell me the rest of it."

His eyes lifted to hers, like arrows sent swift to the mark. Emma felt herself go very still. "What would you have me tell you, Lady Wynford? That she was a rare creature of beauty and a fiery passion that set men's souls afire with wanting her? It was rumored at the time that Henry himself had an eye for her—which was undoubtedly why her guardian saw fit at last to send her home to Badenoch. A pity he put it off until too late." Revelstoke tore his eyes from

Emma and, leaning an elbow along the top of the mantlepiece, stared into the fire. An oddly bitter smile played about the corners of his mouth. "He was one of those Scotsmen, who, like the Earl of Angus, entertained a liking for most things English. He fell at the Battle of Ancrum Moor, one of the few Scots to die in that greatest of Scottish victories over the English. Ironic, don't you think?"

Emma, struck by the chiseled hardness of his face, remained silent, hardly knowing what to say. If she did not know better she might have supposed he was recalling people he had actually known and for whom he had cared not a little. Indeed, she drew herself up short when it came to her that she was laboring under an unfamiliar desire to chase the bleakness from his eyes. It was a strange sensation, one that she little liked. "And the girl?" she said finally.

Revelstoke glanced up from the fire, his expression unreadable. "She was killed not far from here, leading a band of Scots on a raid into Northumberland. It is said she came to avenge the murder of her intended." He looked at Emma strangely. "I believe you are not unacquainted with the tale."

A shock went through Emma. She was not unacquainted with it, of course. How could she be? Everyone in the county knew that particular legend. "Maggie Macpherson," she said, her eyes going to those of the young woman in the portrait. Then, driven to it, "Why is her likeness here?"

Her tone was flat to hide the confusion of emotions that warred in her breast—disbelief among them, and a sudden quickening of her heartbeat with the first stirrings of an excitement she did not wholly comprehend. It was all too sudden—her little understood compulsion to return to Moorsgate, her need to visit the grave, Revelstoke's strange proposition, and now this. Faith, it was all too coincidental, or was it?

A myriad of questions clamored in her brain for expression, but Revelstoke had already straightened and pushed away from the fireplace.

"That, I'm afraid, I cannot tell you," he said, his face once more bafflingly impenetrable.

"Cannot, my lord?" Emma demanded, incredulously aware that, having presented her with the intriguing elements of a puzzle, he was now making it plain he had no intention of satisfying her curiosity.

"It occurs to me that your tea will be waiting," he answered instead, as if that ended the discussion.

The devil, to tease her! fumed Emma, a stinging retort on the tip of her tongue to the effect that, if he thought she intended to leave the subject there, he was sadly mistaken.

The utterance died unspoken at sight of the faint, mocking light in his eyes. To her dismay, she choked on an unwitting burble of laughter. The rogue! How dared he make her laugh when she was out of all patience with him. But then, it was hardly worth making a cake of herself to state what he obviously knew already. Unclenching her anger, she lifted cool green eyes to his.

"Quite so, my dear," Revelstoke murmured, insufferably sure of himself—and of her, it was readily apparent, the devil take him. Pointedly, he offered her his arm. "And, now, if you are ready? The others are undoubtedly anxious to meet you."

Startled, Emma drew back. "Others? I was not aware you had other houseguests."

"No, how could you," Revelstoke agreed, "when I myself had no expectation of it? As it happens, a Colonel Everston along with his wife and daughter and a—er—Mr. Pinkney, I believe, were on their way to Kielder last night. When the storm drove them off the main road to search for shelter, they had the added misfortune to break a wheel on their coach. It was purely by chance that they found their way to Revelstoke and prevailed upon my staff to grant them asylum from the weather."

"By chance, sir?" Emma queried lightly, amused at the

realization that he was less than pleased at having uninvited guests invade his privacy. "Why is it I find myself doubting that anything to do with you is ever entirely by chance?"

Revelstoke's hooded glance came to rest on Emma. "I'm sure I cannot say, ma'am," he answered with uplifted eyebrows. "I assure you I am powerless to affect the weather or the course, in general, of people's lives."

"Are you, indeed, my lord?" Emma flung dryly back at him. "You cannot know how relieved I am to hear it." Her own glance mocking, she laid her hand on his sleeve.

Col. Rolph Everston, formerly of the East India Company, was, it soon proved, on his way to Saughtree at the invitation of his cousin to indulge in an apparent passion for trout fishing. He was a bluff gentleman, tending to a portliness that somehow suited what seemed an expansive nature, as did his wife, a plump matron of middle years with weak blue eyes, distorted behind thick-lensed spectacles, and who wore a motherly aspect. She greeted Emma's entrance with what seemed a heart-felt relief to which Emma responded with a gay warmth in sharp contrast to Revelstoke's distant civility.

No doubt, Emma surmised, smiling faintly to herself, Revelstoke's daunting immanence in addition to the castle's less than cheerful surrounds had begun to weigh somewhat on the poor woman's spirits, and little wonder. Not even the generous fire crackling in the cavernous Gothic fireplace could dispel either the gloom cast by the heavily draped windows or the damp chill that permeated the room. Emma could not but note that Miss Clarissa Everston, a blond-haired, blue-eyed innocent who could not have been overly long out of the schoolroom, looked to be on the verge of succumbing to a fit of the high fidgets, and not even the reassuring presence of a very young and foppish Mr. Pinkney, her intended, was sufficient, it seemed, to allay her misapprehensions. In no little amusement, Emma suspected that, Revelstoke, far from being sympathetic to his guests' discomfort, was taking a perverse pleasure in it.

Indeed, she was made sure of it when, meeting his eyes across the room, she detected a sardonic gleam in their depths.

"Ah, Clarence," she said, carried on an irresistible impulse to address the butler who was just on the point of withdrawing after having delivered the earl a fresh decanter of brandy. "It seems a shame to waste the daylight, does it not? And the castle does command a magnificent view, after all. I wonder. Would it be too much to draw back the drapes before you go?"

If she had asked him to murder them all where they sat, Clarence could not have presented an aspect of greater or more profound alarm. His normally impassive features blanched to the color of ash, and his ponderous jowls demonstrated a sudden and distinct nervous tic.

"The drapes, m'lady?" He swallowed and appeared studiously to avoid glancing in his master's direction.

"Indeed, Clarence," Emma answered, "the drapes. Is there some reason why they cannot be opened?"

"In the East Indies, we always kept the shutters closed," Mrs. Everston interjected perhaps a trifle too hastily. Her glance slid from Emma's and sidled to her husband. "The sun was dreadfully hard on the furnishings, was it not, Colonel?"

Everston coughed to clear his throat. "Oh, aye. Dreadful. Faded everything. No need to put his lordship out. Perfectly comfortable with things the way they are."

With an effort, Emma stilled a swift stab of impatience at what seemed very like unctuousness on their part. Indeed, she began to wonder if Everston were a colonel at all. He would seem to be decidedly lacking in fortitude.

Fortunately for Clarence, who gave the impression of a fly caught fast in a spider's web, Revelstoke chose just then to intervene on his behalf. "But I am not in the least put out, Colonel," murmured the nobleman. "Indeed, I should be a poor host to object to anything that contributes to the comfort of guests in my house. I beg you will forgive my butler, Lady Blythe. He was merely obeying my orders. I suffer a condition that renders me particularly sensitive to sunlight. However, if you will indulge me." Extracting from a pocket a pair of eyeglasses, darkened to a nearly impenetrable hue, and sliding them on his face, he inclined his head ironically to Emma. "I shall manage to contrive. Pray, open the drapes, Clarence."

An expression of profound relief, mingled with a telltale hint of surprise, washed over the butler's normally austere features. "As you wish, m'lord," he intoned and proceeded with alacrity to do as his master ordered.

An earlier occupant, it would seem, had had an eye to making the ancient keep rather more habitable. An entire wing in the Elizabethan style had been added to the original structure with two great bay windows on either end and more windows spanning the entire front facing the west. Bathed even in the muted sunlight of an overcast day, the drawing room took on a whole new appearance, revealing a richness of color and an exquisiteness in taste that dispelled not only the gloom, but, in large measure, the almost preternatural chill about the place.

"There, you see?" said Emma, her glance embracing the Oriental carpets, caffoy-covered chairs and sofas, occasional tables of burnished rosewood and mahogany, not to mention the tastefully arranged objects d'art that frequented them. "It is every bit as delightful as I knew it must be. Indeed, all that is missing is roses to fill the vases. For shame, Revelstoke. A room like this deserves better than to be cast in the shadows."

"I bow to your judgment, ma'am," murmured Revelstoke, who remained, despite the pale flood of sunlight, obscured behind a compelling barrier of aloofness.

That afternoon, the rains came again, transforming the roads into a hasty-pudding, so that even if the new wheel from Kielder had arrived, it would have made little difference to Everston and his family. They had little choice but to remain Revelstoke's uninvited guests, whether he or they wished it or not. And it seemed patently clear to Emma that Revelstoke, in spite of his chilling courtesy, little relished their continued presence.

Emma herself was not displeased at the additional company. There was, after all, a certain safety in numbers, and she was not at all convinced she was ready yet to be utterly alone with her host—in spite of the fact that he was undeniably the most fascinating man she had ever encountered *and* the most compellingly attractive.

Indeed, she could not but admit that the merest touch of his hand was enough to arouse a bewildering array of sensations in her, not the least of which was the effect of having a galvanizing shock wave sent through the length of her or of experiencing what gave every evidence of the sudden onset of a slow-mounting fever. One look from those smoldering eyes, and her knees went suddenly weak beneath her and she felt herself flush all over like the veriest schoolgirl. Faith, a single kiss from the Earl of Revelstoke had been sufficient to persuade her to fling all caution to the wind and to place herself at the mercy of a man who was a complete and total stranger to her! Little wonder if she mistrusted her own ability to keep a level head when it came to being alone with Revelstoke.

It was not that she was afraid of him, she told herself firmly. She had never allowed herself to be afraid of anyone or anything in her life, and she was not about to start now.

And, indeed, it was not fear that he inspired in her, but something quite on a different order. For the first time in her life, she felt herself on the verge of something she had long since ceased to believe could ever happen to her.

She was not such a simpleton as to call it love. It was simply too absurd to suppose she could lose her heart to someone she had known less than twenty-four hours, one, moreover, whom she was not even sure she liked very well.

It had come to her, however, that she might easily lose *herself* to Revelstoke, and she was not at all certain that was something to be devoutly desired. After all, she had not survived with her spirit and soul intact the worst that Wynford could do to her only to gladly relinquish to another that which she had come to prize most in the world—her independence.

The truth was, however, that no matter how strongly her highly developed sense of self-preservation called out to her to flee Revelstoke, whatever it was that attracted her to him held a far greater sway over her. Indeed, she had the strangest feeling that events were already out of her hands.

No doubt it was due to some perversity in her character that Emma found that possibility rather more exhilarating than daunting. But then, she had ever been the sort to relish adventure, oftentimes to her subsequent downfall. Such had been the case with her most recent peccadillo with the Duke of Kittering, who, a member of the Carleton set, had sworn, as she laughingly informed the Everstons, he could pass her off to Prinnie himself as a young Hungarian nobleman and thus gain her admittance to a prize fight being staged on the outskirts of London. All had been going splendidly until Prince Esterhazy had insisted on exchanging pleasantries with one presumed to be a fellow countryman.

"Oh, I say," exclaimed Mr. Pinkney, who, in spite of the scandalous nature of the tale, had obviously fallen victim to its narrator's lively charm, "a bit of rotten luck, that."

"Yes, it was, wasn't it," Emma agreed, laughing. "Still, I could hardly hold it against the Hungarian Prince for exposing Count Zoltan as an imposter. The prince was far too engaging. Besides, he was not only greatly entertained to discover a woman had stormed the bastions of that staunchest of gentlemen's gaming events, but he was gracious enough to escort me himself from the premises."

"And His Grace, the Duke of Kittering?" asked Mrs.

Everston, glancing keenly over her needlepoint at Emma. "What had he to say for his part in this episode?"

"Why, nothing. I believe he had succumbed to an overindulgence of spirits by then and was in no case to say or do anything in my defence. Not that I *had* any defence." Emma, rising from the sofa, took a seat before the pianoforte and began to run her fingers absently over the keys. "I was clearly guilty of gross misconduct for a woman of gentle birth." On that note, Emma launched into a lively tune, which quite effectively forestalled any further comments on the infamous exploit that had ruined her.

Emma had not been ten years in London society without learning how to alleviate even the most awkward of social situations. Before the afternoon was greatly advanced, she had so far succeeded in easing the tension in the withdrawing room that Col. Everston was brought to relate a wide range of anecdotes concerning his lengthy sojourn in Madras. In this, he was amply abetted by Mrs. Everston, who inserted an editorial comment in all the appropriate places, and by Mr. Pinkney, who kept the well primed with any number of leading questions. Even Miss Everston so far forgot herself as to entertain the company with a song from India rendered in a sweet, if somewhat less than voluminous, soprano.

Revelstoke, obscured behind his impenetrable eyeglasses, surprised them all by displaying a subtlety of charm and wit that must have dispelled his guests' earlier misgivings. Indeed, had Emma been less well versed in the nuances of society manners, she might have been fooled into thinking Revelstoke did not view the Everstons as commonplace and therefore prone to contribute to his ever-threatening onset of boredom. Hardly of the sort to concern himself over the comfort of people in whom he had little or no interest, he was, she realized with a great deal of perplexity and not a little amusement, exerting himself to be agreeable for her sake.

What a strange man he was, to be sure, she reflected, not in the least taken in by his unhesitating suggestion that Miss Everston entertain them with a second rendition.

Emma, nevertheless, could only be relieved when Mrs. Everston gathered up her needlepoint and announced that she was feeling a little tired after the previous evening's harrowing adventures and thought she would retire for a nap before dinner. The colonel, taking his cue from her, recalled that he had some correspondence that needed his attention, upon which, Mr. Pinkney, pointing out that the rain had stopped, invited Miss Everston to go for a stroll about the grounds in order to view the sunset.

Emma, smilingly refusing Pinkney's polite suggestion that she join them, found herself alone with Revelstoke.

She was made immediately aware of the sudden pall of silence that settled over the withdrawing room and of Revelstoke, seated in the wingchair near the fireplace, one long leg stretched out before him as he appeared to contemplate the brandy in a glass held in one shapely hand before him. She played the pianoforte absently, her fingers picking out a meaningless medley of tunes, and all the while, even though she could not see past the cursed eyeglasses, she could feel Revelstoke's eyes on her.

Abruptly she let her hands go still.

"I find myself wondering, my lord," she announced, turning her head to look directly at him, "why you lured me here. Oh, I know." Giving an impatient gesture of the hand, she stood up. "You decided you must have me. Naturally, that must make everything perfectly clear, mustn't it. Why, for example, you have been humoring me these past two hours by playing the charming host to the colonel and the others, when you know perfectly well you have been wishing them all at Jericho."

"You seem surprised," observed his lordship. "Did you think I should not fulfill my obligations as a host?"

"I think, if not for my presence here, you would not hesitate to send the colonel and his party packing, my lord. If I am wrong, I shall naturally beg your pardon."

"As it happens, if you were not here, there would be no need to send them packing. Still, you are not wrong. I should gladly consign them all to the devil. And so, I do not hesitate to suggest, might you, Lady Blythe, if you are wise. You should know, better than most, how little to trust in appearances."

Emma stared at him. It was a warning, couched in riddles, like everything else about Revelstoke. And like everything she had thus far encountered, it made little sense. Turning her back on the nobleman, she looked out on a flower garden that, left untended, had been allowed to grow rife and wild. There could not possibly be anything in the innocuous Everstons of which to beware, she told herself wryly, save, perhaps, for the distinct possibility of coming down with an acute case of dyspepsia from excessive exposure to their overabundance of virtue. No doubt he meant only that she should be wishing the others gone that they, two, might be alone at last.

All of which brought her to the real question that had been nagging at her.

Abruptly, she came around to face Revelstoke. "Do you make it a practice at every ball you attend, my lord," she asked without preamble, "to single out an unattached female for your particular attention, or have I the honor of being the only one to whom you have made your outrageous proposal?"

The answer came chillingly direct. "You are the only one, never doubt it."

Emma was struck with the peculiar feeling that he had been waiting for her to ask that very thing.

Without warning, he set the glass aside and, unfolding his long length from the chair, crossed to her with a long, purposeful stride. Emma fought the impulse to back before him as his tall form loomed suddenly, large and forbidding, over her. Next to him, she felt ridiculously small and vulnerable. But then, she would rather die than let him see that. Her head came up, and unconsciously she straightened to her full five feet three inches in height.

Furiously, she saw a smile flicker at the corners of Revelstoke's mouth, and suddenly she was not in the least afraid. A curse on his arrogant self-assurance, she thought. He would discover she was no wilting hot house flower.

Hardly had that thought crossed her mind than strong fingers closed about her arms. "But then," he said, drawing her deliberately to him. "You already knew that, or you would not be here."

Emma arched an inquisitive eyebrow. "Here, at Revelstoke?" she queried, a devil in her eye. "Or, here, in your arms, my lord?" Resolutely ignoring the persistent voice in the back of her head that warned against giving rein to irresistible impulse, Emma ran her hands upward over Revelstoke's chest and clasped her arms provocatively about his neck. Her hand at the back of his head, she lifted her face to his and pulled him down to her.

At that moment she did not care where her actions might lead. It was far too late, after all. Revelstoke had unleashed the devil in her. Her lips parted to meet his. "Tell me, sir, do you intend to kiss me or not?"

Revelstoke's smile was singularly mirthless. Bloody hell, she was priceless, was the fearless Lady Blythe. She was taunting him, daring him to do his worst, when, by all rights, she should have been in mortal fear of him.

Ruthlessly, his fingers closed in her hair. "I intend to do much more than kiss you, Lady Blythe," he said, relishing the sudden leap of her pulse at the base of her throat. His own blood burned with a fierce, pulsating desire that threatened to consume him, and she had the audacity to press her soft woman's body against him.

By the devil, he thought, she did not know with what she was dealing!

Chapter Five

Revelstoke's mouth covered Emma's in a burning kiss that aroused in her a response quite unlike anything she could ever possibly have imagined. Indeed it was passing strange, she mused, rather like suddenly discovering one was beset by a great unquenchable thirst one did not previously know one had or like finding at one's center a wholly different person of whose existence one had never been remotely aware before. Revelstoke's lips moved over hers, ruthless and demanding, and yet with an odd sort of passionate tenderness that seemed to kindle flames in the most peculiar places within her. Enthralled, she abandoned herself to the pleasurable sensations his hands and lips aroused in her. Faith, it had never been like this with Wynford, she thought deliriously. With an unwitting groan, she molded herself to Revelstoke, her body and soul awakened to needs and emotions that she had never before known she possessed and which, once brought to her awareness, she had no wish to resist.

She was hardly prepared to have Revelstoke's hands clamp suddenly around her wrists or to have him drag her arms forcibly down from around his neck.

His voice rasped in the stillness, harsh with barely controlled passion. "You tempt me, Lady Blythe. By all the fires of hell, you tempt me. But the time is not now."

Releasing her, he wrenched violently away to stand with his back to her. His broad shoulders rose and fell as he struggled with whatever it was that drove him.

Emma stared at him without comprehension. She felt dazed by the sheer savagery of the emotions that had swept over her, only to be brought so abruptly to a halt. Her heart beat wildly beneath her breast, and her limbs felt trembly and weak. Indeed, she knew herself to be shaken to the core by things she had sensed, even glimpsed, while in the throes of what she half-suspected to have been a state of utter madness.

The whole experience had left her feeling both unsettled and yet exhilarated, baffled and yet peculiarly clearheaded. Strangely, the one thing she did not feel was fear.

"For a man who has sworn he will have me, you certainly have a strange way of going about achieving your ends," she observed, her laugh hollow even in her own ears. "While I behaved in a perfectly reprehensible manner, you, my lord, have remained the perfect gentleman." Then, "Why, Revelstoke? Surely you must have sensed I was yours for the taking."

Her heart leaped as Revelstoke came sharply around, his eyes a pale glint through the dark-tinted lenses.

"No doubt I hate to disappoint you, Lady Blythe. The truth is, however, that you have always been mine for the taking. I suggest you remember that and do not try me again. I have sworn to wait for the time when you will come to me willingly, Emma, but even I have a limit to my self-control."

Stung by his arrogant assumptions, Emma stifled a gasp. Her lips parted to deliver him a stinging retort, but before she could utter it, Revelstoke bowed cynically and, informing her that he would no doubt see her at dinner, spun on his heel and left her to stare after him, her eyes flashing green sparks of resentment.

Damn Revelstoke, she fumed, resisting the urge to snatch up a priceless Wedgewood Portland vase and send it crashing after him.

This was all *his* fault, she told herself. It was, no doubt, an unfortunate quirk in her character that, when goaded, she had always been prone to react with a perverseness well known to her intimates, and bloody well damn the consequences; but that did not alter the fact that he should never have presumed to believe that she would ever play the shrinking violet for him. And yet that was what she had seen in his eyes—and once having dared to presume she was afraid of the power he had over her to fascinate and arouse her more primitive passions, he had inevitably unleashed the imp of perversity in her. She had flung herself at him and in the true style of the Scandalous Lady Blythe had dared him to take her.

The devil! Had she not vowed long ago that she would never submit to being anyone's willing victim? And, indeed, why should she? She belonged to no one, but herself. She had kept to that vow with all of the numerous men in her life who had taken a perverse pleasure in invoking fear in the hearts of those they deemed in their power. No doubt she had been a sad disappointment to Wynford, who, knowing she would have no other recourse but to suffer his notions of authority, had offered for her. He could hardly have known that, even when he was to exert himself to the fullest, she would refuse to give him the gratification of seeing her so much as flinch from him. She had not done so even when he had at last gone too far, she reflected bitterly.

She could take grim satisfaction in knowing that Wynford had won her loathing and her undying contempt, but never the fear and subjection he required to feed his particular appetites. Revelstoke, however, baffled her.

What the devil did he want from her? To have her come to him willingly? Faith, she had just flung herself at him with an utter wantonness! What greater demonstration of her readiness to sink herself beneath reproach did he require from her?

But then, that was it, was it not? she marveled.

Revelstoke had not lied when he said he had decided to have her, she realized with a peculiar sensation in the pit of her stomach that might have been outrage, but resembled more a soft thrill not unlike a delectable presentiment of danger. It was not enough for her to offer herself in an act of defiance, which would not be giving herself at all. He would not come to her bed unless she wanted him there without doubts or reservations. Indeed, Revelstoke would settle for nothing less than her complete capitulation.

Why? What possible difference could it make to him why she gave herself to him so long as he had what he had said he wanted? She was not fool enough to believe he was in love with her. It simply was not possible. He had never laid eyes on her before the previous night's encounter, and she had never been one to believe people fell in love at first sight. No, there was something else going on here that she did not understand.

But she would understand it, she vowed with an ominous jut of her delightfully pointed chin. Indeed, she had the strangest feeling that it was crucial somehow that she resolve the mystery that was Revelstoke.

The half-light of gloaming was collapsing into night when Revelstoke burst out on to the parapet walk as if pursued and began to pace in the manner of one in the grip of powerful emotions.

A bitter curse seemed torn from him as abruptly he came to a halt and, laying his hands on the parapet wall, stared out over the darkening forest spread out below the castle.

Damn fate! And damn the bloody curse that had brought him to the toil in which he now found himself. Possessed of a beauty and fire that surpassed even those of the legendary Maggie Macpherson, Emma Blythe was a deal more than he could possibly have anticipated.

Indeed, it had seemed the final irony to be drawn from his fastness by the first stirrings of awareness of her to discover a woman who had the power to make him forget who and what he was. By the devil, he had even found himself warning her away from him—the greatest sort of folly for one who had been waiting an eternity of hell for the one who could release him.

Subsequent exposure to her sweet fire had done little to dispel the madness which gripped him. Forced to watch her weave her spell over the fatuous colonel and his toadying companions, Revelstoke had seen what he had neither thought nor wished to see. In addition to the fearlessness and fierce passion he had already known she possessed, the incomparable Lady Blythe was gifted with a discerning heart and a generosity of spirit that could not but change her in his eyes. She was hardly what her reputation had painted her.

Hell and the devil confound it, he had not been too long in the darkness not to realize that she was as good as she was innocent, never mind that she was a widow with a name that was notorious across England. What was more, he had seen in the way he had into her very soul.

The beautiful Emma was one of those rarities—a creature of nobility and courage who did not deserve to be corrupted by one of his kind. She was all dazzling light and sweet fire. She had awakened in him primal impulses that he had thought beyond resurrection. She was the one woman he was sworn to possess. How ironic that the dark Earl of Revelstoke should find himself moved by the primitive male instinct to protect her from the evil that stalked the moldering castle, indeed, from himself. Yet he had, and that was nothing to the madness to which he had committed himself this day.

Revelstoke's harsh laugh rang out over the parapet. The end of his torment had been within his grasp. Lady Blythe herself had opened the door to him, and he, like a fool, had turned suddenly noble. He would not take her until she came to him willingly? Bloody hell. The truth was that, even in the throes of a searing torment of desire, he could not bring himself to subject the singular Emma to that final embrace. Rather than have her see him as he truly was, rather than have her *become* as he was, he had suddenly found himself pushing her away. He had known then that, if it were not for the greater threat to her posed by the presence of his unexpected houseguests, he would even have gone so far as to send her away, never mind that it would mean the end of Revelstoke.

But then, in the final analysis, what did it really matter? he speculated darkly. He had already brought destruction down on one woman and ruin upon himself. Perhaps it was time it all came to an end. Revelstoke smiled cynically. At least he would have one good to record against all the bad, a final shred of the honor that had once meant something to him.

Emma could only be grateful for the earl's excellently trained staff as she slipped into a rose linen tunic gown embroidered around the hem in a Greek pattern. If not for one of the maids who had seen that her gowns were shaken out and pressed, she would have been made to appear in a sadly rumpled state. A pity Clara, her abigail of long-standing, had shown craven the last minute. The abigail could always be depended upon to keep her mistress's wardrobe up to trig.

At least, blessed with hair possessed with a natural tendency to curl, Emma need not worry overmuch about her coiffure. Indeed, she had only to run a comb through the fashionably short tresses before, with a last glance in the oval lookingglass, she judged she was ready to descend to the dining room. Taking up her folding fan and slipping the strap around her wrist, she let herself out of her room and made her way slowly down the corridor.

She felt in no great hurry to join the others, presumably assembling in the withdrawing room. Her thoughts were on the riddles that enveloped Revelstoke, chief of which were Maggie Macpherson and her portrait, mysteriously hanging in state in Revelstoke's private study, and the earl's exceedingly odd behavior toward Emma herself. Somehow she could not shake the feeling that the two puzzles were actually somehow one and the same and that in solving one, she would inevitably solve the other. And yet what possible connection could there be between Maggie Macpherson, a woman who had lived and died over two centuries before, and herself? Other than Emma's own fascination with the tale, a fascination that had had its origins in a child who had had little else but a vivid imagination to relieve the bleakness of her life, Emma could not think of a thing that would tie them together.

Or had that been the real reason she had been drawn to steal out on moonlit nights to visit the grave of Maggie Macpherson? Emma mused suddenly. In view of the exceedingly strange events that she had experienced in the past two days, she was no longer quite so certain. Perhaps there was some truth in the rumors the gossipmongers had delighted in concocting about Emma Headley. Perhaps she *was* touched by the devil. Toward the end, Wynford, after all, had become fond of referring to her as a witch and a demon wench, and she could not deny that it was hardly grief that she had felt upon gazing over the broken balustrade at his quite obviously lifeless body, sprawled grotesquely on the parquetry tiled floor a full story below her. She had wished him dead, indeed, had prayed for it without the smallest feelings of remorse. And how not? He, after all, had finally gone beyond the pale.

Had she as well? she wondered, her thoughts turning once more to the events of that afternoon. Certainly since meeting the Earl of Revelstoke, she had conducted herself in the shameless manner of a Cyprian, an eventuality that she could not but find rather amusing in light of the fact that she had led a singularly celibate existence since Wynford's demise. It had even occurred to her, as Revelstoke held her in his arms, that there might be some advantage to being a widow with a tarnished reputation, one, moreover, who had been rendered utterly incapable of ever bearing children. At least, she thought with a sardonic twist of the lips, if she allowed her newly discovered appetites free rein, she need not worry about either her reputation or the possibility of producing a nameless offspring.

Her thoughts were interrupted by the sound of her own name couched in a breathless feminine voice. "Lady Blythe? Lady Blythe—"

Emma, coming about, espied Miss Everston, hurrying toward her from the far end of the corridor. Dressed in a pale blue evening dress whose ruffles and ribbons were not only lacking in sophistication, but were sadly demode, Miss Everston contrived to appear even younger than her admitted seventeen years. It was obvious that she had not had the opportunity since arriving home from India to refurbish her wardrobe. Or perhaps the colonel was not quite so plump in the pocket as he made out to be, speculated Emma with a pang of sympathy. There was a time when she had known what it was to be without a feather to fly with.

"Thank you for waiting, Lady Blythe," exclaimed Miss Everston, as she came up to Emma at the head of the stairs that separated the east from the west wing. "I am running a trifle late, I fear, and Mama and Papa have already gone down without me." The girl blushed in embarrassment. "I was ever so glad to see you come out of your room. I-

I should never complain after his lordship's kind hospitality to us, but I confess that I should be grateful to have someone to walk down with me."

Emma smiled, wondering how Revelstoke could have found anything remotely sinister in a female of Miss Everston's delicate sensibilities. Still, he had said to beware of appearances, she reflected, gazing thoughtfully at the girl's perfect, if somewhat insipid, features. "But of course. I understand perfectly, Miss Everston." Turning, Emma started down the stairway with her youthful companion. "Revelstoke's Gloaminggate is a trifle gloomy, is it not. Especially, if one is used to the sunnier climes of India. If you were at home, in Madras, you would undoubtedly be experiencing the end of the rainy season, when the northeast monsoon cools everything down quite comfortably."

"You are familiar with Madras, Lady Blythe?" queried Miss Everston, glancing sideways in apparent surprise at the older woman.

"Only vicariously, through books and various acquaintances," Emma replied with a vague wave of the hand. "My late husband had an interest in the East India Company," she added in the way of explanation. No one, save herself, could possibly have known that she had just finished doing extensive research on the Orient, along with numerous other places, with the possible intention of traveling to some exotic foreign land when she left England. "Do you miss your former home, Miss Everston?"

"Perhaps, as you said, when the northeast monsoon has made it rather more pleasant," Miss Everston replied with a nervous flutter of her fan. "Otherwise, I am glad to be back in England. Mr. Pinkney and I plan to take a house in London after we are married," she added, turning the subject. "Nothing grand, of course, but sufficient for our needs. He has taken a position with Messrs. Hildegrant and Carstairs. Perhaps you have heard of them."

"Not Mr. Phineas Hildegrant? Why, we are old acquaintances. He and his wife used to come occasionally to tea when Wynford was still alive. Such a distinguished-looking gentleman, Mr. Hildegrant, with that steel grey hair and those black bristling eyebrows. I confess I found him altogether intriguing."

"Why, I suppose he is, rather," agreed Miss Everston with an air of uncertainty. "Although I fear you have mistaken him for Mr. Carstairs. Besides being a confirmed bachelor, Mr. Hildegrant is rather portly and quite bald, poor man."

"Dear, how very foolish of me," Emma said, laughing. "You are right, of course. What could I have been thinking? I must indeed have mixed Carstairs up with Hildegrant. But then, it was a very long time ago, and I have never been the least good with names," she glibly lied.

Miss Everston smiled sympathetically. "Pray think nothing of it, Lady Blythe. We have all made similar mistakes at one time or another. And who is to say Mr. Hildegrant cannot be distinguished in his own way? I myself was in a positive quake when I was first introduced to him. Still, he has proven most kind to Mr. Pinkney."

"Yes, he would, naturally," Emma murmured, glancing away from the girl's distinctly smug expression. Miss Everston had seemed exceedingly ill at ease until Emma's deliberate *faux pas*, but then Emma would have been greatly surprised had the younger woman not been a trifle off set. In any discussion of the Orient, the girl was obviously out of her depths. "Was Mr. Pinkney in India?" Emma instantly queried. "Is that where the two of you met?"

"Oh, heavens, no. The Pinkneys are old friends, part of the family actually. Gerald and I knew one another as children, and, well, when the colonel brought Mama and me back to England, we met again in the natural course of events. I suppose it was always expected that we should eventually be wed."

It was, in point of fact, an arranged marriage, Emma surmised, which might explain the seeming lack of any great affection between the newly betrothed couple, a curiosity that Emma had noted early on about Miss Everston and Mr. Pinkney. Even for one who was not marrying for love, Miss Everston would seem to demonstrate a remarkable tepidity at the prospect of her approaching nuptials. Indeed, had Emma detected in the colonel's daughter the least antipathy toward Mr. Pinkney, she might have suspected the girl was being coerced into the match against her will. As it was, however, the only outstanding eccentricity one noticed about Miss Everston's temperament, apart from her tendency to nervous distraction, was that she seemed strikingly devoid of any but the most prosaic of emotions. This vapidity, Emma had previously attributed to extreme youth and possibly the result of being coddled by over-protective parents. Now, however, she was not so certain.

The party assembled in the withdrawing room was markedly lacking in merriment, Emma could not but observe as she made her entrance with Miss Everston. If anything, there would seem to be a pall on the company. It occurred humorously to Emma as she met Revelstoke's hooded look from across the room that he had been quite right when he warned that she might soon be wishing the colonel and the others at Jericho. They would seem to have an absolute gift for putting a damper on any social gathering.

Mrs. Everston, demonstrating a sudden annoying tendency to gabble on about the most inane of topics, was discussing the merits of pork jelly as a restorative for those recuperating from a high fever, when she was interrupted by Emma, who apologized for making everyone wait.

"Miss Everston was just telling me how lovely it must be in Madras, now that the rainy season has ended," she murmured to Revelstoke a moment later as he bent over her hand. "I believe I am quite tempted to go and experience it for myself. I have always wanted to travel," she added, smiling up into the earl's suddenly piercing glance, "and, now, it seems there is little to keep me from it. Have you ever seen the Orient, my lord?" she queried as he escorted her into the dining room.

"In my extreme youth, I was, as a matter of fact, part of an expeditionary force to the Far East, Lady Blythe," he answered dryly. "Which is why I am aware that the northeast monsoon does not descend upon Madras until November. In case you are unaware of it, it is now the month of August. I daresay you would soon find yourself all wet were you to venture forth in Madras at this time of the year." Pulling out the chair at the place of honor next to the head of the table, Revelstoke waited for Emma to be seated.

"It would seem, my lord," Emma retorted, her glance lifting to his as she took her seat, "that it is not *I* who am all wet. Unless I am mistaken, one of your guests has not studied her geography lessons thoroughly enough."

A single arrogant eyebrow arched toward Revelstoke's hairline.

"You intrigue me, Lady Blythe," he murmured. "Although I am hardly surprised. I was reasonably certain you would not rest until you had proved me either right or wrong about my uninvited houseguests."

"I have done neither yet, my lord. I have only uncovered a flaw in what would seem to be a carefully contrived character. Or perhaps it is only that this particular person is one of those creatures with more hair than wit who go through life without the smallest notion of what is going on around them. I have met more than a few like that in my time."

"Is that what you think she is, Lady Blythe?" queried Revelstoke, eyeing her impassively.

"No," Emma admitted honestly. "On the other hand, I do not know yet what to think, except that nothing at Revelstoke would seem to be quite what it is made out to be. Even you, my lord."

If she had meant to win a reaction from the maddening earl, she was to be sadly disappointed.

Revelstoke smiled dispassionately. "Especially me, Lady Blythe. But then, I have already given you fair warning on that subject, have I not?"

Emma was prevented from answering that singular observation by the proximity of the colonel, who, after seating his wife and daughter on the far side of the table, had taken the chair next to Emma.

Straightening, Revelstoke took his place at the head of his guests.

The meal that followed was not notable for its scintillating conversation, Emma was to muse sometime later as, pleading the onset of a headache, she made her way to her room. The earl had withdrawn behind his maddeningly impenetrable barrier of aloofness, leaving Emma the task of playing hostess.

The earl had done nothing to ease what was fast made an unbearably awkward situation. At least, the various courses had been excellent in spite of the fact that Revelstoke, with what she must assume was a characteristic perverseness, had eaten of them sparingly. All in all, Emma could only be relieved when at last the sweet meats had been sampled, signaling the end of the wretched meal. She was left feeling exceedingly weary of the entire company, Revelstoke included.

Unfortunately, she was not in the least tired physically. Quite the contrary, she was filled with a restlessness that precluded even the thought of seeking her bed.

No doubt it was the need to escape for a time the stifling confines of the castle that prompted her to snatch up her cloak and, flinging it around her shoulders, steal out of her room and down the stairs to the Burgundy Room, which overlooked the garden she had earlier noticed. Letting herself out of French doors, she stepped out into a riot of daffodils, hollyhocks, dewdrops and crocuses, all rendered peculiarly chimerical in appearance by trailing tendrils of knee-high mist.

Immediately she drew in a deep breath, savoring the scent of the mist-laden air. For the first time since arriving at Revelstoke's Gloaminggate, she felt herself free of the oppressive sense of waiting for something lurking just beyond her comprehension. Indeed, had it not been for her fascination with the Earl of Revelstoke and the aura of mystery that surrounded him, she was very nearly certain she would have ordered the horses set in their traces and dared the treacherous road back to civilization rather than spend another minute at Gloaminggate. Really, nothing had gone at all as she had envisioned it would when she set out to take up Revelstoke's challenge.

Bending her steps down a nearly overgrown walk paved in flagstones, Emma strolled, lost in admiration, beneath spreading elms and ancient oaks, their low-hanging branches cascading luxurious vines of wisteria and celandine. It occurred to her that once the garden must have been a magnificent example of its kind. Still, she thought, smiling to herself, she rather preferred it the way it was now. It was somewhat like finding oneself in some primeval wood, which should, by all rights, have been haunted by wood sprites and elves or any number of other supernatural creatures.

Hardly had that thought crossed her mind than she was startled by a sudden, unmistakable rustle of underbrush ahead of her. She drew up short, the nerves tingling at the nape of her neck. Deliberately she probed the dense jungle of trees and vines, made more impenetrable by shadows and mist. A hint of movement like the brush of wind through branches caught her eyes, and she stilled, her mouth suddenly dry.

The air lay thick and heavy around her, without even the whisper of a breeze to disturb it. Someone or something was there, she knew it. She could sense eyes on her, watching, she was sure of it. Indeed, she had the strangest feeling that who or whatever it was wished to frighten her into turning back the way she had come.

"Who is it?" she called sharply. "Who is there? Pray come forward and show yourself."

The silence stretched unbearably, along with Emma's nerves, into what seemed an eternity of waiting, but which could not have been more than ten seconds or more. At last Emma's unease gave way to impatience.

"Oh, very well then," she declared aloud to the shadows. "Have it your way. I, however, have no intention of waiting around for you to make yourself known."

Her shoulders back and her chin tilted at a defiant angle, she strode boldly forward along the path. She was damned if she would show craven now. Nevertheless, she could not but be tinglingly aware that she was preceded every step of the way by a distinct rustling in the undergrowth. Unconsciously, she quickened her step, heedless of the hidden snags and branches that tore at the fine linen of her gown, and, always, she could hear the telltale sound of movement before her.

Suddenly the mist parted, and for a fleeting instant a magnificent creature, wolf-like, lean and wild, appeared to her. She drew a sharp breath. Then it was gone again, swallowed up in the mist as if it had never been.

With a low cry of triumph, Emma clawed her way in pursuit of the creature through a tangled curtain of vines. Tearing free of the grasping branches, she stopped, her breath coming in shallow gasps and her eyes fixed and staring on the thing that loomed out of the mist before her.

The tomb of grey marble brooded in the midst of clinging ivy and towering yews. A doorway gaped, the marble slab that had once sealed it lying in a broken mass of rubble as if it had been blasted outward by some powerful force. A glowing lamp in a niche beside the gaping maw appeared to beckon Emma onward. She shivered, thinking it rather had the look of a gateway to the netherworld.

But how absurd, she told herself firmly. The place was nothing more than the family vault. As she approached the blasted doorway, she saw, carved in ornate letters over the arched portal, the words: *In death we are in life.* It was, she realized, a corruption of the familiar quote from the *Book of Common Prayer:* "In life we are in death." The original was meant as a warning of the transitory nature of life, which lay ever in the shadow of death. She frowned, wondering what possible meaning could be construed from its corruption.

At last, her curiosity greater than what should have been a natural antipathy to entering a tomb in the dead of night, Emma took up the lamp and let the light play over stone steps, descending into gloom.

She did not hear the furtive step at her back as she halted on the threshold. Nor was she aware of the shadowy figure looming suddenly behind her.

Chapter Six

Emma, lifting the lamp high, hesitated, suddenly uneasy. She could not quell the feeling that the epitaph inscribed overhead was somehow vital. People did not generally, after all, make it a habit to memorialize a last resting place with any old thing pulled out of a hat. Surely it did not mean what it would seem to mean, that there were those for whom death was as transitory as was life to the living. She was not one to jump to conclusions, and yet the thought that there might be dead people walking around in the guise of the living was not one that she found particularly conducive to comfort.

It was, in fact, all perfectly absurd, she told herself, and yet perhaps the solution to the puzzle did lie below, though she could not imagine what a coffin or, worse (she could not quite stifle a shudder), a moldering corpse could possibly tell her. Still, she was here, she reflected. She might as well fling her heart over before her and take the jump. It would be absurd not to see for herself what lay below.

Squaring her shoulders, she took the first step.

* * *

The hand came out of nowhere to clamp on her shoulder.

Emma uttered a wholly unladylike epithet and came about face, delivering a roundhouse swing as she came.

Her would-be assailant, no doubt startled to receive a blow to the most vulnerable, not to say protuberant, part of his facial anatomy, uttered a muffled oath and, clasping a hand over his injured member, fell, stumbling, back a step.

"Why, Mr. Pinkney!" exclaimed Emma, instantly recognizing Miss Everston's intended, revealed in the spill of lamplight. Torn between annoyance at the gentleman for having stolen up behind her in the dark and dismay at the mounting evidence that she had drawn his cork for him, she regarded Pinkney with no little perturbation. "What in heaven's name are you doing here?"

"Sh-h-h, not so loud, beg you," pleaded Pinkney, attempting to stem with the hasty application of a linen handkerchief the flow of blood from his ill-treated nose. He eyed Emma out of watering eyes. "Beg your pardon, Lady Blythe," he continued in a muffled voice. "Saw you leave the house and followed you. Hoped to have a word with you."

"That is no doubt all well and good, Mr. Pinkney," observed Emma, drawing forth from her sleeve her own lacy excuse for a handkerchief, "but you really should not have startled me. Dear, I do hope I have not broken your nose."

"Nothing to signify, assure you," Pinkney rumbled, assaying a brave display of masculine fortitude. "Lived through worse and lived to tell of it."

"No doubt, Mr. Pinkney," Emma observed dryly. "Here," she added, dipping the small square of dainty fabric in a clean puddle of water left behind by the rain. "Very often a cold, damp compress at the back of the neck is beneficial in such cases."

"Kind of you, my lady, to be sure." Pinkney's eyes rolled

toward the yawning maw of the sepulchre as Emma struggled to place the wet handkerchief inside the victim's collar, which, besides being heavily starched, was of an absurd height that gave Pinkney somewhat the appearance of a turtle emerging from its shell. "Only, not my nose that concerns me."

"No, of course it is not," agreed Emma, who, having noted the dandy's nervous preoccupation with the crypt, thought to spare his masculine sensibilities. "Now, pray be still, Mr. Pinkney. You are not making my task any easier."

At the commanding note in Emma's voice, Pinkney flushed, but obligingly ceased to squirm. "Beg your pardon, my lady. Never meant to be a bother."

"No doubt you relieve my mind, Mr. Pinkney. I confess I was not in the least certain what you intended."

"Be happy to explain it to you, Lady Blythe," replied Pinkney with a nervous tic of an eyelid, "if only you will come away from here with me. Now, before it is too late."

"Too late?" Emma, having succeeded in wedging the damp handkerchief between Pinkney's collar and his neck, stepped back to favor the gentleman with an amused look. Really, instead of his collar, the man should try a bit of starch in his backbone. He would seem to be afraid of his own shadow. "Too late for what, Mr. Pinkney? Surely everyone is in bed asleep by now."

"'Night, having sleep, the brother of Death,'" Pinkney intoned in what could only be described as funereal tones.

"I beg your pardon?" demanded Emma, little wondering at Miss Everston's lack of warmth for the gentleman. Pinkney's propensity for cryptic utterances would have cooled the most ardent of hearts.

"Er—nothing." Pinkney swallowed and ran a finger around the inside of his collar. "Only something I picked up somewhere."

"Indeed, I recognize it. It is from Hesiod. *The Theogony*, am I not mistaken." She was on the point of demanding to know what his purpose was in quoting it, when Pinkney jumped and let out a shrieking gasp that sent cold chills clawing down her back.

"Good God, did you hear that?" he uttered in a shrill whisper. Clasping her arm, he assayed to pull her away from the crypt.

"Pray get a grip on yourself," ordered Emma in ill-concealed disgust. Obviously Pinkney was one of those people who entertained an unnatural terror of graveyards and anything to do with the dead. "I heard nothing, Mr. Pinkney. Unhand me, if you please. I fear you are letting fancy run away with you."

"Must have heard it, Lady Blythe," Pinkney insisted, unloosing her arm with obvious reluctance. "A rush of wings through the trees. Not mistaken, assure you. Liable to swoop down on us any time now. Must get away from here."

"No doubt it was only an owl," Emma insisted, digging her heels in. "Still, I should no doubt be happy to oblige you, sir, were I convinced I could trust you. As it is, I am not at all sure I wish to go anywhere with you. It occurs to me that you and your companions have not been entirely truthful about yourselves."

"Happens you are right, Lady Blythe," Pinkney baldly admitted. "May we go now? Beg you. Might be discovered any moment."

"Very well, if it means so much to you," said Emma, taking pity on Pinkney, who, having gone deathly pale, appeared on the verge of a sharp decline. She replaced the lamp in its niche. "I warn you, however, that I shall not hesitate to draw your cork again if you try anything."

"Mean you no harm, my lady, promise you," Pinkney hastened to assure her, even as he took her arm and pulled her away from the brooding sepulchre with its gaping maw. "Quite the contrary. Came to warn you."

"Warn me of what, Mr. Pinkney?" Emma demanded.

"A moment, my lady," replied Pinkney, apparently not

yet satisfied that they had put enough distance between them and the clearing. He shot a darting glance over his shoulder as if in anticipation of being set upon at any moment from out of the shadows.

Emma, however, had had quite enough. "On the contrary, Mr. Pinkney," she said, coming to a halt before a marble bench set beneath a burgeoning grape arbor. "I shall not take another step until you have explained to me why you saw fit to follow me from the keep, not to mention startling me out of half a year's growth, not once, but twice. Just exactly what is it that you wished to tell me?"

Mr. Pinkney, who did not appear at all happy with the spot she had chosen for a contretemps, favored Emma with a look very nearly resembling dislike. "Needn't fly at me, Lady Blythe. Risked a great deal, after all, just to meet you like this. Shudder to think what would happen if the others knew what I was about." Suiting action to words, the gentleman noticeably shivered, even as he darted another glance over his shoulder. *"She* wouldn't care for it at all. A regular brimstone, she is. Devil of a temper. No telling what she'd do."

"Indeed?" queried Emma, who, no matter how hard she tried, could not quite picture the delicate Miss Everston in the role of a termagant. But then, Mr. Pinkney did not impress her as being precisely the forceful sort, she reasoned. Perhaps it was a simple matter of relativity. "Still, you will admit, Mr. Pinkney, that the others would have every reason to be set on end if we were discovered in what could only be construed as compromising circumstances."

"Daresay you are right," replied Pinkney with a most peculiar expression. "Hadn't thought about that. But, no," he said, appearing to give pause for reflection. "They'd never go for it, depend on it." Assuring himself with a final sniff behind his handkerchief that his nose had at last ceased its bleeding, Pinkney stuffed the square of soiled linen in his pocket and squared his shoulders. "Better to get on with it."

"Indeed, Mr. Pinkney. Pray do not be afraid to open your budget."

Pinkney stole one last darting glance at the shadows around him. Then deliberately he leaned close to Emma. "The thing is, Lady Blythe, ain't safe for you here. Might be if you were to leave now, wouldn't be any reason for anyone to follow. Stands to reason, don't it? Only a danger if you're here, after all."

"Danger, Mr. Pinkney? Are you saying *I* am a danger to someone?" demanded Emma, who was having difficulty making sense out of her companion's elliptical utterances.

"Said so, didn't I? Not that it's any of your fault. Couldn't know about the bloody curse, could you. Never wanted to hear about it m'self. But what would you. I'm here now, and ain't bloody likely I'll be let to cry off. Bad *ton* and all that. Still, couldn't help but do what I could to warn you."

"What curse? And pray to whom am I a danger. Mr. Pinkney, pray explain yourself. Who will not be moved to follow me?"

It was immediately apparent, however, that Mr. Pinkney not only was not listening to her, but he had reached the end of his courage. "Well, then," he declared with a heavy sigh of manifest relief, starting to edge away from her. "Said what I came to say. Just be on my way now," he added, his glance flickering to the shadows. "Stayed away too long as it is. Daresay they will have missed me. Best if you leave Gloaminggate. Now, Lady Blythe. Wouldn't even bother to pack if I were you."

As he had by this time turned and begun a headlong retreat along the overgrown walk that led back to the keep, this last trailed, wisp-like, over his shoulder.

The next instant, he was gone, swallowed up in the darkness and fog.

Only then did it occur to her that Pinkney had failed to explain what he had meant when he readily admitted the Everstons were not what they appeared to be. "Now, what the devil," Emma muttered to herself. She hardly knew whether to be alarmed or amused at her encounter with the young dandy. Certainly, Mr. Pinkney had left her with far more questions than answers.

Suddenly, as she stared, frowning, into the darkness where Pinkney had vanished, she sensed she was not alone. She did not have to look to know who had come up behind her. She knew by the quiver that coursed through her belly.

"Pinkney is right," observed Revelstoke's soft, thrilling voice at her back. "You must leave Gloaminggate. Tonight, before the others suspect what you are about."

"Why?" demanded Emma, coming about to face him. "Pray do not tell me you are suddenly concerned about my reputation, for I shan't believe you. Besides, it is far too late for anything so patently absurd."

Revelstoke's eyes appeared opaque in the faint glow of moonlight through the silvery mist. Emma could read nothing in them. She felt her heart, suddenly cold beneath her breast.

"Why is of little significance. Suffice it to say that, much as I regret the imposition, I find I have changed my mind. It was a mistake to bring you here. Nothing will be served by prolonging your stay."

Emma stared at him with a keen sense of incredulity. "I see," she said. "I have not lived up to your expectations. And, now, having decided you no longer wish to make me yours, you have decided to rectify your error by sending me away in the dead of night, is that it?"

"Brava, Lady Blythe," Revelstoke drawled cynically. "You would seem to have grasped the essentials. If you leave directly, you can make it to Moorsgate by morning. No doubt your cousins will not deny you their hospitality for one night."

For a moment Emma stood perfectly still, aware of the heat flooding her veins. The devil, she thought. Not for one night, not even for one hour. She would die first before petitioning Wilfred for a roof over her head. It really was too much when she found even the man for whom she had cast the last shreds of her reputation to the wind suddenly wished her at Jericho. Indeed, it was the height of absurdity.

Emma, however, did not feel in the least like laughing. She was not sure what she felt. Anger and resentment paled before the sickening sensation of having been kicked in the stomach.

She turned away to pace a step. Good God, if she did not know better, she might think she was more hurt than humiliated at Revelstoke's unexpected change of heart. In spite of the fact that she had felt drawn to the infuriating nobleman from the very first or that the attraction she felt for him had grown rather than lessened with subsequent exposure to his compelling presence, she would not allow that she was losing her heart to him. And yet, she could not deny that he had a most unsettling effect on her emotional and physical equilibrium.

The truth was that she had never met anyone who intrigued her in the manner that Revelstoke did. He was, in fact, everything she might have looked for in a man—intelligent, well-read, and possessed of a lively sense of the ridiculous that was every bit as keen as her own. With Revelstoke, it was as if they shared at any given time the same thoughts and feelings. She had never met anyone before who seemed to understand her as Revelstoke did and, furthermore, to accept her for what she was. Or, at least, that was what she had come to think until now.

Hell and the devil confound it! She *could* not be mistaken in what she had sensed in him. On the contrary, his sudden change of heart would seem on the surface to make little sense.

"Well, I do not believe it," she declared, rounding on the earl with flashing eyes. "Pinkney claimed I posed some sort of a danger, but only while I am here, at Gloaminggate. I do not suppose you can tell me what he meant by that?"

Even in the gloom, Emma sensed Revelstoke raise his guard. His voice sounded, edged with caution beneath its velvet softness. "No, how should I? Pinkney is a bloody fool."

"Perhaps, but he was frightened, and, still, he managed to find the courage to warn me." Deliberately, she closed the distance between them. "And now *you* want to send me away." She laid her palms against his chest, felt his strength held in check by an unbreakable will. Still, she had to try. Shamelessly, she leaned her weight against him. "A bizarre coincidence, wouldn't you say?" she speculated. A tremor shook the earl's powerful frame. Emma knew a heady sense of triumph. "The truth, Revelstoke," she whispered, letting her hands slip slowly up around his neck. "You swore you would never lie to me." She tilted her head back, allowed her gaze to linger provocatively on the stern lips. Then at last she looked into his eyes, which, no longer opaque, appeared to burn with an amber fire. "Is that danger to you, my lord?"

Revelstoke's laugh rang harshly in the silence of the garden, followed by a groan of anguish. The next instant Emma felt herself ruthlessly crushed in arms of steel.

"The truth, Lady Blythe?" Revelstoke's fingers in Emma's hair forced her head back, baring her neck to him. "The truth is that you have proved my undoing."

Emma glimpsed the savage gleam of eyes like amber flame, of bared teeth in a face that had been transformed by torment into something unrecognizable. Indeed, it was as if some great and terrible power had been unleashed, usurping her will and rendering her utterly vulnerable to it—to the thing that was Revelstoke. And through it all, she could feel his anguish as if it were her own.

The pain and torment of more than two centuries of terrible exile shattered her defenses and stripped her of the false logic that had served to blind her to the truth. Thoughts crowded her mind, the threads of a dread secret on the point of raveling. She loved him; indeed, had always loved him. All along, it had been Revelstoke on the edge of her consciousness, Revelstoke in the dreams that had come to her at night, Revelstoke who had drawn her to Dunnecombe and the grave of Maggie Macpherson. She knew it with utter certainty. No longer need she wonder at the emptiness that had been waiting to be filled. She had been born to love Revelstoke.

Revelstoke lowered his head toward her.

A shudder coursed through him as he found the throbbing pulse at her neck. Life and blood flowed maddeningly within reach. The gnawing hunger, the torment of desire clawed at his belly. Emma was vital, warm, pliant in his hands, her strength pulsating, hot in her veins. He had only to take her.

Savagely, he pressed his lips to her neck. His tongue savored the subtle taste of her. Her groan, her fingers clenching in the fabric of his coat inflamed his senses. Her woman's scent mingled with the perfume of violets intoxicated him, threatened to drive him beyond reason. He inhaled her sweetness, felt the dark rush of animal lust sear his veins. His blood roared in his ears, deafening him to all but the beat of Emma's heart beneath her full, rounded breast.

He groaned, knowing how near he was to being utterly lost.

Revelstoke wrenched his head up. Emma's face, blurred through a red veil of mist, loomed in his vision, pale with realization. A bitter pang pierced his heart as he realized he had accomplished what he had set out to do. He waited for her revulsion.

What he did not expect was to hear his name upon her lips.

"Revelstoke," she whispered, her eyes shimmering with tears. Her hands lifted to cradle his face with infinite tenderness. "My dearest love. Faith, what did they do to you?"

Chapter Seven

Clinging, still, to Revelstoke, Emma sank down on the bench beneath the grape vines. "I remember. Like fragments of someone else's dream. Maggie Macpherson's dream." She lifted her head to look at Revelstoke. "How is that possible? How is any of this possible?"

Revelstoke stood over her, his gaze turned outward into the night. "Who is to say what shapes reality? Dreams, visions of things beyond this world, a power that exists in the shadows beyond our physical senses? In you flows the blood of the highlander clans. Perhaps through such a kinship, it is possible for one to reach across the passage of time to another of a kindred soul. I know only that nearly three hundred years ago Maggie Macpherson led her clan into battle to avenge the death of her lover, a man who was not dead and cannot die. At least not in the normal course of events. She rode to her death because of a lie."

"Magnus Ferguson's lie," murmured Emma, knowing without knowing how she knew. "She went to the clansman of Lothian to beg him to release her from her promise to wed his son. Her heart, she said, had been won by another. Aye, by an English lord, he answered. All the world knew. But she would not be allowed to bring shame on the Fergusons. Her lover was dead, fallen to the executioner's axe, and she would wed the heir of Ferguson. Instead, she rode in grief against the English to avenge the murder of her English lover." She raised her eyes to Revelstoke. "Your death, Revelstoke. You were her lover."

"But I, as you see, am not dead."

"Indeed, my lord, you would seem to be very much alive. But then, you are not like the rest of us," Emma gravely pointed out. Really, she wished he had not withdrawn so thoroughly into his dark fortress. He might at least look at her. "What are you, exactly, my dearest Revelstoke?"

He did look at her then, his wonderful eyes piercing in the moonlight. "I am a monster, Lady Blythe. A *vampire* I believe is the current term. A beast born of darkness who survives on the blood of others. Hardly a pretty concept. You should run from me."

Emma smiled tolerantly. "Naturally, you would say that. After all, you have determined to frighten me away, have you not? Why, my dearest love? I promise I am not in the least afraid of you. Indeed, I must warn you that you will fail in any endeavor to send me off. I am a deal more stubborn than your marvellous Maggie Macpherson, I promise you."

"You, Lady Blythe, are a fool. The devil, Emma. I told you I should never lie to you." He wrenched around to impale her with his eyes in which the mysterious power shone, the power of the dark lord of Revelstoke. "You see me now as I am. Speak no more of love. You haven't the least notion of what you are saying."

If he had thought by that to bring her to her senses, he was to be sadly mistaken. Emma's lovely gaze never wavered.

"You may glower at me as much as you wish, Revelstoke," she informed him in the most prosaic of tones. "I am not in the least put off by it. What I see is a man in torment. A man who has been made indestructible by some terrible pain. The curse is one you brought on yourself. Why, Leopold? Maggie Macpherson would never have demanded such a price simply because she died and you did not."

Revelstoke, veiling his power behind drooping eyelids, marveled at Emma's ability to see straight to the heart of a matter. It was, in fact, her most unnerving attribute. He doubted not she would not rest until she knew the whole of it, but by then it would be too late for her to follow what would undoubtedly be her inclination to save him. "Perhaps," he said, his voice cold-edged and mocking. "But then, Maggie Macpherson did not expect to die by her lover's hand. Ironic, don't you think? My sword pierced her heart through. No doubt she was gratified to have the distinction of breathing her last in my arms."

Emma lowered her eyes. What a fool she had been not to see it coming. After all, Revelstoke Castle alone had stood guard against Scottish forays into Kielder Forest and beyond. When the alarm sounded, the lord of the keep would naturally have ridden forth to do battle. Neither he nor the highlander woman who had loved him could have known what fate awaited them on that grey morning in Dunnecombe.

It would seem to explain a great deal about Revelstoke, and, still, it was not enough. She did not believe for a moment that grief alone had transformed Leopold Smith into the creature of darkness who, in showing himself to her only moments before, had awakened her to the realization that he was the only man she could ever love. With a man like Revelstoke, it would have taken a great deal more to so thoroughly break his faith as to drive him to embrace powers that must forever condemn him to walk in the shadows.

"You buried her in Dunnecombe, and then you withdrew into your fortress and refused to ride out again against the Scots," she said, recalling the bits and pieces he had grudgingly confided. What had happened then? No doubt there had been a long struggle with grief and the torment of guilt. However, strong men of intellect like Revelstoke did not succumb to such emotions, even when they were also men of great passion. Something else had intervened to interrupt the healing process, but what?

And then it came to her. Leopold Smith had been executed in 1548, not for treason against his king, but for the practice of witchcraft!

"My God!" she exclaimed huskily, her lovely eyes expressive of horror and compassion. "My poor, dear Revelstoke. They tortured you, and then, when you would not confess to that which was not true, they executed you in any one of a number of the dreadful methods reserved for those accused of witchcraft. At least they did not burn you at the stake. I daresay no one, not even a vampire, could have survived such a fate."

Revelstoke uttered a startled laugh at her eminently practical deduction. "You are right, of course. Fire is one sure way of ridding oneself of a vampire. On the other hand, I was not yet committed to my present course. That came when I was interred in my tomb. I was fortunate, you see. My executioners chose to bury me alive. I was given a deal of time to reflect on the ironies of fate."

Emma went deathly pale. "Good God," she breathed, "how long?"

Emma stilled at the touch of Revelstoke's hand beneath her chin. A wry smile twisted at his lips at what he read in her eyes. "Not long in the cosmic scheme of things, I assure you. Two hundred years or so. And then you came to Maggie Macpherson's grave, drawn by the yearning for your highlander kindred. You swore on her grave you would one day have the love that Maggie Macpherson had known. It was your voice, your passion, that drew me from the fastness. I have been waiting ever since for you to come back again to Moorsgate, to Dunnecombe and Maggie Macpherson."

Emma felt a cold prickle of dawning realization. She had been seventeen at the time, and her uncle had only just informed her that she was to be wed to Wynford—for material gain, for the marriage settlement that would save Moorsgate from going under the gavel. She had made the vow in a rebellious rage. And then she had gone to Wynford, who had been far worse than even she could have imagined.

"I knew," she said, staring at the hard planes of Revelstoke's face with new eyes. "The first time I saw you at my cousin's ball. It was against all reason and, still, I could not stop the way I felt about you. It was simply too illogical to accept that I should be in love with a man I had never seen before. But, now—"

"Now." Revelstoke dropped his hand. "It is even less logical now," he said and turned away from her, his gaze on the shadows, distorted by moonlight and mist into a landscape for dreams. "Unfortunately, it is now too late to avoid the inevitable. It seems the rest of my 'guests' have decided to join us. I do not suppose I could persuade you to withdraw to the stables and order your coachman to take you away from here while I deal with this?"

"I'm afraid not, my lord. It is, after all, one of the final pieces of the puzzle. I am all eagerness to discover where they fit in all of this."

"They, my dear Lady Blythe, have no place at all, save for the one they would usurp for themselves. I'm afraid the last of the Dernes was not so astute as his predecessors. As you can see by the examples of his former butler—Mr. Everston, who was never a colonel and who I am reasonably certain has never been to India, and his wife, who served in the capacity of housekeeper. Mr. Pinkney, you may be interested to learn, was formerly employed as Derne's man of affairs. I am, of necessity, a nocturnal creature, which is why they no doubt thought I should have been in ignorance of their former capacities in my house. A grave misjudgment on their part. Poor Rupert paid the price. But then, he always was a wretched judge of character."

"No, how can you say so, my lord?" blustered Everston, who had with a crash of underbrush lumbered into view. "I must take exception," he added, brushing twigs and leaves from his person. "Mrs. Everston and I served Rupert Derne with the utmost loyalty right up until the end. It's a pity he had to discover Mrs. Everston going through his private papers. But what would you? We could hardly let him give us the boot. Not with a vault full of treasure for the taking. He left us little choice but to despatch him."

"Which we did, my lord, in as merciful a fashion as we could devise," Mrs. Everston appended, dragging the hem of her skirt free from a grasping rosebush as she, in the company of a disgruntled Clarissa, made her appearance. "And now there's only you and the lady to know. A shame you had to turn up when you did, m'lady. It's almost the time of the gloaming. Without you, his lordship would have been in a very short time little more than ashes and dust, and there would be a tidy end to it."

"Ashes and dust." Emma felt a chill hand touch her heart. "Revelstoke, what is she talking about?"

"Quite simple, assure you. All here, in fact, in Derne's journal." It was Pinkney who strode out of the darkness to stand significantly behind Emma, only a Pinkney Emma had not seen before. The dandy's round blue eyes no longer reflected a vague bewilderment at the complexities of the world around him. They were sharp and cunning, and she did not care in the least for the way they lingered on the soft swell of her bosom. "With the first light of dawn, will have been ten years to the day since you drew Revelstoke here from his tomb." Pinkney shrugged. "Afraid it's all the time allotted to him—unless, of course, you were to grant him a new lease on life. Happens, you, Lady Blythe are the only one with the power to save him. Naturally, however, we cannot allow that to happen."

"Really, Pinkney, is all this talk necessary?" demanded

Clarissa, eyeing with disgust her ruined finery which had suffered the ill-effects of a traipse through the garden in the dark. "Why not just cut her stick for her and be done with it."

"Beg your pardon, Lady Blythe, for Miss Everston's unfortunate manners," Pinkney offered ingratiatingly. Seating himself on the bench next to Emma, he lightly stroked the side of her face with his hand, in which resided a pistol, obviously primed and loaded.

Emma remained perfectly still, her eyes on Revelstoke, and marveled that Pinkney could remain so utterly oblivious of the danger he was courting. Even knowing what Revelstoke was, he clearly had not the least notion of with what he was dealing.

"Isn't necessary for you to make such an extreme sacrifice," he was saying. "Assure you. Never saw any woman more beautiful. Should consider it a shame to have to put a period to your existence."

"How kind of you to say so, Mr. Pinkney," retorted Emma, not bothering to conceal her contempt for him. "And you, I must suppose, have an alternative to offer."

"Do, as a matter of fact. Was born to better things, my lady—the younger son of nobility. Haven't forgot what it is to be a gentleman. Honor and the knowledge of what's due a lady. The thing is, Lady Blythe, I want you to be my wife."

"Here now, what's this? Your *wife?*" demanded Mrs. Everston, rounding on her erstwhile future son-in-law to the accompaniment of a feminine shriek of outrage from the demure Clarissa, who, but for her mama's intervention, would undoubtedly have launched herself at Pinkney, claws extended. "You'll have a wife, certain enough. Our Clarissa here, just as you promised. Don't think we'll stand idly by while you up and toss her aside. Well, don't just stand there with your mouth agape. Tell him, Rolph Everston."

Everston, looking as if he had been made to swallow

something of a particularly disgusting nature, coughed and cleared his throat. "She's right, y'know, Mr. Pinkney. Can't have it said our only daughter was jilted. It just wouldn't be seemly. Must ask you to take back your offer to Lady Blythe. We shall only have to despatch her anyway. Can't have her around, knowing what she knows."

"Can't put a period to her existence either," Pinkney stubbornly maintained. "Thought it all through. Bad *ton*, going around wringing ladies' necks for them. Besides, seven thousand a year's nothing to sneeze at. You'll have your share of the gold when we find it. Should be enough to buy a husband even for Clarissa."

"Oh, you sniveling rogue!" screamed Clarissa, straining to break past Mrs. Everston's matronly bulk to more properly express her obvious disaffection with her intended. "You—you scoundrel! You miserable excuse for a man. Buy me a husband, is it? Even for the likes of Clarissa Everston! I'll see you never look at another woman when I get my hands on you."

Pinkney, having perceptibly paled, bolted to his feet, pistol extended, no doubt intending to more forcibly demonstrate his determination to cry off from the engagement. "Hold on, now. No need to fly up in the boughs. Never cared for me all that much anyhow. Plenty of other fish in the sea and all that."

In a fury, Clarissa lunged, but it was Mrs. Everston, wearing what could hardly be described as either a kind or a motherly aspect, who clearly intimidated him. Backing, he waved the pistol in her direction.

"Keep your distance, both of you. Taken all I mean to take from the likes of you. Waspish old woman with the tongue of a viper. Not the sort one would wish for a mama-in-law."

Emma, finding herself no longer the center of attention, took the opportunity to remove herself from Pinkney's immediate vicinity. With a stab of dread she realized that the cypress tree before her had grown noticeably more distinct and that the sky was paling toward the dusk before sunrise.

Her eyes sought Revelstoke, who, in spite of the cold fury held rigidly in check, had remained a surprisingly impassive witness to the farce just then unfolding. It came to her with a paralyzing flash of insight that he intended to do nothing to save himself.

Damn his cursed honor, she thought. He would rather die than allow her to give herself to him with all that that must surely entail. Why could he not see that, far from viewing it as a sacrifice, she knew it to be her heart's desire?

No doubt it was some dark instinct born of desperation that prompted her to fling herself at Pinkney.

It was all rather like a dream, she thought. The pistol going off with a resounding crack, the sharp blow like that of a savage fist to her side that not only knocked the breath out of her, but hurled her in a wholly undignified heap to the ground. She did not think it in the least strange that she should hear the savage howl of a wolf somewhere behind her or that Pinkney should suddenly appear to be plucked from his feet as if he were a ragdoll and flung, screaming in abject terror, out of sight through the air. The crash of underbrush and the high-pitched wails of feminine fright receding in the distance told their own story.

It was Revelstoke, of course, she told herself, hoping that he would not be too long in coming back to her. She felt strangely heavy and yet light-headed, and she was aware of a spreading moist warmth along her side.

She felt the cold edge of fear as, above her, the stars, glimpsed through thinning mist and the branches of an oak tree, dimmed and receded in the first faint blush of gloaming. Where the devil was Revelstoke? she fretted, afraid he had decided not to come back to her. She struggled to lift herself, but had not the strength. Her head spinning, she fell back in a faint.

Consequently, she was only vaguely aware that someone had come to kneel beside her and, lifting her in powerful arms, bore her swiftly away from the scene of Pinkney's debacle.

There was, she decided, drifting in and out of awareness, something exceedingly satisfying about being held against a hard chest. She was quite sure she had never felt so snug or so marvelously secure before.

It came to her that, if this was all a dream, she had no wish to awaken.

Chapter Eight

The shriek swelled out of the depths of the night, a scream unlike anything Emma had ever heard before.

Startled, she jerked to full wakefulness and then, with an unwitting groan, to the pain, like a firebrand plunged into her side.

Revelstoke's curse rent the air.

"Good God," gasped Emma. "What in heaven's name was that?"

Grimly, Revelstoke kept to the pace. "Pinkney, if I am not mistaken. It would seem he has been made to realize the price of his noble intentions at the hands of his future in-laws."

"But then, they are alive, Revelstoke," she persisted, aware of a swift pang of joy at the realization, "you did not put a period to their existence."

She was awarded a mirthless smile for her astute observation. "I had other, more important matters to attend. Now save your strength. We are not out of the woods yet."

It seemed that Revelstoke was possessed of a peculiar ability to see in the dark as he made without pause through a maze of thickets and shrubs. Emma, who had lost all sense of direction, was more than a little startled when moments later she found herself once more before the marble tomb.

Unwittingly, Emma stiffened as Revelstoke made directly for the yawning maw.

His eyes, amber-lit with power, pierced her through. "The danger is not in there. It is behind us and drawing closer with every second." Holding her near, he peered into her face. "You must trust me, Emma. It is the last thing I shall ever ask of you."

Emma returned his look steadily. "But I do trust you, Revelstoke. You would never hurt me. It is the one thing I have known from the moment I laid eyes on you."

A shadow flickered across Revelstoke's strong features. "Then you are a deal greener than I imagined," he uttered harshly. "It was my intent to ravish you."

Revelstoke went abruptly still as Emma reached up to touch her palm gently to the side of his face. "I know," she said simply. Then, smiling, "Why do you think I came to Gloaminggate? I must say, my lord, so far, you have proven something of a challenge. I begin to wonder to what lengths I shall have to go to overcome your gentlemanly instincts."

"Little devil." His strong arms tightened about her. "You haven't the least notion what you are inviting."

"Perhaps not, my lord," Emma returned, suddenly sober. "On the other hand, I want very much to understand, if only you will instruct me."

Revelstoke stared into her face, turned gravely up to him. "I fear, Lady Blythe, you are about to learn a deal more than you bargained for."

Emma, however, appeared singularly unmoved at the prospect. Indeed, if anything, she gave every evidence of being entranced at the idea, Revelstoke noted wryly.

"I am about to become as you are, is that so bad?" she demanded tenderly. "Who is the monster—a man who was willing to suffer death for me or Pinkney and the Everstons who, wearing the appearance of respectability, thought nothing of killing your servant? And for what? For greed? My dearest Revelstoke, I have lived with a monster, and, believe me, you do not resemble him in the least."

"The devil, Emma. You are not listening to me. It will mean living always in the shadows, a secret life that sets one apart from all others."

Emma smiled, undeterred. "A shadow, yes. I saw it when you made your grand appearance in Wilfred's ballroom. It was a veil of concealment that drew me to you from the first. Have you forgotten who I am, my dearest Revelstoke? I am the Scandalous Lady Blythe. Feeling set apart is hardly a novelty to me. I daresay I shall not find it in the least burdensome with you at my side. You will have to find a more convincing argument to dissuade me, I'm afraid. And pray do not fling your mysterious powers up at me. I freely confess I find them altogether appealing."

By the devil, she would, his indomitable Lady Blythe, thought Revelstoke, feeling himself on the brink of defeat. "They are powers of which you never dreamed, my little termagant. But they are powers of darkness."

"Oh, Leopold," exclaimed Emma, as close as she had ever been to being wholly out of patience with him. "Are you truly so blind that you do not see? I have been living in darkness for as long as I can remember, and now at last I am neither alone nor afraid. I look at you, and I see, not a monster, but the man I was destined to love. If that is darkness, then I most willingly embrace it."

The words seemed to hang in the air, like an echo of a promise made long ago. "Willingly would I embrace the darkness, if I knew one day we could be together again. And we shall, Leopold, I swear it. If there is a God in heaven, I will come back to you."

She had come back to him in sweet, fiery Emma, who had just opened the door to him. And, still, the dark lord of Revelstoke hesitated. Once he carried her across the threshold of the gloaminggate, there would be no turning back for her again.

"Think, Emma, of all that you will be giving up for me. If you cross the threshold, it means never having children. You will never know what it is to have a child at your breast."

"I shall never know that on this side either, Revelstoke, and it was not you who took that away from me. It was Wynford in one of his drunken rages. He killed the life that was growing inside of me, and then he had the decency to kill himself. And, now," she added, leaning her head wearily against his shoulder, "I think it is time you accepted the fact that I am yours, just as you promised I should be. My dearest Leopold, I shall most certainly die if you do not soon make up your mind."

"Little devil," growled Revelstoke, stepping across the threshold. "By all the fires of hell, I love you."

"I know, Leopold," Emma murmured wearily back at him. "I have always known. It is what drew me back to Dunnecombe. That and the promise I made to Maggie Macpherson. So long as I live, she will not die. Together, my love, we shall give her the gift of immortality."

The Full of the Moon

Janice Bennett

Chapter One

Miss Juliana Wittingdon froze beside the green velvet drapes at the edge of the ballroom. The dance floor, unusually crowded for so dark and dreary an October night in the Little Season, offered no hope for escape. She could only stand stiff and forbidding as Captain Lysander Woolsey—Captain Sharp, more like—bore steadily down on her.

It was she he sought, no doubt of that. He wended his purposeful way through the outermost line of dancers in their silks and laces, his burly figure forcing ladies and gentlemen alike from his path, his steady gaze never wavering from her. She turned away. She dreaded the thought of a confrontation here, where her ready temper would betray her into unseemly behavior. Such as scratching his eyes out. Appealing, of course, but it wouldn't be at all the thing.

She had taken no more than two steps back the way she had come when a hand closed over the tiny puff sleeve of her amber crepe overdress. The unwelcome tenor voice demanded: "Miss Wittingdon, a word with you."

She directed a chill gaze over her shoulder. "A word? That much I can allow, but you have already used more than that, I fear."

His full lips formed a smile that failed to reach his eyes. "Ever the jokester, are you not?"

"I usually mean exactly what I say." She inclined her head in a dismissive gesture. "If you will excuse me? I am looking for my cousin."

"He is in a set on the far side of the floor, you will not be able to speak with him at the moment. I, on the other hand, am not only available but very eager to have a word—ah, you objected to that phrase already, as I recall. Let us say a quiet coze, then, shall we?"

The devil take Bertram for leaving her in such a pass, she fumed, with a want of propriety that would have put her gentle aunt, had she known of it, to the blush.

Captain Woolsey glanced around, and determination gleamed in his dark eyes. "The perfect place. And not a soul is looking our way." He swept back the heavy velvet hanging to reveal an open French door leading onto a tiny balcony which overlooked Half Moon Street.

Juliana pulled away, but he transferred his grasp to her elbow and thrust her through into the cold night air. The dark green folds of cloth fell behind him as he joined her on the narrow ledge with its cast iron railing, and she shivered. The strains of a country dance drifted after them, almost muffled by the babble of voices.

He stood squarely in front of the doorway, blocking any hope she might have of escape. "Much better," he announced.

"That's a matter of opinion," she snapped back. "Is it your desire to create a scandal, sir? Or simply to have me catch a chill?"

He held up a hand. "Pray forgive me. I desired a few moments of your undivided attention, that is all."

"Are you so sure of that?" she muttered, but not for him to hear.

THE FULL OF THE MOON

Unctuous charm oozed from him. "I have been speaking to your cousin Bertie."

"More's the pity," she stuck in, using that same low tone.

If he heard her words, he ignored them and forged ahead. "He tells me you took exception to that harmless little expedition on which I escorted him."

"You took him to a gaming hell! Any person of sense would object to that."

"Miss Wittingdon—Juliana, if I may—"

"You may not!" she interrupted.

His smile stiffened, but never left his face. "Miss Wittingdon," he resumed. "You misunderstand the situation. Mrs. Newbury's is not some establishment but simply a house, no more than that, on my word of honor. A house where card parties are held upon occasion. There is no harm in that."

She fixed him with a steely gaze. "I may be a miss fresh from the country, but I am not the naive rustic for which you take me. I am perfectly aware what sort of establishment that is, *and* what sort of people frequent it."

"I assure you, it is of the highest *ton!*"

"And so is your Mrs. Newbury? I am fully aware of the meaning of the expression 'Haymarket ware', Captain Woolsey."

He flushed. "That is hardly seemly—"

"I also know the meaning of 'uphills', and I can recognize an 'ivory turner' when I see one."

His color deepened. "My dear Miss Wittingdon, what you can possibly know of such matters—"

The curtain parted behind him, and he broke off and spun around. A wave of menace washed outward, and Juliana took a step back, pressing herself against the metal rail.

In the doorway stood a tall, broad-shouldered Corinthian, elegant in a coat of burgundy velvet, black satin knee breeches and white stockings. His fair hair, striking in its thickness and unusual length, curled back from his high forehead. His neckcloth, crisp with the perfect creases of the Mathematical, gleamed white at his throat. A single blood red ruby nestled in its folds. Juliana's hands gripped the iron support behind her.

The Corinthian's penetrating gaze swept dismissively over Captain Woolsey and came to rest on Juliana. Her throat dried, and she swallowed convulsively. Little frightened her, these days, and people, never. Before her stood the exception.

"Miss Wittingdon, is it not?" His deep voice commanded attention without being raised. "I thought I could not be mistaken. How pleasant to encounter you again so soon."

Pleasant for whom? The hazy thought drifted through her mind. With an effort, she shook off the mesmerizing effect he had on her and stared blankly into a face that seemed all sharp angles and planes. The myriad candles in their glittering chandeliers stood to his back, shielding his shadowed face from a closer scrutiny. Here on the balcony, not even starlight filtered through the clouds on this moonless night. Yet she could see him well enough to know she did not recognize him. Uneasiness rippled through her at this total blank that filled her mind, at the dreadful possibility she might have suffered another lapse of memory.

Woolsey stirred. "You interrupt, sir," he said, though his tone lacked conviction.

The man ignored him. With his disconcerting gaze still on Juliana's face, he raised his eyebrows. "I am chagrined, Miss Wittingdon. I seem to possess no hold on your memory. I am Ramsdell, and I had the pleasure of making your acquaintance only a few nights ago, at Lady Lowestoft's."

"You attended Lady Lowestoft's soiree?" Woolsey demanded of Juliana, his voice tinged with envy.

Juliana cast him a withering glance and turned back

to the gentleman who still blocked the curtain. He had reassured her about herself, at least. Now if she could only be sure of him, of why he unnerved her, and why he pretended to an acquaintance they certainly did not possess.

Playing along to find out threatened an element of danger, yet it seemed infinitely preferable to remaining in the company of Captain Lysander Woolsey. Mastering her unaccustomed trepidation, she extended her hand. "Of course." But the smile that accompanied her words held a wealth of challenge.

Ramsdell bowed over her fingers, taking them in one hand while he continued to hold back the curtain with the other. "A breath of fresh air becomes a necessity, does it not? As does a glass of lemonade for a parched throat. Would you care to accompany me in search of refreshment? You must be quite chilled by now." He released her and offered his arm.

Her decision took no more than a moment. She awarded Woolsey a dismissive nod. "Pray hold me excused."

The gamester's mouth tightened, but he made no attempt to keep her. She took Ramsdell's arm and accompanied him back into the ballroom; no impropriety there, he had stood so as to be clearly visible the entire time. Discretion? He seemed to her a man who would not care a fig for the opinion of others. Or perhaps one of whom others would not dare to hold opinions. An instinct to turn tail and run mingled with fascination. He intrigued her—and she very much wanted to know what he was about.

She fluttered her lashes in a deliberate mockery of flirtation. "Perhaps you will be so good as to explain the reason for your effrontery? I am not so much as acquainted with Lady Lowestoft, and I certainly did not attend her soiree."

"Neither did I," came his amused response. "Like you, I have not yet been introduced to the lady."

That brought her to a stop. "Nor have you been to me," she pointed out. She would have remembered him, no matter the circumstances; of that she no longer entertained any doubts. The piercing smile he directed at her left her breathless, but whether with nerves or interest, she couldn't tell. He filled her awareness, making the music, the flickering lights, the subtle scents of perfumes and pomades seem to vanish. Only one scent reached her. His. And she couldn't place its subtle yet compelling components.

She dragged her attention back to the matter at hand. "How did you know my name? To my certain knowledge, I have never met you before."

"Not yet." He spoke softly, but his tone possessed a force that somehow made the simple words a vow. Then a smile glinted in the depths of his turbulent blue eyes and suddenly—unexpectedly—spread to encompass his entire being. "I heard him speak it through the curtain before I intruded. I acted out of the purest chivalry, I assure you."

She stiffened. "If you mean—"

He stopped her with no more than a quirked eyebrow. "I saw him accost you, I saw you pull away, and I saw him propel you through the curtain."

"You— Oh, the devil take the man! Do you mean he made a spectacle of us? The entire ballroom—" She cast an appalled glance around to see if even now she were the cynosure of condemning gazes. She could *not* let her aunt be so distressed.

"No." Amusement rippled just beneath the surface of his words. "I noticed you by the merest chance. No one else saw. Would you care for that lemonade, now?"

She glanced at him sideways. He disturbed her, in a manner that made her want to escape from his company as quickly as possible—yet also to remain at his side. The latter, she decided, might prove far too dangerous. Steeling herself, she awarded him an artificially bright smile.

"When we haven't been properly introduced? I am not so lost to all propriety." She inclined her head and strolled away.

But not without a pang of regret.

Chapter Two

It took Ahlric, Lord Ramsdell, only three minutes to reach the side of his hostess in the crowded ballroom, but over twenty minutes more passed before he secured her services to perform the desired introduction. Everyone present, it seemed, had chosen this precise moment to exchange words with, or seek assistance from, the Dowager Lady Leeds. Ramsdell could drive them away at once, of course, but he had no desire to instill terror in these poor, sheep-like people. Instead, he tried to compose his soul into patience, only to discover he possessed very little of that commodity. He compromised by planting subtle suggestions into yielding minds, suggestions that took many of the inopportune guests elsewhere, though they would never, later, be quite sure why.

At last, the woman's impressive figure, swathed in yards of purple satin, turned from a doddering old roue. A gleam lingered in her eye as she looked Ramsdell up and down appraisingly. "Enjoying yourself?" she demanded in the forthright manner that had earned her the enviable position as the *ton's* most original—and devastating—hostess.

"Can't say I've ever been to an Italian ball, myself. Finding our ways strange?"

"Refreshing. I have a favor to ask," he said, cutting straight to the chase. "Will you introduce me to a certain young lady?"

Lady Leeds snorted. "Should have known. That's all you young bucks ever want. That, or a tip on who to back in the next race or prize fight. Which young lady, then?"

"Miss Wittingdon. I believe she is here with her cousin." Whose name, unfortunately, he didn't know.

Not so his hostess. Lady Leeds nodded, setting the dyed pink ostrich plume in her turban swaying with vigor. "The Paigntons. Bertie, the cousin would be. Well, where are they, then?"

She started forth without awaiting his answer, and her guests moved from her path as if clearing the way for a battle ship under full sail. Just as well, Ramsdell reflected as he strode in her mighty wake; tonight he did not suffer the vagaries of others with any tolerance. Odd, when he had long ago learned to regard the world with a calm detachment.

Lady Leeds paused, frowning, looking about her gratifyingly crowded room. "Now where—?" she murmured.

Ramsdell closed his eyes, listening for a vocal tone he would not forget, reaching with preternaturally keen senses. Somewhere, he would detect her presence. Somewhere— Then cutting through the babble of irrelevant voices came the sound of laughter, *her* laughter. The throaty, captivating ripple of amusement carried to his straining ears, drawing him like a siren's call.

But it held an underlying note of sorrow, of hollowness. Something bothered this delightful creature, and that fact caused him an unexpected wrench. Had he, on that balcony, interrupted a situation more serious than an importunate jackanapes inflicting his unwelcome person on a young lady?

He grasped Lady Leeds's arm. "This way," he announced, and started forth. He continued to focus his hearing, and caught the musical cadence of Miss Wittingdon's speech though not her actual words. The thought flashed across his mind that he could listen to that sweet sound for hours.

A scarlet-coated half-pay officer blocked their way. Fuming at this further delay, Ramsdell implanted a silent suggestion in the man's mind; the lieutenant looked about, then strolled off aimlessly as if he had forgotten what he was doing. Ramsdell paid him no further heed. He guided Lady Leeds forward, and there sat Miss Wittingdon at the edge of the dance floor, her head bent close in animated conversation with a youthful gentleman whose most commanding feature appeared to be his good-natured countenance. Their matching dark auburn hair, high cheekbones and straight noses bespoke the closeness of their familial relationship.

As if the intensity of his mood touched her like a physical force, she looked up, straight at him, startled surprise clouding her warm brown eyes. The eyes of a puppy, the thought flashed through his mind.

Lady Leeds strode forward, wasting no more than an acknowledging nod to young Paignton. "Miss Wittingdon," she declared, ignoring mere pleasantries. "May I present Lord Ramsdell to you as a suitable partner for the next set?" She cast an amused glance at Ramsdell. "That what you wanted?"

Ramsdell awarded her a half bow. "It will do very well. If Miss Wittingdon is willing?"

Young Paignton leaned a fraction closer to his cousin. "Well, Jewel! The mysterious baron, no less. You're doing well for yourself this night," he mouthed in a tone that would defy normal hearing.

Ramsdell, as his acquaintances had occasionally remarked, possessed the uncanny hearing abilities of a night-hunting predator. He pretended to take no notice. Instead, he held out his hand to Miss Wittingdon, his eyebrows quirked in amused challenge. "Is this sufficient introduction for you?"

"You are very prompt, sir." Soft color tinged her pale cheeks a becoming rose. She met his steady gaze fleetingly, then lowered her scrutiny to the clenched hands of her kidskin gloves.

"Go on, ninny!" Again, young Paignton whispered the words, this time accompanying them with a nudge of his elbow.

Miss Wittingdon cast her cousin a fulminating look, then rose, shaking out the creased skirts of her gauze overdress. The material clung gently to her slender figure, and Ramsdell's blood stirred. Prudently, he transferred his gaze to her face, which seemed to be filled by her incredible eyes. He'd been right; they were like a puppy's, deeply soulful and filled with warmth and understanding. When he looked into them, he saw all the love and sorrow that usually only came to one with old age. They fascinated him.

"It is quite warm in here, is it not?" she said with demur blandness. She placed just the tips of her fingers on his offered elbow.

The sheer insipidness of her remark piqued his curiosity. He murmured a polite rejoinder as he led her toward the floor, and noted how she maintained a decorous distance between them. Where was the fiery miss he had encountered little more than half an hour earlier? Now, in comparison, she seemed a shadowed, unworthy copy of the original.

Or a sorely troubled one.

Just what had he interrupted on that balcony? If he were any judge of character—which he knew himself to be— she was more than capable of handling any number of mere importunate fools. Determination welled in him to discover what troubled Miss Juliana Wittingdon. And that fact set off alarum bells within his head.

She took up her position opposite to him in the lines

that formed. "It is quite crowded for this time of year, is it not?" Her lashes lowered, hiding from him those sorrowful windows into her soul.

So, she intended to keep him at a distance. That knowledge annoyed him. Normally, the pattern of movements of a country dance, so ideal for casual flirtations, suited him to perfection. Not this time. He seethed as they separated, exchanged partners with another couple, then returned to their original positions.

"The weather has turned quite chilly for so early in October, do you not think?" This time, she accompanied her words with an artificially sweet smile as they briefly came together.

"I find it stimulating," he shot back when next they drew close.

If she noted the sting of his words, she made no sign. "I believe I heard someone say that you had but newly arrived from Italy."

Never before had he experienced such frustration in small talk; he gave shorter shrift than usual to his tale of living his entire life abroad and now coming home to this unknown land to claim title and estates. And never before had the lies appeared so patently transparent to his own ears. Miss Wittingdon murmured the correct responses of no more than polite interest, and it was with considerable relief that he heard the string quartet end the last measure.

Now, perhaps, he could make some headway; he wasn't the least bit ready to relinquish her. He cast his thoughts about for some reason to detain her, some way to break through her reserve. Some way that did not involve his subtle forms of coercion. He wanted to learn more about what could subdue such a vital spirit as hers, but he wanted the information shared willingly.

"If you will excuse me?" She started to draw away.

"Wait." Only one idea occurred to him. "Will you join me in a game of cards?"

Her eyes flashed. "I do not find that the least bit amusing."

Ahhhh.... A return to the liveliness he found so enthralling. He allowed his lips to twitch into what he hoped to be a disarming smile. "I may be out of practice by your standards, but I assure you, I am not thought to play that ill."

Again, becoming color rushed to her cheeks. "I didn't mean—Oh, the devil! You couldn't know, could you?"

"Not if you don't tell me," he pointed out.

At that, she actually smiled, albeit faintly. "You perhaps recall that so-called gentleman with whom I conversed earlier? He is a gamester. A Captain Sharp. I believe the term is," she added hastily.

He nodded. "And having dealt with one, you are not anxious to take on another? You may see for yourself I am not of his ilk."

She hesitated. "I suppose there could be nothing wrong in a hand. It has been such a while since I've had an able opponent." A touch of longing crept into the last words.

Again, he offered his arm, and this time, to his pleasure, she placed her fingers on his elbow willingly enough. As he led her from the ballroom, he asked, "Does your cousin not play?"

She gave a short, bitter laugh. "Let us say he does not play well enough."

The card room—normally a large, elegant drawing room appointed in shades of crimson and gold—stood across the narrow hall. Only four elderly gentlemen sat about one of the numerous tables in the far corner, intent upon a game of whist. Ramsdell led her to the opposite end of the room. He seated her, then picked up the provided deck and sorted out the lower pips.

She folded her hands on the green baize cloth before her and watched him through narrowed eyes as he began to shuffle. "You're certainly no stranger to the pasteboards."

"I'm no gamester, either." Yet, to tell the truth—which

he wasn't about to do—he'd spent far more hours than he cared to remember at this pastime.

She inclined her head in acceptance of his statement, and he experienced a rush of satisfaction. He had cleared the first hurdle; she no longer held him at a cool distance. For that matter, she showed no missish constraint or embarrassment at being virtually isolated with an unknown gentleman. All in all, a unique young lady.

He dealt, flipping two cards at a time into place with practiced ease, and watched covertly as she examined her hand. She was no stranger, either, it seemed, to the intricacies of piquet. Not for a moment did she hesitate over her choice of discards, and no trace of a betraying expression touched her features as she drew two replacements from the stock.

His own hand would do quite well, he decided. Declining his turn to discard, he instead turned an enigmatic smile on Miss Wittingdon. "Your point?"

"Six," came her prompt response. "Will that do?"

"Only if they score more than fifty-eight."

"Yours, then," she conceded. "What of a run of five?"

"You have the better of me, there." His gaze rested on the serenity of her face. Artificial, of course. A measure of tension remained within her, strong enough for him to sense across the narrow space that separated him. Not fear; no, nothing so blatant. Unease. But not on his account. Something disturbed her, and he sensed her determination to resolve the matter in short order.

"Will three aces serve?" she asked.

Her soft voice drew him out of his reflections. "Not against all four kings, I fear."

They declared their scores, and Miss Wittingdon led to the first trick. She took it, and as she led again, he ventured, "It is your cousin that troubles you, is it not?"

She stiffened. "It is naught that need concern you."

"But it does you?"

She met his gaze squarely, her eyes cold. "My dear sir—"

she began, only to break off and look away. "It is of no moment." She drew a card at random from her hand and tossed it on the table.

His words, it seemed, had hit home. He took the trick with studied casualness. "It is no easy thing to see one so young in the hands of a gullcatcher."

"How—?" She broke off. "Is it so obvious?"

"A lucky guess. I have encountered Captain Woolsey, you see." He smiled. "And young gentlemen are notoriously loathe to listen to advice from their female relatives. In fact," he added, musingly, "the better the advice, the more reluctant they are to listen."

That brought a fleeting smile to her lips. "You speak from your own experiences, I must suppose?"

"My own lamentable experiences. Has he no other well-wisher who might intervene for you?"

"My uncle—" For a moment, a touch of fondness softened her expression, only to fade at once. "He thinks Captain Woolsey"—she said the name with a tinge of disgust—"a capital fellow. Uncle William is such a dear, only so unworldly."

As if she, who could be no more than a mere eighteen, and by her own confession a country miss into the bargain, were up to every rig and row in town. "He'll be guided by no one but this so-called captain?"

"He thinks the world of him!" An exasperated sigh escaped her. "He believes him to be a regular out-and-outer, a—a cool hand, a veritable Trojan!"

"Whereas you know him to be a curst rum touch." Their game having ended, almost unnoticed by either of them, he swept the cards together and shuffled once more.

She watched with an abstracted frown creasing her brow as he dealt the cards. "What I need," she said at last as she examined her new hand, "is to get poor Bertie to see the truth, to realize what a—a *nodcock* he is being!"

"I can think of only one way," he said slowly, surprising himself, "to do the trick." Damn it all, what the devil was he contemplating? To go against a lifetime's policy of avoiding involvement? And for what? A pair of puppy eyes that threatened his security—his hard-won control? That could only lead to danger—and not for himself.

She leaned back in her chair, her brow furrowed in thought, but her remarkably soulful eyes gleaming with a sudden flicker of alertness. "Have you a suggestion?"

A prudent man, he told himself sternly, would murmur something vague and withdraw at this juncture. And over the years he had become, above all else, an extremely prudent man. What absurd impulse had induced him to contemplate intervening in the affairs of people who only an hour or so ago had been completely unknown to him? And what induced this strong-willed young lady to look upon him—*him* of all people!—as a potential ally?

"You will need the help of a gentleman," he heard himself saying.

"Nonsense!" She hunched an indignant shoulder. "I am very well able to take care of my own."

She even gave him the chance to retreat! Irrationally, this only increased his determination to be of assistance. He studied his cards for a moment, then folded them together. "Very well, if you think you can hold sway over your cousin in a matter he is bound to see as a gentleman's pursuit, I wish you every success. Should you decide you need help, I shall be happy to offer my services."

Her teeth closed about her lower lip, giving her a touchingly vulnerable look. Still, her eyes flashed her irritation. Abruptly she rose. "I thank you for your offer, but I most fervently hope I shall not need to trespass on your kindness. If you will excuse me?"

He caught her gaze, allowing himself one brief moment of compelling force to hold it. "We will speak again later."

She returned no answer. She merely stared at him, her expression unreadable, until the silence became palpable between them. Then with a curt nod, she turned on her heel and strode from the room.

His gaze followed her retreating figure, lingering on the animal-like grace of her movements. A young lady of fire and determination, of spirit and pride. And they *would* talk again later.

He didn't know whether to be pleased or angered at his having assured that one more conversation with her.

Chapter Three

Ramsdell stood before the gilt-edged mirror in the card room and glowered at his reflection under the pretences of adjusting the intricate folds of his neckcloth. What the devil had possessed him? he wondered. That he—*he,* of all people—should have offered to interfere in a matter that had no bearing upon himself.

His fingers slowed in their creasing. Only one reason existed for his having behaved in so unprecedented a manner. He had *wanted* to help.

That fact took several seconds to sink in. He had actually wanted to help someone. What, in the name of all that was holy, had happened to him? Many more years ago than he cared to count, he had learned the necessity of remaining remote from his fellow creatures. He tried not to injure anyone, of course, but circumstances had forced him to design his life around himself and his own demanding needs. This had been his way for so long, he'd forgotten what it was to put himself out for another. It terrified the life out of him.

Terrified the life out of him! He gave a short, hollow laugh, attracting fleeting glances from the elderly occupants across the room. If only something *could* terrify the life out of him—or for that matter, remove its never ending, frequently torturous, presence by any other means! He, Ahlric, ninth Baron Ramsdell. Ninth baron, indeed. Fourth, more like. Not to mention fifth, sixth, seventh, and eighth, as well. And then there would be tenth, eleventh, and all the rest still to come, further ahead than he had any desire to see.

He turned away, unable to face his reflected image. It hadn't been so bad, thirty years ago. Then society expected a gentleman to paint his face and be fashionably pale. Now, though, one was expected to be a rugged outdoorsman, a Corinthian, a regular top-of-the-trees. No easy feat for a man who lay involuntarily comatose during the hours of daylight.

He strode into the narrow hall where he paused, reluctant to enter the ballroom once more. Only the thought that Miss Juliana Wittingdon danced somewhere within drew him onward. He had no intention of letting her slip away without speaking to her once more.

He halted just inside the door of the crowded room, forcing himself to adjust again to the overwhelming sensory onslaught. The crystal drops of the chandeliers glittered with reflected light, casting a dazzling brilliance over the sea of people beneath, hurting eyes adapted for searching through the darkest recesses of the night. The babble of voices and the vibrating resonance of the strings assaulted ears attuned to the faintest rustling of leaves or twigs. Ramsdell made the conscious effort to protect his hypersensitive senses, to isolate himself. And to isolate *her*.

Lights, colors, sounds, all faded back to bearable levels. He moved forward, feeling for her with his mind. Nowhere did he hear the melodic strains of her voice, the laughter that sent an unexpected warmth through him; still, an awareness of her nearness filled him. Unerringly, he turned to the left, and found her in a set on the far side of the room, partnered by an eager young officer. Satisfied, Ramsdell strolled to the refreshment table to wait.

When the music at last stopped, he simply stared at her. Not by any sign did she indicate if she were aware of his unwavering scrutiny; she merely disentangled herself from her erstwhile partner and wended her way through the milling crowd directly to Ramsdell's side.

He held out a glass of lemonade which he had waiting for her, and she took it with a word of thanks. She led the way toward the curtained balcony, then stood before the velvet drapes and took a long swallow of the beverage. Only the slightest tinge of perspiration touched her brow and cheekbones, but it bestowed a softly highlighted glow to her delicate features that caused his pulse to increase. A totally unrelated gleam lit her eyes.

"I fear," she said at last, and with considerable reluctance, "that the assistance of a gentleman will indeed be necessary."

"And that fact causes you no little distress."

Her lips twitched into a reluctant smile. "I would rather manage affairs on my own," she admitted. "But the world takes a dim view of females taking such matters into their own hands."

"Possibly the world fears the result," he murmured.

"And well it should! If I could get my—" She broke off and stared at her gloved hands, with their long slender fingers. "Yes, I would dearly love to deal with Captain Lysander Woolsey. But it would not be *comme il faut.*" She sighed.

He repressed a smile. "I am sorry if it distresses you so greatly."

She shook her head. "I would not cause my uncle and his dear wife the agony of a scandal. So I am forced to accept your kind offer. If, in fact, you meant it?" She cast him a sideways glance through thick auburn lashes.

"I never offer something I don't mean." More fool he.

Again, her lips twitched. "I gained the impression you

generally do just as you please. Now," she went on in a hushed, determined tone. "I've concocted a plan."

"Why," he mused aloud, "do I have the feeling I should run while I'm still able?"

"Idiot!" She turned her gaze on the new sets that formed on the dance floor. "I could not help but notice that you seem to be rather good with a deck of cards."

He inclined his head. "I am not one to be flummoxed."

"But you could do the—er, *flummoxing*, should there be a need?"

Comprehension dawned. "You would have me play the role of a wolf in sheep's clothing to your cousin's downfall?"

A deep flush spread across her cheeks, and her hands clenched the stem of her glass. She took a rapid sip of the liquid. "That—that's one way to put it, I suppose. And yes. I want you to lure my Cousin Bertie into an evening of cards. And I want him to lose heavily—so heavily, he won't have any doubts about the trouble he is in. I want him to fear both you and the consequences. And—" She broke off, glanced at him, then away quickly. "I want you to do the same for Captain Woolsey, just to prove to Bertie how fallible his friend is. Do you think you could outflummox a man who earns his livelihood at plucking deluded and gullible pigeons?"

Ramsdell made a show of considering, though in fact it would be no difficult feat at all to implant subtle suggestions into the mind of the easily led Bertie Paignton—or even that of the dislikeable Woolsey. At last, he inquired, "Have you decided on when and where this fleecing is to take place? Or for that matter, how I am to issue the invitation to two gentlemen whose acquaintance I have not had the honor of making?"

"As soon as possible," she declared, answering the first of the questions. "As for where, I believe I know of a quiet house where card parties are held, and a gentleman may hold his own bank at faro."

His eyebrows quirked up. "How on earth would you know anything of the sort?"

She drained her glass, then studied the empty cup. "I've heard it mentioned. A Mrs. Glasdon's, off Jermyn Street. It is most discreet, but I believe we would be granted *entre.*"

"You amaze me. And the introduction to your cousin and his despicable friend?"

"Why not now? They are just heading out the door. If we move quickly," and she started forward as she spoke, "we might catch them before they embark on a game of cards."

And that, he noted as he followed her determined figure, she seemed anxious to do. Across the room, he could just see the tall, dark-haired figure of Captain Lysander Woolsey disappearing through the doorway with the shorter, auburn-haired Bertie Paignton at his side. Ramsdell increased his pace, overtook Miss Wittingdon, and led the way once more across the hall and into the card room.

The two men were just seating themselves at a table when Miss Wittingdon hurried toward them. Bertie Paignton looked up, and an amiable smile lit his young face. "Jewel!" he cried gaily. "Didn't think anything would take you away from the dancing. Care to join us?"

Captain Woolsey had also glanced up, but Ramsdell would describe his expression as calculating rather than welcoming. The man rearranged his features to speak an affable word to Miss Wittingdon, but he did not add his own invitation to her cousin's.

"Oh, I've already had a game of piquet this evening," Miss Wittingdon assured her cousin blithely. "It was quite delightful. So much so, that I made certain you would like to meet my opponent. Lord Ramsdell," she turned courteously to him, "I should like to present my cousin, Mr. Bertram Paignton, and his friend, Captain Woolsey. Bertie, he's such a dab hand, you really must play him!"

"Really?" Bertie flushed as he gazed up into Ramsdell's

face. "I—I should like that of all things, of course, but at the moment I'm promised to Woolsey, here."

Ramsdell offered up his most affable smile. Miss Wittingdon, he noted, withdrew a trifle; yet he sensed her penetrating gaze on him—judging, no doubt, whether or not she had been saddled with a competent co-conspirator. Well, she would see.

He sprang his trap. "Pity. In Italy I found little opportunity of playing anything other than piquet with my father. I've been quite looking forward to trying my hand at faro. Perhaps one of you could introduce me to a likely partner?"

Woolsey's eyes narrowed. "Good heavens, man, you've never played?"

Ramsdell shrugged negligently. "Once or twice. My father felt I should know the rules, but he wasn't the least bit keen on it, himself."

"Look, Woolsey." Bertie Paignton leaned forward. "Why don't you start a bank? Low stakes, what do you say? It'll be fun."

The silly cub was a trifle above par, Ramsdell realized. Just muddled enough to believe himself to be still level headed. Ripe for plucking. Though if Woolsey sought to entangle another, perhaps Paignton would be spared this night.

Woolsey studied Ramsdell for a long moment, then nodded. "Unless you would like to hold the bank?" he asked, which Ramsdell declined.

Miss Wittingdon, who had stood a little apart, stepped forward now, wide-eyed and suspiciously innocent. "Might I join? Oh, please, Bertie, I should like it of all things, and there can be nothing wrong, playing at a private ball, and with my own cousin!"

Ramsdell threw her a veiled but forbidding look. "I doubt—" he began.

"By Jove!" Bertie exclaimed, interrupting in his delight.

"What a girl you are for surprises. No milk and water miss, are you? Woolsey, we will be four."

Woolsey explained the game, with frequent additions and digressions from Bertie, creating a confusing result. Ramsdell listened with pretended concentration, all the while watching Woolsey set up a layout from the spade suite of a spare deck. Bertie shuffled, to Miss Wittingdon went the honor of cutting, then Woolsey took the pack and ran his hands lovingly over the pasteboard surfaces. To Ramsdell's certain knowledge, two cards subtly changed places. An experienced cheat, as Miss Wittingdon suspected.

But not as experienced as he, Ramsdell reflected some half hour later. Woolsey lacked finesse. Tonight, though, the time was not yet ripe to turn the tables and fleece this wolf.

Smiling cheerfully, Ramsdell placed another bet and watched it evaporate like the vast majority of the preceding ones. Miss Wittingdon lost with pretty dismay, and cried out with untrammeled delight on those rare occasions when her penny wagers resulted in success. An excellent dissimulator; Ramsdell filed that fact away for later contemplation.

Only Bertie seemed distressed by his meager losses. "Always the same," he fumed as the last turn ended. "It's not the amount," he protested as his cousin pointed out that he had lost barely a pound. "It's my curst luck!"

Woolsey laughed. "My friend, it cannot stay bad. Tomorrow, undoubtedly, you will come about."

"Perhaps a change of venue might help," Ramsdell suggested. He drew a chased silver snuff box from his pocket, flicked it open with his thumb, then offered it to Bertie. The young man stammered his thanks, took too big a pinch, and went off in a fit of sneezing. Woolsey took a more decorous amount, and Ramsdell helped himself before snapping the box shut. Bertie had flushed scarlet in embarrassment, and bore every resemblance to a hunted creature searching for a hole in which to go to earth.

"Do you know," Ramsdell went on as if the idea had just come to him, "tomorrow I think I should like to visit a rather exclusive little house I've been hearing about this night. Why don't you join me, Paignton?"

"An exclusive house?" Bertie's crestfallen demeanor fell away. "By Jupiter, I should rather think so! The only place I know is the one where I go with Woolsey. That is—" He broke off, casting a dismayed glance at Woolsey. "You see, we'd already decided—"

Woolsey frowned. "I'm rather partial to Mrs. Newbury's. You're welcome to join us there, Ramsdell."

Ramsdell shrugged a careless shoulder. "I hear this new place is all the go. You might like to give it a try, Woolsey."

Bertie, still flushed and flattered, turned eagerly on his friend. "Why don't we, Woolsey? Maybe the change is just what I need!"

Ramsdell rose. "You have built up my confidence. Tomorrow, I shall hold the bank. Promise me you will lend me your company."

A muscle near the corner of Woolsey's mouth twitched, as if he tried to contain some emotion. "It sounds a delightful evening," he relented at last. "I feel certain we will not be missed in the least from our other engagement. I must thank you."

"Then it's settled." Ramsdell named the time and location.

Miss Wittingdon artfully smothered a yawn. "Bertie, I beg of you, find your mama. I am quite done in, I fear." She bestowed a dazzlingly false smile on Woolsey and Ramsdell. "You must hold us excused."

Bertie, apparently oblivious to her neatly removing him from Woolsey, bounded off to find his parent.

While the Paigntons and Miss Wittingdon made ready to depart, Ramsdell lingered near the main hall, watching. The cousins showed affectionate and teasing solicitude in assisting the older woman on with her shawl, and the words that reached him held a bantering note. There could be no mistaking the love and caring between them.

An ache crept through him at so simple a joy as having close relatives. He'd had two sisters once, so very long ago. Mary had died of a fever before she'd reached her twelfth year. Catherine had married and borne three children before succumbing to complications with that last birth. Her children had married and produced families of their own before he'd lost track of them. Somewhere, he mused, he probably did have relatives. But they would hardly welcome him with open arms.

On that depressing thought, he took his leave of his hostess and wandered out into the chill October night, heading for his rooms on Albemarle Street. He passed beneath the glow of one of the gas-lit street lamps, then back into the comforting darkness. Clouds hung low in the sky, obliterating the stars. There wouldn't be any moon; tonight it was in its phase of full darkness. A night of near safety for the hunted creatures of the earth. A night when his own predatory instincts lay almost dormant. A good night.

A few minutes of stretching his legs served to restore his spirits; he'd long ago grown reconciled to his solitary state. He even, in an odd sort of way, had come to enjoy this peculiar life he led. Though parts of it he found more enjoyable than others.

Such as coming home to England again. These English autumn nights were agreeably long, ideal for the dusk to dawn existence he must lead. He drew a deep breath, luxuriating in the feeling of the chilled droplets of fog filling his throat and lungs. Every scent, every sound, reminded him he was once again in England, land of his birth. He would willingly spend the rest of his days here—if that were not impossible.

His pace slowed. To spend the rest of his days in this one place, in his own home. He hardened his heart to that insidious longing. After all, his existence wasn't one of unalleviated wandering. He could remain in one place for the span of a normal life—provided he were careful with face paints and never kept a curious manservant too long in his employ. But there invariably came a time when his current gaming cronies began to comment that although his hair had turned gray, his countenance showed remarkably few of the ravages of age. And then, once again, it would be time to move on.

This time it had happened in Munich, toward the end of June. He had paid off both his mistress and his valet, washed the dye from his hair and the theatrical makeup from his face, and once again bore the visage of a young man not yet thirty.

And this time, he had regarded the prospect of starting over again with eager anticipation. The last twenty-eight years he had spent on the Continent; that meant he now could return to England and to Ramsdell Grange, the estate he had inherited from his father in 1596. As soon as he had set foot on his native soil, he had headed directly to his beloved home, to view the changes—and rejoice in what had remained the same under his steward's guardianship.

And all the while, he had to maintain the pretext of viewing his property for the first time. As far as his servants knew, he was his own son, born on a mythical Italian estate to a mother none of them had ever met. He had repeated this farce far too many times during the course of his long and lonely life. Since that long regretted night in 1591, when a fatally attractive gypsy girl had shared with him her curse of vampirism, his life had been one long, complex lie.

At least now he was home again—if only for a few years. So why did he have to add to his difficulties, beleaguer this relatively short span of time he could remain in England? He had no more sense than one of those idiot peacocks who strutted about the Grange, forever tripping over their own tails while trying to impress the peahens. How could he have been so foolish as to pledge himself to play the role of hero for some damsel in distress?

Because she was a very delectable damsel in distress.

But not a helpless one. A very lively and determined young lady, this Miss Juliana Wittingdon.

For the first time in decades, he experienced the stirrings of emotions. Like a moth to a flame, he found himself drawn to her passion and intensity of spirit. Yet he knew full well it would be she who ultimately would be burned if he didn't keep his distance.

Which dictated his next move. He had better find himself a compliant and unexciting mistress here in London before his driving instincts overrode his control and he did any serious damage to the enticing Miss Juliana Wittingdon.

Chapter Four

She shouldn't have come, Juliana reflected. With an effort, she forced herself to listen with apparent rapt attention to the young lady plucking with painstaking accuracy at the strings of a harp. About her, a polite silence reigned, though many of the attendees to Lady Albany's musical soiree shifted restlessly in their seats. Juliana tried not to emulate them. All her thoughts concentrated on what would occur later this night, at a very different sort of entertainment at a very different sort of house.

The piece ended to polite and relieved applause. Bertie, who had spent the last ten minutes squirming at her side, sprang to his feet. "Lemonade," he announced in a voice of desperation, and dove for the door.

Her aunt Lucilla Paignton, her petite figure swathed in ells of the most becoming lavender gauze, resignedly watched the back of her retreating son. "I don't suppose he'll bring us any, do you?"

Juliana smiled. "I wouldn't put a wager on it. Would you like me to fetch you some, dear Aunt?"

"Sweet child. By all means." She leaned closer in a cloud

of the lavender scent that lingered on her lace caplet with its violet satin ribands and embroidered roses. Silvering hair fluffed out beneath, curling about the delicate bloom of her cheeks that defied time, giving her the appearance of a young matron rather than a mature woman in her mid-forties. "But first," she said in a lowered voice, "you might tell me who that gentleman is, the tall, fair one standing by that far door? He came in just after Miss Thornsby started that dreadful piece, and I would swear he has not taken his eyes from you since."

Juliana's heart gave an odd tug, then seemed to double its efforts in speed and force. She allowed herself no more than the most fleeting of glances, but that served well enough. She was not likely to mistake him. And now that she knew he was here, it didn't seem possible she had not been aware of his presence at once.

"Lord Ramsdell." Juliana kept her voice cool. "Did you not meet him at the ball last night? He is but newly arrived from Italy."

"So that's the mysterious baron." A gleam of interest lit Aunt Lucilla's eyes. "You danced with him? What is he like?"

"What have you heard?" Juliana countered.

Aunt Lucilla's brow puckered in concentration. "Miss Dryden pronounced herself quite terrified of him, but then she is such a poor little dab of a creature. Old Mr. Pottsworth declared him to be civil enough, but not, apparently, a sportsman. So he had little use for him. Lady Sophia called him dangerously attractive, though to her any eligible male is a matter of extreme interest."

Out of the corner of her eye, Juliana caught movement, a predatory pacing that could only be his. The tiny hairs tickled at the base of her neck at her awareness of his approach. "You may judge for yourself, for I believe he is coming this way." She turned to face him fully as he stopped just before their chairs. "Lord Ramsdell." She offered him only the blandest of smiles. "I hadn't expected to see you here. I do not believe you have made the acquaintance of my aunt."

Ramsdell bowed low over Lucilla Paignton's hand, with an elegance sure to win the approval of a middle-aged lady with a preference for manners and propriety. His dress appeared modish with the austerity of a Brummel rather than the excesses of a tulip. Like the night before, a blood red ruby glittered in the folds of his neckcloth, his only jewelry aside from a rather heavy signet ring on his left forefinger. The deep mulberry wool of his coat set off the breadth of his muscular shoulders.

Aunt Lucilla studied him with undisguised interest. "Are you enjoying the music? Or," she added *sotto voce*, "do you find it as tedious as we do?"

A deep, disarming chuckle escaped him. "Very much so," he responded. "But such an evening is far more enjoyable when shared with someone one knows."

He could have picked on no better approach to the motherly woman. Instantly, her face lit with expressive concern. "But of course, you must be acquainted with so few people in England! How dreadful that that horrid little Napoleon kept you isolated so far from your real home. Pray, won't you join us? My son—have you met Bertie? He will be back with us in two shakes of a lamb's tail, I make no doubt. Juliana, my love, were you not going in search of lemonade? I am perishing for a glass. Do find Bertie and bring him back."

"Allow me." Ramsdell offered his arm as Juliana rose.

She took it, though with a measure of reluctance. It would be too easy to enjoy his unsettling company. "What brings you here?" she asked as soon as they were out of earshot of her aunt.

"To see if you had any last minute instructions for me."

She cast him a sideways glance. "Now, why did I think you would prefer to manage this on your own?"

His eyes danced. "I could say the same about you."

"I bow to necessity."

"Odd," he murmured. "I gained the impression that you might make necessity bow to you."

She stared straight ahead. "Whatever makes you say anything so absurd?"

He looked down on her from his much greater height, and the corners of his mouth twitched. "Recognition of a kindred spirit, perhaps? Come, I see your cousin. We had best capture him before he makes good his escape again."

They returned to Lucilla Paignton with both the promised glasses of lemonade and Bertie just as two young ladies took up their positions at the pianoforte. One, seated on the bench, began to play, while the other, undoubtedly her sister, began to sing an old ballad in a soft, quavering voice. Juliana began to count the minutes until the appointment at the gaming house with Woolsey would necessitate their departure.

Somehow, her aunt had rearranged their seating so that Ramsdell now occupied the chair at Juliana's left. She shifted away; that she should be so very much aware of him when she barely knew him seemed absurd. Yet there it was. Contact with him caused her pulse to race and her chest to feel tight when she breathed. His mere proximity dominated her thoughts, made everything else seem of no consequence. The man awakened yearnings in her that she knew he would lead her to regret.

Even now, sitting at apparent ease as he listened to the music, she sensed a tension in him, a tautness of mind and body. As if a coiled spring occupied the chair next to her. Was it only she who reacted to him like this, or did others sense the overwhelming power of the man when he entered a room?

For the sake of her peace of mind, she should have as little to do with him as possible. Yet here she had gone and enlisted his aid, albeit with considerable reluctance. She would prefer not to be bound to this man in any way at all; yet her love for her cousin demanded she make her best effort to save him, at whatever cost to herself.

She looked down at her hands, at the delicately boned fingers and the neatly trimmed nails. Why had Ramsdell ever offered to help? This was a man, she sensed, who was accustomed to please himself. In what way could this affair of Bertie be of any benefit to him? He was not, she would swear, a gamester. But nor was he a bear-leader by nature. So what did he want?

An obvious possibility struck her. Did he hope to place her firmly in his debt, with the purpose of seducing her? Yet that would not be the action of an honorable man.

Of course, she had no reason to believe he *was* an honorable man. Only her instinct told her to trust him. But instincts—even hers—could prove wrong. No woman in her right mind should trust a man who set her pulses racing and whose slow smile touched her as intimately as a caress.

No, she'd been right to label him dangerous. At the moment, her attraction to him created a treacherous peril. He was not a man who would settle for a safe and well-bred flirtation. He was far more like to seize whatever he wanted, allowing no one to say him nay. Definitely, Ahlric, Lord Ramsdell, did not fall under the category of a safe sort of person for an innocent young lady to know. Before this little episode of Bertie and Woolsey had ended, he was like to cut up her peace, lead her a merry dance, and end by breaking her heart.

When the two young ladies finished their piece, Ramsdell rose and turned to Lucilla Paignton. "You must forgive me for stealing your son from you, ma'am. He has been gracious enough to agree to accompany me to a small party."

Aunt Lucilla eyed him with pleasure. "The very thing. Do take the troublesome boy off before he disgraces me by falling asleep and snoring. Juliana and I shall probably leave shortly ourselves."

"I'm going with them, dear aunt." Juliana caught Ramsdell's sharpened gaze and held it. "It will be quite proper for Bertie to escort me, I assure you. We may be somewhat late getting back, but that will not signify. I know for a fact we are not pledged anywhere at all tomorrow, not until evening, and so we may recover at leisure from our outrageous revelries."

"Outrageous, indeed!" Aunt Lucilla laughed. "My lord, I haven't a scrap of faith in my son. Do see that Juliana comes to no harm, will you?"

"There is no need!" Juliana protested. "I am quite accustomed to looking after myself, I assure you."

"Oh, on your deserted moors. My dear, I assure you there are far more treacherous occurrences for a young lady here in town than ever you might meet in the wilds of Yorkshire."

"She will come to no harm, madam." Ramsdell's steady gaze locked onto Juliana's for a moment, then turned to Lucilla Paignton. "You have my word on it."

"Gallantly said." She nodded her approval. "You must call upon my husband one day soon, for I make certain he would wish to thank you himself. He is confined to Paignton House at the moment. So silly, but he will rush his fences, so I suppose a broken arm is a small price to pay. But he would be delighted to receive a morning visit from you, and Hampstead Heath is no very great distance from town, after all."

"I—spend my days in seclusion." He offered her a deprecating smile. "I fear I am a creature of the night."

Lucilla Paignton laughed. "So are all you gentlemen when you come to London. Very well, you shall come to dinner some night soon."

Ramsdell thanked her, repeated his assurances for Juliana's safety, then led the way to find their hostess to make their excuses. Juliana, glancing back toward her aunt, noted that the woman had already moved to join a mother and daughter and appeared to be settling in for an agreeable coze. She need have no further worries about Aunt Lucilla, it seemed. Her aunt would be highly entertained for the next hour and more, then the carriage would take her safely home before returning for Juliana and Bertie.

After taking leave of their hostess, Ramsdell led the way to the entry hall, and Juliana braced herself to receive his wrath. Bertie she removed by the simple expedient of dispatching him to fetch her cloak. She was almost prepared when Ramsdell turned to her, his eyes burning with an annoyance that for a terrible moment caused her determination to falter.

"This is a necessary part of my plan!" she informed him before he could speak.

"Then perhaps your plan had better change." His eyes narrowed. "You may well be compromising yourself by visiting such a house."

"I would not have suggested one that I did not feel it safe for me to enter," she countered.

He paced away a step, then turned back to her. "None of this need be necessary," he said at last. "I could remove the problem, quite easily."

"You mean remove Woolsey." She swallowed. "I—I feel certain you would be quite capable of it. And that you would carry it off with subtlety and finesse."

"Then allow me to do it."

"I've considered it." She looked up into his face, and her treacherous heart fluttered within her at the strength of his features and the sheer force of the gaze that rested on her. "But it wouldn't serve, you know. You've met Bertie. He's so—so *trusting*. Another, and possibly wilier, gullcatcher would replace Woolsey soon enough, and then he'd be no better off than he is now. Worse, possibly, for I doubt whether he would confide in me so freely a second time."

"It would be cruel to place any barrier between you and your cousin, would it not?" A lopsided smile tugged at the corner of his mouth. "Very well, then. We will play the hand your way. I take it you have something more in mind than you have already revealed to me?"

"Only to teach him a modicum of worldly wisdom. He doesn't see in the least how foolishly he has been behaving. But I think that if he were to see another, and one dear to him, fall into the same trap, it might open his eyes."

"You." Ramsdell frowned. "I cannot like it. You might well—"

"Hush, he's back." Juliana moved away from Ramsdell, hurrying forward to receive the warm folds of her wool cloak as Bertie draped the garment casually about her shoulders.

This would be no easy evening if she were constantly at loggerheads with her accomplice. Not for the first time she experienced qualms about their plot. But she pushed them aside, knowing she had no other choice.

Still, it dawned on her that Ramsdell was a force to be reckoned with, who made his presence felt in every way. If she were not careful, her fragile control of this situation might slip into his hands. And would her own person be that far behind?

For her safety, she had better take steps to keep him at a distinct distance.

Chapter Five

Mrs. Glasdon's house off Jermyn Street, Ramsdell decided shortly after their arrival at this establishment, was much better than he had dared to hope. It exuded a subtle and unexpected air of respectability. In his experience—which when it came to gaming houses was vast—one could hope for little more than a glittering, and very thin, veneer of gentility.

But then he shouldn't have been surprised. Miss Wittingdon, after all, had been the one who suggested it.

It bore every appearance of being the private home that in fact it was. A very proper *major domo* opened the door to them, bowed them inside, took their cloaks, and requested their names. He then led them through a hall decorated with gilt-edged mirrors and vases filled with arrangements of autumn flowers and branches. A rather good landscape hung on a wall papered in discreet tones of gold and cream. A less penetrating eye than his would easily miss the chipped veneer on the pier table, or the darning of a hole in the lace runner that imperfectly covered it.

Their escort ushered them up a flight of stairs and into

a large drawing room decorated in shades of deep green, cream and gold. The figurines on the mantel shelf were excellent copies of costly originals, Ramsdell decided. Whoever had decorated this place had done so with taste and elegance—but a limited budget.

A number of gentlemen already occupied both this room and its twin, which Ramsdell glimpsed through the adjoining double doors that had been thrown wide. He even, to his further surprise, noted two ladies, though not innocent chits in their first blush of youth, like Miss Wittingdon. Nor were the rooms crowded, but comfortably filled, as one might expect at a card party given by a lady of minor consequence in the *ton*.

Ramsdell spotted their hostess even before the *major domo*, who had paused in the doorway to scan the apartment. She stood beside a faro table, a tall, gaunt figure, dressed in an elegantly simple gown of emerald satin, ruched in a single line about the hem. Sheer sarsnet, fastened at the throat by a brooch, filled the low decolletage. A confection of lace and green ribands perched amidst the soft rolls of white hair that waved back from her high forehead. She leaned forward, one gloved hand just resting negligently along the back of one of the upholstered chairs, as she exchanged a friendly word with one of her guests.

"There is Mrs. Glasdon," Miss Wittingdon exclaimed with an unexpected touch of pleasure in her voice.

Ramsdell's eyebrows rose. "You've met her before?"

A soft flush tinged her cheeks. "She has been described to me. And it is not as if there are many ladies here this evening."

"There should be one less," he muttered as he followed the servitor to their hostess's side.

Mrs. Glasdon listened to the *major domo's* introduction, then directed the penetrating gaze of her gleaming eyes upon each of the trio in turn. "The name of Paignton is familiar to me," she said at last. Her voice, deep and gentle, held a smile as if she found her world amusing. Her gaze strayed from Bertie to linger on Miss Wittingdon, and suddenly she nodded, satisfied. "You are the very image of your mama, my dear girl. You are most welcome."

"Your mama?" Ramsdell demanded in a murmur as he ushered them toward a table.

"Dash it all, Jewel," Bertie blurted out. "Do you mean to say your mama came here? I'll swear my papa never knew!"

Miss Wittingdon threw him a look brimful of laughter. "My dear Bertie! Whoever do you think brought her here in the first place? Times were somewhat different then. But don't you go telling him you know. The poor darling would be so mortified, now. He has become such a paragon of respectability."

Bertie chuckled, but Ramsdell studied Miss Wittingdon covertly. Under his scrutiny, the delicate color rose once more in her cheeks. For all her attempts at worldly sophistication—for that matter, for all her seeming confidence and determination—she really was naught but the veriest innocent.

He settled them at a piquet table and invited Bertie to join him in a hand or two while they awaited the arrival of Woolsey. Miss Wittingdon seated herself at her cousin's side, professing herself delighted to watch. A servant poured wine for them, left a bottle near at hand, and departed. Ramsdell sorted out the lower pips, all the while involved in his delicate task of scoring the upper ones with his thumb nail, then shuffled and dealt. The hand progressed very much along the lines he had planned.

As they announced their final scores, Bertie flushed with pleasure. "I say, Jewel, I've won! Perhaps my luck has turned at last. Good notion of yours, coming here tonight, my lord. Shall we raise the stakes this time?"

Miss Wittingdon fluttered her lashes in wide-eyed innocence. "Is that wise? It's still rather early in the evening."

Bertie laughed. "Oh, it's a maxim of Woolsey's to always

bet heavily the entire evening when the first hand goes to you." He drained his glass and refilled it.

Miss Wittingdon's brow wrinkled. "But if your luck turns bad, is that not dangerous?"

"Oh, Woolsey says that's when you should double your bets," he assured her. "Because fortunes are bound to change soon, and then you'll win back all you've lost so far."

So following this rule, he bet more. Ramsdell eyed him for a long moment, then accepted the fate that Miss Wittingdon—and his own perverse offer to help—had thrust upon him. He dealt with care, and Bertie lost.

"Who'd have thought you'd hold back that king," Bertie declared, blithely accepting his defeat. He reached once more for the bottle and topped off his glass. "Don't pull so long a face, Jewel. Next time should be the charm for me, you'll see. Shall we double the stakes, Ramsdell?"

Ramsdell shuffled once more, handed the pack to Miss Wittingdon to cut, then dealt with unexpected reluctance. With every card he flipped skillfully from the bottom, he actually felt himself tainted! The thought was absurd, of course, but there it was. The penalty, he supposed, of having indulged in the foolishness of involving himself in the affairs of these ordinary, short-lived people.

Yet there was something most pleasantly *uno*rdinary about Miss Wittingdon.

That was not a line of thought he cared to pursue at the moment. The possibility of engaging in a flirtation with her intrigued him, but some remnants of common sense warned him off. Any flirtation with this young lady would not likely remain casual for long. It could all too easily come to mean something to him, and that was an eventuality, for her safety, he dared not allow.

He took the last trick, saw Bertie's crestfallen expression, and had to harden his heart. Usually he could afford to indulge his whims of allowing a partner to win whenever the fancy took him. But not this time. He was, he reminded

THE FULL OF THE MOON

himself, teaching this young paper-scull a much needed lesson.

"May I try a hand?" Miss Wittingdon begged, all bright-eyed eagerness. "Perhaps taking a break will do you good, Bertie."

"But Woolsey always says—" Bertie began.

"Nonsense," she broke across his protest. "A break will help. You'll see."

And so it would, Ramsdell reflected, making a mental note to allow Bertie a tidy victory in their next encounter. He faced his new opponent, and found his thoughts too easily distracted by the lovely picture she presented. With an effort, he dragged them back to the task at hand. "And what shall we wager?"

"Five pound points?" she suggested, equaling Bertie's last misguided venture. Her eyes danced with mischief at him from across the table.

"I say, Jewel!" Bertie protested. "That's dipping rather deep, don't you think?"

Miss Wittingdon laughed. "What a ninny you must think me! It's only what you wagered, after all. If it is agreeable with you, my lord?" she added, turning back to Ramsdell.

He inclined his head. "As you wish."

Bertie frowned, but made no further objection. He moved behind his cousin, the better to watch her play, Ramsdell guessed. She would not be able to help him by displaying any lack of skill; he would have to arrange to win on his own. Conceiving an active dislike of this chiseling pastime, he felt for the marks he had placed on the cards, shifted their positions with finesse, and dealt a hand that would assure him the victory by sufficient points to cost her a tidy sum.

As she tossed down the last of her cards in response to his lead, she gave a sigh of half exasperation, half amusement. "I've never held such an unhelpful hand. Really, my lord, you are to be congratulated on your luck. Now Bertie, what does Woolsey say? Am I to double my bet for the next hand, or merely increase it?"

Her cousin's brow furrowed, and for a long minute he stared into space. "It's not really the thing for a lady to do," he announced at last.

"Pray don't talk fustian. Where is the difference whether it is you or I who places the bet? Surely the principle makes no allowance for play by the weaker sex?"

An expression perilously close to a pout settled over Bertie's features. "I don't know. It just don't seem right."

"If it's right for you, then it's right for me. Woolsey wouldn't steer you wrong, would he? I know he's your friend."

Bertie brightened. "That's right. You should double your bet, because you didn't win your first hand."

She didn't win the next, or even the third, thanks to Ramsdell's adroit handling of the deck. Still, she remained smiling and professing faith in Bertie's system—with an enthusiasm that would have appalled Ramsdell had he for a moment believed her sincere. He did not, however; the determination that glittered in her soulful, puppy-like eyes had nothing to do with the gambling.

As he began to deal the fourth hand, Woolsey arrived at last. He strode toward the table, his gaze traveling about the drawing room, his expression assessing. "Never been here before," he pronounced as he reached them.

Ramsdell noted the unease in his voice. Did the man fear being out of his familiar haunts? Perhaps the proprietor of his normal hunting grounds turned a deliberately blind eye to any discrepancies in the manner of his play. Here he would have to watch his step.

"I believe I promised us all faro," Ramsdell said, and rose.

Miss Wittingdon sprang eagerly to her feet. "Yes, please. No, do not worry, Bertie. I *know* I should continue at piquet until I have won back all my losses. This will only be a temporary break, I promise. We may go back to our game later, may we not, Lord Ramsdell?"

"Of a certainty." Ramsdell watched Bertie's worried expression with satisfaction. Not a bad lad at heart; he certainly cared for his cousin's welfare. That boded well for their eventual success.

The pleasure he felt at that surprised him. What foolishness was this? He had learned two centuries ago the folly of caring for people. It seemed he barely got to know them before they were claimed by the ails and laments of old age, and then death. Always, he found himself alone in the end—and lonely, if he'd been fool enough to allow himself to like someone.

They located a table set up for faro. Woolsey offered to hold the bank, but Ramsdell claimed that right as his own, offering a sum that caused Woolsey to raise his eyebrows. Ramsdell knew full well it was extravagant, but as his late father had been fond of saying so long ago, one didn't catch big fish without big bait. He allowed the first game to go without his interference, with the result that Woolsey and Juliana each came out ahead by a few pounds, while Bertie lost.

Miss Wittingdon, in her role of innocent dupe, pronounced herself delighted. Ramsdell congratulated her. It surprised him how easily he could read her true feelings. Almost, the thought crossed his mind, as if they shared some part deep within themselves.

The first stirrings of his senses began, and his hands stopped their rapid shuffling of the cards. Then the all-too familiar—and dreaded—aching began in his teeth. A soul-wrenching longing coursed through him that could only be satisfied with blood. *Her* blood.

Yet only one day had passed since the dark of the moon. He could still control his bloodlust. But if he were to continue keeping company with Miss Wittingdon—

He had better not waste another night before finding a suitable mistress. He preferred ones of weak intellect, whose memories would fuddle with ease. He didn't want any vivid dreams of fangs in necks lingering to mar the cordiality of his business relationships.

His business relationships. He had long since lost count of the mistresses he had kept during the course of over two hundred years. Yet at the moment, the prospect of entering into another of these dull but necessary arrangements suddenly held little appeal. Why should he experience any scruples now?

Because, he realized the next moment, for the first time in a very long while, he wanted something more in his dealings with a woman than the mere satisfaction of his bloodlust. He wanted caring. He wanted passion. And that thought only fed his bloodlust all the more.

Resolutely, he concentrated on cards.

As he intended, all three of his victims quickly lost what money they had brought with them and were reduced to scribbling their vowels. Bertie—reluctantly, to his credit—taught this art to Miss Wittingdon. Ramsdell deplored her learning this questionable skill, but could say nothing.

When the gong sounded in the depths of the house announcing an informal supper, Miss Wittingdon stared at the pile of paper promises that were hers, then raised her uncertain gaze to her cousin. "What am I supposed to do about these?"

He squirmed in his chair. "Debt of honor," he announced. "Have to redeem 'em as soon as possible. But don't you worry, you'll win most of 'em back before the night is over. Not a doubt of it, if we follow Woolsey's system."

"Well, I must say, I'm glad to hear that. It looks the most dreadful sum." She smiled brightly, her worries apparently vanishing.

Ramsdell gritted his teeth. How could that nodcock be so utterly brainless as not to realize the trouble into which she could so easily be falling? But that, he reminded himself, was the lesson she hoped to teach him.

They made their way down the stairs and into the supper room, and Miss Wittingdon looked about in delight. "But this is superb!" she exclaimed. "Are all establishments like this? It is no wonder you spend so many nights gaming, Bertie."

She was only play-acting, Ramsdell told himself, clenching his jaw. Yet he hated hearing such words coming from her lovely mouth. If he had his way— He broke off that thought. What he was beginning to want from Miss Wittingdon could well prove her demise.

Bertie, a bit on the go, grinned owlishly at his cousin. "Just see how those chandeliers sparkle." He pointed to them with pride, as if he were in some way responsible. "And just have a taste of this salmon mayonnaise!" He fell silent, for he had discovered another tray of delicacies.

Woolsey took a perfunctory bite of something fished from the depths of a heavy sauce, then looked around the premises with a slight sneer twisting his mouth. "I prefer Mrs. Newbury's establishment."

Ramsdell regarded the array of dishes through his quizzing glass. "Indeed? I rather like this one. Why do you not all join me here again tomorrow?"

Miss Wittingdon looked up with a regret that did not seem to be feigned clouding her brow. "We are pledged to a dinner party and will not be able to break away. Then the night after that is an informal hop that is being given for the daughter of a special friend of my aunt's, and we cannot get out of it. The night after that"—she smiled, showing just the touch of a fascinating dimple in her right cheek—"we will come, and gladly."

They lingered at the table, sampling a variety of dishes, until the mantel clock struck the hour of two. Miss Wittingdon looked up, startled. "The time! Bertie, we really must be getting home. It's such a long ride to Hampstead Heath, and the poor horses—and coachman—will have been waiting all this time."

Woolsey lounged back in his chair. "I was just going to

suggest to Bertie that we toddle along to another little place I know of."

Bertie, bleary-eyed from the amount of wine he had consumed, shook his head. "Got to escort Jewel. Promised m'mother."

"Then by all means, you must." Ramsdell rose. Woolsey and Bertie fell into a low-voiced argument, somewhat confused by the evening's potations, and Ramsdell took the opportunity to draw Miss Wittingdon aside. She looked up at him, a triumphant smile tugging at her lips. "Yes," he said, forestalling her. "We have done well this night. So there will be no need for you to repeat this indiscretion."

"Indiscretion?" Her brilliant eyes widened. "You mean coming here? Pray, do not be absurd!"

"No matter how genteel, this is still a gaming house. You would be wise not to forget that."

"If it weren't a gaming house," she pointed out with exaggerated patience, "there would have been no point in my coming, would there?"

"No young lady of quality should come anywhere near such an establishment."

She waved her arm, taking in the remainder of the room. "But there are others here."

"Considerably older than you. And married. That makes all the difference."

Her nose wrinkled. "That's silly."

"It's the way of the world. A young miss in her first season is expected to follow certain rules of behavior. You may well ruin yourself with this venture, and I want no part of that."

"Just help me keep Bertie from ruining himself, and I will be satisfied. No, don't look daggers at me." She shivered. "I promise you, I don't want a scandal. I have my dear aunt and uncle to consider, so I will be careful. But as long as Bertie is with me, no real harm will be done."

"The world may not look as kindly on your actions as all that," he pointed out.

She shook her head, and her soulful eyes shadowed as if with some remembered pain. "Then I can always return to the wilds of Yorkshire where no one will care how badly I've behaved."

Ramsdell opened his mouth to object, but Woolsey chose that moment to take his abrupt leave of them. Miss Wittingdon, possibly fearing further argument, excused herself to find her cloak. Ramsdell grasped Bertie by the arm, hauled him down the last flight of stairs, and propelled him into the privacy of a tiny empty salon on the ground floor.

"Does your cousin not have the least comprehension of the importance of the opinion of society?" he demanded.

Bertie gave this his undivided—if fuddled—attention. "Don't care a whit," he pronounced at last. "Won't be led, she says. Complete innocent, of course."

"Has no one instilled in her the consequences of suffering a damaged reputation?"

"Not Jewel." Bertie shook his head emphatically. "She takes care. Won't come to any harm."

"What the devil were her parents thinking about?" demanded Ramsdell. "To turn an innocent chit like that loose among the wolves of society—"

"Father died before she was born." Bertie slumped against the wall, the fatuous smile still plastered to his face. "Brought up by her mama. Odd sort of woman, by all m'father says. Suffered some sort of disease right after she was brought out. Disfiguring, apparently. Pity, she was only eighteen. Retired to a cottage she'd inherited from her own mama, up in the wilds of the Yorkshire moors. Married this Mr. Wittingdon, who died a few months later. Then Jewel was born, and her mama kept her isolated up there no matter how often m'papa begged her to let the girl come and visit. Never succeeded, till now. Gather he threatened to go up there himself and fetch her."

So this was Miss Juliana Wittingdon's first excursion from her isolated home. No wonder she doted so on her relatives; she'd probably longed for them all her life. And now here she was, an innocent raised by another innocent. No matter what she might believe, Miss Wittingdon was very much in need of protection.

Especially from himself.

Chapter Six

The candles in Mrs. Glasdon's elegant drawing room burned with a trace of tallow blended in with the beeswax. Another cost cutting measure of which only the rarest of her guests would be aware. Ramsdell knew himself to be unique in his sensory abilities. And little good it did him.

The faro table at which he sat had become peculiarly his own during the course of the past eight days. The four of them—as unlikely a quartet as he could imagine—had turned a visit to this establishment into a nightly ritual. But their plan had progressed more slowly than they had hoped.

Bertie Paignton, desperately clinging to the faulty maxims taught him by his professed friend, had begun to take on a gaunt and haunted appearance. Yet still he persisted. Captain Lysander Woolsey came as if against his will—which in fact he did, appearing only in response to Ramsdell's subtle persuasions. Loudly he bemoaned a losing streak which he—but not Ramsdell—found inexplicable. And Miss Juliana Wittingdon turned a distressed face to her cousin, trembling over the amount of her supposed losses, while all the time her eyes danced with the mischief of impending triumph.

Nor would Ramsdell have been anywhere else in the world. These sessions at the faro table, plagued as they were by the necessity of fleecing two lambs and a wolf, provided his sole contact with Miss Wittingdon. He found himself every bit as addicted to her as her cousin Bertie had ever been to gaming. He relished these few hours spent in her presence. The other portions of his night ceased to have any meaning for him except as time spent either in anticipation or reminiscence of the few brief moments in which they could speak alone.

He shuffled the cards he had just gathered. His gaze drifted from Bertie to Woolsey to Miss Wittingdon—and away from her, at once. Even the simple pleasure of looking upon her grew too dangerous. Eight nights, and each one brought them inexorably closer to the full of the moon, when his need for blood would be at its greatest. Three nights from this, he would no longer be able to control his desperate need. Yet he had made no move to find a mistress, to find a safe and emotionally uninvolving outlet for his driving lusts.

Woolsey pounded his fist on the green baize cloth, setting the wine glasses rocking. "I'm tired of this house!"

Ramsdell steadied the bottle. "Then why do you come?"

Woolsey's haunted gaze faded to blank, then he rallied and glared at Ramsdell. "Never had such a rotten run of luck. Something not right about that."

Bertie snorted. "You're always telling me it goes like that. Just double your bet, that's what you say." He glowered at his erstwhile friend. "Don't see you doing that."

"Go to another house." Woolsey nodded. "That's what we should do. Go back to Mrs. Newbury's."

Bertie waved his glass, tilting it at a perilous angle. "Don't matter where I go. Lose everywhere."

"I don't." Woolsey pushed back his chair, but made it

no farther. He just kept nodding his head. "Go somewhere else. 'Way from here."

"Then go," Bertie snapped. "There's no one keeping you here."

Woolsey started to rise, then sank once more into his chair, his expression deflated. He reached for the bottle of claret, almost knocked it over, then managed to refill his glass with only a few spilled drops. "I *want* to go," Woolsey muttered, and had long recourse to his wine. "Least to 'nother table."

"Oh, stop complaining." Bertie hunched a shoulder, half turning from his former friend. "Stay or go, 's all the same to me. Only just *do* it."

Woolsey threw him a darkling glance, then slumped back in his chair. "What are you waiting for?" he demanded of Ramsdell. "Get on with it!" He slammed another vowel over one of the cards on the placard.

Minds, Ramsdell reflected as he cut the cards, could be so easily led. With one like Woolsey's, so self-absorbed as to make it inconceivable to him that another might influence him, it was child's play. No sport in it at all. He would have abandoned the project within a scant half hour if it were not for Miss Wittingdon. And her cousin. Just this once, it did no harm to actually do a kindness to someone. Perhaps, in some obscure way, this one altruistic act might serve as mitigation for some portion of his wholly self-serving life.

At the moment, Miss Wittingdon sat in a dejected posture, watching the turning of the cards in despair. She placed another wager, lost again, and drained her glass. Her eyes glittered as she slammed the sturdy crystal on the table and spun on Woolsey. "Your system is worthless!" she exclaimed. "This mode of betting you encourage serves no one but the bank."

Bertie stared at her. "It can't! He always advises me to play that way. He wouldn't—"

Ramsdell implanted a thought into Bertie's mind, and waited.

"But," Bertie resumed slowly, as if struggling to work out some tangled line of reasoning, "either Woolsey holds the bank, or we play at only one house, where he's well known." He broke off, casting Woolsey a look of horrified speculation.

Ramsdell let it drop for the moment. With a mind as far muddled with wine as Bertie's, too much revelation would simply seep through the cracks and evaporate along with the alcohol fumes. Enough that he'd planted the first seed on ground prepared by Woolsey's constant whines and complaints.

"Oh, let us quit!" Miss Wittingdon pushed away the bottle of ink with which they had all been scribbling their vowels. "I am tired this night. Bertie, will you fetch my cloak for me? I want to go home."

Woolsey looked up, his eyes gleaming, but whether with hope or wine, it was impossible to tell. "Still early," he pronounced with care. "Come on, Bertie, let's go back to Mrs. Newbury's. Just see if your luck don't change."

Bertie shot him a glance filled with distaste. "Do whatever you like. I'm escorting m'cousin home."

Woolsey snorted, glared at Ramsdell and Miss Wittingdon, then lurched to his feet. "I will wish you," he said indistinctly, "a good night." And with that, he swaggered away, bumping into chairs and tables as he went.

"Half sprung," Bertie sneered, as if he himself weren't perilously close to that state. "Fetching you something, wasn't I, Jewel? Right back." With that, he sauntered off with only a slight weaving to his step.

"Do you think he'll remember it's my cloak he's gone after?" she asked.

"Doubtful." Ramsdell moved to the vacated chair beside her. This was the time for which he waited, when they would discuss the progress of their plot. Her presence filled him, just as her spirit haunted him. For the past week, he had emerged from his comatose daylight slumber, returning to his senses each dusk with an unfamiliar sensation that he had at last identified as anticipation. For the first time in two hundred years, he looked forward to something. His nights were no longer an endless round of simply getting through time, with the occasional distasteful variation of fulfilling his macabre needs.

He allowed his gaze to move across her face as he said, "We seem to have made a major advance this night."

"Yes." She didn't look at him.

"Do not be concerned." It took an effort not to touch her hand. "It cannot be much longer. He will shortly realize the hopelessness of his position—and yours, as well. And then we may tell him the truth and relieve his mind."

"Yes," she said again, and her voice rose on an impassioned note as she added, "And it cannot happen a moment too soon, as far as I am concerned."

But it was not worry for her cousin that prompted that outburst. Something else troubled her, haunted the depths of those lovely, puppy-like eyes of hers. He studied her profile—she kept her face averted from him—and experienced the waves of tension that emanated from her.

Not tiredness, but a repressed anger and yearning raged within her. Taken aback, he probed subtly, searching for the cause of her distress, and encountered a blazing desire within her that mirrored his own. She acknowledged the unspoken attraction that vibrated between them, and chose to reject it.

That made her stronger than he. He longed to indulge it. He found himself existing just to hear her laughter or see her smile. His teeth ached with longing for her slender neck—and the havoc she played on the rest of his anatomy came nigh to destroying his rigid control.

He could seduce her, of course. It would be easy. He didn't even need to implant the suggestion of desire in her mind; it existed there already, strong and palpitating, responding to the desperate hunger for her that filled him.

Alarums rang in his mind, warning him off. Possessing her would prove fatal for her. Making love and drawing the blood that sustained him were intertwined, inseparable. Only his control made the difference between life and death for his victim.

And that control, as he had learned to his bitter regret in his very first encounter, evaporated in the face of passion. Since then, he had selected only mistresses who left him emotionally uninvolved; his bloodlust was curbed, but he was never fully satisfied.

For two hundred years he had remained in control, but now here sat Miss Juliana Wittingdon, vibrant, alive, as pulsatingly aware of him as he was of her. And in three scant nights, the moon would reach its fullness, and the madness for blood would overpower any sense or reason.

He clenched his fists, fighting the urge to reach out and trace the delicate line of her jaw. Sweetness such as hers was alien to him; he coveted it.

For that matter, he coveted everything about her. Her full lips, the silkiness of her auburn hair, the softness of her cheek. . . . With one finger, he barely touched her.

She flinched, and jerked around to stare at him. For one long moment, she gazed at him with longing intermingled with unmistakable fear. Then she murmured an unintelligible excuse, leaped to her feet, and hurried away. Halfway across the room she slowed, then turned to look back at him over her shoulder.

The mixture of yearning and misery contained in the depths of those vulnerable puppy eyes tore at him. Yet he had done nothing, he would swear, to drive her away. So it ran deeper than his actions. She was sensitive, aware. Had she begun to suspect the darker, fiendish side of his nature? How right she was to fear him—yet he could not bear the thought of losing her.

He loved her. That realization came as a jolt, carrying

with it both elation and despair. He had thought himself incapable of such a deep and pure emotion. Over the long, lonely years, he had become devoted solely to himself. Yet from the moment he had laid eyes upon her, some long buried part of him had longed for her warmth.

Desire surged through him, overpowering—yet tempered with love. Juliana. His beloved. For her sake, he must master his desires, not succumb to the passion she kindled within him, that threatened to drive him as mad as did his bloodlust. Yet neither could he regret this love, whatever pain it cost him. For the first time in over two hundred years, he truly cared for another. And for the first time, he wished he were still human so he could indulge in the luxury of marriage and a family.

But he wasn't, and he couldn't.

He had to take steps to assure her safety. He had to sate some portion, at least, of his lust, before he lost control and destroyed her with it.

There was only one direction for him. Restless, hating himself, he strode through the darkened streets toward Covent Garden, where the narrow alleys would be filled with ladies of negotiable virtue. No one troubled him; people moved instinctively from his path. Once, that had amused him. Now, he saw it for what it was—one more sign of how unfit he was for any form of human society.

Even now, so far from Juliana, his control hovered on the brink. She had driven his soul half mad with longing for her.

He looked around to see several of the poor women of the streets seeking their customers; yet not one dared to approach him. In his present tortured state, he must radiate danger and terror to them. Was any woman, even the most unappetizing of these doxies, safe with him this night?

He approached one at random, a sorry wretch with straggly, greasy hair escaping from beneath a mobcap, and a dress soiled and torn. His sensitive nose recoiled, yet his driving needs, whipped into a frenzy by the approach of the full moon, forced him on.

No, not even with this poor specimen, so unlikely a target of passion, would he be able to control his feeding frenzy. He turned away, sick with the savage combination of desire and self-loathing. He increased his pace, walking faster and faster, until at last he broke into a desperate run, seeking the elusive semi-oblivion that only utter exhaustion could bring him now.

Chapter Seven

Ramsdell stood before the cheval glass, setting the final creases in his neckcloth. In two nights it would be the full of the moon. He would have to make sure his servants were well away from the house in case some madness overcame him. He turned away from his reflection, hating it, and reached for the small pile of invitations that awaited his attention.

He ripped open each one, examined it, then set it aside to be refused. Only one, he noted, requested the pleasure of his company for a breakfast. Word had gotten about that he shunned the daylight. One silly chub, in fact, had actually gone so far as to try and emulate him, claiming Ramsdell to be correct, that in London the only decent time to be astir was after dark when the town glittered with parties and gaming.

So it seemed that what he regarded as a hateful necessity might set a fashion. Lord, what fools these young men were, not to appreciate sun and light for the glorious gifts they were. He would give much to be able to see them once more.

But the choice was not his. As dawn approached, his body became sluggish, his mind numb. He could barely get himself within doors and to the comparative safety of bed before he slipped into an unconsciousness that nothing, no calamity, could disturb. It left him vulnerable, and he knew it, but there was naught he could do about it except trust to well-paid servitors to assure no one tried to disturb him—or more important, that no fire broke out.

One invitation caught his eyes, and for a long moment he weighed it in his hands. An engagement ball, given by a friend of Mrs. Paignton. Juliana would be there. And so, he reminded himself, would be Bertie. That meant the furthering of Juliana's plot would have to be postponed. A waste of the night, in fact.

If he had any sense whatsoever, he would welcome this chance to be away from her. He might simply remain at home. Or more urgent, seek a mistress. Perhaps, without Juliana's presence to drive him into a frenzy of lust, he could still control himself sufficiently to drink enough blood to slake his desperate need without damaging his poor victim.

Yet nothing, he knew, could distract him from his obsession with his love. Juliana. He spoke her name aloud, rolling it around his mouth like a caress. Her Cousin Bertie called her Jewel, and that was what she was. A very precious jewel. And one he could never possess.

What a fool love made of him! When it came to her, he lost whatever sense he had ever possessed. Rational thought seemed foreign to him; his urges ruled his usually careful existence. And right now, his urges prompted him to see her one more time, at whatever cost.

He changed his garments, adopting the satin knee breeches, long-tailed coat, silk stockings and slippers suitable for a ball. After donning a thick cloak, he dismissed his manservant Drury until the following morning and set forth. At least he could venture alone into the streets freely, without any fear of footpads.

The walk through the chill night air stimulated him, making him vividly aware of his surroundings. The unevenness of the cobbled stones pressed through the soles of his shoes. The cries of linkboys and jarveys, and the clop of hooves on paving, rang in his ears. Pungent aromas of horse, man, and refuse mingled to assault his nose.

A stroll of about twelve blocks brought him to the elegant house in Grosvenor Square. He had no trouble identifying the location; the house blazed with lights, and lanterns spilled out the door, down the red carpeted steps, and along the carriage-lined road. Noise. Bustle. All the things he most detested. He entered, relinquished his hat and cloak, and went to make his bow to his hostess.

The formalities satisfied, he paced off, tense. The glittering crystal drops on the flickering chandeliers nearly blinded him. The scent of so many human bodies, packed so closely together, sent a wave of nausea through him. He was a predator, a creature of solitary habit, a hunter who relied on the dark stillness of the night to seek his prey. He was *not* a Tulip who basked in the approval of society.

People moved away from him, and he took a deep breath, willing himself under control. The hairs on his arms stood on end; the moon came so close to full, he could taste it. It brought a fresh wash of bloodlust rushing through him. Or was that because *she* was near?

He didn't have to search. Instinctively he turned toward where she stood to one side of the room beside a rather insipid young lady. He could tell she was bored, though she gave no outward sign of it, so well did he know her. He started forward, unable to hold himself back, only to draw up short as a young officer strode up to her and took her hand to lead her to the floor.

That cacophony that assailed his ears had actually been the string orchestra warming up, he realized. They now struck the opening bars of a country dance. Around him, sets formed. Driven by the desire to simply be near Juliana, he turned at random, spotted a young lady to whom he knew he had been introduced, and asked her to dance. He positioned them at the far end of the long line in the same set where Juliana stood with her officer. At the moment, it was as close as he dared come to her. The movements of the dance would rectify that—and all too soon. Or was that never soon enough?

The couples, arranged in groups of four, exchanged places with each repetition of the movements, one pair from each group moving up the line, the other down. As the dance progressed, Juliana came nearer. Abruptly she looked up, straight at him, as if sensing his presence. A wariness crept into her eyes, and she turned back to her partner. Even from the distance that still separated them, Ramsdell could see the brittleness of her smile.

He frightened her. All too clearly he recalled the consternation in her face, the yearning and trepidation as she left him sitting at the faro table the night before. He drove her away, and it was all for the best. He was a fool— nay, a villain!—to crave any contact at all with her, even friendship. Yet with every passing hour his control grew weaker and weaker.

They moved into positions that made them part of the same quartet. He couldn't concentrate; he moved without conscious thought through the familiar steps. She filled his being as his needs built within to a fiery rage.

"I hadn't expected to see you," she said as they passed on a diagonal.

"I knew you would be here," came his ragged response.

Her gaze flew to his, then dropped. "It's not wise," she whispered the next time they passed.

"Nor preventable," he breathed.

He hadn't thought she would hear, but her startled expression showed otherwise. They separated with the next rotation, but he could feel her gaze straying toward him again and again, and still again, along the length of the line. How truly could they ever be separated? he wondered. In some strange way, she belonged with him.

But that was impossible. What could there be between them? Never, with her, could he control his bloodlust. If he were ever such a fool as to take her in his arms, even just to kiss her as he longed to— No, it would never stop there, not until he had claimed her body, her blood—and ultimately her life.

Only if she were as immortal as he, could she withstand what every fiber of his being demanded of her. Only if she, too, were a vampire. For one moment—one brief, surging moment—he allowed the possibility to enter his mind, that he could turn her into a creature like himself, the mate for which he craved.

But to reduce a being of sunlight and love and laughter to a being like himself, one of darkness and emptiness, who only inspired fear in others—

That would be an act too cruel, too hateful to inflict upon any living soul. How could he curse her with this semi-life, when he loved her so much? And even if he did sink to such depths of depravity, the vile deed would take more control over his bloodfeeding than he could manage at this time. No, whatever his intentions, he would only prove her death.

The dance ended, he returned his partner to her seat, then his longings got the better of him. With a muffled groan, he prowled to Juliana's side. He saw her stiffen even before she turned to face him; she wouldn't meet his gaze, looking first down, then away, as if eager to find any excuse to escape. With a mental force greater than he'd intended, he pushed everyone away from her, leaving her standing isolated in the center of a small circle.

He closed the distance between them; she stood waiting, her hands clenched together before her, her expression an agonized mixture of longing and despair. "Just one dance," he breathed.

"I—" she began, only to break off. Then, "One," she agreed in a voice half strangled by emotion. "But not yet."

He had to wait through a country dance, a reel, and a waltz. She came off the floor breathless from this last, her face delightfully flushed. He almost snatched her from her partner, and his gloved hand closed tightly about hers. The material might not have been there at all, so aware was he of her fine bones—and especially of the blood that pulsed through the delectable veins of her wrist.

She pulled free from his touch. "Let— May we sit this one out? I—I need a moment to rest."

"Some lemonade?" He offered his arm, and after a moment she placed the tips of her fingers on his elbow. As they threaded their way toward the refreshment table, she took considerable pains to avoid bumping into him.

"I've frightened you," he said, unable to keep the anger from his voice.

"No!" Her gaze flew to his face, then dropped so she stared resolutely at the floor.

"It bothers you that I watch you."

She gave a short, mirthless laugh, and when she spoke, her tone mocked them both. "You mean you stalk me? Like some poor field mouse hunted by a hawk?"

It never seemed to occur to her to think he might be paying her court. No, in her eyes he stalked her. And so he did. She sensed that much about him, at least. Enough to know she had need of fear. "An owl, more like," he said with a touch of bitterness. "I do my hunting at night. Have you not noticed?"

She shivered, although the room was uncomfortably warm, and he clenched his fists in frustration. More fool he, to seek her out in so crowded a location. There could be no opportunity to tell her anything. And if there were, what did he think he could say? That he loved her to distraction? That he was a vampire, a creature of terror and the dark? That he was unfit for her companionship? Silently and angrily, he vowed to leave London the moment he completed his service to her. Never again would he venture anywhere near where she might be found.

They reached the refreshment table, and she broke away from him at once. Breathing deeply to control himself, he selected a glass and handed it to her. She took it, careful to come into no physical contact with him.

She sipped the contents, not looking at him. "Do you think we can complete our plan tomorrow?" she asked.

She must be eager to see the last of him; he'd noted the desperation in her voice. But try as he might, he could not detect her feelings. No one had ever been a mystery to him before. Yet now, when he most needed his fine-tuned senses to alert him to her mood, only chaos reached him. In her presence, he had become hopelessly muddled.

He gathered his control around him like a suit of armor and focused on her question. "It might be possible. How does your cousin go on?"

"The poor dear," she said, and for a moment warmth filled her voice, dispelling her rigid aloofness. "He is distraught. Do you know, he would not come this night, saying he felt poorly? But I know it is from worry. He actually counted the sum of his vowels! He has never kept track before. And he wanted to know the extent of my losses. He actually shouted at me when I told him I had no idea. I will be glad when this is over," she added. "I do hate to see him so upset."

"It *is* for his own good," he pointed out.

"I know. But I have to keep reminding myself of that." She drew a deep breath. "And I cannot relent too soon. He must learn this lesson well and truly. We will have to time it with care."

At the moment, the only time concerning Ramsdell was that involving the cycles of the moon and the bloodlust that filled him. He studied her profile, and the longing to drag her into his arms almost overwhelmed him. He retained just enough sense—barely—to prevent that tragedy.

The dance ended, and Juliana's next partner came to fetch her away to the floor. She managed a bright smile for the young officer, and for all Ramsdell could tell, she might truly mean it. The fellow looked exactly the sort of gentleman she should know: handsome, normal, and safe. Ramsdell would—*must*—be glad to see her courted and wed to someone worthy of her. Someone who would give her a happy, normal, enjoyable life. What could he ever offer her but pain and heartache—or more likely, almost instant death?

He turned blindly to leave. What good did it do him to torture himself by gazing upon her? He strode out into the night. He needed to run again, to exercise some part of this fever out of himself. He increased his pace until he raced through the darkened streets, but with every step his entire being craved Juliana.

Chapter Eight

He only had tonight to live through, Ramsdell reflected. Tonight, he would bring this farce with Bertie to a close, terrify the boy, leave him in no doubt as to the folly of his ways, then return his vowels to him and leave. He had no intention of being anywhere within fifty miles of Juliana on the following eve, with the moon at its fullest. If he could be rid of the whole situation by two A.M., perhaps three at the latest, that would still leave him several hours of darkness in which to race to Ramsdell Grange. He could make it before dawn; it would be cutting it close, but with a good pair harnessed to his curricle, it would work.

If only he could ride! But no horse could be induced to carry him with his bloodlust so intense. Controlling a pair would be tricky enough. It would be best to leave the driving to a coachman, but a carriage would be too slow. He must be secure within doors before first light rendered him comatose.

Ramsdell glanced at Drury, his valet. "We'll be traveling to the Grange tonight."

"Yes, m'lord." Expressionless, the wiry little man

brushed a lingering hair from the shoulder of Ramsdell's coat.

"Pack enough things for a few days. Then get some sleep. If I'm not back here by half past two, I want you to bring the curricle to meet me. You know the direction?"

"I do, m'lord." Drury stood back, regarding Ramsdell with the critical eye of the perfectionist. He gave a short nod. "Will that be all, m'lord?"

Inestimable man. He was paid well not to question odd orders, and had been warned of his master's peculiar habits and fancies, but that had not stopped others from prying a little too closely into Ramsdell's personal nightmare.

Drury handed Ramsdell his hat, made a final adjustment to his cape, then turned to the cupboard where he had stored the portmanteau and valises. Ramsdell left him to it, secure in the knowledge that all would be completed to a nicety.

Half an hour later, when he mounted the steps to the drawing room at Mrs. Glasdon's, he saw that the other three had already arrived. That hadn't been easy to assure. He'd been forced to use very strong mental coercion to drag Woolsey there. Ramsdell's lip curled. The strain of being so subtly compelled against his will certainly showed on the man. He could hear him complaining clear across the crowded, noisy room.

"I'd rather play somewhere—anywhere!—else," came the lament, clear to preternaturally acute ears.

Bertie, who slumped in his chair in an attitude of utter dejection, glowered at his companion. "You've been saying that for the past twenty minutes and more."

Ramsdell had been forced to compel Bertie to come, too, though it took less effort with a mind so compliant. Perhaps the silly gudgeon would start to regard gaming as a dreaded addiction to be avoided. One fact pleased him: Bertie and Woolsey did not wile away the time they waited in playing piquet.

And Juliana. . . . He'd waited to look at her, savoring the

moments of anticipation. So beautiful, so alive—so very much the opposite of being *un-dead*. She, too, slumped in her chair, flipping cards in a desultory manner. If he hadn't known better, he would think her sunk in the depths of despair.

As he took his accustomed seat, she looked him square in the face and said, "This one last time. If I lose—" She broke off, but such misery rang in her voice, it would have wrenched his heart if he hadn't known she was play acting.

"Oh, God, Jewel, I'm sorry!" Bertie buried his face in his hands. "I should never have dragged you into this."

Woolsey gave a sharp laugh. "It's this cursed house. We do nothing but lose here!"

Ramsdell, driven by the devil within him, allowed them all to win. Not much, just enough to raise their hopes.

Juliana stared in well-acted delight at the small pile of chips he pushed toward her. "Bertie, you were right all along, this way of betting does work! No, I *don't* want to use it to buy back my vowels. I'm going to win more. You'll see, we'll win it all back!"

Bertie picked up his own meager winnings, fingered them for a moment, then looked from Juliana to Woolsey. With a sigh, he scattered bets across several cards.

On the next play, Ramsdell assured all three of his victims suffered heavy losses. But as the night wore on in this same manner, he sensed only resignation and despair from Bertie. Why could the young nodcock not stiffen his backbone and walk away? Would he always allow himself to be led? He had to be brought to see that some of those who appeared to be gentlemen and worthy of trust were, in fact, the exact opposite.

He, himself, was a prime example.

A glance at the clock spurred him onward. They had been playing for some time; already it neared half past one. He must settle matters quickly, or he would be tied to the city one more night. And that next night, of all nights. The full of the moon. A sense of horror, of dread at what could all too easily happen, seeped through him.

A gong sounded in the depths of the house, announcing the supper. Now, Ramsdell thought, and turned his compelling attention to Woolsey.

The man scrawled a vowel, then suddenly his fingers clenched the paper. He looked up, directly at Ramsdell, his eyes glazed with a wild anger. "I don't believe in your curst luck!" he hissed. "You're just more adept at fiddling than I am. That's the only possibility!"

Ramsdell directed a mental prod toward Bertie.

The young man straightened, staring at Woolsey. "Fiddling? What do you mean *more adept than you?*"

Woolsey slammed to his feet, knocking over his chair. "The man's a damned cheat, though I don't see how he does it. I thought I knew every trick!"

Subtly, Ramsdell fed the anger.

"I'm one of the best! Never known a man I couldn't swindle, but damme if he don't put us all to shame."

Bertie blinked. "You're a—a professional *leg!* Jewel, Woolsey's nothing but a—a—"

"A pigeon-plucker," Juliana stuck in, indignant.

Bertie turned on his erstwhile friend in disgust. "You—you sicken me!" he exclaimed. "How I could have ever let you get your damned claws into me— I trusted you! I followed your advice!"

"You actually believed we could win at gaming!" Juliana inserted, not one to miss an obvious cue. "And only look how deeply we've fallen into debt because of him!"

Bertie shook his head. "Jewel, I— Ah!" He rose and staggered away from the table without a backward glance.

Abruptly, Ramsdell released Woolsey from the enthrallment that had held him at the table. Woolsey stared at him for a long moment, blinking and disoriented.

"Go home," Ramsdell breathed. For this one moment, he directed against this man some portion of the threat and terror that lay at the core of his being.

Woolsey stepped back, his face gaunt and haunted. A desperate expression flickered in his eyes. He took another step back, then turned and fled.

Juliana, her eyes, wide, stared after him. "How—"

"Fear of exposure," Ramsdell said quickly. For the moment, at least, he had himself back under control. "He'll probably make himself scarce in London for awhile."

She started to rise, then sank back in her chair. She didn't look at him. "That's cured Bertie of Woolsey, at least. But will he fall into the hands of another gull catcher?"

"I don't know," he admitted. "For one so compliant, he has an amazing streak of stubbornness in him."

She gave a short, humorless laugh. "We Paigntons are a stubborn stock. It takes a great deal to stop us. We are known to be fools when something we want is at stake." Bitterness sounded clear in her voice, mingled with longing.

It proved more than he could bear to see her so unhappy. He leaned forward, his fingers brushing her cheek where a single tear slipped over the lower lid of her eye. She blinked it away; his fingertip caught it. His entire being centered on her with a longing for fulfillment that only she could bring.

Already, the majority of the room had emptied to seek the delicacies below. In only a few more minutes they would be completely alone. *Not safe. Not safe.* The words echoed through his mind. But he could no more bring himself to leave than he could to drive her away.

Her hands clenched together on the table top, and he dropped his to cover them. "Juliana—" The harshness of his longing filled his voice.

She shook her head without looking up. "Don't," she whispered. "Don't."

She was right, of course. Her instincts to avoid him were sound. Her increasing aloofness, her patent unhappiness— She must be repelled by him, by the savage, animalistic part of him that gained strength with the waxing of the moon.

"Juliana," he began, wanting to warn her away for the morrow. "You cannot—" But the words wouldn't come out of him. He simply could not force himself to give the warning that would frighten her away from him for all time. His rational mind knew he must, yet his bloodlust had grown so great, it wouldn't allow it.

A new fear grew within him, greater than any he had ever known, that on the full moon he would be unable to prevent himself from savaging and destroying this one person he truly loved.

Slowly her gaze rose to his face, a puzzled, strained expression in her soulful eyes. He must be radiating his torment, but though he willed himself to do it, he could not use it to drive her away. Instead, horrifyingly, it seemed to fascinate her. Almost as if of its own volition, her hand rose to his cheek, resting against it.

He couldn't help himself. He turned his face just enough so that his mouth found her palm. His lips pressed a kiss within while his teeth ached with a fervency that drew a groan from him. Instinct raged wild within him, and the remnants of his rigid control snapped. He half rose, dragging her against himself, his mouth straining toward her throat. He knew himself evil, a fiend, the worst sort of devil, but the bloodlust ruled him.

A strangled cry escaped her, and she struggled. Her hand, still on his cheek, clenched, and her long nails scratched deeply as she pulled herself free of his embrace. For one long moment she stood frozen, her expression aghast, as she stared at him. Slowly, she lowered her gaze to her fingers, where only the faintest trace of his blood tinged her nails. She shook her head, a strangled sob escaped her, and she spun around and fled.

He lurched forward in pursuit, until the stinging of his cheek penetrated the lust-filled fog that engulfed his mind.

He slowed as he neared the door, then came to a stop. His hand brushed across the gash, encountering the fine droplets forming there. She had wounded him. For the first time in over two hundred years, he shed blood of his own.

Remnants of an almost forgotten humanity returned to haunt him. This one great gift she had given him.

He had done enough damage to her. If by any means he could spare her more torment, he must. He loved her, more than he had ever believed possible.

And he must never see her again.

Chapter Nine

The full moon. Ramsdell sat in his curricle with his man Drury at his side, staring up at the facade of Mrs. Glasdon's. He knew Bertie would come; the lad hadn't enough strength of will to resist Ramsdell's mental summons. But what if Juliana came with him?

The horses sidled uneasily on the cobbled street, all too aware of the tension that raged within their handler. Ramsdell relinquished the ribbons to Drury and swung down. "I won't be long."

"No, m'lord," came the stolid response.

He would have to give the man a substantial raise in his wages, Ramsdell reflected. Not one word had the valet uttered about the postponement of their trip the night before. He might sit as far away as the narrow bench of the curricle allowed, but he showed no outward fear. Ramsdell kept him under only the subtlest of enthrallments; he'd had other valets, held under far greater spells, who'd run screaming from his presence near the full of the moon.

The *major domo* admitted him like the well-established patron he had become, but moved hastily away, casting him a sideways, uncertain glance. Ramsdell drew in several slow, stilling breaths. In his present condition, he'd drive all the other customers from the rooms as soon as he walked in.

He turned to the *major domo,* who was disappearing rapidly down the hall. "Would you ask Mr. Bertram Paignton to come down to me here? I may use this front room?"

"Yes, m'lord. Of course." As if relieved not to have Ramsdell venture upstairs, the man hurried to throw open the indicated door to the tiny front salon. From a wall sconce he retrieved a candle.

Ramsdell took it from him. "Thank you. I'll see to the lights."

The *major domo* bolted out of the room and up the stairs.

Ramsdell used the taper to light only a single candelabrum. The less clearly young Paignton saw him, the better. Deep in the moon's thrall, desperate for blood, he was no fit company for anyone.

The door opened a short time later. Ramsdell, who stood tense before the fireplace, looked up. Bertie, the image of stoic determination, had stopped just over the threshold, his back straight, his fists clenched at his sides, his complexion deathly pale. Almost, he might have come to his execution. With this wildness upon him, Ramsdell might all too easily make that true.

Bertie swallowed. "I— My lord. I—I have been a complete fool." He blinked rapidly, then rushed on with what was obviously a rehearsed speech. "I can only throw myself on your mercy and beg for time to cover what I owe you. And Juliana, too."

Her name commanded his instant attention, and an instantaneous, unbearable response in his body. "Is she here?" If she were— Yet he didn't sense her presence. He had to finish this business, properly for her sake, then put as many miles between them as he could.

He must find another woman, any woman— No, how could he? In his current, frenzied state, he would only feed too deeply and drain the poor creature's life. No, this time, he would have to abstain. It would sicken him not to partake of blood this lunar cycle, but that would only be for the best. In a weakened state, a couple days past the moon's fullness, he could find some doxy on the street. He would be too drained, then, to do more than drink just enough to keep himself alive. Then once more in control of himself, he could feed in safety for all concerned.

"My lord?" Bertie remained across the room, but he regarded Ramsdell with a touch of concern. "Did you hear me?"

"No. A—a momentary lapse." With difficulty, he focused on the business at hand.

"I—I said I know how great is the sum of our vowels, and we both know it to be a debt of honor. I speak for my cousin, as well, I assure you, when I say that every penny will be paid. Only—only we will need a little time."

"She's not here." For Ramsdell, only this one point mattered.

"No. She wasn't feeling quite the thing. She's at home tonight."

Home, on Hampstead Heath. And the road to the Grange lay in the opposite direction. He would pass nowhere near her this night.

"My lord? About our debt?" Bertie peered anxiously at him.

"Are you likely to game again?" Ramsdell demanded. It took a considerable effort to think of anything but the driving desperation to feed that filled him.

"No!" Bertie said the word with such loathing, there could be no doubting his word. "I've learned my lesson. Oh, a card game or two with a friend, there'd be no harm in that. But I'll never again fall into the hands of one of Woolsey's ilk, you may be sure of that. I'm no longer a pigeon ripe for the plucking. But if you will only give me terms, my lord—"

Impatience to be done with it overwhelmed Ramsdell. "There is no debt."

"No— I don't understand, my lord."

"You heard Woolsey last night. I cheated. On purpose, to teach you a lesson. And you say you learned it?"

"You—" Bertie shook his head, bewildered. "All that—"

"You were too gullible, and that worried your cousin. So I arranged this little charade to open your eyes. You owe me nothing."

"Nothing." The word came out on a whisper. "You mean—nothing? All those thousands of pounds—"

"Nothing," Ramsdell snapped. In moments, he would lose control and feast on the first woman unfortunate enough to pass near. His nails dug into the palms of his hands as he clenched them. Juliana. . . . He needed to know her safe, beyond his reach. "Where is she? Your cousin? In the house? Locked in her room?"

Bertie shook his head, his expression so relieved and grateful as to be comical. "No, not in the house. In that tower of hers. No, you haven't seen it, of course. It's a stone thing that my grandfather built for her mother. She's locked herself in there and refuses to see anyone. Upset like me, of course. She'll be so relieved when I tell her."

No, she'd locked herself away because she was terrified of him. Of that, Ramsdell had no doubts. That bitter knowledge drove away the last remnants of his reasoning control. Desire and bloodlust, fanned by the fullness of the moon, inflamed him. "Leave her to me," Ramsdell said in a strangled voice, and stormed from the room.

In the street, he dismissed his valet with an anguished word and swung into the carriage. The moment his hands touched the ribbons, the near horse reared and the other lashed out with a hoof. Ramsdell gave them the office and lost himself in the physical and mental exertion of controlling a pair maddened by his mere presence.

Only a very few vehicles traversed the streets at this late hour. The drivers moved aside at the frenzied clattering of his horses' hooves on the cobble stones. Ramsdell was beyond caring, beyond even thinking. He drove by instinct, simply *knowing* where he would find Juliana. His pair, their coats gleaming with the sweat of terror, careened onward, past the fashionable district, past the outlying regions, then on to the Heath itself.

Tree-lined lanes branched off the main road, leading to small estates. At one of these he reined in his blowing cattle, then set them speeding along their new course. One portion of his mind registered that the moon rode low in the sky; it would sink beneath the horizon soon. But he had no delusions that its setting would lesson its control over him.

Nearer . . . nearer. . . . He pulled into a narrow drive, where a wrought iron gate blocked his path. No such measly barrier could keep him out. He abandoned the curricle. The horses could wander, cooling themselves; at the moment, they were far from his mind. He strode to the latch, freed it with only the slightest effort of will, and entered the estate.

The house stood only a scant hundred yards ahead, a medium-sized Georgian edifice covered in ivy and surrounded by trees. He turned from it, knowing she was not within. He slipped silently through the brush, a hunter keen with the scent of his prey, as he circled around to the far side of the property.

The tower, actually a single, turreted room, rose from the shrouding midst of trees and bushes. Moonlight glinted off the rough-hewn stone, gleaming silver and cream. Tall windows lined the walls, as narrow as medieval arrow slits. The structure stood isolated, as far from the main house and the neighboring properties as possible.

He crept closer, all stealth, all predator, his supernatural instincts holding full sway. Not a sound reached his ears, no night birds rustling through branches, no nocturnal animals making their rounds. They had abandoned this hunting ground at his approach.

THE FULL OF THE MOON

Then a low growling, followed by a snarl and a whine, broke the stillness of the night. He froze, alert, every sense reaching out for the source of this unexpected sound. The growl repeated, half anguished, half threatening, and he focused on the source. The tower, where Juliana, defenseless and alone, had sought refuge.

Somehow, an animal, a wolf by the sound of it, had gotten in.

A low, echoing howl emitted from the room, followed by the scrabbling of claws on stone, and a sound that might have been a scream.

Juliana.

Chapter Ten

Juliana. Fear for her overcame Ramsdell's maddened bloodlust. He strode forward, filled with a new and very different need to reach her, and took hold of the handle on the door. Bolted, from within. He didn't stop to think or reason. He simply grasped the iron and rammed his shoulder against the massive oak paneling, using every ounce of his unnatural strength.

For a long moment it held, straining against his efforts, then from within came the unmistakable sound of splintering wood. The door swung inward on well-oiled hinges, and Ramsdell stumbled inside.

A giant auburn-colored wolf paced the chamber, its sharp claws clicking and scratching with every measured step. As he crossed the threshold, its great head swung to face him, its teeth bared in a snarl that would have driven a lesser man mad with fear. With a howling cry, it leapt for him, its front legs catching him in the chest, sending him staggering backwards into the wall.

As he collided with solid stone, part of his mind registered that the great beast wore a loose muslin night dress.

Another part recognized that while the savage animal kept him pinned, it wasn't hurting him. Instead, its tongue licked frantically at the long scratch on his cheek caused by Juliana's nails, and the muzzle nuzzled his face rather than tearing out his throat.

Shaken, confused, alarmed for Juliana, he focused on the wolf's face, on its huge, brown eyes. Puppy eyes. For a long moment he stared, numb with shock, while the unbelievable truth dawned on him.

"My God," he breathed, without a trace of irreverence. He freed his arms, then closed them about the wolf, gathering the thick fur and wiry muscle of the animal close against him. An incredulous laugh started deep within him as he buried his face in its—*her*—thick ruff, and gently stroked the head. All this time he'd feared she would guess the terrible truth about him. All this time, he'd thought her withdrawal to be her natural fear of his *unnaturalness*. And all this time, she must have been terrified about what *he* might be guessing about *her*.

No wonder she'd grown more nervous with every day that brought the fullness of the moon upon them. Not because of his bloodlust, but because of what she knew it would do to her. He'd been so blinded by his own personal tragedy, he'd never seen what must otherwise have been obvious to him.

He caught her forepaws and lowered them to the ground. She whined, burying her head in his hands, rubbing against his knees. With the door once more closed, and a portion of the bolt replaced to assure her safety, he crossed the room to the large bed that stood against the far wall; she leapt up on it, circled twice, then settled partly across his lap as he sat on it.

With his arms wrapped about her neck and his face buried in her ruff, his mind raced. The Yorkshire moors. A wild, savage place. Yes, she could have encountered a werewolf there. And her mother—

Fragments of her cousin Bertie's words came back to

him. Her mother had suffered a disfiguring disease. His grandfather had built this stone tower to give his daughter privacy. No, *not* her mother, but Juliana, herself. She must be Bertie's aunt, not his cousin.

But Bertie—and apparently his parents—had no idea. That would be possible, had Bertie's father been away at school when his sister's tragedy took place. His father built the sanctuary on the estate to house—and hide—her. But her lycanthropic instincts must have become too great to conceal. Like his own. At the full of the moon, he might as well wear a sign announcing himself to be a vampire. And she, how constricting it must be in her animal form to be locked away in this tower.

It was no wonder she banished herself to an isolated cottage where she could howl to her heart's content without fear of being overheard. Her parents would have left her alone while they lived. But then her brother, himself married and with a son being presented to society, must have thought of the long-missed sister whose letters had told a tale of a marriage and a daughter—as mythical as Ramsdell's own fictions. So her brother must have determined to bring out his "niece", which nearly proved her undoing.

How long he sat there, cradling her, he had no idea. Slowly he became aware of a returning darkness in the room as the offending moon dipped below the horizon. He felt her shiver, then she kept on trembling, as her metamorphosis back to human form began. He watched, seeing her beautiful features re-emerge, seeing the lupine form fade. Within minutes he held not an animal but a shaken and lovely girl in his arms.

With the touch and scent of her, his own instincts raged once more to the forefront. A groan from deep within shook him, and he gathered her close, his mouth seeking hers as his driving passions took over. She melted against him, clinging, returning his kiss with a frantic need that inflamed him all the more. His teeth ached with the need for her blood. He rolled with her, tumbling them across the bed, and his hands dragged the flimsy material of her night dress from her body.

Then miraculously, he felt her small hands pulling free his cloak, tugging at his neckcloth, dragging the folds from his neck. He released her enough to struggle out of his coat, and she came with him, fumbling with his shirt. With the first surge of joy he had experienced in two hundred years, he allowed the last vestiges of his control to fall away, and succumbed to the surging desire that overcame him utterly.

He claimed her, for the first time in remembrance without fear or restraint, and sank his teeth deep into her neck. She moaned with pleasure, holding him ever closer while he sated his desperate need. Then she twisted her head so that her mouth could seek his throat. Her bite drove him to new heights.

Not until the pre-dawn did he rouse, when his instincts called him to assure his shelter for the coming daylight hours. He lay with one arm sprawled across her, holding her close. A slow smile tugged at the corners of his mouth, and with a sudden grin, he picked several lupine hairs from between his teeth. Gently he stroked the auburn mane back from her face, revealing her delicate features. She made a lovely wolf, too. And she was his, in every sense of the word.

His lips trailed across her skin as he re-examined the long-absent sensation of happiness. Her eyelids fluttered open even as she reached for him, and the warm glow of her smile provided all the light he needed. He kissed her, thoroughly, then leaned back on his elbow so he could simply look at her.

"A vampire," she whispered, and regarded him with an expression of unadulterated love. "And to think I was so afraid of what I might do to you."

"A werewolf." His soft laugh sounded in his voice. "You

must be the only woman in England I can't harm. Which is fortunate, because you're the only one I want."

She snuggled closer. "I never dared hope there could be someone for me. Someone who wouldn't be horrified by what I am."

He rolled to his back and pulled her on top of him. "You need never fear again. I can guard and control you at the full of every moon, and you can run free at my side."

"And I can protect you during the daylight hours."

"When I'm at my most vulnerable," he agreed. "We're made for one another." That was true. His bite could never harm her, for she was as immortal as he. With her, he never need restrain the passion that would bring them both joy for the rest of their never-ending lives. "Which," he added slowly, "leaves us with two matters to attend to."

She leaned down to kiss the base of his throat where the marks of her teeth already faded. "And what might those be?"

"Obtain a special license as quickly as we can. And," he added, "find a vicar who won't mind performing a ceremony at night."

Her eyes gleamed with sudden laughter. "We'll have to hurry a little, then. My family will insist on being present, you know. This will be one undertaking that's best completed by the *dark* of the moon."

He wrapped a long tendril of her auburn hair around one hand. "There's one thing I'll never be quite certain about."

"And that is?" She trailed her fingertips along his chest.

He caught them, and drew her down against himself. "Which one of us is really the wolf in sheep's clothing?"